Looking for Love

Rosie Harris

arrow books

This edition published by Arrow Books in 2005

Arrow Books
The Random House Group Limited
20 Vauxhall Bridge Road, London, SW1V 2SA

Random House Australia (Pty) Limited
20 Alfred Street, Milsons Point, Sydney,
New South Wales 2061, Australia

Random House New Zealand Limited
18 Poland Road, Glenfield
Auckland 10, New Zealand

Random House (Pty) Limited
Isle of Houghton, Corner Boundary Road and Carse O'Gowrie,
Houghton, 2198, South Africa

The Random House Group Limited Reg. No. 954009

www.randomhouse.co.uk

A CIP catalogue record for this book
is available from the British Library

Papers used by Random House are natural, recyclable
products made from wood grown in sustainable forests.
The manufacturing processes conform to the environmental
regulations of the country of origin

ISBN 0 09 191100 1

Printed and bound in Great Britain by
Bookmarque Ltd, Croydon, Surrey

Patsy of Paradise Place

For my grandchildren:
Susie Harris, Kathryn Sak, Michele Harris,
Nicola Sak, Hayley Harris and Robert Harris

Acknowledgements

My sincere thanks to Rhona Caretti for specialised information, and to my Agent, Caroline Sheldon, for her help and advice.

Also to Kate Parkin, Kirsty Fowkes, Georgina Hawtrey-Woore, Lynne Drew, Joanna Craig, Anna Dalton-Knott, Beth Humphries, and everyone else in the Heinemann/Arrow team who have all played such a supportive role.

Chapter One

'Dad . . . Dad? Is it really you?' The skinny tousle-headed child, swinging from a rope tied to one of the lampposts in Paradise Place, scraped her clumpy boots along the pavement to slow herself down.

She peered through the murky gloom of a mid-December night in disbelief as a tall, muscular man carrying a heavy canvas kitbag on his shoulder came striding down the road towards her.

The next moment, Patsy's exclamation of surprise and astonishment ended in a wild scream as the man dropped the kitbag and she found herself being swung high in the air by a pair of strong arms.

'What do you think you are doing out here on your own at this time of night?' he asked in a voice laced with concern.

'Waiting to see if anyone else was coming out to play.'

'At this time of night?'

Patsy giggled. 'Sometimes Janie Grant or Maureen Murphy pretend to go to bed early and then they sneak out so that we can play chasers in the dark or creep up the jowlers and spy on some of the older boys and catch them smoking ciggies.'

'Does your mam know about this?'

Patsy shrugged, but ignored his question. 'Anyway, I don't care if they come out now or not. You've come instead and that's even better,' she said fervently as she hugged him.

'I'm not going to let you go away ever again!' she vowed, locking her hands behind his neck and smothering him with kisses.

'So if I stay at home will you promise not to sneak out in the dark to play?' he asked, lowering her back on to the ground.

Feet placed wide apart, hands on hips, Patsy Callaghan tipped back her head and stared up at the giant of a man who towered over her, her green eyes wide with astonishment.

'Do you really mean that?' she asked in disbelief. 'You really mean that you're never going back to sea again?'

Patsy thought she must be dreaming. The last time her dad had come ashore he had been at home for three weeks and he'd taken her and her mam out for a day that she would remember as long as she lived.

He'd bought her a new green dress, some white shoes and a bow of green ribbon to tie in her hair and when she was all dressed up in her new clothes he'd taken them on the train all the way to Chester. They'd walked along the city walls and they'd sat by the river with a bag of buns and a bottle of pop and had a picnic.

John Callaghan stretched out a hand and ruffled her mop of unruly red curls. 'It's like I say, me darlin' girl, I'm not going away any more. From now on I'll be living at home with you and your mam.'

'For ever?' she gasped.

'For ever and a day,' he told her gravely.

Patsy drew in a deep breath. Father O'Brian must be right after all and your prayers did get answered if you prayed long enough and hard enough. 'Does me mam know?' she asked cautiously.

John Callaghan laughed, a loud jovial sound. 'Not yet, so why don't you run along indoors and tell her?'

Patsy hesitated, then slid her tiny hand into her father's massive one. 'Why don't we do it together,' she said and her face split into a wide grin.

'Whatever you say.' John Callaghan swung his kitbag up on to his shoulder and let his young daughter lead him by the hand towards the back door of the terraced house that was their home.

Patsy paused in the scullery and looking up at her father held a finger up to her lips. 'Hush, don't make a sound!' she whispered. 'Let's surprise her. You wait here a minute.'

John Callaghan nodded. Carefully he lowered his kitbag to the flagstone floor leaning it against one wall.

As Patsy moved towards the door that led into the living room, walking in an exaggerated fashion on the tips of the toes of her laced-up boots so as not to make a noise, John Callaghan looked round him in distaste.

He sighed. Maeve had never been house-proud,

3

which was something he couldn't understand because she was so finicky and meticulous about her own appearance.

Her fastidiousness seemed to end there. It never seemed to trouble her in the slightest what Patsy looked like. Even when she was a tiny baby she could be filthy dirty and dressed in grubby rags and Maeve hardly seemed to be aware of the fact. Today he'd noticed that Patsy's frock was soiled, and the hem hanging down, her pinafore was torn and the toes of her boots were badly scuffed.

He looked around him and even in the dim light filtering through from the main living room he could see that everywhere was utterly filthy. Dirty dishes and saucepans were piled up high in the stained sink, leftover food lay around uncovered and a distinctly unpleasant smell hung in the air.

Patsy had left the door slightly ajar and he could see his wife standing in the living room, leaning over the fireguard that was draped with clothes that she'd washed out and hung there to air, peering into the mirror above the fireplace.

A pretty woman with shoulder-length strawberry-blonde hair, she was attractively slim yet enticingly curvaceous. She was wearing the very latest silk jumper blouse in leaf green over a matching pleated skirt. The lower edge of the blouse had an elaborate crochet border that emphasised her shape and the cap sleeves were trimmed in the same way.

Her face was heavily made up and she was concentrating on outlining her mouth with a

4

bright pink lipstick as Patsy entered the room.

'Mam, there's someone to see you,' Patsy told her.

Maeve ignored the intrusion until she had finished applying her lipstick then turned briefly. 'If it's your Uncle Peter then tell him to go on to the pub and I'll see him there like we arranged. I'll be another five minutes at least.'

'No, it's not him. I bet you'll never be able to guess who it is . . .'

'Not now, Patsy, I'm trying to get ready to go out and I haven't time for your silly games,' Maeve told her peevishly. Then, as she looked back into the mirror and caught sight of the figure standing in the doorway she gasped in disbelief.

'John?' She swung round to face her husband. 'This is a surprise! You nearly frightened the life out of me! What are you doing here?'

'Hey, what sort of greeting is that for a man who has been at sea for almost a year?' He grabbed hold of his wife, pulling her into his arms and kissing her hungrily.

Breathlessly, Maeve wriggled free. 'Hold on, John, do be careful, you're ruining my make-up!' she complained, raising her carefully pencilled brows as she peered over his shoulder into the mirror.

'You've got me mam's lipstick all over your face,' Patsy giggled as he released his hold on her mother and stepped back.

John Callaghan wiped his mouth with the back of his hand and then stared down at the vivid pink stain.

'Why do you put that bloody muck on your face,' he muttered.

Maeve gave him a withering look. 'It's what women do to make themselves look more attractive when they're going out,' she said sarcastically.

His gaze darkened as his eyes swept over her, taking in the low neck of her dress, the shining beads, dangling earrings, the pale silk stockings and the high-heeled shoes laced with coloured cords in the same shade of green as her dress.

'Going somewhere special, were you?'

'I certainly was,' she told him as she turned back to the mirror and began repairing the damage he had done to her make-up.

'And what about young Patsy, then? he asked in a steely voice.

Maeve gave him a puzzled look. 'Patsy. What about her?'

'If you were going out then what was Patsy going to do? Judging by the state of her and the way she is dressed you weren't exactly planning to take her along with you.'

Maeve's mouth twisted as she looked across at Patsy in her grubby cotton dress, torn pinafore and cumbersome boots. 'You know bloody well that I wasn't taking her with me!' She laughed. 'Patsy is a big girl now, in case you hadn't noticed, aren't you, luv? You don't mind staying on your own if I go out for an hour or so, do you, pet?'

'An hour or so? You mean for the entire evening and half the night, don't you?' John commented.

Maeve shrugged. 'An hour or two or the entire evening, what difference does it make?' she said

6

lightly. 'Once Patsy's tucked up in bed and I've kissed her good-night she's soon fast asleep so she doesn't know whether I'm here or not.'

'If she is asleep. More likely she'll be lying there fretting and worrying, too scared to go to sleep,' he argued. 'A nine-year-old shouldn't be left in the house on her own.'

'Well, she won't be on her own tonight, will she?' Maeve smiled smugly. 'She'll have her dad here to keep her company.'

'And for every night in the future.'

Maeve paused with her lipstick in the air, her mouth agape. 'Yer wha'?'

'I've decided that I'm not going back to sea any more.'

Maeve remained silent as she completed the task of outlining her mouth in brilliant pink but her brain was working overtime. What was he saying? Not going back to sea again? She couldn't even begin to think of what that was going to mean. If John was to be at home all the time from now on then it would turn her life completely topsy-turvy. She felt annoyed. She hadn't expected him home for another few weeks and this meant the end of her freedom for the near future.

As things stood, apart from the few weeks two or three times a year when he came home on shore leave she was free to do as she pleased. While John was away she didn't bother to do any cooking and cleaning unless she felt like it, or if she was entertaining one of her many men friends.

If the place was a tip most of the time it didn't

matter, because there was only Patsy there to notice it. Maeve's lips tightened: she'd soon cured Patsy of complaining about the state the place was in by making her help with the cleaning and clearing up.

If John was at home all the time though, that was another kettle of fish completely. He was a stickler for order and he'd expect the place to be clean and tidy all the time. He'd expect her to wash his clothes, iron his shirts and put food on the table at regular times. What was even more to the point, he wouldn't approve of her gadding off out on her own three or four nights a week. In fact, he'd probably try and put a stop to it.

Now was probably not the time to let him know how much she resented his decision, she decided. As she turned from the mirror there was a feigned look of delight on her pretty face.

'John, this is wonderful news,' she cooed as she twined her arms around his neck and her glistening pink lips curved into a tantalising smile. 'You're really going to be home for good from now on? I can't believe what I'm hearing!'

Patsy had been holding her breath as she waited for her mother's reaction to the news. Now she let it out in a cautious sigh of relief.

From now on things would be so different, she thought happily. They'd be a proper family. She wouldn't have to fend for herself when she came home from school, or spend long evenings sitting at the window staring out into the dark street, wondering when her mother would be coming home.

8

She was so afraid of being in the house on her own that she could never sleep. As soon as her mother had kissed her good-night and she heard her go downstairs and the front door slam and she knew she was on her own there were all sorts of strange noises and shadows that she never noticed when her mother was there. The rustling, scuttling noises as mice and cockroaches scurried about, and even the house seemed to creak and groan as if it was alive.

She'd once tried to tell her mother about her fears. Maeve had simply given her a hug and told her not to be so fanciful and then packed her off to bed early, telling her to get to sleep before she went out.

She had lain there with her eyes tight shut trying desperately to fall asleep, but it hadn't worked. She was still awake when her mam came up to kiss her good-night and the moment she heard the front door slam she'd been out of bed and huddled by the window as usual, watching and waiting until she saw her mother coming home again.

When she saw her approaching, if she was on her own, then Patsy would scuttle back into bed and pretend to be asleep in case she came upstairs to check up on her.

With her dad at home all the time that would stop, she told herself gleefully. There would be no more lonely nights.

She couldn't have had a more wonderful father, Patsy thought as she studied him. With his lean tanned face, shock of dark brown hair and gentle blue eyes he was the most handsome man she'd ever known. Her heart felt as if it was bursting with love and pride and she looked forward to boasting about the fact that he was home for good when she went to school next day.

She'd make him promise to come and meet her after school ended and that would stop all the teasing she had to put up with because he was so often away from home.

He was so tall and broad shouldered that he made her mother look slim and dainty as they stood there embracing. She had her arms locked round his muscular neck and she was gazing up at him with her wide-set green eyes as if she adored him.

Patsy sighed again. She knew only too well that those limpid green eyes could become emerald hard and the soft curving lips tighten into an unforgiving line. And the dainty fingers that were at this moment stroking the blue stubble on John Callaghan's cheeks could inflict a stinging slap, or curl into a fist that left bruises on her arms and chest when things didn't go the way Maeve wanted them to do.

There were times, Patsy reflected, when she wished her mother was fat and blowsy like some of the other women in Paradise Place. They seemed to be content with their lot and stayed home at nights, and were always around for their kids when they came home from school. They were there waiting to give them a hug if they were unhappy because they'd been bullied, or console them if they'd been told off at school.

Nevertheless, she took a pride in the fact that her mother looked so lovely. She wished her own red hair shone like gold and that she was as neat and dainty as her mother instead of being so clumsy. She always boasted that her mother was as beautiful as a princess. If, sometimes, their house was so filthy that she was ashamed for anyone to see it, she always managed to dream up some excuse or the other as to why she couldn't bring her friends indoors.

Now things would be different. Her dad liked things spotlessly clean and everything neat and tidy. 'Ship-shape and Bristol fashion' he called it, and he was always telling her that was how things had to be on board ship because there was so little space that everyone had to be tidy.

'A place for everything and everything in its place,' he would scold whenever he found their living room or scullery in a shambles.

Her mam couldn't be tidy if she tried and she would laugh when he started ranting on about it. Then she would light up a cigarette, perch on the arm of a chair or the edge of the table, and watch as he picked things up and put them away.

With her dad at home they'd have to stop piling up the dirty dishes in the sink and simply rinsing off a cup or plate when they needed it. They'd have to wash up after each meal and dry the dishes they'd used and put them away on the dresser or in the cupboard.

There'd be no more running off to the chippy for a fish supper or foraging around to see what scraps she could find in the larder when she was hungry and her mam was out at the pub. Instead, they'd sit down at the table to eat their meal every night and on Sunday there'd be a roast dinner and she'd be so full up afterwards that she would hardly be able to move.

Yes, she thought happily, life was going to be very different. If her dad was at home all the time her mam wouldn't need to go out at nights because she was fed up and lonely. And she wouldn't be bringing any of her strange friends home either.

Patsy shuddered as she thought about some of the uncles who came to the house. Most of them had unpleasant beery breath and she hated it when they tried to kiss her. She hated it even more when they tried to cuddle her because they usually had hot sweaty hands that seemed to roam all over her body. Or else they made her sit on their lap and then they held her so tightly that she could hardly breathe.

Most of the time though they didn't seem to want her around. Some of them gave her a few coppers and told her to take herself off and get lost for an hour or two. If she came back too early she found the front door and the back door locked and no matter how hard she knocked, her mam took no notice. Once one of the uncles had given her a shiny silver tanner and she'd been able to buy a bag of toffees and a big bottle of pop to share with Janie and Maureen. And there'd still been enough left over for her to buy them all an ice-cream.

All that sort of thing would be in the past, she

12

thought pragmatically. At long last they'd be all together like a proper loving family.

When the summer came they would be able to have days out together. There would be trips to the park to feed the ducks, or in the summer they might even go across on the ferryboat to New Brighton. She loved it there because there was so much to see and do, so many exciting things going on.

Her dad liked to walk along the shore for miles and miles and watch the huge liners and massive cargo boats coming down the Mersey and being guided into dock in Liverpool by fussy little tugboats. He seemed to know where each one had come from and how long they had been at sea. She liked visiting the fairground where there was music, and brightly coloured swings and slides and roundabouts to ride on.

Sometimes there was a circus in the grounds of New Brighton Tower, with ferocious wild animals in huge iron cages and her dad would tell her about the foreign places they all came from, where they roamed wild.

She liked the elephants best even though they were so huge and cumbersome that she was afraid they might crush her with one of their enormous feet if she stood too close to them. Some of them did tricks, like picking things up with their long grey trunks, and sometimes they let people have rides sitting up on their backs in special basket chairs.

Patsy sighed happily as she snuggled down in bed that night. There were going to be so many wonderful times ahead now that her dad had promised not to go back to sea ever again. It really was as if all her dreams, as well as her prayers, were coming true at once.

Chapter Two

John Callaghan had suspected that adapting from being a seafarer to becoming a landlubber was bound to present problems. Even in his most uncertain moments, though, he hadn't envisaged anything like those he experienced during the first two months of his change of lifestyle.

His return home in mid-December was so near to Christmas that he decided to leave looking for work until the New Year. He deserved a holiday, he told himself, and he needed time to adjust to being a family man.

Patsy was overjoyed.

'Can I stay home from school so that we can go out together every day?' she asked. Her sharp green eyes shone with enthusiasm. 'We can go looking at all the lovely shop windows in Lord Street and Church Street. They've been specially decorated up for Christmas! And can we make paper chains to hang up in the house and make our own Christmas pudding?' she asked him excitedly.

'You can't stay home from school just for that,' he told her gravely. 'I'll still be here when you break up from school for your Christmas holidays so we can do all those things then if you want to.'

'Of course I want to! I want to do them with

15

you, though, Dad. Me mam isn't interested, except in going round the shops and then she only wants to buy things for herself.'

'Patsy!' John Callaghan frowned disapprovingly.

She pulled a face. 'Well, it's true. You ask her yourself if you don't believe me.'

John Callaghan didn't say anything more on the subject. He suspected that what Patsy had said was probably right even if he didn't approve of her saying such things.

Unlike Patsy, right from the start Maeve seemed to resent his continuous presence in the house. She acted like a caged bird, beating her wings because she had to adjust to his needs and ways, sulking when she didn't want to fall in with his plans.

It wasn't easy for either of them. When he tried to establish some sort of order and routine Maeve accused him of being a fusspot. Sometimes, or so it seemed to him, she deliberately opposed his efforts by leaving her clothes strewn all over the place in the bedroom and dirty dishes piled up in the sink.

As a result of years of strict routine on board ship, John Callaghan was used to rising early each morning. Maeve refused to comply.

On his first morning at home he was up before seven and down in the kitchen making a pot of tea. When he took a cup up to Maeve who was still in bed she struggled up on one elbow, rubbing the sleep from her eyes like a small child. Pushing back her tangle of strawberry-blonde hair from her forehead she stared at him, bewildered. 'What the hell do you think you're playing at waking me up in the middle of the night?'

'It's not the middle of the night,' he told her. 'I know we sat up late last night talking, but it's time we were up or Patsy won't have time to eat her breakfast before she has to go off to school.'

'Breakfast? Have you woken me up at this ungodly hour to talk about Patsy and her breakfast?' Maeve asked sulkily. 'If Patsy wants something to eat she knows where the bread's kept and she's quite capable of putting some margarine on it. Half the time she doesn't bother to eat any breakfast, anyway.'

She pushed the cup of tea away and wriggled back down in bed, pulling the covers over her head.

'Stay where you are then if you're all that tired,' John told her. 'I'll see to Patsy this morning.'

Maeve didn't answer so he went back downstairs. He'd already stirred the dying embers in the firegrate back to life so that he could boil the kettle so now he might as well cook a pan of porridge and cut some bread ready to make Patsy some toast, he decided.

Patsy looked astonished when she came downstairs and found that the dirty dishes from the night before had been cleared from the table and that it was now laid for breakfast for the two of them.

'Is this a special treat because it's your first day home or are we going to have breakfast like this every morning?' she asked in surprise.

'From now on you'll be having breakfast like

this every morning,' he told her crisply.

She grinned gleefully as she sat down at the table and tucked into the food he set in front of her.

'Now go and get ready and I'll walk as far as the school with you,' he said when she had scraped her bowl clean and eaten a slice of dripping toast.

'I am ready,' she told him.

He studied her for a moment in silence. 'You're going to school dressed like that?' he frowned.

'Yeah! What's wrong with me?' She ran the back of her hand across her mouth. 'I've had a wash!' She looked at him sideways to see if he believed her. 'Well, I wiped me face over with a wet flannel before I had my breakfast.'

He shook his head disapprovingly, then decided not to make an issue of it. 'Your dress looks grubby. Hadn't you better go and change it?'

She rubbed ineffectually at the greasy stain down the bodice of the drab blue serge dress. 'I haven't got another one,' she said slowly.

He felt irritated by her prevarication. 'Don't talk silly! You must have more than one dress.'

'Not winter ones. Me mam said she would get me a new one for Christmas.'

'Christmas is weeks away. Are you going to wear that same dress every day until then?'

'I wears one of my summer ones with a jumper over it on Saturdays and then I wash this one and it's clean for me to wear to Mass on Sunday and to school all the next week,' she explained.

John Callaghan opened his mouth to speak then shut it again, his lips tight together holding back the exasperation. He wasn't sure if Patsy was telling the truth or whether she was being cheeky. Maeve had the cupboard in their bedroom packed full of clothes so surely Patsy must have more than just one warm dress.

He looked at Patsy again and shook his head sadly as he noticed the grubby socks with a great cobbled darn in the leg of one of them.

'Well it's Friday so as it's only for today I suppose it won't matter too much. Go and get your coat on or we'll be late.'

'No we won't, because I'm ready now.' Patsy grinned. She reached down a thick red-and-black striped scarf that was hanging behind the kitchen door and began winding it round her neck.

'Your coat,' he repeated patiently.

'I haven't got one so I wear this,' she told him.

'And what about when it rains?' he queried.

'I pulls it up over my head and I run as fast as I can to try and dodge the raindrops,' she grinned.

'Come on, Dad,' she grabbed at his hand. 'I don't want to be late. I want all me mates to see you. Some of them don't believe I have a dad. And some of the others say you run away from home because . . .' Her voice faded away and she bit down on her lower lip and gave him a nervous sideways look.

John Callaghan felt his insides churn. He was pretty sure he knew what she was going to say and he was glad that she hadn't.

'Come on then, let's be going.' He ruffled her

untidy red curls with his free hand. 'Do you want to nip upstairs to say goodbye to your mam?'

'No fear!' Patsy's eyes widened dramatically as she pulled a face. 'She'd skelp me if I woke her this early in the morning,' she giggled.

Maeve was still in bed when John returned from taking Patsy to school.

'You know I'm not a morning person,' she yawned when he went upstairs to waken her. She gave him a provocative smile. 'Why don't you come back to bed and we can have a cuddle and another sleep.'

'No, I'm wide awake and want to get on with things,' he told her. 'I'll go downstairs and start cleaning up. Give me a shout when you decide to get up and I'll cook some breakfast for you.'

She pulled the bedclothes back up over her ears. 'Oh, don't bother,' she snapped. 'I never eat breakfast anyway,' she added with a noisy yawn.

It seemed to set the pattern for the days that followed. No matter what he said or did, Maeve was rarely out of bed before ten o'clock in the morning. Then she would spend ages putting on her make-up and combing her hair. After that she would potter round the house for the next hour or so in her flimsy blue silk dressing gown and pale blue mules with white swansdown trimming looking like a stand-in for Clara Bow. This irritated him even more than the fact that she was a late riser.

If anyone came to the door he would rush to answer it, afraid of what they might think or say if they saw Maeve in that state. Not that she didn't look lovely, seductive even, but that was not the point. He couldn't think of another woman in Paradise Place who was ever seen in a dressing gown. Probably none of them had one, and certainly not a silk one. If there was a middle-of-the-night emergency then they either pulled a skirt or dress on over their nightgown, wrapped a blanket round their shoulders, or put on their outdoor coat.

He wondered what the other women thought about the fact that Maeve was always dressed up to the nines and yet young Patsy's clothes were little better than rags.

The first weekend he was at home he took Patsy out on a shopping spree. He bought her two winter skirts, one navy and one brown, two thick wool jumpers, one blue and one green, and a heavy navy-blue gabardine coat that would also keep the rain out. He also bought her sensible leather shoes to replace the boots she'd been wearing and several pairs of knee-high woollen socks.

Patsy was like a dog with two tails as she displayed all her new clothes for her mother to see, but Maeve was not impressed.

'Complete waste of money,' she said dismissively. 'Have you any idea what she is like with her clothes? When she's swung from a few lampposts and climbed a few walls, or been in a fight with some of the other kids, those things will be in tatters, you'll see.'

'She's only a tomboy because you let her run wild,' John protested. 'From now on she's going to behave like a little lady, aren't you, kiddo?' he murmured, ruffling Patsy's curls.

'Until she gets herself into a scrap with some of the other kids round about and they start fighting and tearing the clothes from her back.'

'Why does she get into those sort of scrapes?' John asked, his eyes narrowing speculatively, as Patsy walked out of the room.

Maeve shrugged. 'How the hell should I know? When she comes home with a black eye or a bloody nose she never tells me how it happened.'

'Have you ever taken the trouble to find out why she won't tell you?'

'Got better things to do with me time,' Maeve grinned. 'If she wants to be secretive about things then that's up to her, luv, now isn't it?'

'She gets into fights because she's defending you,' John told her quietly.

'Defending *me*? Worra she got to defend me about, I'd like to know?' she demanded hotly.

'I think you do know,' John said firmly. 'She doesn't like it when the kids start teasing her, calling her names and saying she doesn't know who her father is.'

'Bloody load of rot!' Maeve snapped. 'Course she knows who her father is.'

'Not when I'm away at sea and you're bringing home a different man every night of the week,' he said bitterly.

'Who youse been gossiping with then?' Maeve asked defiantly. 'Been down the boozer listening to all the local scandal from those beery bastards, have you?'

22

He nodded. 'It didn't take long before some of your so-called friends were putting me wise to the way you carry on when I'm not here.'

Maeve shrugged, but her cheeks were now bright red and her eyes shooting sparks of venom. 'You shouldn't have buggered off to sea and left me on my own for months at a stretch then, should you,' she spat.

John sighed. 'No, I shouldn't have done, but I did it so that I could earn the money to give you and Patsy a good life,' he said flatly.

'Money's not everything,' Maeve told him, her luscious pink mouth curling sardonically. 'I need a man about the place for company and if you preferred to bugger off on your own for months at a time then I had to find someone else to fill your shoes . . . and your bed!'

He flinched as if she had struck him. How could a woman who looked so angelic talk and act like that? he asked himself, struggling to hold his anger in check.

'You didn't have to neglect Patsy,' he said lamely.

'What lies has she been telling now?' Maeve asked, taking a cigarette from the packet lying on the table and lighting it. She puffed out a cloud of blue smoke. 'You don't want to let her wind you up, you know. She's a contrary little madam, likes to go her own way so I let her. She'll tame down in time.'

'If she doesn't land in trouble first! Dressed like an urchin and playing out in the streets at all hours of the night and day she could very easily end up in bad company.'

23

'She's on the ball, that one,' Maeve told him scathingly. 'She's well able to take care of herself.' She stubbed out her cigarette angrily. 'What's brought all this on anyway? You got a guilty conscience about leaving us for months at a time or something?'

John's steady blue gaze levelled with her face. 'Maybe I have,' he said thoughtfully. 'I never dreamed that Patsy was leading the sort of life she is. Or that she was being taunted and teased.'

'Kids' stuff, that,' Maeve told him. 'The little buggers are always picking on each other. One minute they're fighting and the next they've got their arms round each other's necks and you can't tear them apart.'

'I always thought mothers looked out for their daughters and that they cherished them and taught them how to behave and dressed them in pretty clothes. I made you a generous allowance all the time I was at sea so I knew you were all right for money, and I thought you'd be enjoying each other's company.'

'Doing what? She's a kid, she wants to play with other kids of her own age not sit around with me watching me paint my nails!'

'I imagined you'd be taking her to the pictures, or on trips to the shops or even over to New Brighton and places like that. If I'd known for one minute that she was being left on her own at nights while you went gadding off out with other blokes I'd have been home like a shot.'

'And are you telling me that you never went out on a drinking binge with the other fellas on the ship when you put into port?' Maeve jibed.

'Out drinking, no! I looked round the different places we docked in and took in the sights, but I didn't squander my money boozing. You must know that from the amount I was sending home to you.'

Maeve's mood suddenly seemed to change. Her face softened and her sneering was replaced by soft wheedling tones. Her eyes became limpid green pools as she looked up into her husband's face 'What are we quarrelling about, luv? You're home now so why don't we make the most of it?' She reached up, slipped her arms around his neck and gave him a seductive smile. 'I know of far better things we could be doing,' she breathed coquettishly, the tip of her tongue teasing the lobe of his ear.

Chapter Three

For Patsy Callaghan, Christmas 1922 was a mixture of sheer delight that her dad would be at home for Christmas for the first time since she could remember, wonderment that one of her most cherished dreams had come true, and fear that something would go wrong and spoil everything.

She would have given almost anything not to have had to go to school in the week leading up to the Christmas holidays. She wanted to spend every magical moment she could with her dad.

In the past, huddled in the dark waiting for her mam to come home from the pub, or wherever else she had gone in the evenings, Patsy had tried desperately to remember what sort of man her dad was. She wanted him to be strong yet gentle, kind yet authoritative. She hoped he didn't have a temper or shout, but above all she wanted him to be understanding, yet firm.

It was so long, more than ten months, since he had been at home that her memory of him was rather confused. She hardly expected the real man to live up to her anticipations, but it was consoling to daydream.

To her astonishment he seemed to match up to her expectations in every way. Except for the shouting. He hadn't shouted at her yet, but then she had been trying so hard not to do anything that might upset him or make him cross with her.

He had shouted at her mother a number of times and Patsy hated it when he did that, despite the fact that she could understand why it happened. Her mam could be so difficult to live with. In a matter of minutes she could change from being girlish and giggly into being mean and snappy. She could turn the atmosphere from one that was pleasant and relaxed into one that was fraught with tension.

It had happened several times since her dad had been home. Patsy had sensed they'd been rowing before she came into the house. She could hear their raised voices out in the street and then they would stop talking the moment she walked through the door. Her dad would look grim and her mother would be sulky, or pouting, and ignore whatever was said to her.

She'd confided in her best friend, Maureen Murphy who lived only a few doors away, about her mam's moodiness.

'One minute she's all sunshine and kisses and the next minute for no reason at all she's thumping me! Is your mam like that?'

Maureen's blue eyes had widened; her plump pallid face had looked perplexed. 'Not really. Sometimes she boxes my ears if I cheek her, but that's about it. Mostly it's a tongue-bashing I gets. I can shut my ears to that so it don't bother me too much.'

Patsy pulled up the sleeve of her jumper and displayed the bruises at the top of her arms to

Maureen, who shuddered at the sight of them.

'Does your dad hit you, then?' Patsy asked

Maureen pushed her long dark hair behind her ears and shook her head emphatically. 'Me mam wouldn't let him! She's boss in our house and if me or me sister needs telling off then she's the one that does it.'

'So you never get hit, not unless you're being cheeky?'

'Our Megan sometimes slaps me one. She's a right bossy-boots, but then you know that. She tells you off too!'

Patsy shrugged. 'Words don't matter, it's the thumping that hurts. I've got bruises everywhere.'

'What, as well as on your arms?' Maureen asked.

'On me back, me chest and me bum. The new ones are blue but later on they turn a greenish yellow. They don't hurt then and I forget about them. Until the next time.'

Patsy couldn't imagine her dad ever hitting her. She wasn't too sure though whether one of these days he might lash out at her mother. Sometimes she seemed to be deliberately winding him up, teasing him, provoking him almost as if she wanted him to thump her.

Patsy wondered what would happen afterwards if he did. Would she walk out for good as she kept threatening to do when things didn't go her way?

She hoped nothing like that would happen before Christmas. She wanted it to be an absolutely perfect occasion.

Slowly the days to Christmas crept by. She breathed a deep sigh of relief on the day school ended and she knew that from now on she could spend every moment with her dad. He'd promised her he'd help her make paper chains from strips of coloured paper and all sorts of other things to decorate the house. They'd never done that before and she was a bit surprised that he'd agreed, because he liked everything to be neat and tidy. Her mam said she didn't care what they did as long as she wasn't expected to join in or clear up after them.

On Christmas Eve he suggested they go into the centre of Liverpool to look at the decorations in the big shops in Church Street, Lord Street, Ranelagh Street and Clayton Square. Maeve said she would sooner stay at home, but at the very last minute decided she would come along as well.

Maeve wanted to visit Bold Street but John Callaghan said what was the point of looking in shops where everything was so highly priced you couldn't even begin to dream of buying them?

He was far more interested in the shops like Bunney's with their bright window displays that included toys and gadgets as well as clothes and things for the home. He was as keen as Patsy on looking round the toy departments and shared her enthusiasm for wind-up action toys and the Hornby train sets.

'What an utter waste of time this is, looking at toys,' Maeve grumbled. She pulled the fur collar of her dark green coat up around her ears until it was almost touching her green cloche hat. 'Patsy is too big now for such things. She's never played with dolls anyway.'

'Only because I've never had one to play with!'

'Yes you have. For Christmas last year I brought you home a lovely china doll from Spain,' John reminded her.

'You didn't come home last Christmas.'

'Well, no, but I brought it home in February and it was meant to be your Christmas present. Anyway, it settles the point. You do have a doll.'

As Patsy opened her mouth to explain about the doll Maeve grabbed her arm, her slim fingers with their long hard nails penetrating like talons, making themselves felt even through the thick gabardine sleeve of Patsy's new raincoat. She turned quickly to face her mother and shivered as she saw the warning in the icy glare Maeve gave her.

She drew her breath in sharply, pulled her arm away from Maeve's grasp and darted to the nearest brightly decorated window and stared in with feigned interest. But she could see nothing through the mist of tears that filled her eyes.

Her mother didn't want her dad to know what had happened to his lovely present. She doesn't want me to tell him that she burned it in front of me as a punishment because she said I had been rude to one of the uncles.

The memory sent a *frisson* of revulsion through her. He had been fat and smelt of whisky, but the worst thing about him had been his moustache. It had been wet and bushy and it felt like kissing a prickly brown rat. It made her stomach churn even thinking about it.

By the time they caught up with her, Maeve was complaining that her feet were aching and they still had all the shopping for food to do.

'Why don't you cut along to T.J. Hughes or C&A and buy yourself something special for Christmas,' John suggested as he handed his wife a crisp five-pound note.

Maeve hesitated for a brief moment then her gloved fingers curled round the note and she planted a grateful kiss on his cheek.

'Ta! I'll do that and then I'll get the tram home. Me feet are killing me. You and Patsy go to the market and pick up a bird and some veggies for tomorrow. Orright?'

The day took on an even greater magic once Patsy and her dad were on their own. The market was crowded with last-minute shoppers eager to find a bargain for the Christmas dinner. There was music playing and a group singing Christmas carols and even though John and Patsy found themselves being pushed and jostled from stall to stall they enjoyed every minute of it.

By the time they set off for home they were so loaded down with shopping bags and parcels that they could hardly stagger on to the tram.

One parcel intrigued Patsy more than all the others. While they were in the market her dad had bought her a milk shake and himself a coffee and they'd had a mince pie each. He finished his first and had told her not to hurry but to sit where she was at the table as he had forgotten something.

He promised he would be back in a few minutes and told her to guard the parcels and not move from the table.

When he returned he was carrying a large parcel, but he didn't say what it was and although she was curious about it she managed to keep from asking.

To their surprise the house was in darkness when they reached Paradise Place.

'I wonder where your mam is,' John frowned. 'She can't still be in town. Perhaps she's gone upstairs to have a nap. She said her feet were hurting and that she was tired out.'

He left the shopping on the kitchen floor, all except the mystery parcel, which he took upstairs with him. Within seconds he was back down again. 'She's not there. It must be taking her longer to find something she wanted than I thought.'

Together they unpacked the foodstuff they had bought and put some of it away.

'Leave the bags of veggies and the turkey where they are,' he told her, 'and start laying the table ready for tea.'

The time ticked by. Seven o'clock . . . half-past . . . eight o'clock. Patsy began to feel really hungry. It had been a long time since the milk shake and mince pie. 'Can we have our tea, Dad?' she asked cautiously.

He frowned. 'I suppose so. I thought we would wait for your mam, but it is getting late. I can't think where she might be. I'm worried in case she's had some sort of accident. She can't still be shopping or chatting with someone she's bumped into.'

'She's probably met one of the uncles and gone off to the pub with him,' Patsy muttered.

The moment the words were out, Patsy knew she'd said something she shouldn't have done. She thought her dad was going to tell her off, he looked so angry.

'Will you be all right on your own for ten minutes?' he asked. He put a plate of bread and butter and a pot of jam on the table in front of her. 'Tuck into that while I'm gone.'

'Of course I'll be all right, but where are you going, Dad?'

'I'll be back by the time you've eaten that lot,' he told her.

'Can't I come with you?'

'No, you'd better stay here in case your mam gets back and is worried because we're not here.'

Patsy nodded and began to tuck into the food. She really was hungry and she was afraid he might change his mind and say they must wait until her mam was home.

By the time she had cleared the plate, neither of them had come home. It had been well over half an hour since her dad had gone out. She walked across to the window and peered out into the darkness debating how much longer he was going to be.

She was tempted to slip upstairs to see if she could find where her dad had hidden the mysterious parcel he'd brought home. She was sure it was something special for her for Christmas. If she squeezed it she might be able to guess what it was.

'And if I get caught then I mightn't get anything at all,' she told herself out loud.

She took her plate over to the sink and rinsed the crumbs off it, dried it and put it back on the sideboard. Then she put the jam away in the cupboard. She was wondering whether perhaps she ought to go to bed when she heard a scuffling noise outside and then the door opened and both her mother and father were there.

'Give me a hand, Patsy,' her father ordered as he pushed a pile of shopping bags into her arms and then half lifted her mother over the doorstep. 'You hold her upright while I shut the door and then we'll get her up to bed, she's not feeling too well.'

Even as he spoke Maeve heaved and the next moment Patsy found herself covered in evil-smelling vomit.

She felt like bursting into tears. Her lovely green jumper was covered with horrid smelling slime that was bound to stain it, ruin it even.

'Go and take that off and put it to soak in cold water and I'll wash it out properly later on,' John Callaghan ordered grimly. 'Don't worry, luv, it will be all right. I'll see to it as soon as I've put your mam to bed,' he added more gently.

Holding back her tears, Patsy went to do as she was told. She felt so angry inside that her head ached, for it looked as though the special Christmas she had been dreaming about was going to be ruined after all.

All she wanted to do was get into bed, pull the covers up over her head and go to sleep and hope that when she woke up it would all have been a bad dream. Instead, she did as she'd been asked. She took off the smelly jumper, then filled the tin bowl they used to wash up in with water and plunged the jumper into it.

Her stomach heaved as obnoxious yellow slime floated to the top along with particles of food. She tipped the water away and refilled the bowl and then left it for her dad to see to once he'd managed to put her mam to bed.

She knew she ought to go and see if she could help him, but she couldn't bring herself to do so because she didn't want to see her mother like that. She'd never seen her so drunk. In the past when she had been out with one of the uncles and had too much to drink she was usually laughing loudly and singing and sometimes even dancing round the room with her arms held out and her head thrown back like some film star would do. This time, though, she had been more like a rag doll, limp and droopy with her head down on her chest and her legs going all over the place as she tried to walk.

Patsy thought about all the bags of food that she and her dad had shopped for in St John's Market. Some of them were still on the kitchen floor, and tears of frustration stung her eyes. All their plans now seemed to be going wrong.

As she began to unpack them and put them away in the larder she wondered if they would be having a proper Christmas dinner after all. Her dad had splashed out and bought a turkey which he said was even nicer than chicken. She'd never tasted turkey in her life so she was looking forward to it very much.

It was to have been the highlight of their day, but now it looked as if her mother would be too ill to be interested. She wondered if she would even be well enough to get up and go to Mass with them.

Her dad's plan had been that they would prepare the turkey tonight so that they could pop it into the oven to cook the moment they got up. After breakfast, before they all went to the special sung Mass at eleven o'clock, they would prepare the vegetables. They'd put the Christmas pudding on to heat up as well so that when they came home they'd only have to wait for the vegetables to cook and their dinner would be ready.

She was to be in charge of laying the table, and her dad had bought some paper hats for them to wear while they ate their dinner.

Now there was a shadow over it all. Patsy was afraid that her dad might be so disappointed and cross about the way things were turning out that he'd decide to go back to sea again after all.

Chapter Four

To Patsy's amazement Christmas Day looked as though it was going to be every bit as wonderful as she'd dreamed.

She woke early and crept out of bed to look out. The sky was grey and leaden and Paradise Place was deserted apart from the Murphys' black cat, that was picking its way delicately across the cobbles towards home.

There wasn't a sound in the house so, shivering with the cold, she decided to creep back under the covers for a while. As she turned round to climb into bed her foot caught against something bulky. She bent down to pick it up, and saw that it was a pillowcase with several things inside it, and her excitement made her forget all about the cold.

Pulling back the curtains so that she could see what she was doing she dragged the bundle up on to her bed and began to unpack it, eager to find out what was inside.

The first thing she discovered was the bulky parcel her dad had nipped out from the market to buy. She'd suspected it was a surprise for her and was glad now that she hadn't sneaked upstairs to try and find out what it was.

She felt it all over, trying to guess what it could

be. It was something inside a cardboard box and he had wrapped it up in green paper that had holly and robins printed all over it.

Patsy was torn between desire to know what it was, and curiosity about what else was in the pillowcase. Taking a deep breath she put it to one side and began taking out the smaller items.

She spread them out on the bed beside her. An orange, some walnuts, raisins in a screw of pretty paper, a bar of chocolate, a big rosy apple, two bright new pennies that looked like gold coins they were so shiny, a comic, some coloured pencils, a drawing book and a pair of bright red slippers with white pom-poms on the front.

It was a treasure trove of all the things she liked best and she didn't know which to use first. She felt almost too excited to open the other present and even toyed with the idea of leaving it until later. Supposing it was something she didn't like? Then it would spoil everything.

She laughed out loud at the thought. She was being plain silly. How could there be anything she didn't like!

She looked at each of the many presents again, trying to stem her fascination about the one that remained. Then curiosity got the better of her and she began removing the Christmassy paper.

The lid of the cardboard box inside was even prettier than the paper around it and Patsy sat for several minutes entranced by the attractive fairground scene. When she removed the lid she could hardly believe her eyes when she saw what was inside. Very carefully she lifted it out. The colourful carousel was so pretty that she loved it on sight. Eight gaily painted horses, suspended on tiny gold poles, swung out from the brightly coloured central pivot. As she wound the metal key, not only did a tune begin to play, but the horses moved up and down one behind the other. It was a perfect replica of a roundabout she had seen at New Brighton Tower fairground and had described to her dad in detail.

She could hardly wait for him to get up so that she could thank him. The moment she heard him padding down the stairs, and knew he had gone to make a cup of tea for her mam, she followed him.

'Happy Christmas, Dad, and my present is wonderful!' she said happily as she flung her arms round his neck and hugged and kissed him.

'Like it, do you?'

'It's wonderful. Have you heard the tune it plays?'

'Not yet. They had one playing in the shop so it may be the same tune.'

Patsy shook her head firmly. 'No! This has to be a very special one,' she grinned. 'And thanks for all the other things, Dad!'

'Happy Christmas, luv. Enjoy yourself. It's going to be a very special day, you'll see. Now, why don't you run up and get dressed. I'll take your mam up a cup of tea and then as soon as we've had our breakfast you can give me a hand to prepare the vegetables.'

'How is me mam feeling this morning? Shall I go and wish her a Happy Christmas?'

He looked at her doubtfully. 'No, I should leave it for the minute, luv, she's got a bit of a headache. Wait until she's had her cuppa and is ready to get up.'

It set the pattern for the day. Maeve's headache lasted all morning. Patsy tried not to think about it as she and her father peeled potatoes and prepared parsnips and Brussels sprouts for their Christmas dinner.

'Are you coming to Mass with me?' she asked hopefully when they'd finished.

'No, I think you'd better go on your own. I'll stay here with your mam and see to the dinner.'

When she turned away and said nothing he put his arm around her shoulders and hugged her. 'Look, I'll come if it means all that much to you, luv,' he told her gently.

Her face lit up with happiness. She knew the church had been specially decorated for the Christmas Mass and Father O'Brian would be in his most splendid regalia. There would be twice as many altar boys and the choir would sing.

What was even more important, she'd be as proud as punch because her dad would be there with her standing at her side. Everybody would see him, especially all the kids who called her ugly names and said she didn't have a real dad.

'You go and get ready while I baste the turkey and top up the water in the saucepan so that the Christmas pudding doesn't boil dry,' John told her.

'What about me mam? Is she coming to Mass with us?'

Deep down, Patsy didn't want her to come, she

wanted to have her dad all to herself, but she knew her mam ought to be there. Father O'Brian would expect it on such a special occasion.

Her dad shook his head. 'I don't think she's feeling well enough to come. We'll leave her to have a nice quiet sleep and then perhaps she'll be feeling better by the time we get back.'

Maeve was still asleep when they returned from church. When the vegetables were boiling away on the fire and John had basted the turkey yet again and pronounced that it was 'done to a crisp', he went up to rouse her.

She took ages to get dressed and by the time she arrived downstairs the vegetables had been drained and were going cold and the turkey was looking very well cooked indeed.

While her dad dished up, Patsy told her mother all about the carousel and then dashed upstairs to fetch it so that she could see it for herself. When she wound it up and it began to play, Maeve clapped her hands over her ears. 'For God's sake stop that awful noise,' she snapped.

John picked up the carousel and moved it out of the way. 'Leave it for now, Patsy, your mother's head is still bothering her. It's a lovely tune and you are right it is a different tune to the one they were playing in the shop,' he told her. 'We'll listen to it again later on. Let's finish our meal now before it's spoiled.'

Patsy and John tucked into their special dinner with gusto but Maeve barely touched hers. She played around with it until it was cold and then pushed her plate to one side.

She wouldn't even taste the pudding. Patsy and her dad both had a generous helping and Patsy squealed with excitement when she found a silver threepenny bit in her piece.

'Can I keep it?' she asked, her eyes shining, her cheeks pink with happiness.

'Of course you can! Lucky, aren't you?'

'You should have tried a piece, Mam,' Patsy grinned. 'You might have been lucky as well.'

'Oh for God's sake, Patsy, stop being so childish. Your dad probably slipped it in when he was putting the pudding on your plate,' Maeve told her irritably.

'Do you have to spoil everything for the kid?' John exclaimed exasperatedly.

'What the hell are you talking about? If there's any brandy left give me a nip,' she told him. 'Bloody waste pouring it over the pudding.'

'It's traditional, and how else can you light it?'

'So that you could show off! After the amount of turkey that kid stuffed inside her she shouldn't have needed any bloody pudding.'

'Well at least she ate her meal and enjoyed it, which is more than you did,' he told her frigidly.

'Oh yeah! Going to throw that up at me for the rest of time, are you?' she snapped. 'Who the hell do you think you are?' Her angelic face was contorted with rage.

'I think it might be better if you went back upstairs to bed until you are feeling more sociable,' John told her quietly.

'More sociable? More bloody sociable! I was trying to be sociable last night when you came and dragged me away from me friends. What the hell do you think they must have thought when you marched me out of the pub as if you were my gaoler?'

'I helped you out of the pub and brought you home because you were legless and falling all over the place!'

'You mean because you didn't like to see me having a good time. It's Christmas, for God's sake, and that's what friends do at Christmas. They go out together, have a bevvy or two and enjoy themselves.'

'You weren't enjoying yourself, you were paralytic.'

'I was enjoying myself. I stood them all a drink and they were buying me one back.'

'You mean that you wasted that fiver I gave you to buy yourself a Christmas present on buying drinks for that lot?' he asked angrily.

She gave a simpering smile. 'You said buy whatever I liked and that's what I did.'

'Wasted hard-earned money, and we haven't got a lot of that at the moment.'

'Then you'd better hurry up and find yourself a job, hadn't you? If you can't find one ashore then bugger off back to sea. Life was a lot easier when you were away, I can tell you.'

'Easier for you to go gadding off out with every Tom, Dick and Harry, but not so easy for poor little Patsy left at home on her own.'

Maeve clamped her hands over her ears. 'I don't want to hear it.'

Savagely he pulled her hands away. 'You don't

want to but for once you are going to listen. I've been sending home money for you and Patsy to live in comfort all these years and what have you done with it? You've squandered most of it on drink and entertaining your no-good friends. You've not only left her to fend for herself but you've not even clothed her properly. Well, all that is going to stop. Believe me, it is.'

Patsy listened to their confrontation in growing horror. She knew what her dad said was true but she didn't like them fighting over her. She knew her mam neglected her, but she loved her just the same. There were times when her mam was lovely to her. It was the uncles who spoiled everything. She knew her mam loved her but when they came to the house her mam sent her out to play and forgot all about her.

When she was left sitting on the doorstep with a bag of crisps other children envied her. She never told them that it had been half empty when she found it, or that the reason she wouldn't share it with them was because she was so starving hungry that every morsel was precious. She hid her misery and unhappiness behind a cheeky grin and still went on loving her mam.

Patsy knew her mam only went off to the pub and got drunk because she was lonely, but she was lonely too with her dad away. She had thought everything was going to be resolved now that he was back home. She loved him so much, and if her mam felt the same way about him then she wouldn't be lonely ever again either.

She watched in dismay as Maeve tossed her

head disdainfully, her hair glinting in the gaslight. 'So who is going to change things?' she challenged.

'I am!' John Callaghan said forcefully. 'Things in this house are going to be run properly from now on. I'm not having Patsy run wild any more, do you understand?'

'You can't even find work,' she taunted. 'You've been home for weeks and you haven't managed to land a job.'

'I will do, in the New Year,' he told her confidently.

She shook her head, her lip curling. 'You aren't qualified to do any job except go away to sea. The sooner you wake up to that fact and find another ship and sign on again the better.'

'Oh, no! My days at sea are over,' John Callaghan insisted doggedly. 'I'll find myself a job ashore, don't you worry. I'm not leaving Patsy in your charge ever again.'

Chapter Five

John Callaghan staunchly refused to deviate from his resolve to find work ashore. He knew it wasn't the best of times to do so, but he persevered day after day.

He was up early every morning to make sure Patsy had a proper breakfast. He would walk as far as the school with her then head off to the Pier Head to check out if there was anything going down at the docks, before making his way back into town to the Labour Exchange.

Maeve was highly critical of the amount of dole money he received and even though he turned over the bulk of it to her for housekeeping she complained it was not enough to manage on. It certainly didn't leave anything over for the new clothes, make-up and trips to the pub two or three times a week that she'd been used to when he'd been at sea.

The atmosphere between them had settled down and most of the time she was compliant enough. He tried hard to make her life as pleasant as he could, but he knew she longed to go out more and realised that she was so gregarious that his company would never be enough for her.

Now that she couldn't afford to go to the pub every night she flirted with every man in sight.

The postman, coalman, milkman and even the men who were their neighbours in Paradise Place were all targets for her 'come-hither' smiles and flippant remarks. Some replied in the same vein, some ignored her approach, but others, emboldened by her brazen attitude, tried to take advantage of the situation. She was, after all, a very attractive woman. Her strawberry-blonde hair glinted like spun gold, her green eyes sparkled, her lips were enticing and she always dressed in a provocative manner.

Some of the men simply couldn't help themselves. They seemed to think that a stolen kiss, a surreptitious cuddle, or even a slap on her shapely rump were permissible.

Whenever John was around he made it quite clear that they were overstepping the mark. He would put his arm around her shoulders in a proprietorial way and draw Maeve close, kissing the top of her head or her cheek before leading her away from any further temptation.

When he had first done this she had been furious, but realising that she was not going to win her freedom by fighting him she pretended to be contrite and turned all her charm as well as her full attention on him.

Patsy watched this pantomime with a mixture of bewilderment and unease. Why did her mother have to play games like this? she wondered. None of the other married women in Paradise Place flirted with other men and some of them had husbands who, to her eyes, were horrible. Big paunchy fellows with stubble on their faces and lank greasy hair, or wiry little ferret-faced men with piggy eyes and mean mouths. Her dad wasn't like that at all. He was tall and broad and stood head and shoulders over most of the men he came in contact with and he was so handsome that Patsy thought he looked like a film star or one of the models used on advertising placards to sell cigarettes.

Patsy couldn't understand why her mother wasn't as happy as she was to have her dad around all the time, but it was clear from the constant bickering that went on that she much preferred it when he was away at sea.

As each day passed and John Callaghan was unable to find work ashore, Maeve's nagging became more acid.

'Nothing again today,' she would mock when he arrived home in the late afternoon looking tired out and despondent.

When his reply was that he had been tramping from one place to the next in search of work and that in each instance he was too late, or that he had waited with a long queue of other hopeful men only to be told that the position was filled, she would simply shake her head or shrug her shoulders.

'You can always go back to sea if you can't find a job ashore,' she would remind him.

'No, I'm determined to stay here in Liverpool where I can keep an eye on Patsy,' he would tell her grimly.

He meant what he said and towards the end of January he made up his mind that if he couldn't find work in the normal way then he must create work for himself. He still had a small cache of savings left from his final trip which Maeve knew nothing about and so he decided that as a last-ditch attempt he would sink this money into creating his own business. If that failed, then he would have to admit defeat and go back to sea, but he didn't intend to let it fail.

While he had been searching for work on the dockside he had got to know a number of the gaffers who handed out jobs and had studied them closely so that he knew exactly how they worked. His idea was not to apply to them for a job, but to offer them a service that they needed and which they found frustrating and time consuming to locate.

With this in mind he made enquiries about renting a stable that was at the end of the row of houses in Paradise Place. It had been empty for a long time and was in a state of disrepair, but he persuaded the landlord to let him have it at a fairly low rent if he undertook to put it to rights.

It took him another week and about a third of his precious hoard of money to carry out the necessary repairs. Once completed, the stable was warm and dry and spacious enough to house a large horse. There was room in the yard outside for a cart to be left overnight.

Buying a horse was the next step. John had been born and brought up on a farm in Ireland where all the ploughing and farm work had been done with carthorses and it was a heavyweight animal along these lines that he set his sights on.

Samson was a massive dray horse, but his previous owner assured John that he was as docile as a kitten and a steady worker.

'Goes all day as long as you feed him well and treat him right. I'll be sorry to lose him, but I'm giving up. I'm well into my sixties and too old for handling heavy loads. The wife says it's time I stopped workin' an' put me slippers on, so he's yours whacker if you want him? I might even drop the asking price if I know he's going to a good home.'

They haggled amicably, though John would have been prepared to pay the asking price in order to secure Samson if he'd had to do so. Instead he asked if the cart and tack could be included as well.

When the deal had been concluded there were tears in Samson's owner's eyes as he patted the horse goodbye.

'Hold on a minute,' he called out as John started to lead Samson away. 'Since you're having me bloody horse and me bloody cart you may as well have this,' he said, handing John a well-used piece of paper. 'It's a list of the gaffers and companies down on the docks whose goods I've been carrying for the last ten years.'

John couldn't believe his luck. In one stroke he had set himself up in business. Armed with so many contacts he couldn't possibly fail, he told himself jubilantly.

'If you ever want to see Samson, or check that we're doing a good job, you can always look me up here on the dockside. I'll be keeping an eye out for you,' John promised as they finally parted.

As he drove the horse and cart back to Paradise Place, John Callaghan felt like a millionaire. It was a long time since he'd handled a horse, but Samson seemed to be every bit as docile as his previous owner had said he was. He responded to the slightest touch of the reins and the traffic and other street noises didn't seem to bother him at all.

As he settled the horse into the newly renovated stable he couldn't wait to tell Maeve about his new venture. She'd realise now that he was serious about staying ashore and he hoped that she would stop throwing out remarks all the time about him going back to sea.

Maeve was not at home so as it was mid-afternoon John Callaghan decided to go and meet Patsy from school and take her to see Samson.

Her reaction delighted him and confirmed in his own mind that the enormous step he had taken was the right one.

For the first few minutes Patsy was nervous about standing too close to Samson. He was so huge that her mop of red curls barely reached up to his massive chest. When he emitted a noisy snort of air she jumped back in fright and when he put his huge head down and nuzzled her neck with his warm nose she held her breath in terror.

'I thought he was going to eat me,' she gasped as her dad laid a reassuring hand on her shoulder.

'No, he was trying to be friendly. He was hoping you'd have something for him to eat.'

'Like what?' she asked, looking up at her dad wide-eyed.

'I expect he's partial to a piece of carrot or an apple,' he told her. He fished an apple out of his pocket and handed it to her. 'Here, give him this.'

Patsy held the apple gingerly between two fingers and darted her hand out in front of the horse, then pulled it back just as quickly.

'No, no! Don't tease him like that or he might accidentally bite you,' her dad said quickly. 'Place the apple flat on the palm of your hand and hold it out and keep your hand perfectly steady.'

'I can't! He might bite me!'

'No he won't. He'll take it very carefully and all you will feel is his lips brushing your hand.'

Patsy shook her head doubtfully.

'Come on, I'll show you.'

He balanced the apple in the palm of Patsy's hand then, keeping his own hand underneath hers to steady it, held her arm out in front of the horse.

Patsy held her breath and screwed her eyes tight shut as the horse began to lower his head towards her outstretched hand. When, as her father had explained, Samson took the apple and all she felt was his warm lips as he did so, she opened her eyes again in wonderment.

It was the start of a tremendous bond between the huge brown-and-white horse and the diminutive red-haired girl. Patsy took an immediate liking to Samson and he responded to her voice and touch as if he accepted she was his friend.

Every night after school she would wait impatiently for her dad and Samson to return from their haulage work at the docks. The moment he crossed the cobbled yard into the stable, she had an apple or piece of carrot waiting for the horse and though she now held them out quite fearlessly she never failed to marvel at how gentle the huge animal could be. As soon as Samson's harness was removed she would help to feed and groom him. Maeve hated the horse. She declared him to be a great lumbering, smelly creature and she wanted nothing whatsoever to do with him. She complained bitterly when John and Patsy came indoors after being in the stable that they smelled of the animal and insisted they took their shoes off and left them by the back door.

Now that she knew there was no possible chance of John ever going back to sea again Maeve studiously began to replan her own life. She hated the ordered round of domesticity. She liked to dress up in her prettiest clothes, but there was no point in doing that unless there was someone to admire her and pay her compliments.

Most nights John was far too tired after his heavy day moving cargo down at the docks to want to go out. Even after he got home there was Samson to be fed and watered, the stable to be cleaned out and fresh straw spread on the floor. Even with Patsy doing her utmost to help it usually took well over an hour. Then all he wanted was a good wash, a filling meal and a quiet evening by his own fireside reading the *Echo*.

At first, Maeve contented herself with visiting the pub at midday, but most of the men whose company she enjoyed were working then. The evenings were prime time for company and after a great deal of argument and continuous nagging she managed to persuade John to take her out every Saturday night as well as at least one night during the week.

The thing John Callaghan disliked most about this arrangement was leaving Patsy at home on her own. As spring advanced and the nights became lighter and lighter it was only natural that she wanted to play out in the street after school with her friends. He had no objections to her doing this, but he was well aware that if he and Maeve were out then Patsy was in the habit of staying out until well after dark and he worried in case she ended up in some kind of trouble.

'Stop worrying your head about her,' Maeve told him crossly. 'I've told you before she's well able to look after herself. She's never got into any sort of bother up to now, has she?'

'No, but she is getting older, and prettier, and I don't want her in any trouble,' he would argue.

'Then make her stay home when we go out.'

'I don't like to think of her left here in the house on her own either.'

'Then tell her to have young Maureen Murphy in to keep her company, or Janie Grant. They're both in her class at school.'

When he mentioned this idea to Patsy she wasn't at all enthusiastic.

'Maureen won't want to stay in, she likes playing out and Janie is such a little goody-goody that she's no fun at all. I'd sooner be on my own than have her in here to keep me company.'

'So who would you like to have here with you?'

'You, of course!' she told him with an impudent grin. 'I love it when it's only the two of us and you tell me stories about all the foreign places you visited when you were at sea and about when you were a boy in Ireland. Me mam never tells me anything like that. All she talks about is clothes.'

John felt torn between the two of them. He knew what Patsy said was right, but he also knew that unless he took Maeve out she would either sulk or go to the pub on her own. She enjoyed the company of her friends who drank there, but he found them raucous. He was glad of the excuse to leave early because Patsy was at home on her own.

As he took on more and more work at the docks he felt the need for early nights rather than outings to the pub. Looking after Samson took up a lot of his time and in the end he decided he would have to find someone to help with mucking out the stable and grooming Samson. Patsy was more than willing to do it but she couldn't wield the heavy yard brush or reach up high enough to groom Samson properly.

He talked to Patsy about it and asked if she knew any likely young lad who might be interested.

'Billy Grant would jump at the chance,' she told him. 'He's always asking me about the horse. Billy loves animals. He used to take old Mr Peterson's dog, Nipper, for a walk every night after school, but then it died and Mr Peterson said he was too old to get another one.'

'You mean Janie's brother? I don't think he would be any use. He's not even as tall as you are.'

'Not her little brother, her older brother. He's nearly thirteen and ever so tall. He could reach up to groom Samson and put on his harness quite easily. And he'd be ever so good with him.'

John promised to give Billy Grant a trial. It turned out to be a tremendous success. As well as helping out after school Billy came round early in the morning to give Samson his feed. In next to no time he had learned how to harness Samson up ready for his day's work.

With help at both ends of the day, John found he was less stressed and had far more time for both Patsy and Maeve. As a routine acceptable to them all became established he congratulated himself that things were at last turning out exactly as he had hoped they would.

Chapter Six

Patsy's tousled red head was barely visible over the half-opened door, but the sturdy brown-and-white dray horse whinnied a greeting as she came inside the stable.

'Yer late, kiddo! Samson's been getting restless thinking yer weren't coming,' Billy Grant said mildly as he carried on grooming the horse.

'I know I'm late, Billy,' Patsy sighed as she fondled the warm soft nose that the horse thrust inquisitively towards her hand in search of the apple or raw carrot that was his usual treat.

'So what kept you?' he asked

Patsy shrugged. 'This and that, you know how it is.'

Billy's eyes narrowed as he cleaned out the curry-comb and studied his work on the horse's coat.

'Is yer ma playing up again, then, kiddo?' he asked casually.

'Yeah. She's got a bit of a cob on. Her head's bad and so she spent the day in bed and I had to do all the cleaning. Me dad's nipped out to the shops because I had no money to buy any food.'

Billy shook his head sadly. 'So what are you doing here?'

'Well, Mrs Murphy has just dropped in to see

me mam so I took a chance to pop out and come over to see Samson.'

'Well I'm off home for my tea now,' Billy said as he reached up for the old plaid blanket that he draped over the horse's back after he'd groomed him. 'See yer at the usual time tomorrow.'

Patsy nodded, but said nothing. She felt too choked to speak. She'd been looking forward all day to having a chat with Billy. It mattered almost as much to her as seeing Samson.

Billy Grant was almost three years older than her, sturdy and capable with thick brown hair, light blue eyes and a square jaw with a cleft in the centre of it.

Patsy liked being with Billy because he always treated her as an equal and they had become very good companions. Unlike the other boys she knew at school he never made any derogatory remarks about her red hair or her freckles. In fact, he never teased her at all.

He seemed to understand how much she cared about Samson and didn't laugh at her for bringing the horse an apple or a piece of carrot every night. He encouraged her to tell him what she'd been doing and sympathised with her when, like today, her mam was so hungover that she had to stay in bed.

They met up and talked to each other nearly every day and she often wished he was her brother. She felt she could tell him anything and he always seemed to understand her problems even if there was nothing he could do to help her.

What was more, he confided in her, telling her things he said no one else in the world knew. She knew exactly how he felt about school and his teachers, which ones he liked and which he hated. And he told her about his mates and warned her which ones to avoid because they were bullies.

Billy had also told her that he intended to leave school the minute he was fourteen and old enough to do so. It worried Patsy because she was afraid she wouldn't see very much of him once he went to work.

'Why don't you let my dad know when you'll be leaving school and ask him if you can work for him full time?' she had suggested.

Billy shook his head. 'He probably couldn't afford to employ me full time,' he told her. 'I want a job where I can earn a really good wage because I'm saving up for something special.'

It had taken her almost a week of deft probing to find out exactly what it was that Billy was saving up to buy. She'd turned it into a guessing game, naming everything from football boots to a cricket bat, or even a wireless set, but he'd shaken his head each time and his lips had remained sealed.

Then one day, out of the blue, he said he was going to tell her what it was. First, he swore her to secrecy. He said he didn't want anyone to know what he was saving up for, certainly not his sister Janie who would be bound to tell his mum and dad.

'I won't tell a soul. Cross my heart and hope to

'die,' Patsy promised and held her breath waiting to hear what it was.

'I'm saving up to buy a Harley-Davidson,' he confided.

'A Harley-Davidson?' Patsy looked blank, then her green eyes danced with excitement. 'You mean a motorbike?'

Billy nodded. 'That's right, but not any old motorbike. I want a Harley-Davidson. I know they cost an awful lot of money, but since I'm not old enough yet to ride one, that doesn't matter. I want to have the money saved up ready, though, so that on the day I am old enough to ride one I can go out and buy it.'

'They're those great big powerful bikes!' Patsy exclaimed in awe.

Billy's face lit up with enthusiasm. 'A Harley-Davidson is the most expensive motorbike in the world and that's because it's the very best motorbike in the world, too.'

Patsy frowned. It seemed a pretty daft thing to her. 'Have you ever been on one, Billy?' she asked dubiously.

He shook his head. 'Not on a Harley, but I have ridden pillion on a Rudge. The Harley is ten times better though.'

'How do you know it is if you've never been on one?'

'A chap who has been on both of them told me so.'

'Will you give me a ride on it when you get it?' she asked hopefully.

He laughed. 'Yeah! I'll make sure it has a Buddy

seat fitted so that I can take you for a spin on it,' he promised. 'You'll love it.'

'Ta! You would still consider working for my dad full time when you leave school if he was to pay you a proper wage, though, wouldn't you?' she persisted, her eyes anxious.

Billy looked thoughtful. 'Well, I might consider it,' he grinned.

'Samson would like that,' she insisted.

'What about you?'

'Yeah! I want you to,' Patsy told him eagerly. 'I'd miss you a lot if you left.'

'Well, that's nice to know,' he said. 'Afraid you're going to miss me now as well, kiddo, because I'm off home to get me tea. Come on,' he went on as he propelled her towards the door. 'I want to lock up the stable.'

Despondently Patsy now walked back across the cobbled yard that separated the stable from the street. She couldn't bear the thought of not seeing Billy every day. He was so very much part of her world, the best friend she had ever known.

She cheered up slightly when she saw that Maureen Murphy was sitting on the front doorstep waiting for her.

'Been sneaking out to the stable to see Billy Grant then?' Maureen teased.

Patsy blushed, her face flaming, making her freckles look like a sprinkling of brown dots over the bridge of her nose. ''Course not, I always take an apple or something over to Samson at this time every day.'

'Oh, yeah? And what about an apple for Billy?

Or perhaps he gets something better, like a kiss and a cuddle,' she said archly.

'Don't talk daft!' Patsy said crossly.

'You telling me you've never kissed him or had a bit of a cuddle?' Maureen persisted, tossing back her long dark hair and staring at Patsy intently with wide blue eyes.

'Of course I haven't,' Patsy told her indignantly, her own eyes flashing angrily.

'Why not? He's ever so handsome. I bet you'd like to kiss him,' Maureen sniggered.

Patsy looked thoughtful, holding her lower lip between her small white teeth. 'Not really,' she said slowly, 'but I like him as a friend.'

'Yer daft, you are!' Maureen told her. 'He's in our Megan's class at school and she said most of the girls are dotty about him.'

'Your Megan would be dotty about anything in trousers,' Patsy scoffed.

'Oh no she's not!' Maureen defended her. 'She wouldn't even give Billy Grant a second look. He might be good looking but he's too scruffy. He smells, too, of that horse. You wouldn't notice that, though, because you stink of that old horse the same as he does.'

Patsy shrugged her scrawny shoulders. 'What are you doing here, anyway?' she asked as she hunched down on the front doorstep alongside Maureen.

'Waiting for me mam. She's having a jangle with your mam. Probably wants to know what's up with her this time.'

'Me mam's got one of her bad heads,' Patsy muttered evasively.

Maureen gave her a sideways look. 'Do I look that daft that I'm going to believe that?' she smirked. 'C'mon, what's really wrong with her?'

'She's got a bad head!'

'I heard what you said first time,' Maureen snapped. 'I ain't stupid, you know, nor deaf.'

Patsy didn't answer, and she avoided Maureen's sharp look.

'You weren't at school again today,' Maureen said accusingly. 'Miss Richardson was asking where you were.'

'Me mam was bad in the night so me dad said I might as well stay home as someone ought to be with her.'

'My mam says if her headaches are as bad as she makes them out to be then she should be in hospital being properly looked after and getting her head examined and put right.'

'She is properly looked after,' Patsy said defensively. 'I look after her better than they would in any hospital. Anyway, it's only headaches she gets and she'd sooner be at home than in one of those places.'

Maureen shrugged. 'I don't suppose they'd take her anyway. The headaches she keeps on getting are because she has hangovers all the time and that's because she drinks too much.'

'What do you mean by that, Maureen Murphy?' Patsy drew in her breath sharply and her expression changed to one of anger. 'I suppose that's why your mam's here, isn't it? Poking her nose in! Come to read me mam the riot act, has she?' Her voice rose hysterically. 'She needn't bother!

Father O'Brian and me dad can do that without any help from anyone else.'

Tears of outrage spurted from her eyes and she wiped them away on her sleeve. Then she scrambled to her feet and pushed past Maureen.

Blindly she stumbled up the stairs to the front bedroom where Mrs Murphy was sitting by the bedside talking to her mother. She paused in the doorway of the darkened room, her breath catching in her throat as the smell from the vinegar-soaked compress that her mother insisted on having on her forehead stung her throat.

'Is that you, Patsy?' her mother asked in a tremulous whisper. 'Could you get me a drink, lovey, I'm absolutely parched. It must be all this talking.'

Patsy nodded, too choked to speak. When she returned with the mug of water she noticed that there were dark shadows beneath her mother's green eyes, that her hair was mussed into a straggly mess, her cheeks drained of colour and her skin a sickly yellow.

'Give it here, chuck.' Bessie Murphy held out her hand for the water.

Short, plump with very dark straight hair, blue eyes and a round florid face, she contrasted so sharply with the woman lying in the bed that for a minute Patsy hated her. Why should Maureen and Megan's mother be so fit and healthy when her own mother was so sickly? It didn't seem fair, Patsy thought rebelliously. Deep down, though, she knew her own mam could be as fit and well as anyone else if she didn't drink so much.

'There, come along then, let's prop you up so that you can take a sip of this,' Bessie Murphy encouraged Maeve as she slid an arm under her shoulders and effortlessly raised her into a half-sitting position.

'You go on down and talk to our Maureen then, Patsy, I'll only be another minute or so. Your mam and me are having a little talk, private like.'

Patsy bit her lip. She knew now why Bessie Murphy was there and she didn't like the idea one little bit. She wanted to be the one by her mam's side, holding her hand and comforting her. She wanted to be the one to tell her that she must stop drinking because next to her dad she mattered more than anything in the world. Even Samson wasn't as important to her as her mam.

She loved her dad best because since he'd stopped going to sea she felt so safe and happy. If he ever went away again she didn't know where she would be. Sometimes, though, she found it was hard work trying to please him all the time.

She wondered if it was the same with her mam. Perhaps the drinking bouts were her way of dealing with things when living up to what was expected of her, and keeping her feet on the straight and narrow, became too much for her, Patsy reflected. She wasn't really a bad person, it was just that she couldn't be bothered about day-to-day things, like keeping the house clean and having meals on the table, things that other people considered important. She sighed. And sometimes her mam would lose her temper and lash out for no reason at all.

Her casual way of doing things had started when her dad had been at sea. Without him coming home at regular times she'd lost the habit of keeping to a routine. She simply did what she had to, but only when she felt like it.

When I was a very little girl, Patsy mused, whenever my dad was coming home on shore leave Mam would dress me up in a lovely new dress bought specially. When he arrived home I'd sit on his knee, all clean and pretty with a bright ribbon in my hair and I'd be wearing shiny black shoes and white socks, and feel like a princess.

For the first few days that he was at home it was like a wonderful party and friends and neighbours would pop in at all hours to see him and join them in a drink.

Then, Patsy recalled, just as she was growing used to this tall stranger with the smiling face and deep warm voice he would go back to sea. Her mam would be in tears for a few days and then things would drift back into chaos again.

At night, after she'd been sent to bed, she would lie in the dark thinking back on all the fun and laughter there had been while he'd been at home.

Within a week or two her mam would become moody and miserable. She would start going out at night or bring friends home. So many different ones that Patsy had never been able to remember their names so they were all 'uncles'.

It all seemed so long ago, yet it was only a little over a year since her dad had decided it was time to give up going to sea and had bought Samson. His haulage business moved cargo from ships when they docked at Liverpool to the warehouses along the quayside, or transported loads to the other side of the Mersey to businesses in Wallasey or the Wirral.

Patsy thought back to the old days when sometimes she didn't even bother to wash her face and her hair had been tangled and dark for want of washing. Her dresses had been stained and grubby too and their home had been dirty and smelly a lot of the time.

All that was in the past, she reflected. Since he had hired Billy Grant her dad had more time to notice these things. Their home was probably one of the cleanest in Paradise Place and she had more clothes than Maureen Murphy or Janie Grant so she was always nicely turned out.

Her dad had restored order and routine to their lives. They went to Mass together on Sundays and when the weather was nice they went out as a family on trips to the park or over to New Brighton.

Mrs Murphy's mouth pursed impatiently as Patsy still lingered by her mother's side. 'Go on, then, do as I say,' she reiterated sharply, breaking into Patsy's thoughts. 'Go and talk to Maureen, there's things your mother and me want to say to each other that are not for your ears.'

Resentfully, Patsy did as she was told, but inwardly she was seething at being sent away.

She didn't want to talk to Maureen, not after the things she'd been saying about Billy Grant. She'd always thought of Billy as being like a brother and now Maureen had spoiled it all by talking all soppy about kissing and cuddling with him. Patsy's face flamed just thinking about it.

Chapter Seven

John Callaghan was a very happy and contented man. It was his thirty-sixth birthday and he was more than proud of the fact that since he had stopped going to sea some four years ago he had managed to build up a haulage business as good as many men would have achieved in a lifetime.

Being handed a list of possible customers by Samson's previous owner had been a stroke of good fortune, of course. It was still the nucleus of his business, but he had more than doubled the number of customers that he'd had in those early days and he was still expanding. He'd never advertised; it had all happened by word of mouth. Fair prices and reliability and his attention to detail had all helped.

Billy Grant was another great asset. He'd been quick to learn, he was polite and efficient and always looked clean and smart. He didn't say a great deal, but people liked him. And so did Samson. He and Billy made a splendid team.

Things on the home front had gone well too over the last four years, John reflected. There had been a rough patch with Maeve at first. She'd resented losing her freedom, but he was sure that in her heart she understood his reason for staying ashore and knew it was the right thing to do.

Another couple of years and young Patsy would have been completely uncontrollable or in trouble with boys or the police. It wasn't that Maeve didn't love her, but she seemed to have no idea about how to bring up a child. She'd let Patsy run wild and she'd neglected her.

Now, she was thirteen and she had grown into a little beauty with Maeve's green eyes and red hair, but Patsy's hair was a darker red and a riot of curls. She was taller than her mother, tall and lean like him. She wasn't doing as well at school as he would have liked, but then that wasn't entirely her fault. She did try hard, but she had missed out on so much of her schooling in the early days that it seemed it was impossible for her to catch up.

That did bother him, because he would have liked her to be a teacher or perhaps work in one of the big shipping offices in Liverpool, but he knew she'd have to be pretty bright to do either of those things.

He didn't want her to leave school and become a Nippy in a Lyons tea shop like Billy's sister had done and he didn't want her working in a factory, as so many of the girls from Paradise Place ended up doing. When it was a little closer to her fourteenth birthday he might ask around at some of the firms where he made deliveries to see if there was any opening for her as a receptionist or telephonist or even as a typist. She'd have to start at the bottom, of course, and she would probably have to go to night school in order to train for such work, but it would be a real step up in the world for her.

He'd tried talking to Maeve about it, hoping she would be of the same opinion and have a word with Patsy, but she'd not really agreed with him over Patsy's future.

'With her looks and figure she'd be better off going for something more glamorous like being a dancer. I can see her as an actress. She's got my looks and she's tall so she'd be perfect as a show-girl. That's if she doesn't get married first. I can see the lads will be round her like bees round a honeypot once she stops messing about in the stable with that old nag of yours. Her clothes stink to high heaven most of the time after she's been there feeding it and letting it rub its face against her.'

Maeve still didn't like Samson. 'Great lumbering creature,' she called him and nothing would persuade her to go within six feet of him.

'If he accidentally put one of those great hooves down on you then you'd be crushed to death and if he turned nasty then with those great teeth of his he could bite your arm off before you knew what was happening.'

Nothing Patsy or John told her about how gentle Samson was made any difference. Grudgingly she admitted that he was an asset as far as work was concerned, and that without him there would be no haulage business, but that was as far as her acceptance of Samson ever went.

Maeve could be very stubborn when she wanted to be, John thought resignedly. He'd found

71

that persuading her to conform to what he expected from her as a wife and mother had been hard work.

The trouble was that her friends were not his friends. He liked a drink as much as the next man did and he wasn't averse to a game of darts, but he didn't want to spend every evening doing that. He liked to read, to listen to his wireless set or simply to sit and talk over the day's happenings.

This was never enough for Maeve. She craved excitement and she needed to be laughing and joking with an admiring crowd all around her. He sensed the constant restlessness in her and the frustration she felt most of the time because she could no longer carry on like that.

For all her faults, he still loved her as desperately as he had done when they'd first met in Dublin. She'd been a slip of a thing then, her red-gold hair halfway down her back and her green eyes challenging.

He'd spent his brief shore leave with her and she'd agreed she'd be waiting for him when he returned. She'd kept her promise. Eight months later when his ship had put into Dublin she was on the quayside to greet him, only this time she wasn't the slim, lithe girl he'd kissed goodbye. In fact, if it hadn't been for the flowing red hair and vivid green eyes he wouldn't have recognised her. She was as plump as a suet duff and he suspected the worst even before she flung herself into his arms, tears streaming down her face, and announced that she was expecting his baby.

'I was so afraid you wouldn't be back in time

to marry me before it was born,' she sobbed as she clung to his arm.

He felt as if he had been hit midships by a northeasterly gale. He was only twenty-two; he'd no intention of marrying and settling down for years. He loved his present life too much! Going to sea had been his dream ever since he'd been a young boy. The life was strenuous, but he enjoyed the company of the men he sailed with and the excitement of putting into strange ports and seeing new sights. He'd already sailed halfway round the world, but there were still places he hadn't visited.

Settling down ashore and being saddled with a wife and family was for older men, not for young blokes like him. Anyway, there was a whiff of trouble in the air and they might well be at war within the next few months. Life would be hazardous enough at sea without having responsibilities at home.

Yet he knew his conscience wouldn't let him desert her. If, as she said, it was his child she was carrying then he had to do something about it, but marriage was out of the question. He drew the line at that.

Three weeks later, though, they were married. It had been a quick, simple ceremony. His parents were dead and hers, being strict Catholics, had turned her out the moment they knew she was pregnant.

They'd left Ireland immediately.

'We'll start afresh in Liverpool,' he told her. 'I'll see you settled in somewhere before my next trip.'

'Promise me you won't go until after the baby's born,' she pleaded in a little-girl voice that he hated, but found hard to resist.

One of the men he had known on his last ship had come from Liverpool. The name of the place where he lived, Paradise Place, had always intrigued John Callaghan so they went there first to see if he could recommend anywhere they could find a place to live.

'You've come at just the right time, boyo,' Davy Williams greeted him. 'The wife has decided she doesn't want to stay on yer in Liverpool. Too lonely, see, with me away so much. She wants to move back to Cardiff, to be near her own family. We're in the throes of packing up our things and I was about to hand in the rent book.'

'So how does that help us?'

'I'll put a word in for you with the landlord, boyo. He'll want a new tenant, now won't he?' He winked broadly. 'He's bound to prefer one who comes with a reference for being a good sound payer rather than take on a complete stranger.'

Davy Williams's plan had worked. The day he moved out of Paradise Place John and Maeve moved in. Maeve had been like a little girl playing at house. They'd bought new curtains and rugs and bits and pieces of furniture until his wallet was almost empty.

'I'll have to go back to sea and earn some more if we go on like this,' he'd warned.

Her face had clouded and she'd pouted and clung to him with tears in her eyes. 'You can't leave me all on my own, not now when the baby is due any day.'

He'd promised he would stay until after she'd had the baby and he'd kept his word. When Maeve had gone into labour on a scorching hot August day the full realisation of what was happening, and the enormity of his responsibility, hit him like an avalanche as he went with her to the hospital.

As he paced to and fro outside waiting for news the thought of taking off, getting a ship and disappearing out of her life was so strong that he had to force himself to go back into the hospital.

When they told him he had a baby daughter he wanted to run a mile. He was a man's man, a sailor, and the thought of having a wife and a daughter was too frightening for words.

He was told he could go in and see them both, but his legs felt leaden. He'd faced all sorts of dangers and strange situations both at sea and abroad, but none of them compared to this.

Maeve, her hair fanned out on the pillow like an exotic shawl, looked pale and exhausted after her ordeal. His heart thudded with love as he bent to kiss her. He was glad he hadn't succumbed and taken flight.

'It's a little girl,' she whispered. 'Is that what you wanted?'

John felt perplexed. He hadn't given it any thought until that moment. A baby was a baby, a shawl-wrapped bundle that cried when it was hungry and slept the rest of the time.

Then he looked at the baby in the bassinet at her side and his heart not only thudded, it turned over. The baby was asleep and it looked like a life-sized doll. It had Maeve's heart-shaped face and its head was covered with a soft red down.

As he'd stood there gazing down at the tiny bundle, trying to collect his thoughts, the baby had suddenly moved and stretched. Opening her eyes she had looked straight at him and it was as if an invisible thread was joining them. He felt a huge surge of protective love for the fragile little creature that he had helped to create.

They'd named her Patsy and for the next few weeks life took on an entirely new meaning. Nights as well as days seemed to revolve round the baby.

It was with the greatest reluctance he went back to sea, but they needed the money and it was the only life he knew.

During the time he was ashore they had got to know some of their neighbours in Paradise Place. There were several families with babies almost the same age as Patsy so he knew Maeve would have company and people to call on if she needed help with the baby.

He had managed to get a short run and was home again before Christmas. Maeve was looking fit and well and Patsy, now almost four months old, was a complete joy. He was happy to take her out, or sit and watch her as she lay cooing and gurgling to herself in her cradle. Maeve seemed to be besotted by her so he went back to sea in the New Year with a contented mind.

Patsy was a year old when he next came ashore. An active lively little thing, who, now that she could crawl, didn't stay in one place for more than a few minutes.

Maeve made it quite plain that she found Patsy a handful and was adamant that she didn't want any more children. Because he was so besotted by his little daughter, John promised he'd have one more trip and then he'd come ashore for good.

War intervened. All shore leave was cancelled. Then the ship he was on was torpedoed and after drifting for days in an open boat he was finally washed up off the coast of India. Getting another ship home was impossible. He couldn't even get word through to Maeve. All he could do was hope and pray that she was receiving the allowance he had made over to her so that she had enough money to live on and to feed and clothe Patsy.

He was stranded in India until the war ended. When he finally docked in Liverpool he was almost four years older, Patsy was already at school and Maeve almost a stranger.

If she had missed him she made no mention of it. The soft kittenish manner had been replaced by a brittleness that he found disturbing. She'd even changed the colour of her hair. The fiery red was now a strawberry-blonde shade and she wore far too much make-up.

At first their reunion was strained. It was almost as if she resented him coming home. Then she flung herself into a whirlwind of activity, organising a constant round of parties, and inviting her many friends in. Repeatedly he told her that all he wanted was to be with her and Patsy and to relax; to get used to his freedom and adjust to being back at home again. But Maeve took no notice.

Patsy had accepted him without any questions about his absence. He knew she couldn't possibly remember him because he had been away for the greater part of her young life.

Apart from the shock of red curls and the huge green eyes, she too had changed completely. Instead of being a chubby round-faced baby she was now a skinny little girl with bony knees and sharp elbows. It saddened him that she had such a grubby unkempt air about her and she appeared to be extraordinarily self-sufficient for a five-year-old.

At first whenever he spoke to her she simply hung her head, or looked the other way. She was fiercely independent and didn't like being kissed or cuddled. Whenever he went to pick her up she shrank into herself or shivered violently as if she couldn't bear to be touched. He blamed this on his long absence and although it saddened him he took great care not to force her into accepting him.

It irked him when she called him Uncle instead of Dad, but as he met up with Maeve's wide circle of men friends, and saw the way Patsy called all of them Uncle, he gradually began to understand the situation more clearly.

He didn't know how to handle it or how to rectify it. It wasn't his fault that he hadn't been able to get home. He supposed, if he was honest, he had to admit that it wasn't altogether Maeve's fault either that she had adopted a lifestyle that he didn't like.

None of the other women in Paradise Place had been left on their own for such a long time, not even those whose menfolk had been called up into the army. Their husbands had come home on leave from time to time, as well as writing home regularly. He'd not been able to do any of these things. As far as Maeve was concerned, receiving the allowance he made her regularly was the only sign she had that he was still alive.

As soon as possible he had gone back to sea. He felt he needed space, the wide sea and the open sky to sort his mind out and decide what he was going to do about the future.

Almost as soon as he was out of port he wished he could go back. Leaving Patsy behind tore at his heartstrings. He knew she needed his care and protection and that he was deserting her.

He had the same feeling of guilt when it was time to leave on each of his next home visits. By then, he and Patsy had not only accepted each other, but the bond between them had become increasingly stronger. The moment he saw the mute pleading look in her eyes when he said goodbye, he felt sick with apprehension because he knew the sort of life he was condemning her to while he was away.

Patsy was running wild and it was up to him to do something to change that before it was too late and Patsy ended up in trouble. It was not something he could accomplish in a few weeks, or even months, which was why he had stuck to his determination to take a shore job and be a proper father to Patsy.

In some ways he had been more successful than he could have ever hoped and their special outing tonight to celebrate his birthday was proof of that. He was taking Maeve and Patsy to see a show at the Empire Theatre.

Chapter Eight

Regardless of the fact that she was wearing the new blue-and-white spotted voile dress her dad had bought her specially for their celebration night out, Patsy flung herself down on the pile of straw in the corner of Samson's stable and buried her face in her arms.

Tears that had been threatening for the last hour gushed from her eyes and rolled down her cheeks unchecked.

'So what's up now, kiddo?'

Patsy jumped as if she'd been shot.

She'd thought she was alone in the stable and for a moment as she looked up at the tall broad figure of Billy Grant, who was standing only a few yards away from her, regarding her with concern, she felt angry about the interruption.

'What are you doing here at this time of night, Billy Grant?' she snuffled crossly.

'I dropped by to see how Samson was. His ribs got a bit of a bashing when we were down at the ferry today. The boat pulled away a bit sharp like and he wasn't standing four square and he caught himself against the deck rail. He seems to be OK now though, don't you, old boy?' He reached up and fondled the horse, patting its thick neck affectionately.

Samson blew down his nostrils and whinnied in appreciation as he nuzzled against Billy's shoulder.

'What are you doing in here anyway lolling around on the straw when you're all dressed up to the nines?' Billy asked, staring at Patsy. 'I thought that with it being your dad's thirty-sixth birthday you were supposed to be going to the Harry Lauder Show at the Empire Theatre.

Patsy sniffed back her tears and wiped her eyes with the back of her hand. 'We did go to the Empire.'

'Then why are you so glum? Wasn't Harry Lauder any good?'

'Yeah, he were absolutely great! The whole show was good!'

'Why the tears, then?'

Patsy shrugged. 'It was after the show ended that things began to go wrong. Me dad took us for a fish and chip supper and that's when me mam started griping. She wanted to go to the Grafton afterwards for a bevvy and he said he'd sooner go home. They started arguing and she said he was ruining everything because all her mates were waiting there for them.'

'So he gave in and they came back to the pub?'

'Yeah!'

'And you got sent home because they won't let kids of your age in the Grafton?' Billy said softly.

'That's right,' Patsy snuffled. 'A smashing evening out and then I get sent home to bed on my own. Me dad wanted to come with me and make sure I was orright, mind, but me mam grabbed his arm and said I was big enough to put meself to bed without a nursemaid.'

'And so you are,' Billy grinned. 'Anyway, you've been putting yourself to bed while your mam goes off down to the pub for years, so why are you making such a fuss?'

'No I haven't! Not since me dad's stopped going to sea.'

She stood up and brushed away the straw from her dress, then walked over to fondle Samson.

'Come on, I'll walk back to your place with you,' Billy offered. 'I'll even put you to bed if you like,' he added with a wide grin.

Patsy's face flamed. 'You needn't bother, you cheeky bugger! If I told my dad what you said he'd boot you out,' she added threateningly.

'He couldn't manage without me.' Billy grinned flexing the muscles of one arm.

Patsy's lip curled. "Course he could!'

'How do you make that out?' Billy demanded.

'I'd help him, wouldn't I!'

'Huh! I'd like to see you lifting bales of cotton up into the cart or trying to handle some of the other heavy loads,' Billy teased.

Patsy tossed her head, making her red curls dance around her ears. 'I could hold Samson's head while me dad loaded up.'

'Oh yeah?' Billy's grin widened.

'I do now when I come out with you on Saturdays and in the school holidays, don't I?'

Billy nodded solemnly. 'I was only teasing you, kiddo, trying to get you to stop crying and give us a smile. I like it when you come out with us.

We have some good times, don't we?'

'Yeah,' Patsy agreed. 'And as soon as I can leave school I'll be coming out with you and me dad all the time.'

'You sure about that?' His blue eyes held hers in a puzzled stare and he looked uneasy.

'Yes, why shouldn't I be?'

'Well . . .' Billy ran a hand through his thick brown hair. 'I think your dad has other ideas about what sort of job you'll be doing.'

Patsy frowned. 'How do you know that?'

'He talks to me a lot when we're working.'

'So? What's he been saying then?'

Billy rubbed his chin doubtfully. 'I'm not sure whether I should be telling you or not.'

'Go on,' she prompted impatiently. 'What's my dad been saying?'

'I think he has plans for you to stay on at school and pass exams so that you can become a teacher or something.'

'Oh, no!' Patsy's eyes clouded. 'He's not serious about that, is he?'

'He sounds serious to me. He seems to be very proud of the fact that you won't have to go and work in a factory like Megan Murphy, or a shop, or even become a Nippy like our Janie.'

'What's wrong with being a Nippy?' Patsy asked in surprise. 'Your Janie seems to love it. She looks real posh in her uniform. She's always going on about what a good time she has at work and about all the interesting people she meets.'

'Don't forget about all the money she earns and the tips she gets,' Billy laughed.

'Well, there you are then.'

'Yeah, but she's only been working a couple of weeks, hasn't she. She mightn't think it's so wonderful once the novelty has worn off. Anyway, it's not what your dad wants for you. He has plans for you to do something much grander.'

'Well, I don't. I want to come out with him and you and Samson.' She looked up at the horse and patted his broad neck.

'Forget it, Patsy. Your dad doesn't want to see you working down at the docks every day with us and I bet your mam wouldn't be very pleased about it either.'

'She'd probably love it if she thought me dad was against it,' Patsy said glumly. 'She likes nothing better than winding him up.'

'She loves winding most people up,' Billy grinned. 'My dad says she's always doing it when she's in the Grafton, especially when she's had a few drinks too many.'

Patsy bit her lip to stop herself saying anything. Billy knew quite a lot about what went on between her and her mother, but she didn't want him or anyone else critising her mam or feeling sorry for her.

Things had been pretty good at home lately and so she preferred to forget about the past when her dad had gone to sea and her mam's moods had swung madly from one extreme to the other.

A shudder went through her as she thought back to when she was small. One minute her mother would be kissing and cuddling her and brushing her hair and dressing her up in fancy

85

frocks. Then she'd be off down the pub and forget all about coming home to give Patsy something to eat or put her to bed.

Even worse had been all the men friends her mam had brought home. Thin men, fat men, little men, big men – she'd lost count of them. She'd hated every one of them.

Patsy sighed. She still couldn't understand why her mam needed to go out to the pub. In the past she'd always said that she only liked going to the pub and bringing the uncles home because she was lonely. Now that her dad was home she couldn't be feeling lonely any more so why couldn't they have a normal sort of life like the other families in Paradise Place?

She was pretty sure that her dad felt the same way about it as she did. In the evenings after a hard day at work all he wanted was for them to sit round the fire and read the *Liverpool Echo* or listen to the wireless.

She'd gone with him to buy the wireless and it had been the most expensive one they had in the shop. The man explained that it was battery powered and that it cost so much because it had an Armstrong TRF superheterodyne receiver to ensure better fidelity. Neither of them had been too sure what that meant, but it sounded impressive.

How exciting it had been when they took it home and connected it up to the accumulator and he had let her be the first to turn the tuning dial! It had been like magic moving from one wavelength to another. Sometimes there was music, at other times people were talking, and in between there was a swishing sound like waves on a far-off shore.

Her mam didn't think very much of it, especially when it began oscillating and sending out high whistling sounds so that for a minute or two they couldn't hear the music or what people were saying. Her dad thought even that was interesting and would sit there moving the dial a fraction one way and then the other until he had fine-tuned it and it was working perfectly again.

Whenever he started doing that, her mam went and put her coat on and announced she was going out to the pub where there were real people to talk to and music as well if old Sammy was there with his fiddle, or Phil with his squeeze-box.

'Well, are you coming, Patsy? Do you want me to walk as far as your door with you or not?'

'I dunno!' Patsy came back to the present with a deep sigh.

'Well, I do. Come on, or you won't be home let alone in bed before your mam and dad get back and then you'll be in trouble.'

'Do you have rows going on all the time in your house?'

Billy shook his head. 'No! What me old man says goes. He's boss and nobody ever argues with him.'

Patsy turned this over in her mind. Joe Grant was about the same age as her dad, a heavily built man with a bald bullet head. He looked more like a boxer than a docker with his prominent nose and a cleft in the centre of his square jaw. She'd heard her mam say that he was aggressive and pig-headed.

Billy must take after his mam, Patsy decided. Elaine Grant was a plump, motherly woman with a fringe of fair hair framing her grey eyes. She had a smile and a cheery greeting for everyone although she always seemed to be bustling about looking after her family.

As well as Billy and his sister Janie there was a younger boy. Freddie was something of a terror at school, but his mother would never believe it and always took his part no matter what mischief he'd been involved in.

'Does your mam ever go to the pub on her own?'

'She never goes to the pub. Me dad wouldn't stand for it. He likes his beer, mind you, but he only goes to the pub on a Saturday night and he never gets plastered.'

'Do you go to the pub, Billy?'

He laughed and shook his head. 'Can't afford to go drinking.'

'Why not? You don't have to give your mam all your wages, do you?'

Again he shook his head. 'I'm saving up for the Harley-Davidson, remember? It will be ages before I can afford to buy it. Don't you tell anyone, mind, not even your dad. Promise?'

Patsy nodded solemnly. 'Am I still the only one who knows your secret, then?'

Billy grinned. 'You and Samson. I tell him all my secrets, the same as you do. He never argues or lets me down. Come on, he needs his sleep even

88

if you don't,' he told her, pushing her towards the door.

As they walked across the cobbled yard and the short distance to her front door in silence, Patsy was suddenly conscious of how tall and broad Billy had become in the last few months. She could see from their shadows that he was half as tall again as she was. He might be kind and gentle like his mam, but he was built like his father, she thought, as she glanced sideways at him. Not for the first time she wished he was her brother instead of someone who only worked for her dad.

'Well, your place is in darkness so either your mam and dad are still both down the boozer celebrating his birthday, or you're so late back that they're home and in bed,' Billy commented.

Patsy pushed her hand through the letterbox and retrieved the doorkey that was hanging there on a piece of string.

'They're probably still at the pub,' she said glumly.

'So do you want me to come in and keep you company until they get home?' Billy asked.

'Gerroff! Do you think I'm daft?'

She would have liked to ask Billy to come in, but she thought it best not to. If her mother was tipsy when they came home there was no knowing what she might say or do and it would be embarrassing for Billy to see her mam like that.

'Tara, see you tomorrow then,' Billy said and began to walk away. He paused and called back over his shoulder, 'By the way, you look smashing in that frock, kiddo. It suits you!'

Patsy felt her cheeks burning. No one had ever paid her a compliment like that before and she didn't know what to say so she pretended not to have heard.

She dashed upstairs and undressed as fast as she could. She wanted to get into bed as quickly as possible so that she would still be able to hear his voice saying 'you look smashing in that frock, kiddo,' as she fell asleep.

Chapter Nine

It was a cold murky Saturday morning in late March. John Callaghan had agreed to collect a heavy consignment from a factory in the Wirral, bring it back to Liverpool and then have it loaded on to the SS *Maybury* before the ship sailed on the mid-morning tide.

'You can come along as well and give a hand with Samson while Billy and me handle the load if you like, Patsy,' her father told her.

'Yes!' Her face lit up. There was nothing she liked better than to sit perched up on the long narrow seat of the cart, wedged in between Billy and her dad. While they loaded or unloaded she would hold Samson's head and talk to him, calming him if there were any sudden noises.

'It's going to be a six o'clock start and there's no hanging around waiting for you if you're not ready, so you'd better get an early night,' he told her.

'You give me a shout when you get up and I'll be out in the stable harnessing Samson before you've got your boots on,' she told him with a wide grin.

'There's no need for you to do that. Billy will be coming in well before six to get Samson fed and ready. You'll still need to be up early, though.

It's a cold night so it will be frosty in the morning. Make sure you've time to get a good breakfast inside you.'

'And you'll both have to get it yourself,' Maeve told them peevishly. 'I'm not getting out of bed to cook anything for you at that ungodly hour.'

Patsy pulled a face, but John signalled to her with a shake of his head to say nothing. They knew that Maeve never got up in the morning to cook them breakfast whether it was John going off for the day around seven or Patsy going to school an hour or so later.

'Wear something warm, remember,' her dad told her. 'It's freezing cold at that time of the morning.'

Their trip went extremely well. They caught the six-fifteen ferryboat and were in Wallasey soon after six-thirty. The river was as still and grey as the sky so the crossing was calm.

It was bitterly cold and damp so John Callaghan insisted that Patsy went inside one of the salons to keep warm. He and Billy took it in turns to shelter in there with her while the other one stayed with Samson.

Half an hour later they were at the factory gates. Their consignment was ready for them and there were two burly men to help load up the wagon.

'With any luck we'll be back in Liverpool docks again before eight o'clock like we promised,' Billy said confidently, as they climbed up on to the cart.

'Don't be too optimistic,' John warned as he picked up the reins. 'There seems to be a mist starting to creep in from the sea.'

He was right. Even before they reached Seacombe ferry the mist had thickened and slowed down their progress. The River Mersey was shrouded in fog and warning klaxons and ships' hooters sounded from all sides.

'We'll miss the eight o'clock sailing at this rate,' John said worriedly.

Fortunately for them there were very few travellers on the ferry at that time of day. One of the crew on the *Royal Daffodil* saw them coming down the slipway and waited for them.

'Too early to have the roads aired,' John joked with a deckhand as the ferryboat pulled alongside the Liverpool landing stage and they started to tie up.

'Yeah, and it's a tidy old load you got there,' the man told him, eyeing the piled-up cart. 'You'll need an extra horse to get that lot up the floating roadway. If you hang on a minute I'll see if they've got one working yet. They don't always start very early on a Saturday.'

Their luck was in. A carthorse far bigger than Samson was brought out from the stables under the floating roadway and hitched up in front of Samson. The deckhand led him forward, leaving Billy and John to make sure that Samson walked directly behind him and that their load remained steady.

Patsy scampered on ahead of them and was breathless by the time she'd reached the top of the steep slope. She liked to be there to watch when they unhitched the carthorse, gave him a slap on the rump and left him to turn round and take himself back down the narrow gangway. It was a routine he did a dozen or more times a day, but she still marvelled at how clever he was to be able to make his own way down the long narrow passage at the side of the floating roadway on his own.

Safely on land, John and Billy checked over the harness before making their way along the dock road to where the SS *Maybury* was waiting.

'Youse lot is bloody late,' the gaffer snarled when they eventually drew up alongside the boat.

He signalled to a couple of dockers to give them a hand to unload and get the cargo aboard. It was an exhausting hour's work for them all, but they managed to meet their deadline with half an hour to spare.

'I think we've earned ourselves a break,' John told Billy and Patsy. 'Come on, there's a café just along the front here with space outside where we can tie Samson up for half an hour. The place is a bit rough, but they do great bacon butties and a decent cuppa char.'

'I put a nosebag on board for Samson. He didn't have time for a full feed before we left,' Billy told them, 'so he'll be glad of the chance to stoke up.'

The bacon butty was every bit as good as her dad had said it would be and although the tea was much too strong for her Patsy didn't complain. She was content to be sitting there in the small, overheated shack with them.

Thinking back to the conversation she'd had with Billy on the night of her father's birthday Patsy wondered how she could break it to her dad that this was the life she wanted. She didn't want to be a teacher or to work in an office where she would have to go all dolled up every day.

She knew it was going to be hard to convince him that she liked wearing thick woollen stockings, a tweed skirt and a heavy coat with a muffler around her neck for extra warmth. She liked riding high on the cart, holding Samson's head while they loaded and unloaded, and, above all, she enjoyed being with her dad and Billy.

They made a wonderful team, she thought as she watched them enjoying their food and tea and talking about the work they would be doing in the coming week.

Not for the first time, she wished Billy was her brother. He could well have been, she thought as she studied them more closely. Now that he was fully grown he was more or less the same size as her dad in height and in a few more years, when he'd finished filling out, he'd probably be much the same size.

There were other similarities too, she noticed. They both had thick hair that they brushed back from their forehead; though Billy's was much fairer than her dad's. They both had blue eyes, but Billy's were a lighter, brighter blue. They had long faces with square chins and looked solid and dependable, and when they smiled there was a warmth and kindness in their expression.

She could have sat there all day, studying them and letting her thoughts wander, but her dad had other ideas.

'Come on,' he ordered, draining his cup and standing up. 'Time we were making a move.'

As they emerged on to the dockside the damp and coldness shrammed them. While they'd been inside the café the sea mist had crept in and now it mingled with the grey city smog so that they could hardly see a few feet in front of them.

Billy made his way over to where Samson was tethered, a bulky grey shape in the yellow half-light. He removed the horse's nosebag, which was now completely empty, and than climbed up on to the wagon.

'You get up there and ride with Billy,' her father told Patsy. 'These cobbles are as slippery as glass with this mist on them and since you can hardly see your hand in front of your face I'm going to lead Samson until we get back on to the main road.'

Their progress was slow as the icy cold, damp fetid mist shrouded them. Samson plodded along snorting uneasily, as if in protest at the strange noises from all around them. Strident warning sirens and blaring klaxons sounded from the ships on the river and these made him shy, prick up his ears and whinny noisily as if in fright.

'Come on, Samson, let's get out of here and up on to the main road,' John Callaghan muttered, urging the horse forward. As they turned into the main stream of traffic, however, the conditions grew even worse. Huge Green Goddess trams loomed up out of nowhere, their bells clanging noisily. As John guided Samson out of their way they found themselves in the path of cars and motorised lorries that came so close that they almost scraped the sides of the cart.

The clamorous blare of one horn spooked Samson and he reared up. The animal threw his head back so hard that although John Callaghan clung to the reins with all his strength, he lost his balance. His feet sliding on the slippery road surface, he fell right in the pathway of an enormous lorry.

From her seat high on the cart Patsy heard the dull impact and her first thought as she peered through the dense smog was that Samson had been hurt. Scrabbling down to the roadway she ran towards the front of the cart.

She stopped in horror. Samson was unharmed but a man's body lay pinned under the rear wheel of the lorry and her head reeled with shock when she realised that it was her dad.

From then on Patsy felt she was living in an ever-increasing nightmare. There was commotion around her as people came running from all directions and for a few minutes there seemed to be utter chaos.

Several policemen arrived on the scene and traffic was brought to a stop as they shouted orders and moved the crowd back. An ambulance was sent for and decisions were made about what to do next.

Patsy felt Billy's arm go round her shoulders and she turned her face away so that she couldn't see what was happening. She didn't want to accept that it was her dad lying there motionless, pinioned beneath the wheels of the lorry.

A crowd of dockers, under police supervision, manhandled the lorry off her father's crushed body moments before the ambulance arrived. Even without medical knowledge it was obvious that there was nothing they could do for John Callaghan. The doctor who had arrived with the ambulance, after a cursory examination, declared him to be dead.

Dry eyed, but numb with grief, Patsy turned to Samson. He stood dejectedly between the shafts, his head down, as though he knew he was partly to blame for the accident.

Patsy fished around in her coat pocket to find the apple she'd brought out to give him and as he munched stoically on it she patted his broad neck. 'It wasn't your fault,' she whispered, burying her face in his mane.

Billy placed a hand consolingly on her arm. 'I'd better get Samson back to his stable,' he told her. 'Are you coming home with me or are you going in the ambulance to the hospital?'

'No!' Patsy shuddered. 'There's not much point, is there?'

'Billy put his arm around her shoulder again. 'Come on then, you ride and I'll walk. Samson is probably feeling nervous so I'll lead him until we're clear of the main streets.'

Shrouded in fog and gloom, Patsy had no clear idea of their journey back to Paradise Place. When Billy pulled into the small yard and opened up the stable doors she remained where she was, frozen in body and mind.

'Come on,' he said as he helped her to the ground. 'You'd better go and tell your mam what's happened.'

The colour drained out of Patsy's face. 'I can't do that on my own,' she protested. 'You'll have to come with me.'

Billy hesitated. 'I ought to see to Samson, he's soaking wet, cold and probably frightened by all that's gone on this morning,' he prevaricated.

'Then I'll stay and help you,' she told him.

Before he could protest she had started unhitching the cart.

'Leave that,' he said, pushing her to one side. 'You put down some dry straw and fill up his feeding trough and see there is fresh water for him.'

Working together they made the horse as comfortable as they could. Patsy picked up the curry-comb ready to start grooming him but Billy took it from her.

'We'll just dry him down and put a blanket over him, then leave him to rest and settle down. I'll clean him up properly later on,' he told her. 'Come on,' he said. He propelled her towards the stable door. 'It's time we faced your mam and let her know what has happened.'

Patsy hung back, shivering and shaking her head. 'I can't do it,' she whispered.

'You've got to,' Billy insisted. 'I've said I'll come with you, if you like.'

She stared at him, her eyes dull with despair and the freckles across the bridge of her nose standing out like a brown band against the chalky whiteness of her face.

'I'm not even sure that it's true,' she shuddered. 'That . . . that thing lying there in the road, not moving, not breathing, that couldn't be my dad!' she exclaimed shrilly.

'Oh, Patsy!' Billy held her close, smoothing down her red curls. 'I know how terrible this is for you, it's been an ordeal for all of us, but you've got to be brave. You must tell your mam what has happened.'

She looked up into his face pleadingly. 'Couldn't you tell her?' she begged.

He shook his head. 'I'll come with you, I'll be there to give her the details if she wants to know them, but you should be the one to tell her,' he said firmly.

Chapter Ten

For Patsy the days that followed the accident were a long, never-ending nightmare. She and Billy had to make statements to the police. There were countless messages of condolence to be acknowledged, from the companies John Callaghan had acted for as carrier. At the same time there were constant visits from neighbours in Paradise Place, all of whom wanted to help.

Bessie Murphy came in several times a day to see if Maeve was all right or if there was anything she could do. Her husband, Daniel, even went across to the stable to see if Billy needed a hand.

Maeve Callaghan was bearing up remarkably well. When Patsy and Billy had first told her what had happened she was too stunned to speak. A short time later the police arrived and Maeve gave way to a fit of uncontrollable weeping.

She was quite hysterical after they left and Patsy was so concerned that she asked Billy to send his little brother Freddie to fetch Father O'Brian and the doctor.

'Let's hope that one or the other of them will be able to pacify her,' she said worriedly.

By the time a reporter and photographer from the *Liverpool Echo* arrived on the doorstep half an hour later Maeve had made a swift recovery. She insisted on renewing her make-up before she saw them in case they wanted to take a picture of her and then proceeded to deliver a voluble account of what had happened and how she felt about it all.

On the day of the funeral, Maeve dressed from head to toe in deepest black and concealed her face with a heavy black veil.

At first Patsy had said she wasn't going to attend the funeral, but Father O'Brian had been shocked and insisted that it was her duty to be there to support her mother in her hour of grief.

Eventually she agreed, but only on condition that the coffin was carried on their cart with their own horse pulling it. She insisted on helping Billy to drape the cart with crape and to groom Samson for the occasion.

They worked in silence until Samson's coat gleamed and his harness glittered. Patsy washed the fringes around his fetlocks and even blackened and polished his hooves so that he looked as though he was entering for some championship prize. Between them they decorated his massive head with black ostrich plumes that dipped and swayed as he plodded majestically towards the church, led by Billy.

It was a magnificent turnout. Patsy and her mother walked directly behind the cart, followed by almost everyone in Paradise Place. Dockers and deckhands who had grown to know and like John Callaghan joined them as they approached the church.

Father O'Brian, resplendent in his full regalia,

conducted a sung Mass which took over an hour. Then the cortège moved to the newly dug grave in the adjoining cemetery. Later the *Liverpool Echo* carried pictures of the impressive funeral procession and another lengthy report of the accident.

After the internment Maeve seemed quite composed though very pale. Throwing back her heavy black veil she invited Father O'Brian and everyone else there to take part in the wake that had been organised in honour of her husband's memory.

Silent and distressed, Patsy accompanied Billy as he took Samson back to the stable. She found immense comfort from being with them and ministering to Samson's needs. Even after they'd fed and watered him she wanted to stay on in the stable, but Billy insisted she must leave and offered to see her home. She looked so sad and unhappy that he longed to take her in his arms and comfort her.

The wake was still in progress. Loud voices, peals of laughter and bursts of song assailed their ears as they reached Patsy's house.

'I can't go in there,' she muttered, turning away. 'How can they be laughing and drinking and carrying on like that when me dad's lying dead in his grave?'

'It's the way some people cope with grief,' Billy told her gently. 'Your dad was a wonderful man, a lot of people were very fond of him and this is their way of celebrating his life and saying goodbye.'

Patsy shook her head, her green eyes burning

with anger. 'Well, it's not mine,' she said stubbornly.

Before Billy knew what was happening she had taken off, running down the street and disappearing into the distance. He made a half-hearted attempt to go after her then decided that perhaps it was better to let her have some time on her own. She needed to come to terms with what had happened, say goodbye to her father and grieve in her own way, he thought sadly.

Although Patsy had appeared to remain dry eyed and stoic ever since the accident, as if determined to remain in control of her feelings, Billy knew how upset she was. To carry on like that and keep all her emotions bottled up inside her would serve no purpose, he reflected. She needed to purge them from her system and convince herself that even though she was missing her dad desperately her life still had to go on.

He thought about all the dreams and plans her father had nurtured for her. What did the future hold for her now, Billy wondered? Or for himself, if it came to that. His future was as much in the balance now as Patsy's was, he thought uneasily.

Tomorrow he would call on Maeve Callaghan and, if she was sober enough to talk about such things, see if he could find out what she intended to do about the haulage business. He had been working for John Callaghan for four years now, counting the time when he'd still been at school. He'd been over the moon when he'd been old enough to leave school and work full time. He'd been so happy that he'd never considered looking for any other job.

John Callaghan had always treated him very fairly and he'd learned a tremendous amount from him. He'd been a splendid boss and they'd made a first-class team. Now the thought that it might all be ending worried him greatly.

What would happen to Samson if Maeve decided to give up the business? He was such a docile and reliable creature that it would be terribly sad if he was sold off to someone who wouldn't care for him like he did, Billy thought. He could hardly sleep that night. He went over and over in his mind the things he could say to Maeve Callaghan to try and persuade her to keep the business going. If she did agree to do so, would he be able to manage all the carting and keeping track of all the accounts and orders? He wasn't used to paperwork. John Callaghan had handled all that side of things himself.

He wouldn't have to let Maeve Callaghan know that, of course, Billy decided. He'd been pretty bright at school so he was confident that he could pick it all up if he had to. Anyway, Patsy would probably be able to help him.

Thinking of her diverted his thoughts into another channel. He wondered what time she'd come home and where she'd gone when she'd run off like that. Her dad had been everything to her so he knew how she must be hurting. Running away wouldn't solve anything, though. He'd have to talk to her tomorrow and try and make her see that.

Next morning, Billy felt at a loss about what to do. He went through the normal routine of feeding and grooming Samson and mucking out the stable, but he knew he ought to go and talk to Maeve before he went down the docks.

He waited until Patsy would have left for school before knocking on their door. He wanted to see Patsy, but he felt it would be more sensible to talk over business matters with Maeve first.

He knocked twice and was about to walk away when Maeve opened the door. She had make-up on and her hair was combed, but she was wearing a bright red silk wrap and he could see she was still in her nightclothes.

'Sorry, Mrs Callaghan, I didn't mean to disturb you' he mumbled awkwardly, 'but I thought I ought to speak to you before I took Samson . . .'

Maeve cut him short. 'Look Billy, if it's business you've come about I'm not interested,' she told him sharply and started to close the door.

'Hold on, there's arrangements John made and I don't know what to do about them.'

'If it's things to be collected and delivered then go ahead and do it,' she snapped. 'Don't bother me about it now. You can come back later and talk to me when you've done them.'

This time the front door was firmly slammed shut with such force that that the frame rattled.

Billy didn't know what to think. Did this mean she was going to carry on the business? Did it mean that he was in charge? If he couldn't cope on his own would she let him hire someone to help?

The questions buzzed round in his head like a swarm of wasps as he hitched Samson up to the cart and set off for the docks.

As he had told Maeve Callaghan, there was work already booked so he went to attend to it. The gaffers were pleased that he had turned up because there had been no time to find anyone else to do the work. They were as co-operative as they could be, making sure he had help with both loading and unloading, but he knew they were making this special concession because of what had happened. In the near future he would have to find someone to help him as there was no way he could manage single-handed.

He made his way back to Paradise Place at the end of the day with these thoughts uppermost in his mind, and puzzled over the best way of explaining it all to Maeve Callaghan.

Perhaps he had done the wrong thing in going to see her when she was on her own. It might after all have been better if Patsy had been there. She would have made sure that her mother listened to the things he had to say. What was more, she would have been able to support him when he explained to her mam that he was going to need help of some kind.

As soon as he had tended to Samson he made his way to the Callaghans' house again. This time Maeve had the door open almost before he could knock. She still wasn't interested in anything he had to say about the business; it was Patsy's absence that she was concerned about.

'Are you saying that she hasn't come home from

school?' Billy asked, twisting his cap uneasily in his hands.

'Come home from school! She hasn't even *been* to school! In fact, I haven't set eyes on her since the funeral yesterday. The last time I saw her she was walking over to the stable with you and that damn horse. Now where is she?'

Billy shook his head. 'I've no idea, Mrs Callaghan. I walked her back to the house after we'd settled Samson, but she took herself off for a walk because she didn't feel she could face all the people that were here.'

'Huh! She couldn't face them! What about me? I had to face them, didn't I? I had to give them all food and drink, and listen to their maudlin conversation until almost midnight. Selfish little madam, clearing off like that and leaving me to look after them.'

Billy looked puzzled. 'So are you saying that Patsy didn't come home at all last night?'

'I've already told you she didn't!' Maeve snapped. 'Can't you listen to what I'm saying? Here I am worried out of my senses and you stand there and keep asking me the same question over and over again.'

Billy shook his head in despair. 'I'm sorry. It's just that I find it hard to take in. Have you any idea where she could be?'

'That's what I'm asking you, isn't it,' Maeve snapped. 'I thought she might have decided to take the day off school. You know, play truant and go out with you and that horse like she's sometimes done in the past.'

'I haven't set eyes on her, not since last night when she said she was going for . . .'

'Oh shut up, you great oaf, you've already told me that a dozen times,' Maeve snarled, her green eyes icy.

Billy was uneasy. He suspected that either Maeve was still under the influence of all the drink she'd had at the wake, or that she had been hitting the bottle again this morning. Either way, it wasn't helping them to find Patsy.

As if reading his thoughts Maeve made a valiant attempt to pull herself together.

'If you want to help, Billy, then the best thing you can do is get out there and look for Patsy,' she told him.

'I'll do that willingly, Mrs Callaghan, but I've no idea where to start. Have you any idea about where she might have gone?'

'If I had I'd be out there myself bringing her back home, wouldn't I,' Maeve told him exasperatedly. 'Surely you must know where she goes, who her friends are and what she gets up to when she's not at school.'

'Have you asked any of her school friends if they know where she might be?'

'Only Maureen Murphy, and she's about as useless as you are. Anyway, according to what Maureen tells me you see more of Patsy than she does.'

'The only time I see Patsy is when she comes to the stable with an apple or carrot for Samson or when she comes out on the cart.'

'Well, there you are then. Try and think of some

place you visit where she might have gone. Just do something! Don't stand there with that hangdog look on your face! Go and find her.'

'Perhaps we should tell the police that she's missing?'

'Call in the scuffers? You must be out of your bleedin' mind,' Maeve told him. 'Don't you think I've got enough on me plate without having the law sniffing around?'

'They might be able to help,' Billy repeated doggedly. 'She might have been in some sort of accident and been taken to hospital, they'd know about that.'

'If she'd been in an accident they'd have been hammering on my door long before now.'

Billy rammed his cap back on his head. 'I've no idea where to start, but I'll take a look around,' he promised.

'Yeah, well you do that. Use your brain if you've got one, but don't go asking the scuffers anything. Understand?'

Chapter Eleven

For several days Billy searched every imaginable spot where he thought Patsy might be. He had hardly any sleep for worrying about whether or not she was safe. At the back of his mind was the fear that she might have done something foolish like stowing away on a boat and he might never see her again.

John Callaghan's funeral had taken place on a Thursday. Billy had spent most of Friday unaware that Patsy was missing, doing the deliveries that John Callaghan had booked in before his accident. When Maeve told him on the Friday night that she hadn't seen sight nor sound of Patsy since the funeral he had spent all day Saturday, and again on Sunday, searching for her, but he could find no trace of Patsy.

On Monday morning Billy was so tired through lack of sleep, and so worried about having to try and cope with running the haulage business single-handed, that he found it difficult to concentrate on what he was doing.

Hitching Samson up to the cart he set off, leaving the tin of sandwiches his mother had made up for his midday snack behind in the stable. By the time he realised what he had done he was already driving along the dock road to make his first pick-up. Going back for them was out of the question.

'You're going to be in luck, Samson, when we get back,' he told the horse. 'They'll be an extra treat for you tonight.'

When he returned that evening, though, the sandwiches had vanished. He looked for the tin but couldn't find it anywhere. Puzzled, he decided he must have forgotten to pick it up from the kitchen table before he'd left home that morning.

His mother was equally baffled. 'Where's your snack tin then?' Elaine Grant asked when she cleared away the evening meal and began making up the family's sandwiches for the next day. 'Have you left it behind in the stable?'

Billy frowned. 'Are you sure I took it with me this morning?'

'Of course you did! I packed you up two bacon butties and a cheese and pickle one. And I put an apple in so that you could give half of it to that old horse,' she added with a smile.

He shook his head in bewilderment. 'I thought I took it with me, but when I got down on to the dock road I couldn't find it so I thought I'd left it in the stable. Then when I got back there I looked high and low and couldn't find it so I thought I must have forgotten to pick it up from the table before I left this morning.'

Billy knew it wasn't like him to be forgetful, particularly where food was concerned and the problem flickered in and out of his mind all evening.

Next morning he made sure his snack was safe

in his coat pocket, then at the last minute, before he left the house, he picked up a couple of extra apples to take along with him. He'd promised Samson a treat so he'd make sure that this time there would definitely be one at the end of the day.

When he left the stable half an hour later Billy placed the apples on a ledge where he could see them so that he wouldn't forget to give them to Samson when they got back.

Working single-handed became harder as the day wore on. The loads seem to become either heavier or more difficult to handle. He found memories were short. Many of the men who had given him a hand freely on the previous Friday now held out their hand for a reward after helping him.

He knew he would have to talk to Maeve Callaghan and try and explain the situation to her, but at the moment, with Patsy missing, he didn't think she'd listen. Anyway, he wasn't sure she would understand what he was on about. Patsy would, because she had been out on the cart with them so many times in the past.

'If ever a horse deserved a reward then you do,' Billy told Samson as he unhitched him and led him into the stable at the end of the day.

He went straight to the ledge where he'd left the apples then frowned when he saw it was empty. He searched in the straw on the ground underneath in case they had fallen off, but there was no sign of them. He couldn't understand it. He was quite sure he'd put them there first thing that morning.

On his way home he called in to see Maeve Callaghan but she still had no news about Patsy.

'Nothing else I can do,' she shrugged. 'If she wants to run off then that's up to her. You go on looking for her if you want to, kiddo, but I've got my own life to get on with.'

Billy had noticed the moment she'd answered the door that she was heavily made up, but he'd thought that was to put a brave face on things. Now, though, he saw that she was dressed up to the nines in a knee-length green silk dress, silk stockings and high-heeled shoes that made her look more like a flapper than a grieving widow.

'You off out somewhere?'

Maeve Callaghan tossed her head indignantly. 'Yes, I am, not that it's any of your bloody business, Billy Grant,' she told him tartly.

He flushed darkly. 'I wasn't meaning to be rude, Mrs Callaghan. It's just that I wanted to talk to you about the business . . .'

'Oh damn the bloody business,' she snapped. 'I'm in too much of a hurry to talk about it now. If you can't manage on your own then pack it in, but don't come here whining to me because you're on the dole. I don't give a damn! Understand.'

'If the business packs up what will you and Patsy live on?'

'That's also none of your business, Billy Grant. Anyway, what's really griping you is the fact that you'll be out of a job when I sell that old nag, which is something I intend to do any day now,' she announced vehemently.

'I'm sure I could keep the haulage business

114

going if I had some help,' he told her quickly. 'There has to be someone to hold the horse steady while I load up, like Patsy used to do . . .'

'Then you'd better find her, hadn't you,' Maeve said and started to close the door.

Billy walked away, his hands in his trouser pockets, his head down on his chest. He knew he'd handled it badly. He was very much afraid that if Maeve Callaghan could find a buyer then she would sell Samson without a moment's hesitation. And if she did that he'd be on the dole like she said, he thought dejectedly.

'To hear Maeve Callaghan going on you'd think we hadn't even tried to find Patsy,' he told his father despondently as he related what had happened. 'Patsy hasn't been out of my mind for a single second, but I had to see to the deliveries. Let down any of those gaffers who run things at the docks and they've got memories like elephants; that's what John Callaghan used to say.'

'He was right there,' Joe Grant agreed. 'Bloody gaffers! They think they're God Almighty because they have the say-so when it comes to allocating the work. You should hear the way they treat us men.'

'Don't you get started on that Joe,' Elaine Grant murmured. 'You know it only gives you indigestion and pains in your chest when you gets yourself all worked up about things.'

'What do you know about it, woman!' he muttered. 'You haven't got to stand on the dockside in all weathers, herded together in a bunch like cattle, hoping to catch the gaffer's eye so that you'll be amongst those who are picked for the day's work. Sometimes, when it's stinking fish, or that bloody fertiliser muck they call guano, the smell chokes you to death and you wish you hadn't been one of the lucky ones.'

'Well, it does no good at all to let it worry you. Instead of grumbling it would be better if you spent your energies looking for some other kind of work.'

'Like what?' Joe's jaw jutted out. His stocky frame seemed to double in size as he squared his broad shoulders aggressively.

'Perhaps you should go and have a talk with Maeve Callaghan. If our Billy says she's thinking of selling up then perhaps you could take over. You and our Billy working together might manage to make a go of it.'

Joe ran a heavy calloused hand over his bald head.

'Are you out of your bloody mind, woman? Where the hell am I going to get the money to buy a business?'

'Perhaps if you asked you could work along-side our Billy. He said he needs help,' Elaine pointed out.

'Ask a favour of Maeve Callaghan? She wouldn't give you the time of day unless you paid for it. I wouldn't work for her if I were starving, so let's hear no more about it.'

Billy barely listened to them arguing. His mind was concentrating on where Patsy might be. He'd asked everyone who knew her if they'd seen her, but no one had set eyes on her since the day of her dad's funeral. Somewhere at the back of his mind he felt there was a clue as to her whereabouts. Something someone had said, or something that had happened. But what?

It came to him the moment he woke up the next morning. He felt almost lighthearted as he rushed his breakfast and picked up the tin of food his mother had prepared. He would have liked to ask her to double the quantity, but he was afraid his idea might be wrong and he didn't want to raise false hopes about finding Patsy.

When he reached the stable he went through his normal routine of feeding and grooming Samson and hitching him up to the cart. Before he left, he placed his snack tin and his bottle of cold tea on the ledge where he'd left the apples the day before.

All day his thoughts kept wandering back to the stable. He could hardly wait to get back there to see if the food and drink had vanished as he thought they might do.

Although he was on tenterhooks to find out he took his time in the yard unhitching Samson and rubbing him down before leading him into the stable.

Then his eyes went straight to the ledge. The food had gone! Someone had also drunk the tea but returned the empty bottle. As he fed Samson, Billy's ears strained to hear the slightest movement, but there seemed to be none.

He began searching the stable. It wasn't all that big a place but there were nooks and crannies where they stored fresh hay and the bran and other food for the horse as well as a deep recess where they kept spare sacks, tools and tack.

There was no sign of anyone in any of these places. Then, as he was about to leave, Billy sensed a movement on the platform above the bales of straw. When he glanced upwards he thought he could make out a dark shape or bundle that he was sure hadn't been there before.

Lighting the candle lantern that was hanging behind the door for emergencies, Billy clambered up on top of Samson's stall, holding the lantern aloft so that it threw a beam of light into the space above.

As the light shone on Patsy's dirt-streaked white face he almost toppled backwards.

'Patsy! Have you been hiding up there all the time?' he exclaimed, aghast.

When she didn't answer he called up to her angrily: 'I've been searching everywhere for you! I asked everybody I knew if they'd seen you and you've been right here all the time!'

Waving the light at her he said firmly, 'Come on down then, right this minute. Do you hear me?'

When she made no move a shiver of unease crept over him. Was she hurt and unable to move? Then he remembered that she had obviously been able to come down and take the food he'd left on the ledge so he stood firm.

'If you don't come down then I'll come up there and get you,' he told her.

To his relief there was a movement above his head, a flurry of dust and straw and then a pair of legs in thick black stockings appeared over the edge.

'If you jump I'll catch you,' he offered.

She didn't answer, but began climbing on to the top of Samson's stall then down to the ground beside him.

Billy's relief at seeing her safe and sound turned to anger. 'What on earth were you playing at? You must have known your mam would be worried sick and I've spent days looking for you.'

His heart contracted as he saw how dirty and miserable she was. Her red curls were matted with dust and cobwebs, her face was streaked with dirt where she'd been crying and her clothes were crumpled and grubby. She looked hungry and she was shivering with the cold.

He took off his jacket and wrapped it round her shoulders, then awkwardly he took her in his arms and hugged her.

'Have you been here ever since you ran off after the funeral?' he asked her quietly.

Patsy sniffed and nodded.

'But why?'

'I told you I couldn't go back there with all them people singing and carrying on and me mam acting as if it was a party.'

'That was almost a week ago. Where have you been since then?'

'Hiding out here in the stable.'

'So it *was* you who scoffed my sandwiches, and the apple that was meant as a treat for Samson,' Billy grinned.

'I gave him the core,' Patsy said defensively. She gave a forced giggle that ended in a sob. 'He let me have some of his bran!'

Billy shook his head in mock despair. 'Stealing

119

from the horse, eh? You must have been pretty hungry, kiddo, to do that!'

'I was absolutely starving,' Patsy admitted. 'I still am, if it comes to that.'

'Then you'd better let me walk you home so that you can get out of those mucky clothes and get a square meal inside you.'

Patsy shook her head. 'I'm not ready to do that yet.'

'So what are you going to do then?'

'Stay here while I sorts me head out proper,' she told him.

'How long is that going to take?'

'I don't know,' Patsy shrugged. 'You can help me. You can fetch me some clean clothes and something to eat.'

'How am I going to do that? If I ask your mam for clean clothes for you she'll want to know where you are.'

'Then bring me some of your Janie's clothes,' she pleaded. 'We're about the same size so they'll fit me. Tell her I don't want to borrow her Nippy outfit,' she added with a weak grin. 'Anything will do, it's only a loan for a few days while I work things out.'

Billy stared at her in silence. He didn't want to get involved because he knew once news of it reached Maeve Callaghan's ears she'd blame him for Patsy going missing all this time.

'If I do that will you do something for me?' he asked.

Her green eyes fastened on his face questioningly. 'Like what?'

'Help me over the business.'

'How can I do that?'

'I can't manage on me own. I need someone to work with me, even if it's only to hold Samson's head when I'm loading up. You're good at that.'

Patsy looked doubtful. 'You mean leave school and come out with you every day?'

Billy hadn't thought through the implication of his words but now, eager to keep her interest, he nodded quickly.

'I had something like that in mind,' he told her. 'Your mam isn't interested in the business. She wouldn't even listen when I told her I couldn't manage on my own. All she could talk about was of getting rid of Samson.'

Patsy shook her head sadly. 'She's never liked him, not from the first day me dad brought him home.'

'You're not going to let her do that, are you?' Billy persisted. 'What will you and your mam live on if she does that? What's more, if the business goes then all your dad's hard work will be lost. And I'll be out of a job as well,' he added morosely.

Chapter Twelve

In the months that followed John Callaghan's death life took on a new meaning for Patsy.

In the past she'd had to drag herself out of bed to go to school because her heart wasn't in it. As she sat at a desk listening to things that held no interest for her and which she didn't really want to know about her thoughts had drifted.

Usually they'd been with Samson. She wondered where he and her father were working and if Billy was treating him as well as he should. She knew Billy loved the great dray horse almost as much as she did, but she was also aware that he made him work hard.

It was Billy's job to persuade Samson to pull the heavily loaded cart up steep hills or along slippery cobbled roads down at the docks. It was also left to Billy to see that his nosebag was hitched into place whenever they took a break and that there was water for the horse when puffing and panting had left him parched.

After school each day, instead of going home, or out with Maureen Murphy and Janie Grant, Patsy would rush home, change into old clothes and then go straight to the stable. There was always something she could do to make sure Samson was well looked after. Often she mucked out his stall and spread fresh clean straw in readiness for his return at the end of the working day. If she had time she would scrub out his trough and replenish it with clean water for him to drink.

Billy always welcomed her with a wide friendly grin when he drove into the small yard. While they unhitched Samson from the cart he would tell her about what sort of day they'd had. Then he would leave her to lead Samson into the stable while he cleaned out the cart so that it was ready for work next morning.

Now, all that had changed. Instead of going to school she worked alongside Billy all day. Although she had to be up much earlier she found that was no problem at all. She was eager to be out of bed and start the day each morning. The apathy she'd felt when facing a day at school was a thing of the past.

As the cold, frosty days of April gave way to the milder days of May, with their sudden bursts of sunshine, the whole world was a bright and welcoming place.

The black patch, which had drawn her into its deepest depths after her dad's accident, was relegated to the back of her mind. She still missed him a great deal, and she knew she always would, but after the first few weeks of overwhelming grief she realised that she couldn't sit around thinking about him for ever.

She had Billy to thank for her change of attitude. He had made her see that unless she joined forces with him the business her dad had worked so hard to build up would simply disappear.

Her first battle had been persuading her mam to keep the business going. It hadn't been easy.

'Don't talk such a lorra rubbish, Patsy,' Maeve Callaghan had said derisively when Patsy told her about Billy's idea. 'You're still a kid and Billy Grant's only sixteen so what do either of you know about running a business?'

'We can soon learn!' Patsy told her. 'He knows all the gaffers down the docks that me dad used to do work for and he knows all the foremen and bosses at the factories where me dad collected loads. They all say he was so reliable in the past that they'll give him a chance to go on handling their goods.'

Maeve remained unimpressed. 'The best thing to do is sell out while they still remember who John Callaghan was. If we can find someone who wants to buy the business then that sort of good-will will probably fetch more than that old nag. All he's good for is the knacker's yard, but whoever buys the business can find that out for themselves.'

'There's nothing at all wrong with Samson!' Patsy defended him hotly.

Maeve's mouth curled. 'Then why did he cause the accident that killed your dad, tell me that?'

'The accident wasn't Samson's fault,' Patsy said wearily. She had heard this point of view from her mother over and over and had often tried to explain to her that it wasn't the horse's fault but Maeve would not listen.

'If your dad hadn't been walking along the road because he had to lead the stupid creature then he wouldn't have ended up under that lorry,' Maeve repeated stubbornly.

'It was a real pea-souper of a fog, Mam, I was there, remember! You couldn't see your hand in front of your face, that was why me dad was leading Samson. If he hadn't been doing it then Billy or me would have been leading him.'

'Well, like I say, the sooner we dump him the better,' Maeve insisted doggedly.

'If you sell Samson and get rid of the business then what are we going to live on?' Patsy questioned.

'We'll have the money we get for the horse and business, of course!'

'That won't last very long, especially the way you're living it up these days,' Patsy pointed out.

'Less of your damn cheek!' Maeve scowled. 'I've spent years stuck at home on me own, looking after things for you and your dad. I need company, you should know that.'

'Only too well,' Patsy retorted bitterly. 'I can still remember what it was like when I was a little kid and me dad went to sea.'

The thought of getting rid of Samson greatly distressed Patsy. Without her dad to talk to there was only Samson and Billy. Although Samson couldn't answer she was sure he understood. When she was feeling particularly unhappy he would nuzzle her shoulder, or blow down his nose at her as if to say 'Cheer up, I'm still here for you'.

'If you let me and Billy run the business,' Patsy went on determinedly, 'then you'll have money coming in regularly.'

The argument went on for over a week and Patsy was in despair. There seemed to be no sign of her mother weakening. Then suddenly out of the blue, she gave in.

'Go on, then. I know I'm daft to trust the two of you to run the business, but I'll give you three months to prove you can do it.'

Together all of them had visited the bank and explained to the manager, Mr Mantel – a bald little man with horn-rimmed glasses, who wore a navy blue pinstriped suit and a bright yellow tie – that they were now in charge of the company John Callaghan had set up.

Patsy's heart had sunk into her boots when the first thing Mr Mantel told them was that things would have to be done legally and that because of her age she would not be eligible to run a company or act on behalf of her father. When he insisted that it must all be done in her mother's name she was almost on the point of abandoning the whole idea.

'Couldn't Billy Grant take over my dad's business?' she asked, fighting back her tears of frustration.

Mr Mantel shook his head when he heard that Billy was only sixteen. 'I'm afraid that won't be possible either,' he pronounced gloomily.

Maeve seemed amused by their dilemma. 'You didn't expect the bank to let you two kids run a business, did you? she laughed. She smiled archly at the bank manager. 'Don't worry, Mr Mantel, I'll sign the cheques.'

'You will have to provide proper accounts and

I shall require receipts for every penny you spend,' he told her officiously.

Nevertheless, by the time they left his office, he'd agreed to provide them with banking facilities for the foreseeable future and Patsy could hardly contain her relief.

'Right,' Maeve told them, 'I'll pay you the same wages every week, Billy Grant, for as long as you do a good day's work. You'll have Patsy there to help you, but if I catch you slacking or cheating me in any way then out you go and the business gets sold. Understand?'

Patsy had left school immediately even though she wouldn't be fourteen for another five months. She loved working alongside Billy and they quickly adapted to each other's rhythm and became a perfect team. In next to no time they were working side by side on the docks unloading ships and carting goods to one warehouse or another or transporting them to places in the Wirral, as they'd done when John Callaghan had been in charge.

In the beginning, Patsy tended to Samson while Billy coped with the loads. He was young and strong, but often the load was so heavy or big and cumbersome that she had to give a hand. Often at the end of the day he was almost too tired to talk to her as they drove home.

'I'm knackered, that's all,' he would grin when she asked if he was all right, 'and I bet you are too only you won't admit it.'

She was tired, she had to agree, but she was so keyed up by the excitement of it all that she didn't mind.

After the first couple of weeks, Patsy gave up wearing skirts and now wore trousers. It was not only easier for getting in and out of the cart, but it stopped the wolf-whistles and cat-calls she'd had to put up with when she'd first turned up as Billy's co-worker.

Riding on the cart with her father had been different, because everyone thought she came along for the ride. Actually working alongside Billy, not only holding the horse but even helping him to load up when necessary, gave her a different standing altogether. As far as they were concerned she was fair game for taunting and teasing.

The next thing she'd done was to cut her red curls as short as possible so that from a distance, in her dark blue corduroy trousers, dark donkey jacket and black cloth cap she looked like a boy.

She couldn't disguise her pretty face, hide her big green eyes, or her wide smile. Nor could she help the way when she blushed the peppering of freckles over her nose stood out.

Yet she managed to turn these to her advantage when it came to sounding out the gaffers and foremen over new work. She would do the asking, then Billy would assess what the job would cost and between them they would clinch the deal.

On Saturday evenings and most of Sunday Patsy spent her time writing out the bills-of-lading and the invoices. Billy checked them carefully before putting them into envelopes ready for delivery the next time they were down at the docks, or they would put them in the post to firms in the Wirral.

Patsy hated the way her mam kept them under her thumb yet refused to do anything at all to help, but there was nothing she could do about it. She lived in hope that once her mam grew tired of the novelty of acting like a boss she would leave them to their own devices.

She had to admit that in many ways Maeve played fair. When he realised that he wouldn't be in sole charge Billy began to look for ways of getting a better return for his day's work and insisted that Patsy receive a proper wage. Maeve refused to put his wages up or pay Patsy, but after a lot of arguing she did agree that she would pay them a small commission on all the orders they fulfilled.

This inspired both of them to work even harder. They took on jobs that no other carrier wanted to handle. They were always willing to work away from the Liverpool area, taking loads across on the ferryboat to places in the Wirral where other carriers didn't want to go.

Patsy loved these trips. Leaning on the rail of the ferry, staring out across the Mersey at the great liners docked alongside or being towed out to the Bar in readiness to sail on the next tide, she would let her thoughts wander, wondering where they'd come from and where they were going. Stories her father had told her about his many voyages filled her mind and sometimes she imagined herself on one of them. It was a fantasy that was broken the moment the ferryboat grated alongside the floating roadway at Seacombe or the pier at New Brighton.

It pleased Billy to let her indulge in these flights of fancy. He too had his dreams. He would have liked nothing better than to take them both away to some far-off exotic destination where they could explore new places and see strange sights.

As it was, the nearest they ever came to doing that was when they took a load across to New Brighton. Whenever that happened they always tried to make time to visit the Tower Fairground where there was a menagerie. Patsy loved the great lumbering elephants with their tiny wise eyes. Billy preferred the sleek leopards or the ferocious lions that roared menacingly whenever they went near their cage.

They were such frequent visitors, either conveying or collecting goods or spending a few minutes of relaxation looking at the animals, that they became quite friendly with some of the men who worked there.

It was in this way that Patsy met Bruno Alvarez.

Bruno was in his mid-twenties, a dashing olive-skinned Spaniard with flashing dark eyes and jet black hair. He looked as fit and supple as the lions and tigers he trained.

Whenever they stopped off at the fairground Bruno seemed to appear from nowhere and engage them in conversation. He spoke quite good English, but also used his flashing white smile and expressive hands to convey his message or emphasise his feelings.

Patsy found him intriguing and entertaining, but Billy disliked his bravado.

'Bit of a pansy that Bruno chap,' he commented as he and Patsy made their way back to Seacombe ferry. It was a glorious day in May so they'd decided to take the road which ran alongside the river from New Brighton to Seacombe. He reined Samson to a stop when they reached Egremont Promenade and sat staring moodily out across the Mersey to where the Isle of Man boat was steaming up ready to sail on the next tide.

'You didn't believe any of that guff he was spouting, did you?' he asked, giving Patsy a sideways look.

'You mean about the way he trains the tigers?'

Billy nodded. 'Big cats!' he muttered derisively. 'Who does he think he's kidding? I bet he'll have a couple of whips in his hand when he goes into the cage and a couple of chaps armed with big sticks on the outside ready to rush in to help him if the "big cats" as he calls them start getting nasty.'

'Well, that makes sense to me,' Patsy defended him. 'He knows they can be dangerous so he takes precautions. Anyway –' she pulled a couple of tickets out of her coat pocket and waved them in front of Billy – 'I'll be able to see if you're right or not when I go to the show.'

'Where did you get those from?'

'Bruno gave them to me!'

'You're not going to use them?'

'Of course I am!'

Billy looked taken aback. 'You never go out in the evenings, Patsy. You always say you are too tired.'

Patsy sighed. 'I know, but I think it's time I made an effort. Everyone else seems to have fun at the weekends and all I do is stay at home and catch up with paperwork.'

Billy was silent for several minutes. 'Look, if you're fed up with doing the bills then I'll do them. I used to help your dad with them, but I thought you wanted to do them.'

'I can manage. I'm just saying that it's time I did something else on a Saturday night, that's all.'

Billy felt uneasy. Was Patsy waiting for him to offer to go with her? She had made the point that she had two tickets, but he wasn't sure if that was because Bruno had given her two or whether she had asked for two so that he could go along as well.

Biting his lip he asked hesitantly, 'Do you want me to come with you?'

Patsy shook her head. 'No thanks, Billy. I'm going to ask Maureen Murphy.'

Billy looked shocked. 'You can't come over here on your own on a Saturday night!'

Patsy raised her eyebrows. 'I won't be on my own if Maureen is with me now, will I?' she giggled.

'Two girls coming over here in the evening on their own?'

'Oh, come off it, Billy. You sound like someone's grandmother. What's wrong with Maureen and me coming over here? Safer than some of the places we could go to in Liverpool on a Saturday night. It's not even as if it will be dark when the show finishes, not at this time of the year.'

Chapter Thirteen

Patsy's visit to New Brighton Tower Fairground the following Saturday night was the first of many similar excursions.

She sat enthralled as Bruno appeared, resplendent in a uniform of tight white breeches and a red jacket bound in black silk that was lavishly trimmed with gilt buttons and braiding.

With a sweeping flourish he doffed his white peaked cap, also bound with black silk and heavily encrusted with gold braiding, and then bowed low to the audience before entering the tigers' cage.

There was a tense silence as he proceeded to put the two tigers through their paces. Under his instructions they climbed on to cream and gilt stools, jumped through spangled hoops and performed several other tricks.

When he finally emerged from their cage, which was quickly bolted and barred behind him by the uniformed attendants who had been standing there throughout his performance, there was thunderous applause from the audience.

Patsy and Maureen sat entranced. Patsy would have liked to see it happen all over again, but almost immediately the immense cage was wheeled out of the ring. Five gaudily dressed clowns came rushing into the arena to perform their tumbling act and amuse the audience while the sawdust was raked over ready for the next act. This starred a young girl performing tricks on the back of a white Arab horse.

More exciting acts followed and the entire show lasted for almost two hours. There was an interval halfway through and as people began to make their way to the bar Patsy felt a hand on her shoulder. Wheeling round in her seat, the colour flooded her cheeks as she found Bruno standing there.

'You came to see my act, then?' he smiled. 'Now you tell me you like it, yes?'

'Like it! I thought it was wonderful,' Patsy assured him enthusiastically. Smiling happily she introduced him to Maureen, who giggled self-consciously when he raised her hand to his lips and kissed it.

'Perhaps I take you both for the lemonade, yes?' Bruno suggested. 'Come, this way. We go to the back to be served so that we do not have to wait like all the others.'

The interval was over all too quickly. Bruno had to return to the ring where, he told them, he'd be performing once more, this time with lions.

'You will wait for me after the show has ended so that we take the stroll along the promenade, yes?' he asked, his dark eyes fixed on Patsy.

She hesitated, remembering the pile of invoices and bills-of-lading that she had pushed to one side in order to come out for the evening, then shook her head. 'I'd like to do that, but it would make me very late getting home and then I would be in trouble,' she told him.

'Then you will come again. This time not to see the show but to see me, Bruno. Yes?'

'Billy and me will probably be over this way again with the cart some time next week.'

'No, no, you do not understand!' He gesticulated. 'It is not you and Billy I want to see, Patsy. It is only you! I want to see you again when you are like a young lady, not in the trousers and cap. Understand?'

Patsy understood quite well and she was excited and flattered by his attentions. It made her feel very nervous to be chatted up by someone quite a bit older than her; older than Billy, even. Apart from Billy, no boy, or young man, had ever showed any interest in her before, and she wasn't too sure what to say or do.

She was glad that Maureen was with her, even if Maureen simply stood there as if she'd been struck dumb and was grinning like a Cheshire cat.

'On Sunday there is no work at the fairground, except to see to the animals. People come and walk about and look at the animals in their cages, but there is no performance. You understand?'

Patsy felt her colour rising. 'Yes,' she mumbled.

'Tomorrow is Sunday. So you also come? Not to see the animals but to walk about with me. Yes?'

Patsy shook her head. 'I can't. Not this Sunday,' she said emphatically.

Bruno looked disheartened and his smile vanished. 'You no want to walk about with Bruno?'

'Yes, of course I do,' Patsy told him quickly. 'I

135

can't come tomorrow, though. Next Sunday perhaps.'

'Yes? That is good. Next Sunday then!'

His good humour restored, he took Maureen's hand and kissed it then he held Patsy by the shoulders and kissed her on both cheeks before showing them back to their seats and disappearing behind the scenes.

Patsy sat through the rest of the show in a daze. She was still trying to get her breath back, and come down to earth, when they boarded the ferry-boat.

'You're a dark horse, Patsy Callaghan,' Maureen told her as they found themselves seats in one of the salons. 'Fancy you knowing a chap like that!'

'He's nice, isn't he?'

'Nice! He's absolutely gorgeous! He can kiss my hand any time – or my cheek,' she added, giving Patsy a sly sideways glance.

Patsy looked embarrassed. 'That's just foreigners' way of doing things,' she mumbled.

'So where does he come from then?'

Patsy shrugged. 'I don't know. Billy thinks it may be Spain.'

'So Billy knows him as well, does he?'

'We both know him, we've talked to him a few times when we've been making deliveries to the fairground,' Patsy explained.

'So that's what he meant by "trousers and cap"? If he's only seen you before when you're working then it's a wonder he recognised you when you're dressed as a normal person.'

'Wearing skirts and stockings is not very practical

136

when you have to climb up and down into a cart all the time and help heave loads around,' Patsy pointed out.

'You could get a normal job and let Billy Grant run the haulage business on his own,' Maureen said.

Patsy shook her head. 'No, it's not the sort of thing that you can run single-handed.'

'He could always find a young lad to help him, couldn't he?'

Patsy bit her lip. 'You don't understand, Maureen. It was my dad's business and I'm doing it for him. He worked so hard to make a go of it and I don't want to see it go under.'

'You like Billy Grant, don't you! You always have. Even as a kid you used to go straight to the stable to see him even before you went home at night. Are you still soft on him?'

'We're business partners, nothing else,' Patsy said sharply.

'Oh yes! I bet he doesn't know that you were coming over here tonight to see Bruno.'

'Well, that's where you're wrong. If you must know, Billy was there when Bruno gave me the tickets.'

'So why didn't he come with you, then?'

'For the simple reason that I thought you would enjoy it. Now, though,' Patsy said crossly, 'since you've done nothing but criticise and pick on me, I think I'd have been better off asking Billy Grant after all.'

Maureen wasn't to be silenced so easily. She was far too curious about Patsy's relationship with Bruno.

'Does your mam know you've come over here tonight?'

Patsy shrugged. 'I said I was going out with you, I didn't bother to say where we were going. She's probably not interested. Too pleased to know I'd be out of the house all evening.'

'You mean so that she can entertain one of her men friends.'

The minute the words were out, Maureen clamped a hand over her mouth. 'Sorry, kiddo, I shouldn't have said that,' she muttered contritely.

'It's what everyone else in Paradise Place says, isn't it?' replied Patsy.

Maureen looked uncomfortable. 'Well, she has been carrying on a bit for someone who has not long lost her husband. She's down the Grafton most evenings, or so my dad says.'

'Well, he should know. He goes there every night himself.'

'He drops in for a quick pint on his way home, that's all,' Maureen bristled.

'And no one thinks any the worse of him for doing that,' Patsy said wryly, 'but when a woman goes in for a drink she's suddenly thought of as a Judy or labelled a Mary-Ellen.'

'I never said that,' Maureen declared hotly.

'You didn't need to, luv, I can hear it in your voice.'

'It's not what I meant at all,' Maureen muttered sulkily.

'Look,' Patsy said, and put her hand on Maureen's arm, 'I don't give a damn about what me mam does or about what people say about her.

She likes plenty of company and a good time, that's all there is to it.'

'She likes flirting and all! She's always chatting up the men in the Grafton and letting them buy her drinks.'

'It's her life. As I said, it's nothing to do with me, kiddo.'

'So are you going to tell your mam that you're meeting Bruno next week?' Maureen asked.

Patsy looked thoughtful. 'I don't know. I mightn't go, anyway.' She grinned. 'I've got all week to make up my mind now, haven't I?'

'He's a real hunk, you'd be daft to turn him down,' Maureen declared. She shot a sideways glance at Patsy, 'If you don't want to meet him next Sunday then I will.'

Maureen was right about Bruno and Patsy knew it. She had no intention of turning down his invitation.

She lived in a private dream all the following week. Her absent-mindedness irritated Billy. He suspected it was because she was thinking of Bruno and he felt uneasy about it. Bruno was not only a foreigner, but he was so good looking that in Billy's estimation he was bound to be a flirt. He was convinced that if Patsy wasn't careful Bruno would break her heart and he didn't want to see that happen.

A further point – which Billy wouldn't admit, even to himself – was the fact that he was jealous of Bruno.

He'd had strong feelings for Patsy ever since she had first started coming out on the cart with him and her dad. He knew that in those days she thought of him as the brother she didn't have. As they both grew older he'd secretly hoped that her feelings for him would change and, if he was lucky, become more like those he had for her.

After John Callaghan had died, and Billy had managed to persuade Patsy to leave school and help him full time to run the business, his hopes about their relationship had soared, but he'd decided it wasn't the right time to speak out.

Now he wished he had said something. If he'd told her then that he loved her and that he wanted to marry her, but that he was willing to wait until she was older, she probably wouldn't have given Bruno Alvarez a second glance.

If he said anything to her now about his feelings for her she would think he was only doing it because she had shown an interest in Bruno and had confided in him that she was going across to New Brighton to see him.

Billy felt that the problem was insurmountable. Worrying about what the outcome might be made him tetchy and short tempered. Patsy didn't seem to notice. All week she remained in her dazed trance. The most he could hope for was that her meeting on Sunday with Bruno would turn out to be a flop.

As far as Patsy was concerned it was one of the most wonderful occasions in her life. It was a glorious June afternoon and she was able to wear her favourite dress. She'd bought new white gloves to wear with it and with her curls brushed until they glowed she knew she looked completely different from her hoydenish appearance when she was working alongside Billy.

As the ferryboat sailed up the Mersey towards New Brighton she went up on to the top deck, leaned on the rail and pretended she was travelling to an exciting foreign land.

Bruno was waiting for her by the pier and she saw his dark eyes gleam in appreciation as he took in her changed appearance.

He looked different too in his grey flannel trousers, white shirt and dark blazer. Not nearly so flamboyant as he did when he was working, but still devastatingly handsome with his shock of black hair and olive skin.

He kissed her on both cheeks, making her blush, then tucked her hand into the crook of his arm and suggested a stroll along the Ham and Egg Parade.

'It is a very strange name for a road,' he smiled.

'It's called that because at all the boarding houses along there they serve ham and eggs to their customers,' Patsy explained laughingly.

'Ham and eggs is a speciality? You must come to Spain where I will serve you not one speciality but many. We have wonderful fish, delicious fruits and so many different wines that you would not be able to taste them all if you lived to be a hundred.'

'It all sounds marvellous!'

'There is more, much more!' He waved his hands expressively. 'It is a warm sunny land, full of exotic flowers and wine and so everyone is relaxed and happy because they sit in the sun, drink wine and enjoy themselves.'

'So why did you leave such a wonderful place and come to England?'

'I come here to work,' Bruno explained. 'I want to earn the big money, make myself wealthy, but soon I go back to my home in Almeria.'

'So you are missing Spain and feeling lonely?'

Bruno shrugged expressively. 'In my country people are friendly and oh so welcoming. Here they do not talk to each other very much and they do not like strangers.'

'That's because we like to be introduced to people before we talk to them,' Patsy explained.

Bruno looked puzzled. 'But you talk to me before we were introduced,' he pointed out.

'I know, but look at the number of times we have seen each other when I've been with Billy delivering things to the fairground,' Patsy said. 'That makes a difference.'

'Billy?' Bruno frowned. 'Ah yes! Is this Billy your brother or your boss?'

Patsy laughed. 'Neither! We are partners. We work together.'

Bruno looked puzzled. 'You mean you are married to him?'

'No, nothing like that,' Patsy smiled. 'We're business partners. It's a long story . . .'

'Come.' He took her arm and led her down a slipway on to the shore. 'We will sit here on the warm sand and tell each other all about ourselves. Later, I will take you and buy you the afternoon tea. Yes?'

When Patsy had finished telling him all about herself, and how she and Billy came to be working together, Bruno talked again about the wonders of Spain.

'One day, you will come with me to my home in Almeria and see these things for yourself,' he promised. 'You will meet all my family and all my many friends. You they will love.'

Patsy sighed blissfully as he took one of her hands and cradled it between his. His strong brown fingers stroked her bare arm, sending delicious shivers right through her.

'So you will come there with me?' he persisted.

Patsy smiled but looked doubtful. 'You make it all sound so wonderful, but I have to work too. I have a living to earn the same as you do, Bruno, so it may be a long time before I can ever visit Almeria.'

Chapter Fourteen

During the long warm summer Sunday afternoons of July and August, Patsy became more and more enchanted by Bruno Alvarez and even admitted to herself that she was crazily in love with him.

He was utterly charming, very romantic, and so handsome that he swept her off her feet. He was her first boyfriend and quickly became her lover.

His seduction routine was so smooth that it had happened almost before Patsy realised what a tremendous step she had taken.

During their first two or three meetings Bruno was so restrained that Patsy felt completely at ease in his company. As they walked along the promenade, stopping occasionally to watch a liner being guided by fussy little tugs down the Mersey and into dock at Liverpool, he talked enthusiastically about Almeria.

'Soon I return there when the season here is over. You will come with me, yes?'

His dark eyes were pleading, but his voice was so teasing that she assumed he was joking and happily went along with the game she thought he was playing.

So often she wasn't sure when he was being serious and when he was fooling around. Except when he kissed her. That was serious. When he held her close to his hard muscular body and his firm lips covered hers, the excitement was almost unbearable and she felt her entire being quiver with emotion.

So much so that she felt embarrassed when he suddenly sometimes stopped as they walked along the promenade and took her in his arms and kissed her.

'You mustn't do that,' she protested, pushing him away.

His dark brows drew together in a puzzled frown. 'Why is that, my pretty Patsy? What is it that I do wrong?'

'Someone who knows me might see us kissing.'

'This would matter to you? You have feelings for me the same as I have for you so what is so wrong with my kissing you?'

She wasn't sure why she was so concerned about being seen. There was no one, except perhaps Billy Grant, who really cared what she did or what happened to her. Her mother was too engrossed in her own life. And she could hardly pass judgement, since the things she got up to were far worse.

The only other person who might care was Maureen Murphy and that was only because she was infatuated with Bruno herself even though she had only met him once. She was always trying to persuade Patsy to take her along with her when she went to meet Bruno on Sundays.

'Two's company, three's a crowd,' Patsy would remind her.

'I know that, but surely Bruno must have a friend. We could make up a foursome. Be safer,' she added with a snide smile.

'I'm safe enough as I am,' Patsy told her. 'Bruno is a perfect gentleman,' she added, her colour rising.

Yet she knew that wasn't quite true. On the previous Sunday he had persuaded her that, since it was such a hot day, instead of strolling along the promenade, which was very crowded, they should walk further on towards Leasowe Lighthouse and find somewhere quiet where they could sit and watch the river.

They'd found a secluded spot in a convenient dip in the sandhills and made themselves comfortable. For the first few minutes they merely kissed and cuddled, but then Bruno became more amorous.

At first Patsy made no objection when he lay down full length in the sandy hollow and pulled her down alongside him.

Lulled by the sun's warmth, the gentle murmur of Bruno's voice and the sensual caressing from his long-fingered hands as they stroked the contours of her face and buried themselves in her red curls, she felt totally relaxed, even to the point of closing her eyes. She barely noticed when his hands began to slide gently down her throat and he started fondling the curves of her breasts.

Finding she made no resistance, Bruno became bolder. He unfastened the bodice of her dress, gently cupping each of her breasts in turn, murmuring his pleasure at their warm softness.

Then he buried his dark head between them and delicately circled each of her nipples with his tongue.

'You are so beautiful, Patsy, your skin is so smooth and creamy,' he murmured huskily.

Before Patsy was fully aware of what was happening he had lifted the skirt of her cotton dress and his hands were moving over her bare flesh in an intimate manner that sent warning shudders through her.

Shocked by what was happening she tried to remonstrate with him and to push his hands away, but it was too late. Bruno became even more passionate. His mouth covered hers, silencing her protests. Her own blood pulsed wildly, thundering in her ears; waves of excitement coursed through her as his hands glided over her body exploring every secret crevice.

She knew it was wrong, but now she wanted Bruno every bit as much as he needed her. Her surge of happiness was overpowering, and she found the sensations he was extracting from her body exquisite.

With a blissful sigh she stopped resisting and gave herself up entirely to his touch, revelling in the magic of the moment. It was her very first experience of physical love and there was a moment of sharp, agonising pain when Bruno entered her, but this only heightened her desire.

When he was finally sated and moved away from her she was too overcome by the enormity of what had happened between them to move a muscle.

The true magnitude of their actions didn't register in her mind until much later. That night, lying in bed, letting the memories of the day glide through her mind before she fell asleep, the realisation of what she had done seared her mind, making sleep impossible. Supposing she became pregnant? She pushed the thought away. Refused even to contemplate such a thing.

She wondered what Bruno would think of her for giving in to him so easily. He'd said nothing about marrying her so would he lose interest in her now? Or would he take it as a sign that she really was in love with him and wanted to go back to Almeria with him when his season was finished in New Brighton?

The thought of leaving Liverpool, even for somewhere so wonderful, threw her mind into turmoil.

Yet what had she to lose? she asked herself. Here she was working a long, gruelling day yet most of the money she and Billy earned went to her mother, who spent it on buying drinks for herself and all and sundry at the Grafton.

In Almeria, if what Bruno had said was true, life would be so much more easygoing. The sun shone, the people laughed, danced, drank wine and gossiped with each other. It sounded heavenly and if she was there with Bruno what more could she ask from life?

The only thing that worried her was – could she bear to be parted from Samson? He was so much more than a mere dray horse. She shared her secrets with him; he listened to all her troubles.

He was there for her from first thing in the morning and her loyal companion all day. He was her link with her dad.

Billy would look after Samson, of course, because Billy loved him almost as much as she did, but leaving him behind would create a gap in her life that nothing else could fill.

She'd be leaving Billy behind as well, she reminded herself. They'd been such close friends all these years that it would be a wrench to do that, too. Billy had been the one who had comforted her and stood by her when her dad had died. It had been Billy who had made her see sense and realise that unless she pulled herself together then the business her dad had worked so hard to build up would simply disappear.

Billy was such a wonderful friend. Her feelings for him were so deep and so strong that she sometimes forgot that they merely worked side by side and that there was no other tie between them.

Over the next few days these thoughts surged around in her mind. She was so much on edge that once or twice Billy wondered if she was ill or sickening for something. Usually she sang or chattered to him as they loaded up, or while they drove from the docks to wherever they were taking their load; now she was silent and lost in thought.

He suspected that it was to do with Bruno Alvarez, but was afraid to ask in case she told him something he didn't want to hear.

He had warned her against Bruno often enough. He had seen trouble brewing from the very first time they'd met him. Maureen Murphy had told him all about what went on the night the two of them had gone over to see the show at New Brighton Tower Fairground. She'd let slip the fact that Bruno had asked Patsy to go out with him again the following Sunday.

Since then, Billy knew, she had been going over regularly on a Sunday to see Bruno. All dressed up in her best, her red curls brushed until they gleamed, and wearing white shoes and gloves, she looked so totally different from the boyish young girl in shabby trousers and jacket who accompanied him on his rounds each day.

When he'd mentioned it casually one Monday morning she'd bitten his head off.

'What's it to you, Billy Grant, what I do on a Sunday?' she'd snapped, her face colouring up so much that her freckles stood out like a myriad of dots.

'I was only asking because I wondered if you had a nice time?' he told her mildly.

'We walked along the prom and then we had tea in one of the cafés in Victoria Road and then I got on the boat and came home.' She tossed her head defiantly. 'Is there anything else you want to know?'

He shrugged. 'Not unless there's anything else you want to tell me.'

'Well there isn't!'

'Oh, come on! It's not like you to be secretive. Where does he come from? Is it Italy, France . . .'

'He comes from Almeria in Spain. He told me all about where he lives and it sounds wonderful. It's hot and sunny and there's flowers everywhere and the people sit around drinking wine when they're not singing and dancing. Will that do?'

Although he tried to make light of the matter, inwardly Billy felt churned up. He was so worried about her. He didn't trust Bruno for a second. He was much too old for her, flash, far too handsome and he was a foreigner. What was more, Billy was pretty certain that like most showmen Bruno didn't stay anywhere longer than one season.

He had painted Patsy a romantic picture of his home in Almeria, but Billy guessed that his life there was little better than the one he had in Liverpool. It might be sunny for most of the year, but it was probably just as hard to make a living there. Otherwise why had he bothered to come to England?

Billy wished he'd had the sense to tell Patsy how he felt about her before she had met this Spaniard. Normally they worked in such harmony, but now there was a distinct sense of unease between them. He'd held back because he'd thought she needed time to get over her dad's death and also because he felt she was still too young for a serious relationship. He'd been afraid that if he spoke out it might cause an uncomfortable rift between them.

He couldn't bear the thought of losing her, but he knew he had to tread carefully if he was going to manage to convince her that her future lay here in Liverpool with him.

If her relationship with her mother had been on a sounder footing he would have asked Maeve for advice, or persuaded her to speak to Patsy on his behalf. As it was, to do that would only make matters worse.

Maeve was no help to either of them. She did nothing to help them with the business. In fact, these days she was rarely sober and she was getting a very bad reputation. Other women in Paradise Place objected strongly to the way she flirted with their husbands and Billy was sure that sooner or later she would end up in a fight.

She had never been the motherly type. Even after John Callaghan had given up the sea she had only made a pretence of caring for her home and looking after him and Patsy. Now, although she still lived under the same roof as her mother, Patsy fended for herself so there was nothing really to hold her in Liverpool.

Except him. And, of course, Samson. She loved the old horse dearly – but when it came to a choice between Samson and Bruno Alvarez, Billy had a sick feeling in his gut that it would be Bruno who would win.

Unless he could do something to change the situation. If only he could turn the tables, win her back, show her that he cared even more for her than Bruno did. Show her that he could offer her a good life here in her own familiar surroundings.

His offer to take her to the pictures startled her. 'Whatever do you want to do that for?' she asked him, her eyes wide with surprise.

'I thought you might like a night out at the Trocadero,' he told her.

She hesitated and he could see she was torn between accepting his offer and being disloyal to Bruno if she went out with him.

When she shook her head his spirits fell. He could see it was going to take more than an invite to the pictures to persuade her to go out with him. Most girls would have been won over with a bunch of flowers or a box of chocolates, but Billy felt that it would cheapen his cause to offer such inducements after she'd turned down going to the pictures.

Over the next few weeks the atmosphere between them became more and more tense. Billy sensed that once again her thoughts weren't with him or the job, but with Bruno.

In that he was right. Ever since that warm Sunday in July, Bruno's passion had dominated their meetings. Patsy wasn't sure if she was pleased about this or not. When she was in his arms and he was making love to her everything else was forgotten. But when she got home and relived what had taken place, guilt and apprehension overwhelmed her.

Several times she thought she ought to make him stop. That sort of behaviour should wait until after they were married, or at least engaged.

When she tried to remonstrate and explain this to Bruno he looked bewildered.

'One day we are to be married so why is it wrong?'

'Because we are both Catholics and we both know it is a sin,' she told him primly.

Bruno took her face between his hands and gently kissed her. 'When the season ends, which will be very soon now, you will come back to

Almeria with me. There my family will make you welcome and I will make you my bride.'

'If I'm going to be married then I want it to be here in this country, in Liverpool,' Patsy told him firmly.

He shrugged eloquently. 'We do whatever it is that you wish,' he agreed smoothly. 'You like to have your mother and friends there to see you marry? Yes? Then we will do it in the church here and then we will marry again when we get to Almeria so that all my own family can rejoice in the sight of my beautiful bride.'

Patsy had thought that wonderfully romantic. So much so that she insisted that on the following Tuesday he must come and meet her mother.

Chapter Fifteen

Today, 27 August 1929, was going to be the most exciting day in her life, Patsy Callaghan decided. Not only was it her sixteenth birthday, which was a landmark in itself, but she had promised Bruno that today he would meet her mother.

Patsy could think of nothing else. Dressed in a man's blue cotton shirt and denim trousers, her curls hidden under a cloth cap, she whistled cheerfully as she worked with Billy on the dockside, loading up a consignment of cotton bales.

The midday sun was at its hottest and it blazed overhead, turning the dull Mersey into a sheet of glittering gold. They'd been hard at work since seven o'clock that morning and they were feeling exhausted and ready for a break.

'Let's get this load across on the ferry and then we'll find a shady spot somewhere over on the other side to eat our snack,' Billy suggested.

'Suits me,' Patsy agreed, running her arm across her brow to wipe away the sweat and grime.

'Not much of a way to spend your birthday, is it?' Billy grinned. 'If you're not planning to do anything special tonight then what about the two of us going out somewhere?'

Patsy bit down on her lower lip, her eyes full

of dismay. 'Sorry, Billy, I've already got something planned,' she said.

'Yer mam's throwing a big party for you, is she?' he asked sardonically.

'Well, no, not exactly . . .' She hesitated wondering whether to go on. The idea of asking Maureen Murphy and Billy if they'd like to come to her home for a meal after they finished work had been in her mind all week. The idea of taking Bruno to meet her mam tonight had seemed such a good one when she'd issued the invitation on Sunday, but ever since then she'd wondered if it was going to work out.

She'd never actually confided in her mam about how serious going out with Bruno had become. She'd mentioned his name once or twice, and said he came from Spain, but that was all. She'd never mentioned that they were planning to be married. Or told her that she intended going back to Spain with him when the New Brighton season ended.

Now that the moment of introduction was almost upon her she was beginning to have butterflies in case her mam didn't like him, or in case when he arrived at the house her mam was in one of her moods and was downright rude to him.

Patsy knew she should have told her mam a great deal more about Bruno, but there had never been the opportunity to do so. Lately her mam had been going out earlier in the evening and staying out so late that Patsy was in bed and asleep long before she came home.

Her mam was never up in the morning before Patsy left for work and on the few occasions when they were both at home in the early evening her mam was usually in a foul mood. Lately her moods had been as bad as anything Patsy remembered from the past when she'd been a little kid and her dad had been away at sea.

With Billy and Maureen there at least she could count on Bruno having someone to talk to, and they'd help smooth out any awkward moments. The only problem was over inviting them. Would Billy come? Maureen would jump at the chance, but if Billy wasn't there then Bruno would have three women for company and he might find that a bit overwhelming.

She knew Billy didn't approve of her going out with Bruno and wondered if he already suspected that she might be thinking of going back to Spain with Bruno at the end of the season.

The feeling of excited anticipation she'd had earlier in the day slowly began to evaporate. By late afternoon, when they were on their last delivery, she felt so miserable that she was on the verge of tears. The only way to recapture that feeling of well-being, she told herself, was to ensure that things did go well. To do that she must enlist Billy's help.

'Billy, you know you suggested that the two of us should go out tonight?'

'Yes, it's still on,' he told her eagerly, his blue eyes lighting up. 'Where do you want to go? Anywhere at all. A meal, then pictures or the theatre? Or we could go dancing. It's entirely up to you.'

'Well, it's a bit difficult. I had planned to do

157

something else, but I would love it if you came along as well.'

Billy's jaw jutted out. 'You mean a trip to New Brighton to watch the famous animal trainer at work, I suppose,' he said grimly.

'No, not that, although it does involve Bruno,' Patsy said quickly.

'Go on.' Billy kept his eyes fixed on the road ahead, his lips clamped together in an uncompromising line.

'Well,' she hesitated, unable to find the right words. She didn't want to hurt Billy's feelings in any way because she so desperately needed his support.

'If it's going to be a mystery tour then don't spoil it by telling me,' Billy said sarcastically.

Patsy paused. Then in a rush she said, 'I've invited Bruno over to meet my mam and I'd like you to be there as well.'

'What the bloody hell for?'

It was so unusual for Billy to swear, at least in front of her, that Patsy was struck dumb. He sounded so aggressive that she wondered if she was doing the wrong thing after all in even mentioning it to him. It was too late now: she'd told him enough for him to know what was happening and so she'd have to go through with it.

'I thought it was time they met and my sixteenth birthday seemed to be as good a time as any,' she said lamely. 'I thought of asking Maureen Murphy as well,' she added.

'Why should you want him to meet your mam?'

He shot a sideways glance at her. 'Unless, of course, you're serious about him?'

'We . . . we're friends, you know that.'

Billy was silent for a minute. 'Closer than us?'

'It . . . it's a different sort of friendship,' she said defensively, her colour rising.

His good-looking face hardened. 'Like that, is it! Then I don't see why you need me to come along. Your mam won't want me there for a start.'

'Rubbish, she thinks the world of you,' she grinned. 'She's always saying what a wonderful chap you are and how hard you work.'

'And how much money I hand over to her so that she can afford to go to the pub every night and drink herself silly and treat all her men friends?' he commented bitterly.

'Billy!' Patsy had never heard him talk like this before and it shocked her.

'Well, it's true and you know it is.'

She did know, but she didn't want to talk about it and antagonise him further, not at this moment when she needed his help so much.

'So will you come?'

He shook his head, his jaw set stubbornly, refusing to answer or meet her pleading look.

'Please, Billy. You are my dearest friend.'

'Friend perhaps, but not your lover!'

Her cheeks burned. She'd hoped he didn't suspect quite how serious matters were between her and Bruno. Now that he did there seemed to be nothing else to hide so she might as well come out into the open with him about her future plans.

Billy went chalk white when she said that she

was planning to marry Bruno when the season ended in New Brighton and that she was going back to Spain with him.

'Are you really serious about that? Do you know the sort of life you will be living over there?'

'Oh yes!' she smiled brightly. 'Bruno has told me all about Almeria. The people are friendly. A land of song and sunshine, he called it.'

'You don't want to believe a word of that,' Billy sneered. 'Almeria may be in southern Spain where the weather is warmer than here, but what he hasn't told you is that a lot of the people are so poor that they live in caves on the outskirts of the town.'

Patsy stared at him in annoyance. 'And what makes you think that is where Bruno's home is?' she demanded.

'I'd stake my life on it. That's where the Spanish gypsies live and anyone can see that he is a gypsy.'

'You're only saying that to turn me against him,' Patsy said angrily. 'Of course he's not a gypsy. For one thing, if he was a gypsy, like you say, he wouldn't be able to speak such good English.'

Billy shook his head. 'He probably would, because the kids are taught to beg from the time they can crawl. They hang out round all the ports asking for money and they can do it in half a dozen languages. They're also thieves and vagabonds so you want to watch out.'

'I don't believe a word of that!' Patsy railed.

Billy shrugged. 'It was your dad who told me about what all these foreign places were like. I bet he told you the same things only you've forgotten them.'

'You're making it up to try and make me change my mind about Bruno,' she declared, her eyes filling with tears. 'I don't care what you think or say, though, I'm in love with Bruno and I'm going to marry him.'

'You're going to give up on our business arrangement then as well, are you?' Billy asked in disbelief.

'You'll find someone else to help you on the cart. It will mean you'll be the boss and they'll have to do what you tell them,' she added with a grin, trying to lighten the atmosphere.

Billy was not in the least amused. He stared straight ahead, as though he hadn't heard. Then he gave vent to his feelings by slapping the reins down hard on Samson's back, startling the tired horse into a fast trot. Patsy waited anxiously for him to speak. When he did she was completely taken aback.

'Yeah, kiddo, I'll come to your bash,' he told her in a light-hearted tone. 'Don't bother to ask Maureen, though. Me and your mam, you and Bruno. A cosy little foursome, eh? So what are you planning on doing to make it a special evening?'

'I . . . I don't know, I hadn't thought that far ahead,' Patsy admitted.

'I tell you what, why don't we have a fish and chip supper, that'll give Bruno something to remember about Liverpool. Afterwards, to please your mam, we'll all go to the Grafton and get pissed out of our minds. How does that sound to you?'

'Well . . .' Patsy felt uneasy. It wasn't like Billy to want to go to a pub.

161

He slapped the reins again. 'That's it! Settled! I'll come round to your place as soon as I've scrubbed the muck off and put on a clean shirt. How about that? What time is Bruno going to be there?'

'He's coming across on the seven o'clock boat. He's arranged to take the night off.'

'Really?' Billy gave a long low whistle. 'He must think it's going to be a pretty special occasion then.'

When they reached the stable Billy insisted that he would see to Samson. 'I may as well get used to doing it all on my own again,' he remarked as he unhitched the cart and led the horse towards the stable.

'Billy, please!' Patsy ran after him, grabbing at his arm. 'Don't be like that,' she begged.

He shook her away. 'You dash off home and get yourself ready. It's bound to take you a lot longer than it will me because you'll want to be all dressed up to the nines,' he told her.

'By the way,' he called after her, 'it might be a good idea to warn your mam in advance that this is a very special occasion and that before the evening is out she's going to hear some very special news!'

'I thought I would wait and introduce Bruno to her first before telling her about our plans,' Patsy said uneasily.

Billy shrugged. 'It's up to you, kiddo, how you handle things. It's your big night. I'm just coming along to referee the show!'

Maeve Callaghan looked rather amused when

Patsy told her about the arrangements she'd made for the evening.

'So my little girl is growing up at last and Bruno Alvarez is a serious boyfriend, is he? You never told me that before.'

'I have mentioned his name. I told you he was someone I met when we were delivering in New Brighton. He works at the fairground. He trains the lions and tigers.'

Maeve's light green eyes widened in surprise. 'So is he a foreigner? He must be with a name like that.'

'Well he comes from Spain, but he's very nice. I know you'll like him.'

Maeve raised her eyebrows questioningly. 'So why ask Billy Grant along as well? Are you playing them off against each other, or trying to make Billy jealous?'

'Of course I'm not trying to make Billy jealous, why on earth would I want to do that! I thought it would be better if there were four of us rather than just three,' she explained lamely.

'And we are all going for a fish and chip supper and then to the Grafton for a bevvy?'

'Does that sound all right to you, Mam?' Patsy asked anxiously.

'Suits me. It's your birthday after all so we'll do whatever you like.'

'So you will come out with us, Mam?

'Yeah. If that's what you want,' Maeve agreed. 'Hope you're going to get yourself dolled up a bit,' she added, surveying Patsy's working clothes with distaste.

Patsy grinned. 'Of course I will! It's my birthday.'

'So what's so special about this foreign fella? Training animals is not much of a job. What does Billy think of him?'

Patsy shrugged. 'I think he likes him all right,' she murmured evasively.

'I bet he doesn't!' Maeve laughed gleefully. 'You *are* playing them both along aren't you, my girl? Take after me, don't you?'

Patsy opened her mouth to deny what her mam had said, then she shut it without saying a word. Never, never would she turn to drink and men like her mother had done ever since her dad had gone to sea.

Now was not the time to criticise her mother or to make comments about anything that might start an argument. She desperately wanted her mother to accept Bruno, to like him, and to approve of them marrying.

She'd warn Bruno not to say anything about her going back to Spain with him. She'd break that piece of news to her mam later.

Chapter Sixteen

Patsy found it hard to believe how well her mam and Bruno were hitting it off. She had been afraid that her mam might be critical, unfriendly even. She had been so nervous that she had left it to Billy to introduce them to each other.

To her relief, Maeve had greeted Bruno warmly. In fact, she'd turned on the charm to such an extent that he seemed to be absolutely captivated by her.

As the evening progressed, Patsy didn't know whether she should be pleased or worried at the obvious attraction between them. If Billy hadn't been there she would have felt even more upset, because the two of them practically ignored her.

She should have suspected that her mother was going to go all out to grab his attention when she spent ages getting ready to go out. Maeve had taken a great deal of trouble with her hair and make-up and put on a low-cut black dress that showed her ample cleavage and skimmed her curves like a second skin.

Alongside her mother, even though she was wearing her pretty blue and white spotted voile dress, Patsy felt extremely gauche. She was a good six inches taller than Maeve and because of her very active life her beanpole figure had none of the ripe sexual allure of her mam's plump curves.

She was not able to compete with Maeve when it came to being seductive either. Whatever subject was being discussed, Maeve made full use of her carefully made-up green eyes and her wide smile. Bruno hardly seemed to notice that there was anyone else there.

'Patsy has told me such a lot about you, of course, Bruno,' Maeve gushed, 'but I had no idea that my little girl had such a fascinating friend.' She gave a sexy little shudder. 'I couldn't believe my ears when she told me you were a lion tamer!'

'Lions and tigers,' he told her, smiling.

'Really! How thrilling.' Her green eyes locked with his smouldering dark ones. 'I'd love to see you in action,' she murmured.

'You must come over to New Brighton very soon,' he told her. 'I cannot understand why Patsy hasn't brought you over to see my show before now.'

'Probably because she is so anxious to keep you all to herself,' Maeve smiled.

She focused her whole attention on him, letting shivers of fear and murmurs of awe escape her lips as he told her about his act in great detail.

'And you trained to do all this in your own home country?' she breathed in feigned amazement.

'From a very young age. My father, he too is a lion tamer, one of the most famous in Spain,' Bruno boasted.

'Spain?' Maeve's eyes widened. 'You come from Spain! So romantic!' she said enviously. 'It's a country I've always dreamed of visiting.'

Patsy subsided into bewildered silence as Bruno extolled the wonders of Almeria. She'd heard it all before but watching the simulated rapture on her mother's face was unbearable.

Billy tried to help by introducing other topics but each time he did so Maeve ignored him and turned her attention back to Bruno, fluttering her eyelashes at him, and inviting him to tell her more about himself.

Bruno was so eager to comply that Patsy felt utterly miserable. She could see that Bruno was dazzled by her mam. She felt so miserable and defeated that she wanted to creep away into a corner and hide. In Bruno's eyes her mam must appear self-confident, glamorous and sexy whereas she was simply a gawky naïve kid.

Patsy could only hope that when they moved on to the Grafton, and her mam was surrounded by her own friends, Bruno would realise how much older than him her mam was and that he didn't stand a chance with her.

By the end of the evening he would see her for what she was, a middle-aged woman who liked to drink more than was good for her, Patsy thought uncharitably.

Billy was almost as concerned as Patsy was about the immediate affinity between Maeve and Bruno. He had heard his father constantly criticising Maeve's behaviour in the pub because of the way she flirted and upset a lot of the wives in Paradise Place, but he'd not taken very much notice.

His mother had always been more charitable.

'It's because Maeve Callaghan is lonely that she behaves like that,' Elaine Grant would argue. 'She's a very attractive woman, you have to admit that, with her reddish hair and green eyes and that lovely peaches and creamy skin. She's so very young to lose her husband, she's still only in her thirties, remember.'

'If she's all that wonderful then why doesn't she find herself another husband, not try and pinch some other woman's man,' Joe Grant would argue.

Looking at what was going on between Bruno and Maeve, Billy felt a shiver run down his spine. He saw trouble ahead and he was sure there was going to be heartache for Patsy.

He knew he should be feeling glad, because with any luck it would push Patsy into his arms for consolation, but that was not the way he wanted things to be. He loved Patsy intensely and he wanted her to return his love as a spontaneous gesture not as a last resort.

As the evening progressed, Patsy became more and more despondent. She had always been worried about introducing Bruno to her mam, but for very different reasons. She had thought she might be scornful about her having a boyfriend, might make sneering remarks that would make Bruno uncomfortable, or simply consider the whole thing ridiculous and ignore Bruno.

She had never expected that Maeve would be so attracted to him that she would monopolise him. She watched with growing concern and heaviness of heart as she saw her mam's hand resting possessively on Bruno's sleeve as she emphasised some point in their conversation. Then, as she saw the way her green eyes exchanged unspoken signals with his dark ones, almost as if there was no one else in the room, Patsy looked away in despair, feeling betrayed.

She wanted to go home; to creep into bed and hide her head under the covers and give way to the pent-up tears that had been threatening all evening. She felt an overwhelming sense of relief when the landlord called 'Last orders, please!' She edged close to Bruno, intending to take his arm the moment 'Time' was called so that they could at least spend a few minutes together before he had to dash for the last ferryboat.

Maeve forestalled her by inviting him back for a nightcap before he returned to New Brighton.

'If he does that then he'll miss the last boat,' Patsy said quickly.

'Does that matter?'

Maeve addressed the question to Bruno, her eyes challenging.

He gave an exaggerated shrug. 'I do not have to give a performance until it is the evening. I have only to feed the animals in the morning.'

'So you could stay here overnight and catch an early morning boat?'

'I could, if I had somewhere to sleep,' he agreed.

Maeve gave him a teasing smile. 'Then it's all settled. You stay.'

Patsy could take no more. Turning away, ignoring the hand Billy stretched out to stop her, she made for the door. Tears streaming down her face she headed back to Paradise Place, to the sanctity of the stable.

There, in the darkness, she leaned against Samson's sturdy body and let the tears roll unchecked down her cheeks.

Samson snorted and nuzzled his warm nose into her shoulder as if trying to comfort her.

Running away was only giving in to her mam's wiles, she told herself despondently. Drying her eyes, she made her way home. When she reached her front door she could hear her mam's tipsy laughter.

Determined not to let her mother win Bruno away from her, Patsy straightened her shoulders. She was adamant that she would hold on to him.

They both looked surprised when she walked in.

'I thought you'd come home and gone to bed,' Maeve exclaimed. 'Where have you been? Surely it hasn't taken you all this time to say good-night to Billy?'

'No, and I have no idea where Billy is,' Patsy said sharply. 'He was still in the pub with you when I left. I went over to the stable to make sure that Samson was all right.'

'Samson!' Her mother raised her eyebrows and smiled at Bruno. 'Patsy worries more about that old horse than she does about me,' she pouted. 'He comes first with her every time. He's your secret love, isn't he, darling?'

'He's reliable and can be trusted,' Patsy retorted and then wished she hadn't risen to her mother's taunt because her reply sounded so childish.

'Are you staying here tonight, then?' she asked, turning to Bruno.

'Of course he is! The last boat's gone, what do you want him to do – swim across the Mersey?' Maeve simpered.

'So where is Bruno going to sleep?' Patsy asked bluntly.

Maeve winked at Bruno. 'On the sofa, of course. Why don't you go and find a couple of blankets for him.'

By the time Patsy returned with the blankets Maeve was pouring out a glass of brandy for herself and Bruno.

'A nightcap before we turn in,' Maeve said, waving the bottle unsteadily in the air. 'I know you don't want one because you don't approve of drinking, do you my darling. I'm sure she will change when she's more grown up,' she added as she smirked at Bruno.

Patsy plumped the blankets down on a chair and turned away. She could hardly speak for the lump in her throat.

This was her sixteenth birthday and it was to have been a very special occasion. She felt so miserable that it should end like this. She had intended to tell her mam that she and Bruno were planning to be married and that she was returning to Spain with him. Now all those wonderful plans seem to be in jeopardy, she thought bleakly.

She stared across the living room at Bruno and wasn't even sure she knew him. The way he had behaved tonight, he was not at all like the man she had thought him to be.

When he returned her stare his look was so uninterested that she felt she was being tossed away like an empty cigarette packet.

'Good-night,' she whispered.

Neither Bruno nor her mother answered. Long after she'd undressed and crept into bed she could hear their voices. She dozed fitfully, plunged into nightmarish dreams that left her soaked in perspiration.

When the first streaks of daylight appeared at the side of her curtains she crawled out of bed and pulled on her working clothes. There was no point in lying there tormenting herself. She'd go over to the stable. Samson hadn't been groomed the night before and if she did it now it might take her mind off her problems.

She crept down the stairs as quietly as she could, hoping that Bruno was still sleeping on the sofa. The living room door was ajar and as she peeped in, to make sure she hadn't wakened him, her breath caught in her throat. The sofa was empty. The blankets she had brought down for him were still on the chair where she had dumped them.

She stood in the doorway as if frozen. He could have decided to go back to New Brighton after all, she told herself over and over. She knew it wasn't true. It couldn't be true because the last boat had sailed and there was no other way he could get there.

He probably went down to the landing stage and waited in one of the shelters for the early morning mail boat, she told herself. She knew that wasn't true either.

Holding her breath she crept back up the stairs and stood for several minutes outside her mother's bedroom wanting to look inside but afraid to do so.

Finally, unable to stand the suspense any longer, she turned the handle and opened the door.

What she saw confirmed her worst fears. Her mam and Bruno were both there, in bed together. The bedclothes were in wild disarray and Maeve's bare arm was across Bruno's bare chest.

Covering her mouth with her hand to suppress the bile that was rising in her throat, Patsy rushed headlong down the stairs and out into Paradise Place.

The dark stable was warm and comforting with its familiar smells of hay and horse. Samson neighed a greeting, nuzzling her hand in search of an apple or a piece of carrot.

'Sorry, my old luv,' she whispered. 'I haven't anything special for you.'

She reached for the curry-comb and brush. The rhythmic movement as she groomed him was soothing. Gradually her rapid breathing slowed to normal and her reeling senses calmed. As she talked out loud to Samson about her troubles and problems the bitterness within her slowly dissolved.

Then she froze, not daring to even breathe. There was someone else in the stable.

'Who's there?' she gasped, her heart thundering. To overcome her fear she clung tightly to Samson's mane.

'It's all right, Patsy, it's only me!'

Her breath escaped in an explosion of relief as Billy emerged from the shadows.

'I didn't hear you come in,' she gulped.

'You left the door unfastened. What are you doing here at this hour of the morning?'

'I couldn't sleep.'

He grinned. 'Me neither. Too much to drink last night, I suppose. I'm not used to it, but since it was your birthday bash . . .' He stopped as Patsy broke into sobs.

'Hey, hey! What's the matter? What have I said?' He gathered her into his arms, stroking her red curls as if she was a small child.

'Nothing, nothing,' she sobbed, burying her face in his shoulder.

'Didn't things go well when you got home?' he asked softly. 'Come on, tell me what's gone wrong,' he persisted gently as her tears flowed faster and her body was convulsed by sobs. 'I heard some of what you were saying to Samson so I know there's been trouble. Is it to do with Bruno . . . and your mam?'

Patsy tried to answer, but her voice was too choked and her sobs too violent.

Billy drew her down on to the stack of clean straw waiting to be put down in Samson's stall. He held her close, stroking her hair and kissing the top of her head.

'Oh, Billy, I'm so miserable,' she whispered, resting her tear-streaked face against his. 'How could she do this, my own mother?'

Billy felt afraid to answer. He held her tighter, gently pushing her curls back from her damp brow, stroking her face to try and soothe away her misery. After a while, she began to relax. Her sobs diminished to the occasional shoulder-heaving gulp as she nestled close to him, finding comfort from being in his arms.

For Billy it was utter torment. He loved her so deeply that he hated seeing her so upset. He wanted to tell her how he felt about her, but he was afraid to do so in case it made her pull away from him.

Of their own accord his hands began to move over her body, stroking her shoulders and then moving down her back. When she made no objection he grew bolder. He slipped one hand up under her jumper, his fingers closing over her small firm breasts, gently caressing first one and then the other.

As she turned her face towards his and their lips met he threw all caution to the wind. He returned her kisses with fervour and all the time his hands were exploring her body more and more intimately. He pulled away the cotton trousers to stroke the firm contours of her hips and thighs.

Their passion mounted. He knew he couldn't stop now, whatever the outcome might be. He remembered all the dreams he had harboured of them making love together and in a breathtaking moment of passion he slid into her body. The blissful sense of happiness felt awesome, greater than anything he had ever experienced in his life before.

He would have lain there for ever, cradling Patsy in his arms, but she broke the spell by pulling away from him and sitting bolt upright, a look of astonishment and dismay on her tear-stained face.

'Billy, what have we done?' she gasped.

He reached out, wanting to pull her back into his arms again, but she struggled free. Her face flushed with shame, she avoided his eyes as she moved away from him and straightened her clothes as quickly as she could.

He wanted to assure her that they'd done nothing wrong, that he loved her with all his heart, but it was as if there was an impenetrable wall between them that stopped either of them saying a word.

In icy silence they went about preparing for the day's work ahead. As they set off for the docks, sitting stiffly side by side on the cart, Billy wondered if they were ever going to speak to each other again.

Chapter Seventeen

As September's balmy days turned into October's wet and chilly ones, and the holiday season at New Brighton came to an end, Patsy waited expectantly for Bruno to tell her what he was planning to do and say when he intended to return to Spain.

When the funfair closed down in mid-September the animals had been moved to their winter quarters so she couldn't understand why he had said nothing to her about their date of departure.

She tried talking to him about it, explaining that there was so much she had to do before she could leave home. She had to let Billy know in good time so that he could make arrangements for someone to help him in the business. She had to break the news to her mother that she would be leaving home, she pointed out.

No matter what she said, Bruno remained evasive. Even when she asked if he had changed his mind about returning to Spain he merely shrugged his shoulders, flashed the brilliant smile that could churn her stomach with desire, and told her, 'Later, later, we will talk later, my little flower. Not so much of the hurry. Stop worrying your pretty little head, I will tell you all in good time.'

Patsy did worry, though. She worried about the

way Bruno refused to talk about their future and she worried even more about their relationship. He was still as eager as ever to make love the moment they met on Sundays, but there was a restlessness between them afterwards that concerned her.

She tried to blame it on their surroundings. Inclement weather made it impossible for them to find privacy amongst the sandhills at Leasowe and deserted beach huts, or promenade shelters, didn't have the same ambience.

Recently, even when they made love she sensed that all was not as it had been between them in their first rapturous encounters.

There were so many guilty secrets in her heart. They had never mentioned the night he had spent at her house in Paradise Place. She had never told him that she knew he had slept with her mam and he had never spoken Maeve's name. He never asked after her, never referred to that night at all, and this gave Patsy a vague, disquieting feeling. It was as if it had never happened.

Patsy wished she could adopt the same attitude, but she found that was impossible. When they met on a Sunday, the moment they started to make love, uppermost in her mind was the memory of opening the bedroom door and seeing Bruno lying there in bed with her mam. And what had happened the following morning in Samson's stable also haunted her.

She knew she shouldn't have let Billy make love to her, but she had been half out of her mind with distress at what she had witnessed. The feel of his arms around her had been so comforting, and he had been so gentle that she had been carried away.

It had been a very precious moment, one she couldn't forget. His lovemaking didn't set her afire like Bruno's did, but she had found it wonderfully consoling. It had temporarily alleviated her sadness and shock. Afterwards, although she had felt both guilty and astonished, she had felt at peace. Only Billy and his deep love for her had carried her through the next few days.

When she saw Bruno the following Sunday, she had expected him to confess that he had slept with her mother, and when he did she fully intended to tell him that it was all over between them.

Bruno hadn't said a word. She'd felt terribly confused because no matter how hard she'd tried she'd not been able to broach the matter. She even began to wonder if it *had* all been a figment of her imagination, a result of the wine she'd had to drink.

She blamed the wine for what had happened between her and Billy too. It had been difficult trying to explain that to Billy: he was so convinced that it meant as much to her as it did to him.

She'd tried to let him down gently, but he'd been so angry, so insistent.

'It had nothing to do with having a glass or two of wine. You feel the same way about me as I do about you, only with working together we've always been so close that you haven't realised it,' he protested.

'I think the world of you, Billy, but that's not the same as being in love.'

'And do you think the world of Bruno Alvarez?' he asked, mimicking her voice.

Patsy's eyes softened. 'What I feel for him is different to anything I've ever felt before,' she said dreamily.

'Because he's a foreigner and has a glamorous job,' Billy scoffed. 'You let him treat you like dirt and it makes me sick!'

'I do not!' Her voice rose in indignation.

'You can still claim you think the world of him even after he's slept with your mam?'

Patsy's face reddened. 'He'd had too much to drink as well; he didn't know what he was doing.'

'If you believe that then you'll believe anything,' Billy said scornfully.

'It's what happened! It was all a terrible mistake.'

'Like letting me make love to you was a mistake,' Billy said bitterly.

Patsy reached out and touched his arm. 'I'm sorry, Billy. I never intended to hurt you.'

'I wonder sometimes if you have any feelings at all, Patsy Callaghan,' Billy muttered. 'You know that Bruno spent the night in your mam's bed, but you carry on seeing him as though nothing has happened.'

'I've told you, I love him! If I make a fuss about it I might lose him, and I couldn't bear for that to happen,' Patsy said quietly.

Her mam hadn't mentioned Bruno's name either. She'd not even asked about him the next day. Patsy felt sure that when she'd left the house the following Sunday to go to New Brighton her mam must have known she was going to meet Bruno, yet she never said a word.

There hadn't even been any coolness between her and her mam, Patsy reflected. Life had continued in its usual pattern. Her mam was still in bed when she left for work in the morning, and she was usually getting herself ready to go out when she returned at night.

Her mam didn't say where she was going, but then she never did. Patsy assumed she was off to the Grafton as usual, but she never checked. She was usually in bed before her mam came home so she never knew if she brought anyone back with her or not.

It was as if they were all living in tight little worlds of their own, Patsy thought sadly. Following their one and only lovemaking Billy seemed to be harbouring the dream that she was in love with him, but she was more convinced than ever that it was Bruno she loved.

Unable to stand the uncertainty about the future any longer, Patsy finally asked Bruno outright when they were leaving for Spain. As usual he tried to evade the issue, but she refused to accept his negative shrug.

'I need to know, Bruno. Are we going at the end of this month or next? I keep telling you I have to make plans, tell my mother and Billy.'

Bruno took her face between his hands, forcing her to meet his dark gaze. 'I want to take you home very much, yes? I need to earn the money though to keep you happy, yes? I can earn so much more better money here in England than in my own country so I must stay here a little longer, yes? You understand?'

Patsy pulled herself free, her green eyes blazing. 'That is not what you said back in the summer. You said you would be going home when the season ended,' she reminded him.

'Yes, but my mind I have changed. It is very much for the best.'

'Whose best? Yours or mine?'

'You have the red hair temper showing,' he told her, amusement in his voice.

'I am not in a temper, I am concerned because it means changing all my plans.'

Bruno snapped his long brown fingers. 'Your plans, pouf! It is *my* plans that count. I need to earn good money so I stay.'

'The season is over, there's no work for you here in New Brighton now so how can you be earning money?'

'It will start again soon. It is all arranged. There is to be a circus here at Christmas and my animals will perform. I will be well paid for my act. You will see.'

Nothing she said made any difference so Patsy resigned herself to the fact that all her plans had fallen through. Things had changed between her and Bruno too.

She was sure it had something to do with her mother. The fact that Maeve never mentioned Bruno's name, never asked after him, didn't even enquire if she was still seeing him, filled Patsy with suspicion.

Added to that, Maeve's whole attitude had

changed. She still went out every night but she was dressing with more care. She seemed quieter, more content, less given to moods. Often she was singing to herself, or smiling as if contemplating pleasant secret thoughts. Patsy wondered if she was in love and it troubled her because she had an underlying suspicion that the man involved might be Bruno.

Patsy made vague excuses to Billy about her own change of plans, but he was so relieved and happy to find that she wouldn't be going to Spain that he didn't probe.

Although he'd accepted her pronouncement that what they had done the morning after her sixteenth birthday had been wrong he'd seemed to regard her in an entirely new light ever since then. Whenever the opportunity arose he would take her hand and give it an affectionate squeeze. Often while they were grooming Samson he would kiss the nape of her neck or her cheek.

The look of love in his eyes unnerved her. Things were not going as smoothly as she would have wished between herself and Bruno, but she didn't want to build up Billy's hopes again.

Patsy also had another reason for concern. She'd suspected it for the last couple of months, but now, as the year drew to a close, she knew for certain. She was pregnant.

At first she had thought she'd imagined it, or miscalculated her dates because she was in such a state of uncertainty about her future. She tried to think back; to calculate as accurately as she could, but it only increased her confusion. She waited another month, and then another, and then she knew it was as she feared. She was also aware that she had left it far too late to get rid of it.

She wanted to tell her mother, but Maeve was so secretive, so immersed in her own life that she could never find the right time to do so.

She knew there was only one other person she could confide in and she couldn't bring herself to talk to him about it. She was afraid that if she told Billy she was expecting he might jump to the conclusion that the baby was his.

The only thing she could do, she realised, was to conceal her condition. With it being winter Billy was hardly likely to notice if she wore baggy trousers and even baggier jumpers. He would think it was the sloppy clothes she was wearing to keep warm that made her look fat and shapeless.

She avoided Maureen Murphy and Billy's sister Janie. With their sharp eyes they might guess her secret.

The only time when she was worried that her changing shape might be noticed was on Sundays when she went over to New Brighton to see Bruno. Sometimes she wished he would comment that she was getting fat so that she could tell him why, but either he didn't notice or said nothing even if he did.

Even that no longer became a problem when, towards the end of November, he told her he was going to Blackpool for three weeks to train his group of animals in readiness for the Christmas circus.

'Why do you have to go there?' she asked resentfully. 'If the circus is to be here in New Brighton then why not train the animals here?'

He shrugged. 'Blackpool is the home for the big cats in winter. It is more convenient to do it there.'

Patsy felt bereft. The first Sunday he was away she mooned about the place wondering how to spend her time then finally made for the stable and cosseted Samson.

On the second Sunday she stayed in bed for most of the morning glad of the opportunity to have a rest. Keeping up appearances and not letting Billy know she wasn't really fit enough to do her share of the heavy work was beginning to take its toll. Her legs and back ached badly and often kept her awake at night. Sometimes she felt almost too weary next morning to climb out of bed.

When she came downstairs around midday to make herself a drink before she started to get dressed Maeve was already up and in the kitchen. She stared at Patsy open mouthed as if seeing her for the first time.

'What the hell has happened to you?' she gasped.

'What do you mean?' Patsy rubbed the sleep from her eyes and frowned in bewilderment.

'Look at you!'

'Stop fussing, Mam, I felt like a lie-in. I'll get dressed in a minute,' Patsy yawned. 'There's only us two here, isn't there?'

'Just as well!' Maeve exclaimed cynically. 'God knows what they'd think if they saw you!'

Patsy looked puzzled. Slowly it dawned on her why her mother was so concerned. Desperately she tried to button up the coat she'd pulled on over her nightdress but the edges would barely meet.

'You daft little bitch, you've gone and got yourself up the chute, haven't you?' Maeve spat at her.

Patsy shivered, but made no answer. She didn't know what to say. She knew she should have found a way to tell her mam. Being pregnant wasn't the sort of secret she could keep for ever.

Maeve's face was contorted with rage. 'You feckless Judy,' she railed. 'How could you be so bloody stupid?'

'I . . . I don't know how it happened,' Patsy choked.

'For God's sake!' Maeve's lip curled and the colour drained from her face. 'You don't know how it happened,' she mimicked. 'Don't come that Little Miss Innocence act with me! Of course you bloody well know what you've been up to. You're not a kid and you're not a bloody virgin either, by the look of you!'

Patsy stared at her, speechless. She had never seen her mam in such a rage. She had hoped that when she did eventually get round to telling her she was pregnant her mam would understand and be sympathetic.

'So whose is it? You've been sleeping with that oaf Billy, haven't you, you silly slut!' Maeve screamed.

Dumbly Patsy shook her head. 'Billy doesn't know a thing about it,' she whispered brokenly.

'Then the sooner you bloody well tell him and find out what he's going to do about it the better,' Maeve yelled.

'Mam, it's got nothing to do with Billy,' Patsy protested. 'He's not like that!'

For a moment Maeve looked taken aback. 'Are you telling me that he's a cream poof?' she gasped.

'No, of course he isn't,' Patsy said hotly, 'but my being pregnant has nothing to do with him.'

'Oh yes it bloody well has and the sooner the two of you tie the knot the better. I'm not having any little bastards living under my roof. Your dad would turn in his grave with shame.'

'But, Mam . . .'

'I don't want to hear any more. Just look at you. How many months gone are you? And you have the gall to stand there and tell me you didn't know what was happening? Get up those stairs, get yourself dressed and go and let that stupid oaf know that he's going to be a dad any day now. Tell him he'd better face up to his responsibilities or he'll have me to deal with and . . .'

'But, Mam . . .'

'Sort this mess out before the rest of Paradise Place knows what's been going on. Do you hear me? Does that Maureen Murphy know about this?'

Patsy shook her head, too choked to speak.

'Right! That's something, I suppose. You'd best go down on your knees to Father O'Brian. Billy Grant and his lot aren't Cat'licks, but nevertheless you'll marry him, my girl, I'll make sure of that.'

Chapter Eighteen

Patsy's eyes were still red and swollen when she went to work on Monday morning. Several times while they were fixing Samson's harness she saw Billy looking at her questioningly, but each time she avoided his eyes and quickly turned her head away.

'What's wrong with you today?' he asked jokingly as they hitched the horse up to the cart. 'Too many late nights over the weekend?'

'Something like that,' she mumbled. 'I think I might be going down with a cold.'

'Perhaps you ought to take the day off, then. Why don't you go home and go back to bed, Patsy,' he suggested, his voice full of concern. 'You certainly don't look too good.'

'Perhaps I should,' she agreed.

He sounded so solicitous, so caring, that she had to rub the back of her hand across her eyes to brush away the tears. She wondered what he would say if she told him the truth about exactly why she was not looking too good.

She wanted to tell him and to warn him about her mother's reaction, but she was afraid to do so in case Billy turned against her and then she would have no one to confide in.

She had been stunned by her mam's attitude.

It wasn't as though Maeve was strait-laced or particularly moral herself. Patsy was so dog-tired at night that her mam could have taken umpteen men up to bed and she wouldn't have known. Since she'd found Bruno in with her she'd never opened her mam's bedroom door ever again. What she didn't see didn't bother her.

So why had her mam been so outraged? Patsy wondered. Was it because she feels I should have told her sooner, or was it really because of what she thinks Dad would have thought if he was still alive?

She knew he would probably have regarded it as a heinous sin, because he'd been such a good Catholic, but her mam wasn't. She never goes to Mass these days, Patsy mused, and she never checks on whether I do or not.

The way her mam assumed that it was Billy's baby bothered her. What would she have said if I'd told her that Bruno Alvarez was the father? Patsy wondered.

In the end, Patsy came to the conclusion that her mother was so incensed by the news because the truth had been kept from her for so long and some of the neighbours might already know. Patsy felt guilty about that, but one of the reasons why she hadn't spoken out before was because deep down she wasn't sure whether her mother and Bruno were still seeing each other. It was something she tried to blot from her mind because she had no idea how to handle the situation if they were and she was still so much in love with Bruno that she didn't want to lose him, even though things were far from right between them.

If he noticed that she had put on weight he never mentioned it. They hadn't made love for ages because of the cold weather and since she was always heavily wrapped up against the biting winds that came in off the Mersey her changing shape was well hidden.

She blamed it all on the miserable winter weather. On Sundays there was nothing for them to do except go for a cup of tea in one of the few cafés that remained open in Victoria Street. Having nowhere to go took away all the glamour and excitement.

Sometimes he seemed to be almost indifferent to her. The fire had gone from his kisses; she no longer thrilled to his touch. It was this as much as anything else that made it so difficult to tell him about the baby.

'If you hadn't decided to change your plans then we would both have been in Spain by now,' she said wistfully when they met one Sunday. Bruno had been grumbling about the cold and seemed to be in a more surly mood than usual.

'I had no choice but to stay. My animals are here and there was a show at Christmas time,' he reminded her.

'We could have left for Spain as soon as that was over. The show only lasted for two weeks,' she pointed out.

'I try to tell you that I need the big money. And now I am getting things ready for the new season,' he said curtly. 'It cost too much money to go running back to Spain for a couple of weeks, yes?'

'I thought we were going to be married and we were going to live in Spain,' she reminded him, tears of disappointment welling up in her eyes.

Bruno said exasperatedly, 'The plans, they have to change. It is the money that is important.' He shivered and turned his coat collar up around his ears. 'Next year, perhaps, yes?'

'Next year, the year after, who knows,' Patsy argued miserably. 'You say next year, but what if you change your mind again?'

'I go when my pockets are full and not before.'

'We don't have to wait until you are ready to go back to Spain in order to get married,' Patsy pointed out querulously.

When he spread his hands wide in a dismissive gesture, Patsy felt uneasy. She was alarmed by his apathy. She desperately needed to tell him about the baby, but wasn't sure if this was the right moment to do so. Her thoughts were so jumbled that she couldn't find the right words.

'I'm beginning to think you already have a wife in Spain,' she blurted out.

He laughed dismissively. 'If I have a wife in Spain what would I want with another one here?'

'That's the point I'm trying to make,' Patsy said uncomfortably. 'You don't seem to want a wife here. All you want is someone to make love to while you are in England.'

His dark eyes narrowed and he stared at her calculatingly. 'I cannot understand what your words mean,' he prevaricated. 'You say too much, you confuse me,' he told her as they started to walk up Victoria Road to the café.

Patsy stopped. 'I am not feeling well, I'm going home,' she stated and felt resentment well up inside her when his only reaction was to give one of his infuriating shrugs.

'You have the headache?'

It was the first time since she'd known him that she had ended their meeting early and he showed such little concern that her anger spilled over.

'Headache, backache, my legs ache and so do my feet.' She wanted to add: and my heart aches most of all, but she felt too unhappy to carry on talking to him. Although they had barely spent more than half an hour in each other's company she told him she was going to get the next ferry-boat back to Liverpool.

He didn't try to stop her. Merely raised his eyebrows, then turned and walked back with her towards the landing stage where the *Royal Daffodil* was about to leave.

Patsy had thought he was going to come with her, but he simply stood at the bottom of the gangway and waved farewell as the boat pulled away. He hasn't even kissed me goodbye, she thought bitterly.

All the way back to Liverpool she had felt annoyed with herself that she hadn't told Bruno that she was pregnant. She had to do it and the sooner it was out in the open and he knew, the better.

'Go on then, Patsy, off with you,' Billy's voice cut into her thoughts and brought her back to the present with a jolt. 'Home to bed! Perhaps if you nip this cold in the bud you'll be feeling all right in the morning. If you're not, then stay tucked up where you are.'

She wondered if she dared take Billy up on his offer. She wouldn't go home to bed. If she took the day off she'd go over to New Brighton, find Bruno and do what she should have done yesterday: explain the situation to him. He was a Catholic and once he knew she was pregnant she was confident he would want them to be married before the baby arrived.

'Are you sure you'll be OK on your own?'

'You watch me!' Billy grinned. He put an arm round her shoulder. 'Go on, push off. Of course I can manage without you. There's only a couple of local deliveries to do, not enough to keep us both occupied. I must get going though because the first load has to be picked up from Edge Hill before nine o'clock.'

Patsy decided not to waste time going home to change out of her working clothes. Her mother might be up by now and she didn't want to face another row. She waited until she heard Samson clopping down the road and knew Billy was out of the way then headed for the ferry and New Brighton.

Easter was only a few weeks away and then the season would be opening so there was a great deal of activity in the fairground. It took her some time to find Bruno.

He stared at her for a moment as if he didn't know who she was. 'You are dressed for work so you are feeling better again,' he greeted her. 'Today I not have time to stop and talk with you.'

'What I have to say will only take a minute,' Patsy told him, 'but there is something I must talk to you about.'

'If it is about marrying or going to Spain we must leave such talk for another time. I am busy, yes?'

'No, you are not too busy to hear what I have to tell you,' she insisted stubbornly.

He frowned darkly. 'Come quick and spit it out then.'

This wasn't the way she wanted to tell him her news, Patsy thought. She'd imagined that at least they could find somewhere private. She didn't want to tell him here in the middle of a busy fairground with workmen all around them.

'Can we go somewhere quieter, where there is not so much noise and banging?' she asked.

He took her to a far corner of the fairground. 'Now what is this news that is so important that you must come and interrupt me?' he asked curtly.

She bit down on her lower lip, not sure how to break it to him. 'It is news to make you happy, to make us both happy,' she told him quietly.

He looked puzzled. 'Go on!'

'I . . . I am pregnant, Bruno. I am expecting your baby. It will be born very soon now.'

He stared at her in stark disbelief. 'I do not understand?' His heavy dark brows drew together in a ferocious frown. 'What is this that you are trying to tell me?'

'I am expecting your baby, Bruno.' She pulled aside her jacket. 'Look, see for yourself. Surely you must have noticed that I was putting on weight,' she added crossly.

He drew back, shaking his head in dismay. 'I do not understand. This cannot be so,' he said harshly.

'It's quite true, Bruno. I wouldn't have said so otherwise, now would I?'

He stared at her as if she was a stranger. 'Why now? Why you not tell me yesterday, or the week before, or even the month before. Why now at this busy moment?'

'Bruno!' She was taken aback. She'd not known how he would react to her news, but she had certainly not expected it to be like this.

He spread his hands wide and shrugged. 'What is it you want me to say?'

'I want you to tell me you are happy that we are having a baby. To agree that we must be married as soon as possible.'

He shook his head, his dark eyes unfathomable. 'Pleased, I am not. Shocked, yes! I must have time to do the thinking.'

Patsy stared at him, nonplussed. She couldn't believe what she was hearing, or understand his hostile attitude. She couldn't think of anything else to say. Not unless she pleaded with him to marry her, and her pride wouldn't let her do that.

Re-fastening her coat over her bulky figure, she turned away. 'Very well, I will give you time to think,' she said dully. 'You know where I live, so come and see me when you have decided what we are going to do.'

Without waiting for him to reply she walked away. When she reached the main road she turned and looked back, half hoping that he would be running after her. There was no sign of him.

In a daze Patsy walked the short distance back to the pier. As she waited for the return boat to Liverpool she deplored her own foolhardiness. Perhaps Billy was right after all when he said foreigners didn't think the same way as they did. If Bruno refused to marry her, what was she going to do? She felt bitter and confused. First her mam and now Bruno seemed to be against her.

Patsy was so engrossed in her morbid thoughts that when she came off the boat at Liverpool she didn't notice the horse and cart at the top of the floating roadway. She was jerked out of her reverie when a familiar voice said, 'You might as well have a ride home with us as catch a Green Goddess.'

'Billy! What are you doing here?'

'I've finished the last delivery for today and was on my way home. I couldn't believe my eyes when I saw you coming off the New Brighton boat. I thought you said you were going home to bed,' he commented as she climbed up beside him.

She shook her head. 'No, there was something else I had to do that was more important.'

He flicked the reins and concentrated on the road ahead. 'More important than getting yourself fit for work tomorrow?'

She shot him a sideways glance. 'It was very urgent. Something I had to do.'

'Well, are you going to tell me what it was?'

'I'm pregnant.'

The words hung in the air between them like a ship's pennant.

'I had noticed,' Billy said quietly, 'and I wondered when you were going to tell me.'

Patsy's jaw dropped. 'You knew!'

'Well, it had to be that or else you were getting ready to be the fat lady in the circus,' he joked. 'Come on, Patsy, I'm not blind, you know. You've been getting fatter and fatter ever since Christmas. Lately there's been days when it's as much as you can do to climb up and down into the cart.'

'And yet you've said nothing!'

'I was waiting for you to tell me. After all, I could have been wrong, you could have been putting on weight and then think how embarrassed you would have been if I'd been the one to mention it.'

Patsy didn't answer.

'Have you told your mam yet?'

'She found out yesterday. She went absolutely crazy . . . she thinks it's yours,' Patsy said awkwardly.

Billy swung round in his seat to stare at her. The broad smile on his face vanished when he saw her expression.

'So you've been over to New Brighton to see Bruno, and tell him it's his, have you,' he said in a cold, noncommittal voice.

'Yeah. A lot of good that did me an' all! He didn't seem to want to know,' she added bitterly.

Billy faced her squarely. 'It's your baby, Patsy, no matter who the father is and you've only to say the word and I'll marry you. We'd be happy together, I know we would.'

Chapter Nineteen

When Patsy reached home and opened the front door she found her mam, her hair all over the place, her face red with effort, a half-smoked cigarette dangling from the corner of her mouth, struggling down the stairs with a heavy sack.

'Mam? What's going on?' Patsy frowned.

'You can put that back on,' Maeve told her sharply as she started to take off her coat.

'Why, do you want me to take that sack somewhere?'

Maeve drew heavily on her cigarette. 'You can take the bloody thing wherever you like and yourself with it,' she snapped, breathing out a cloud of smoke.

Patsy looked bewildered. 'What do you mean by that?'

Maeve straightened her dress and smoothed her hair back into place. 'Exactly what I say, my girl! Your clothes and your bits and pieces are all in there.' She kicked disdainfully at the sack with the toe of her high-heeled shoe. 'Now take it and get out of my bloody sight.'

'You mean you are turning me out?' The blood drained from Patsy's face. She stared at her mother in shocked disbelief.

'I'm not turning you out, kiddo, I'm bloody well

throwing you out!' Maeve took another drag at her cigarette. 'I don't want you here under my roof another minute.'

Patsy felt frozen to the spot. She wondered if her mam had been drinking, then told herself that couldn't be the reason for her being so belligerent. Her mam went out drinking most nights and when she came home again she was usually laughing and singing. If she brought someone home with her then sometimes she behaved in a silly manner, but Patsy had never seen her in quite such an aggressive mood as this.

'Did you hear what I said?' Maeve snapped. 'I want you and all your belongings out of this house right now.'

'Mam, be reasonable, I've nowhere to go!'

'Then you'd better find somewhere, or ask that Billy Grant if you can shack up with him since he's the one who's got you into this mess.'

'Billy has nothing at all to do with what's happened. I told you that before,' Patsy said wearily.

'Oh no? Are you trying to tell me you've been playing the field?'

'No, I leave that for you to do,' Patsy retorted angrily.

Maeve's hand came up and made contact with Patsy's face before she could move a muscle. The impact of the resounding slap sent Patsy reeling.

'Mam!' she gasped, her eyes filling with tears, her head spinning, as she staggered back.

What on earth was happening to them both? she thought in alarm. She realised that her mother was upset by the news that she was pregnant so she'd expected to get a tongue-lashing, that was only natural. Once that was over, though, she'd thought her mam would help her and tell her what to do for the best.

'Mam, don't do this to me. I've never needed your help more in my life,' she pleaded.

'You might need it, but you're not bloody well going to get it.' Maeve came closer, breathing gin fumes into Patsy's face. 'I must have been blind not to see what was going on right under my nose. You think I'm a soft touch because I let you and that Billy run the business just as you like. You think you can trick me all ends up, don't you? Well, you're wrong.'

'Mam, just listen to me for a minute,' Patsy begged. 'This has nothing to do with Billy, he didn't even know about the baby until today.'

'No? So whose kid is it, the Tooth Fairy's?'

Patsy shook her head, her red curls dancing like flames in a fire. 'It's Bruno's!'

Maeve's green eyes were glacial as she stared at Patsy. 'You little bitch! I was waiting for you to say that,' she said. 'Only I know different, don't I.'

'It's the truth,' Patsy said wearily. 'We've been meeting every Sunday since the beginning of the summer. Bruno promised me we would be married as soon as the season ended and after that he would take me back to his home in Almeria.'

Maeve shook her head, smiling cynically. 'That's what you told him you wanted to do. Bruno told you that it was out of the question because you were only a kid and too young to leave home,' she added scornfully.

Patsy shook her head. 'No, Mam, that's not true. Wherever did you hear that?'

'Straight from the horse's mouth,' Maeve told her exultantly, 'and I don't mean that old nag out in the stable. I mean from Bruno himself.'

'Bruno?' Patsy stared at her in disbelief. 'When did he tell you this?'

'Several times. The last time was today, only about an hour ago.' Maeve licked her lips, watching the bewilderment on Patsy's face.

'Bruno's only just left here!' she declared triumphantly. He came over here before his evening show started specially to tell me what you'd been accusing him of and to assure me that he'd never touched you. He said that he'd taken you out a few times, before your birthday, but that was all . . .'

'Mam, that's not true.'

'He'd seen you a few times before your birthday but he had no idea what your age was,' Maeve went on, ignoring the interruption. 'He was shocked when he came over here that first time and found out how young you were. He told me that straight after that he stopped having anything to do with you.'

'He certainly did not! We've seen each other every Sunday since my birthday, the same as we did before,' Patsy told her hotly.

Maeve looked smug. 'Bruno told me you had been over to New Brighton every Sunday afternoon pestering him to take you out, but he wasn't having any.'

'Pestering him! Walking to Leasowe sandhills

and making love was pestering him, was it?' Patsy exclaimed bitterly.

'That's what you wanted him to do, no doubt,' Maeve taunted, 'but he wasn't the least bit interested because he knew you were only a kid.'

'And all the promises about marrying me and taking me back to Almeria, I suppose I imagined he said all that, did I?'

'He told you about his home in Spain, so you probably daydreamed the rest,' Maeve laughed.

Patsy's shoulders slumped. 'I don't know how to convince you, Mam,' she said despondently. 'Why won't you listen to me, try and understand that I am telling you the truth.'

'Why should I do that when I know you're not,' Maeve demanded. 'Take a look at yourself!' she said scathingly. 'What do you look like? Dressed in a man's shirt and trousers and an old cloth cap perched on your head. What fella would give you a second look let alone fancy you? I know Bruno's no longer interested in you because he has been taking me out ever since your birthday!' she gloated.

Patsy's face hardened. 'I've been doing my best to forget I found you in bed with him,' she said. 'Not something for you to be proud of, being in bed with my boyfriend, Mam! You're every bit as bad as the neighbours say. And to think I've always stuck up for you when they run you down and say things about the way you carry on in the Grafton when you're pissed out of your mind.'

The colour drained from Maeve's face. 'That will do, Patsy. How I live my life is my own affair.'

'You mean affairs, don't you. One affair after the other, isn't it,' Patsy taunted. 'I can still remember the string of "uncles" you used to bring to the house when I was a little kid, while my dad was away at sea.'

Maeve raised her hand as if to lash out again, but Patsy was too quick for her. 'Oh no you don't!' she said scornfully, backing away.

Her scalp crawled with sweat as she stared at Maeve wide-eyed. 'What's up with you, Mam?' she asked. 'I've done nothing to deserve this.'

'No?' Maeve's lip curled. 'Getting yourself pregnant and bringing a load of disgrace on both of us is counted as nothing, is it?'

Patsy's shoulders slumped. 'I know what I've done is wrong, Mam, that's the reason why I've been too scared to tell you.'

'And you've not given a thought about what all the neighbours will be saying about the way I've brought you up?'

Patsy stared at her, confused. Then she gave a wry smile. 'When have you ever worried about what the neighbours thought or said, Mam? They've had plenty to talk about in the past.'

'Be that be as it may, but I'm not standing for it now. I want you to go. I want you out of this house right this minute and I never want you to come back. So take that sack.'

Before Patsy could argue further Maeve opened the door and heaved the heavy sack out on to the roadway.

'Go on! All your things are there, now get out,' she shouted breathlessly. Refusing to look Patsy in the face, Maeve stood with one hand on the door, face averted, waiting for her to leave.

The moment Patsy stepped over the threshold Maeve slammed the door, so quickly and so violently that she caught it against Patsy's heel, making her yell out in pain.

Patsy stood outside her home feeling stunned and shivering in the April drizzle. She still couldn't believe that her mam had meant what she'd said, or that she really was throwing her out. She turned round and banged wildly on the door, but there was no response.

'Mam!' she yelled, banging again with her fists, 'open up this door, it's started to rain and I'm getting soaked.'

The silence from inside remained unbroken. Patsy crouched down to peer through the letter-box. She could see her mam was still in the hall so she thumped again on the closed door with her fist, but Maeve remained where she was, standing at the foot of the stairs, holding on to the newel post.

Tears streaming down her cheeks, Patsy grabbed hold of the heavy sack and tried to think where she could go for shelter.

Asking Billy for help was out of the question. For a fleeting moment she wondered if Maureen Murphy would help her, but the thought of all the questions Maureen's mother and sister would ask, and the gossip that would result from anything she told them, put her off.

She stifled her sobs. No, she resolved, she'd deal with this on her own. It was bad enough that her mother had turned her out without it becoming common knowledge for the whole of Paradise Place.

The sack was heavy and what had started as an April shower had now turned to heavy rain. She was getting soaked. There was only one place she could go to shelter, Patsy thought wearily, and that was into Samson's stable.

By now he would have been fed and settled for the night so there was no fear of Billy coming back again until morning. That would give her plenty of time to decide what to do and what to tell him, she thought as she dragged the heavy sack along the ground.

It was still only early evening and she was hungry so before taking off her wet coat Patsy went to the corner shop for buns, milk and some apples and then to the chippy.

As she tucked into her fish and chips she wondered if she ought to go across to New Brighton again to try and explain the situation to Bruno. Surely the fact that her mother had turned her out must change things, she reasoned. Even if Bruno didn't want to go back to Almeria right away they could be married here in England.

He was a Catholic, so he knew all about mortal sin and he wouldn't want the baby to enter the world as a bastard. Or should she go and see Father O'Brian and ask him for help? Her spirits lifted. She might even be able to get Father O'Brian to talk to Bruno and persuade him they should be married as soon as possible. Surely Bruno would listen to a priest and do whatever he advised?

Patsy screwed up the newspaper the fish and chips had been wrapped in. She'd tidy herself up and go along to the church right away.

When she opened the door the rain was lashing down and blowing straight at the stable so she closed it again quickly. It would be madness to go out in that lot, she decided. Another day wouldn't make all that much difference. It would give her time to plan out in her mind what she should say to Father O'Brian.

Samson whinnied expectantly as she picked up an apple and rubbed it on her sleeve. She took one bite then lost interest and gave him the rest of it. As he munched away she laid her head against his warm side with a sigh. 'You're the best friend I've ever had, aren't you, Samson?'

Her mind was in such turmoil that her head felt as if it was going to explode. She couldn't think straight and she had no idea what to do for the best. Troubled memories floated in and out of her mind like scattered debris.

If only she could turn the clock back; if only her dad was still here. She thought about all the dreams and hopes he'd had for her future and it saddened her to know that none of them would ever come true. She would never be a teacher as he had hoped she would be, nor would she ever work in one of the impressive Liverpool shipping offices.

Perhaps it was as well that he wasn't alive to know how badly she had failed him, she thought sadly.

She felt so tired and utterly depressed that tears trickled down her cheeks. Her back was aching so much that she wished she could curl up into a ball and never wake up again.

Struggling to her feet she groped around in the fading light for some clean straw and spread it out in a corner of the stable to make a bed for herself. She kicked off her boots, then lay down on it fully clothed and pulled a horse blanket over her for warmth.

Perhaps after she'd had a sleep she'd feel better and would be able to see things more clearly, Patsy thought hopefully as she stared into the darkness. By next morning her mam might have calmed down and she would be able to go back home again.

Chapter Twenty

Patsy fell into an exhausted sleep within a few minutes of lying down on the makeshift straw bed. She slept soundly until the first pink glow in the sky forewarned another day of unsettled spring weather.

When she did waken she ached all over and for a moment couldn't make out what she was doing in Samson's stable. She closed her eyes again and wondered if she was still dreaming.

Gradually her mind cleared and she remembered what had happened the previous evening. She went back over the row between herself and her mam and all the awful things they'd said to each other. It was the first time she could remember her mam hitting her so hard and the memory of the vicious slap across her face brought tears to her eyes.

She was sure it must have all been a terrible mistake and the sooner she went back home and cleared the air the better. Her mam hadn't been herself. Someone else must have done something, or said something, that had really upset her. It couldn't simply be the knowledge that she was about to be a grandmother. Or could it?

Patsy sighed. Her mam wasn't all that keen on babies or small children, so that could have been what had led to her violent outburst. She'd thought she was going to be saddled with a young baby around the place! As well as all the extra work that would bring she was probably worried that it might cramp her style.

Patsy smiled to herself. Her mam must feel she was too young to be a grandmother. She prided herself on how young she looked. She even boasted that with her good figure, fresh creamy complexion and shoulder-length strawberry-blonde hair, people often said she looked in her late twenties.

Patsy eased herself upright. She felt huge and clumsy as she brushed herself down and straightened her crumpled clothes. She couldn't stay here another night without water or facilities of any kind. There was barely any light when the door was shut.

Now that she had gathered her wits together she was eager to be up and sorting things out. The first thing she'd do, she decided, would be to go and see her mam and make her understand that the baby wouldn't spoil her life in any way. And when she'd made her peace with her mam she'd go over to New Brighton and make Bruno understand that they had to get married right away, before their baby was born.

She was on the point of pulling on her boots when the stable door opened and Billy appeared carrying a bucket of fresh water and a bag of feed for Samson.

His mouth dropped open in astonishment when he saw Patsy and he stopped just inside the door staring at her as if she was a ghost.

He ran a hand through his shock of brown hair. 'What on earth are you doing here?' he said, frowning. 'What's going on?'

Patsy grimaced. 'It's a long story, where do you want me to begin?'

'Well, why you're sleeping in here, that will do for a start.'

'Because last night me mam kicked me out –' she pointed dramatically towards the sack – 'and all me belongings with me!'

'You had a bust-up with her?'

'Yeah, you could say that.'

'Do you want to tell me about it?'

'I suppose I may as well.' Some of Patsy's bravado seeped away. 'You'll probably hear about it anyway. By mid-morning I expect there will be rumours flying all round Paradise Place.'

Billy's face remained impassive. He tipped the bucket of water into Samson's trough and shook out the bag of feed for him.

'Go on then, I'm listening,' he said gruffly.

'It's because of the baby,' Patsy said stiffly. 'I don't think my mam likes the idea of becoming a grandmother.'

Billy's jaw tightened and his blue eyes were challenging as they met hers. 'There's a lot more to it than that, now isn't there?'

'What do you mean?' Her voice was sharp. Her green eyes were icy as she stared back at him.

'Well . . .' He thrust his hands into his trouser pockets. 'She's probably upset because you're so pregnant and you've never said a word to her about it until now. If you'd told her a lot sooner then she would have had time to get used to the idea.'

Patsy's lower lip jutted sulkily. 'How could I tell her when I didn't know myself?'

'You must have had some idea,' Billy argued. 'Women usually know these things quite early on.'

'Oh yes,' she tipped back her head and regarded him cynically, 'I suppose you know all about that sort of thing, do you, Billy Grant?'

Colour stained his face. 'I seem to know more about it than you do,' he snapped.

Patsy's face crumpled. 'Don't shout at me, Billy. I thought you were my friend.'

'I'm not shouting,' he said in surprise. 'I am your friend, you should know that, Patsy. I can't understand why you didn't confide in me earlier, though. How do you think I feel now that I know you've been pregnant all this time and I've been expecting you to carry on working as normal? Helping to lift heavy loads, and giving a hand to control a massive great horse, isn't work for a girl at the best of times and certainly not for someone in your condition.'

'Honestly, Billy, I didn't know I was pregnant, not for a long time,' she said emphatically. 'I thought I was putting on weight because it was winter and I was eating so much stodge.'

'And that's why you've taken to wearing such baggy clothes, I suppose?'

'Partly. I didn't want people to see how fat I was getting.'

'Even when you realised why you were getting fat you didn't talk about it to anyone, not even me,' Billy went on accusingly.

'No,' she admitted. 'I didn't because I didn't want to believe it was true.'

He frowned. 'And now your mam has thrown you out because you're pregnant. So what are you going to do?'

'I don't know,' she mumbled. Suddenly the idea of going back home and confronting her mam seemed futile. 'Stay here until I get things sorted out, I suppose.'

'Here? You mean here in Samson's stable?'

She shrugged. 'He doesn't seem to mind.'

Billy grinned. 'Maybe not, but it's not a very good arrangement, is it?'

'Then I'll try and sort something out with me mam. I was hoping she might be feeling different about things today.'

Billy raised his eyebrows questioningly. 'Would you like me to go round and talk to her?'

'No, no! Don't do that whatever you do,' she entreated.

'Why not? She might listen to me.'

'You wouldn't like what she has to say about you.' Patsy muttered.

Billy looked puzzled. 'What do you mean by that?'

Patsy chewed on her lower lip for a moment. 'Well, I told you she thinks you're the father,' she blurted out, her face scarlet.

Billy gave a soundless whistle. His mind sped back to what had happened right there in the stable the night of Patsy's sixteenth birthday and his heart thudded.

He looked at her speculatively. Could it be his

child she was carrying? It wasn't the first time he'd wondered about that and for a moment he felt elated.

Then common sense took over as he realised not only the improbability of that being the case, since they had only ever made love once, but also the problems it would probably cause for them both if it was true. Unless Patsy agreed to marry him, but would she?

'So what did you tell your mam?' he asked cautiously.

'That it had nothing at all to do with you, of course!'

Billy scowled. Alvarez! Of course, Bruno Alvarez must be the father. How could he have thought otherwise? For a moment he saw red. He loved Patsy so strongly that he hated her. Then the feeling went as quickly as it had come and he had nothing but pity for her and the awful predicament she was in.

'Please don't go to see my mam, Billy.'

'I won't if you tell me what you're planning to do.'

Patsy grinned. 'First and foremost I'm going to pinch some of the water you brought over for Samson, if there's any left, and wash my face.'

'Right! I'll hitch Samson up to the cart while you're doing that and we can work out some sort of plan for the future as we work.' He paused and looked at her awkwardly, his face reddening. 'Do you think you should carry on working in your condition?'

'I worked yesterday so I can work today,' she

told him. 'That is if you give me five minutes to sort myself out.'

'Make it three minutes and I'll treat you to some breakfast at the café on the Dock Road,' he promised as he led Samson outside.

As she bent over the horse trough Patsy sensed that something was wrong. Her back had been aching when she'd woken up, but now there was a griping pain and cramps in the pit of her stomach that made her wince and took her breath away.

Knowing Billy was waiting for her outside in the yard she tried to stand up, but the excruciating pain made her gasp.

At the same time she noticed that her clothing was soaking wet and wondered what had happened. Then her heart almost stopped. It could mean only one thing. Gripped by a fresh wave of pain, her fear increased. The baby was coming.

Again she tried to stand up, but her legs felt like jelly. She crouched back on the straw wondering what to do now. Should she call out to Billy or try to manage on her own?

She tried to think what jobs were booked in, and what time their first call was, but her mind refused to function. All she could think about was the pain and what was happening to her body. Her face was wet with perspiration, her clothes were soaked and she couldn't go home because her mam had turfed her out.

Another wave of pain surged through her body and she yelled out for Billy.

'The baby!' she gasped as he came rushing in from the yard. Then another contraction took over her body and waves of pain left her speechless and her mind a blank.

When the spasm was over she flopped listlessly against Billy as he wiped the sweat from her brow and murmured words of comfort.

'I'm going to fetch your mam, Patsy,' he told her as he gently laid her back on the straw. 'It's for the best, she'll know what to do.'

Patsy grabbed at his coat sleeve. 'No, no, you can't do that, she won't come, anyway. You know she's chucked me out! That's why I'm here, isn't it?'

'I'll go and get my mam then. You need a woman here and she'll come and help you, Patsy.'

'No, no!' She clutched at him wildly as a fresh spasm gripped her swollen body. 'I don't want you to do that. I don't want my mam or your mam. You'll have to help me, Billy!'

He held her, mopping her face, murmuring words of encouragement, trying to pacify her, but all the time becoming more concerned. He had no experience of such things and had no idea what he ought to be doing.

Patsy's mop of red curls was dark with sweat. He brushed them back from her forehead and looked down into her glazed eyes. 'I can't do this, Patsy,' he told her awkwardly. 'You need towels, blankets, hot water.' He paused and shook his head from side to side. 'I don't know what we need, but there's nothing at all here. Let me go and fetch someone. Perhaps you ought to be in hospital?'

'It's too late, Billy. The baby's going to be born

any minute. You'll have to help me,' she pleaded. 'Open up that sack – there's bound to be something inside it that we can use.'

'You need a woman here,' he insisted. 'Let me fetch my mam.'

Patsy tried to answer him but a contraction twisted her body in a violent shudder. She clung frenetically to his arm, her green eyes imploring, as she begged him not to leave her.

He took a deep breath to steady his own nerves as he gently loosened her fingers. He was scared. He knew he was out of his depth and that the right thing to do was to get help. Perhaps he ought to send for an ambulance. In hospital she would have all the right care.

As if reading his mind, Patsy grabbed his arm. Her voice was hoarse and frightened as she pleaded with him again.

'All right. I'll do it your way,' he promised quietly. He opened up the sack and tipped out the contents, sorting through her few belongings and putting to one side anything that might be useful. The rest he stuffed back in the sack and moved it out of the way.

Removing his donkey jacket and rolling up the sleeves of his checked cotton shirt, he knelt down beside her and loosened her clothing as another contraction left her gasping for air.

'Try and stay calm,' he said softly. 'It will all be over quite soon.'

She looked up at him trustingly and nodded, but before she could speak her body convulsed violently. She tried to control her screams as pain ripped through her and for a brief moment the world around her was blotted out.

From far off she heard Billy's voice telling her what she must do, but she had no control over her body at all. It was now one seething mass of pain, wave after wave, sending her in and out of darkness.

Then an agitated mewing sound pierced the dark that surrounded her and she wondered why there was a cat in the stable. She drifted in and out of consciousness, tormented by the sound and waiting for Billy to stop the animal from crying.

Vaguely, through a misty haze, she could hear Billy telling her something. He sounded very excited, but Patsy couldn't understand what he was saying. Something that sounded like 'The baby is a boy', but his words meant nothing to her.

She didn't know what he was on about, and she didn't care. Now that the terrible searing pain had stopped all she wanted to do was sleep. She wished Billy would go away and leave her alone. She tried to open her eyes and tell him this, but she was so very tired that it was too much of an effort to do so.

Chapter Twenty-One

For the first three days after the baby was born Billy hardly left Patsy's side. Work was abandoned. He ate and slept at the stable, worrying about the baby, knowing it was probably premature and wondering if he had done all the right things for it when it was being born.

He was torn between whether or not he should tell his mother or someone else about what had happened or whether to comply with Patsy's wishes.

To cover up for his absence from home, and the fact that he was not taking the horse and cart out each morning, he told everyone that Samson wasn't well and that he didn't think he ought to leave him.

No one seemed very bothered, and when he said it was something he could deal with he was left to his own devices. His mother made up a pile of his favourite cheese and pickle sarnies as well as bacon butties each day and left them on the kitchen table for him to collect if she wasn't there when he popped home.

'Can you make me some conny-onny ones as well?' he asked. He remembered they'd been Patsy's favourite when she was little and he hoped they'd tempt her appetite.

'I'll do better than that,' Elaine Grant promised, 'I'll make some wet-nelly and leave you a big wedge of that as well. You've always loved it, ever since you were a little lad.'

When he told his mother that he fancied some soup or stew she expressed surprise, but agreed to have some ready for him next time he dropped in.

'Are you going to sit down and eat it here?'

'No, I'll take it back with me.'

'In that case you'd better take the Primus stove and a saucepan with you so that you can heat it up.'

'Thanks, Mam. I'll take the Valor stove as well if you can spare it.'

She looked puzzled. 'You mean that big one we use to warm the upstairs before we go up to bed in winter?'

Billy nodded. 'You're not using it, are you?'

'Well, no, but it's not like you to feel the cold, son,' she frowned. 'I thought the weather had turned quite mild for April. You be careful where you place it, mind, with all that hay and straw about the place.'

'I'm not the one that's cold. It's to take the chill off the stable . . .'

'You and that old horse,' she laughed. 'You think more of him than you do of your family! Still, I suppose he is almost as important to you as we are. Without him you wouldn't be able to work, now would you.'

Afraid that his mother might become suspicious he didn't dare ask her for any of the other things he required. Instead he visited a junk shop and managed to find a tin bath that he could use to wash the baby, Patsy herself and their clothes in. He also found a shallow wooden chest that he thought would make a cradle.

He needed soap, cotton wool and dozens of other things, as well as warm clothing for the baby. He was scared to buy these from any of the local shops in case someone who knew his mother came in. If they told her what they'd seen him buying she was bound to ask him why on earth he wanted such items.

Billy felt worried whenever he had to leave Patsy and the baby, even if it was only for half an hour. It was risky in case anyone came near the stable and heard the baby crying, but it was something he had to do in order to fetch supplies for them.

Once he'd lined the wooden chest with straw, and then with a warm blanket, he was happy that the baby would be quite safe. It might waken and cry, but it could come to no real harm.

It was Patsy he worried about. For the first couple of days she had a raging fever and drifted in and out of consciousness all the time. In between spoon-feeding Patsy and attending to the baby he put cold compresses on her brow and changed her sweat-soaked nightdress.

By the third day, though, her forehead seemed to be that little bit cooler, her body less clammy. By the afternoon she seemed fully aware of what was going on around her.

While she'd been semi-conscious he'd managed

to persuade her to feed the baby whenever she was lucid enough to do so. He'd placed it in her arms and her response to its cry had been automatic. It was almost as if she was unaware of what was going on, or that it was her own baby she was suckling.

By the third day, however, although she was still so weak that she could hardly sit up, she was fully aware of the baby when he placed it in her arms.

Her expression of gratitude when she saw how well it was thriving embarrassed Billy.

'I still think you should have gone home to your mam, or got someone to come here and help,' he muttered. 'I'm not even sure I did the right things when he was born. You ought to see a doctor, Patsy. You really should if only to make sure you're all right as well as having the baby checked over. He was premature, remember.'

She looked down at the tiny redheaded scrap in her arms. 'There's nothing to worry about, Billy. He's perfect, you can see that for yourself.'

'You don't know that,' he persisted firmly. 'Look, Patsy, how do you think I would feel if anything went wrong with either of you later on? I'd never be able to forgive myself if we found out that it was because of something I hadn't done right when he was born.'

'You're talking daft, kiddo!' she protested weakly. 'There is nothing wrong with either of us.'

'You don't know that for sure,' he repeated doggedly, his square jaw looking stubborn. 'He's a tiny baby and he looks a bit frail to me.'

Patsy laughed out loud for the first time since the baby had been born. 'Listen to yourself!' she teased. 'He's small! Of course he's small. Did you expect him to be the same size as Samson?'

Billy shook his head in despair. 'If you think he's all right then he probably is,' he muttered. 'What are you going to do now, though? You can't stay here for ever.'

Patsy's face clouded and her momentary happiness vanished. Her shoulders sagged and he felt so sorry for her that on impulse he hugged her, holding her close, stroking her curls, and tenderly kissing her brow.

'I'm sorry. I didn't mean to worry you, Patsy, but you will have to make plans for the future, for the baby's sake if not for yourself.'

'You think I should tell my mam, don't you?' she murmured unhappily.

'Your mam or . . . Bruno.' Even saying the name choked Billy, but he tried hard to hide his resentment. 'He should be providing for you and the baby.'

'Yes, I suppose you're right, but then he doesn't know I've had the baby, does he? I intended to go to New Brighton to talk to him before the baby was born.'

'Well, you're in no fit state to make that journey for quite a while yet so why not let me tell your mam?'

She moved free of his embrace and turned to face him, her green eyes pleading. 'I'd sooner you went over to New Brighton and told Bruno about the baby.'

Billy stiffened. Surely she didn't expect him to do that! It was the last thing he wanted to do, even to help Patsy.

'Please, Billy,' she begged.

'I don't know,' he prevaricated. 'I don't think I should be the one to tell him. Anyway, you haven't even given the baby a name yet.'

Her face lit up. 'We'll do it now! You delivered him so you choose a name.'

He shook his head. 'I can't do that!'

Smiling, Patsy pulled back the blanket the baby was wrapped in and studied the child. 'With blue eyes he's the spitting image of me dad,' she said proudly.

'So do you want to call him John?'

She shook her head. 'No, that doesn't seem right somehow.'

They stared at each other blankly. He was afraid she would say 'Bruno' and if she did he would tell her that wasn't the right name for a redhead.

'I like the name Liam,' Patsy murmured.

Billy felt a sense of relief. 'Right, that's it then. The baby is Liam.'

'So now he has a name will you go and tell Bruno?' she urged.

'If that's what you want. It might take me quite some time, though. Will you be all right if I leave you here on your own?' he asked anxiously.

Patsy looked surprised by his concern. 'You've left me here on my own before,' she reminded him.

'I know, only then you were either asleep or out cold,' he told her ruefully. 'I always locked the door and took the key with me,' he assured her.

'I'll stay right here,' Patsy promised. 'I don't want anyone to see me now, do I?'

'Do you want me to lock the door and take the key with me? Or shall I leave it in its hiding place under the stone outside?' he asked as he put on his donkey jacket and pulled on his cap.

'No, take the key with you in case anybody who knows where it's hidden comes looking for you and decides to let themselves in. I'll feed Liam and afterwards we'll both have a sleep,' she promised.

Sitting in the gloom Patsy felt nervous and on edge. There were so many strange noises that she kept looking over her shoulder. She wasn't sure if it was Samson as he munched away at his net of hay, or if it was a mouse, or rat, scuttling in one of the corners.

She knew Liam shouldn't be in such surroundings. Billy was right, she must move out as soon as possible. She'd thought her mam would have come looking for Billy before now to ask if she was all right, but it seemed she hadn't asked after her at all.

Billy had been a real brick and she didn't know what she would have done without his help, Patsy thought grimly. He'd cared for her and done far more to help her than she would have thought possible. Having to assist at Liam's birth must have been a terrible shock for him and she'd never be able to make up to him for the way he'd nursed her ever since.

He'd never had a steady girlfriend. Patsy suspected it was because of his feelings for her and that made her uneasy knowing she didn't feel the same way about him. He was good looking and a hard worker. He'd make some lucky girl a wonderful husband.

It was dark before Billy returned. She'd already lit the candle in the lantern, but it threw up such weird and grotesque shadows that she was starting to get jittery.

'I thought you might be hungry so I brought us some grub,' he said, tossing a newspaper-wrapped parcel on to the straw beside her as soon as he was inside the door.

Patsy's face lit up. 'Fish and chips!' She grinned up at him in delight.

They sat side by side sharing their impromptu supper. Billy had also brought some beer for himself and a bottle of sarsaparilla for her.

Patsy waited patiently for him to tell her how his trip to New Brighton had gone, but in the end she could stand the suspense no longer.

'It's bad news, isn't it?' she asked shrewdly.

He screwed his empty newspaper wrapper into a tight ball. 'Yeah! Well, it's not exactly good news.'

'Go on, tell me what Bruno said when you told him about the baby,' she said flatly.

'He didn't say anything. He wasn't there.'

Patsy stared in disbelief. 'What do you mean by that?' she asked in a bemused voice.

'He's left New Brighton. I asked around, but no one at the fairground seems to know where he's gone. One chap said back to Spain, another one said he'd gone to Blackpool.'

The colour drained from Patsy's face. 'You think

he's cleared off, don't you?' she asked in a strained voice.

Billy shrugged. 'I don't know.'

'He's seemed different lately,' Patsy went on in a reflective tone. 'Sort of offhand. I blamed it on the cold weather and with everything in New Brighton closed down it was so dreary.' She stopped and looked straight at Billy. 'Did they say if he'd gone on his own?'

Billy avoided her eyes. 'I've told you, no one seemed to have any details.'

'So what do I do now?' she asked in consternation. 'I suppose I'll have to stay on here,' she added dully.

'Unless you ask your mam if you can go back home. At least let me go and talk to her.'

'If you must,' she agreed reluctantly. 'Don't bother going to the house, she's bound to be in the Grafton at this time of night.'

Billy returned so speedily that Patsy knew he'd had no luck in finding her.

'Well?' she asked the minute he had closed the stable door behind him.

'She wasn't there.'

Patsy frowned. 'Perhaps it was too early for her. Maybe you should have gone to the house after all.'

Billy shook his head. 'Not much point. The barman said she's gone away. She told people that you'd moved out so she thought she'd take a holiday.'

'Did you check to see if it was true?'

Billy nodded. 'I went to the house, but there

was no one there and the curtains were closed.'

Patsy's green eyes were expressionless for a moment as she digested the news. 'I've nowhere else to go. What am I going to do, Billy?' she asked.

'You'll have to stay on here for the moment, I suppose.' He looked round the stable and shook his head disapprovingly. 'It's not suitable for a young baby though, is it? Or for you, when you have to use a bucket for a toilet and Samson's trough for water.'

'I've no choice,' she said sharply. 'I've hardly any money. You know me mam never gave me a proper wage, only a few shillings a week pocket money.'

Suddenly she was in floods of tears as the sheer hopelessness of her situation hit her like a hammer blow.

'Don't take on, Patsy. I'll look round tomorrow and see what other things I can get to make us more comfortable,' he promised.

Patsy's eyebrows shot up. 'Us? Oh, Billy, you can't stay here with me any longer. Your mam must be wondering why you've been here so long as it is. She isn't going to believe your story that Samson's not well for ever, you know.'

'I can't leave you and little Liam here on your own, now can I?' he blustered.

'And you can't go on living in a stable when you have a comfortable home to go to,' she insisted.

'It's not all that bad here. Anyway, it will only be for a couple of weeks, or so, until I can find somewhere better for you to live. There must be someone nearby who has rooms to rent. Leave it with me,' he told her confidently, 'I'll sort something out.' He pulled her into his arms and hugged her. 'You mustn't worry, Patsy, I'll see you through this. I'll take care of you, I promise.'

Her features softened. 'I know you will, Billy, and I really am grateful.' She kissed him warmly on the cheek. 'I've often wished I had a brother like you,' she told him affectionately.

'Thanks!' His lips rested on the top of her red curls. He couldn't meet her eyes. She might guess from the look on his face that her brother was the last thing he wanted to be. She meant so very much more to him than that, but now was probably not the right time to tell her.

When would there ever be a right time to tell her? he wondered. He spent most of his working day with Patsy, she was the first thing he thought about in the morning and the last thing he thought about at night when his head hit the pillow.

These last few days had been bittersweet. Something he would treasure for a long as he lived. He would happily marry her and take care of baby Liam, but he was afraid to offer to do so in case she thought he was putting her on the spot and taking advantage of the situation she was in.

He wanted her to tell him that she loved him before he asked her to marry him, but he wondered if that day would ever come. If it didn't, then perhaps he'd throw caution to the wind and pluck up the courage to ask her anyway.

Chapter Twenty-Two

Next day, left on her own, without even Samson for company, Patsy found that the hours dragged. She wished she hadn't agreed quite so readily that it was time Billy went back to work before he lost all the goodwill they'd taken so long to build up.

After she'd fed the baby and put him down to sleep in his makeshift cot Patsy took stock of her surroundings. The place was a shambles, she thought as she looked round the stable. It was not only gloomy, but it smelt to high heaven.

She made a start by brushing the floor and mucking out Samson's stall. Too late she remembered that Billy had not only locked the stable door but taken the key with him so the only thing she could do was to brush the dirty straw and droppings into a corner. At one end of the stable there was an archway, as though there had once been another door that was now closed off, so she brushed it all into there.

The place still looked cluttered so she tidied up all the baby's things and her own which seemed to be scattered everywhere. It was the first physical work she'd done since Liam was born and she was surprised at how exhausted she felt. She was so tired that when she sat down for a rest she fell asleep.

She was wakened by Liam crying from hunger. Still half asleep she fed him, changed him and put him back down to sleep.

She dragged the baby's cot as far away as possible from the recess where she'd piled the dirt, but the smell was still overpowering. The only window was a skylight in the roof and although this let in a fair amount of daylight it was so corroded that it was impossible to open.

She wished that she had told Billy to leave the key behind, but when she came to examine the lock on the stable door she wasn't even sure that it would open from the inside.

Patsy began to feel entombed. Her heart started to pound and she found herself gasping breathlessly. More than anything in the world she wanted to go outside and take a mouthful of fresh air.

She started pacing round and round the stable like a caged animal looking for some means of escape. She needed air. She wondered if perhaps some of the draughts they'd complained about over the past days meant that there was another door. They might even be coming from a window that had been bricked up to make the place more secure. That could be why it was always so gloomy.

Slowly she moved round the stable, holding her hand against the walls to try and locate where the draughts came from. The only place where there seemed to be air coming in was around the archway where she'd piled up the muck. Some of the mortar between the bricks appeared to be loose and crumbling, and a cold stream of air was coming in through the cracks.

She felt all round again but decided that it was probably her imagination playing tricks. Even so, if Billy didn't come back soon perhaps she would try and loosen some of the bricks, and see if it led into the street, she thought, sinking back on to the straw for a rest.

Patsy had no idea what time it was and how long it would be before Billy came back. She was feeling hungry herself and he'd promised her he would bring bread, milk and some cheese or a meat pie home with him. Since it must now be quite late in the day perhaps he'd bring fish and chips as well, she thought hopefully.

She strained her ears, listening for the clip-clop of Samson's huge feet on the cobbles outside, but all she heard was the occasional voice as people passing in the road called out a greeting to one another.

The gloom deepened so she lit the candle in the lantern. The flickering flame cast distorted shadows on the walls, which did little to cheer the place up and, as usual, sent shivers through her.

Restlessly Patsy began pacing up and down again. Surely Billy hadn't gone home and forgotten about her and the baby?

As her need to get out of the stable increased she felt more and more alarmed. Billy was the only one who knew they were there. Her mind filled with horror stories she'd heard on the docks about people being trapped in the holds of ships. When they were found days later they were dead.

Some of the dockers had taken a special delight in such gruesome yarns. One middle-aged man had told them about tunnels he'd played in as a youngster. Soldiers returning from the Napoleonic wars had built them under some mansion in Edge Hill and they ran for miles and miles. Some tunnels, he claimed, ran right into the centre of the city and had even been used when trains were first brought to Liverpool, because they were so well built. He said he'd been in them and although you could stand up and walk along in them they were full of rubbish and dead dogs and cats.

His words, 'They say there's an entrance to them through some old stable', kept reverberating through Patsy's head. Was this the old stable? she asked herself. Was that where the archway led? Could she get out if she managed to clear away the muck she'd piled up there?

She stared up at the skylight. It was now quite dark outside and since it was April that meant it must be eight o'clock at least. Billy had never been as late as this, not even when they were working together and had more work than they could get through. 'Even if we're not exhausted Samson is and he needs his food and rest,' he would always insist.

What on earth had happened to make him so late? A thousand possibilities jostled in her head but none of them made any real sense to her.

Liam was restless and she wondered if he was hungry again so she picked him up and undid the front of her blouse. He refused to feed. His body felt hot and damp, as though he was running a temperature, and his cry was thin and plaintive.

Patsy felt panic welling up inside her. She was locked in and only Billy knew she was there. Something drastic must have happened to delay him and make him this late. Now Liam seemed to be unwell and she had no idea what to do.

She walked up and down in the confined space trying to soothe the fractious baby and hoping he would go off to sleep again. All the time her mind was in turmoil. The tales of people being holed up for days and not being found until it was too late scared her.

She had to take some action, but she couldn't think what to do. It was no good banging on the door because the stable was separated from the roadway by the cobbled yard. No one walking by would hear her. She couldn't reach the skylight and even if she could she knew it wouldn't open.

Beads of perspiration trickled down her neck as her terror mounted. She must remain calm, she told herself. She was in a tight spot, but everything would be OK as long as she didn't give way to panic. There must be a way out. All she had to do was stay calm and think.

She concentrated her thoughts on the archway again. Supposing that docker had been right and this was the stable he had talked about. If the archway was an entrance to one of the tunnels then if she could move away enough of the bricks she'd be able to escape.

Filled with renewed optimism, she placed Liam down in his makeshift cot and covered him over. With the rake and shovel she'd used to clean out

Samson's stall she cleared away the dirty straw and muck. Then holding the lantern up high she tried to see the back of the recess more clearly.

Her heart thudded with excitement when she saw from its shape that the brick archway could have been a door that had been filled in. Using the edge of the shovel she banged at the mortar between the brickwork until she managed to dislodge some of the bricks and was able to ease a couple of them out.

She worked feverishly, struggling and banging, tearing at the bricks until her fingers were bleeding. When she held up the lantern again and peered into the gloom of the cavity she'd made she couldn't believe what she was seeing.

There was a tunnel! She peered more closely into the gloom: water was dripping from the top of it and the sides were green with slime but there was a tunnel. She could make an escape she hoped.

She pulled away more bricks to enlarge the opening and then cautiously stepped over the gaping hole into the abyss beyond.

The floor was damp and slippery, covered in green slime like the walls, but the tunnel seemed to be endless, vanishing into the distance. Patsy began walking along it, then stopped. Should she go on her own or should she take Liam with her? Which was the best thing to do?

On her own she could make faster progress, but was it safe to leave him behind in the stable on his own? He wasn't well. Supposing his fever got worse, or he cried so much he choked.

Yet if she took him with her what would Billy think if he came back and found them both missing?

Uncertainty undermined her confidence about what she was doing. Perhaps she ought to be patient and wait a little longer to see if Billy came back.

No, she told herself firmly, she wasn't going to wait. She couldn't stay in the stable a moment longer. When Billy returned he'd spot the hole in the wall and come along the tunnel after them. She'd take the baby with her, she resolved, as determinedly she struggled back through the opening. She couldn't leave the poor little mite there on his own.

Wrapping him securely in a blanket she cradled him in one arm so that she could carry the lantern in her free hand. Back in the tunnel she began walking, trying not to think about where it was leading, but to stay positive that it must be taking her into the city somewhere.

It seemed to go on for ever. She wanted to walk faster, but she was afraid of slipping on the damp greasy floor. If that happened and she broke a leg or knocked herself out, she thought pessimistically, it might be the end of her and Liam because no one, except Billy, would ever think of looking for them down there.

Tired and exhausted, Patsy finally had to stop and take a rest. Although Liam was a very tiny baby, because of her own weak state he seemed to grow heavier with every step she took. Crouched against one of the damp walls she brushed the tears from her face and wondered whether she should retrace her steps. Looking back through the gloom towards the stable, the distance seemed as endless as when she looked ahead so she decided to go on.

Soon her legs were aching even worse than they had been before she stopped. Slowly it dawned on her that it was because she was going uphill. What was more, the tunnel seemed to be loftier and there was more air all around her.

Jubilantly Patsy told herself that must mean the tunnel was about to come out at ground level. Filled with renewed hope she pressed on, straining her eyes, hoping to see a glimmer of daylight ahead. But, she reminded herself, it was probably night-time so even when she did reach the end of the tunnel there would still only be darkness.

Although the tunnel now had a high vaulted roof she found the going no easier. Her path was hampered by rubble of every description from ashes and clinkers from domestic firegrates to all sorts of other household junk that was rotting and stinking. As she tried to pick a way through it a scurrying in the shadows left by the lantern warned her there were rats and mice around.

Patsy pressed on determinedly. It was too far now for her to go back. Her arms ached from carrying Liam. He was still restless and he had started to cough. It was a harsh, dry little sound that ended in a whimper.

Poor little mite, she thought contritely. None of this was his fault. He hadn't asked to be born, or to be condemned to live in a stable. It had been her stupid concern about someone finding them there that had made Billy lock the door and take the key with him.

Where was Billy? she wondered, as she grappled her way through muck and rubbish. That was something she simply couldn't work out. He was always so reliable, so what on earth could have happened?

The last few hundred yards to freedom were the worst she had encountered. The muck that had been thrown down into the cavity was putrid. Decaying fruit and vegetables, as well as wet paper and cardboard that had disintegrated into soggy pulp, stuck to her feet and clothes.

When she eventually reached the roadway the fresh air was cold and damp. Patsy stood there for several minutes simply staring around, trying to work out where she was. It had to be somewhere in the city because of the noise and so many lights.

Discarding the lantern and tightening the shawl around Liam's little body she began making her way towards where she could see people and shops.

From somewhere close by she heard the familiar street cry, 'Echo! Evenin' Echo!' As she drew closer to the news-stand she saw the placard and the words sprang out at her.

ACCIDENT ON THE DOCKSIDE.
HORSE DIES. MAN SERIOUSLY INJURED.

Patsy felt the blood drain to her feet. She swayed and would have fallen if she hadn't reached out and grabbed at the newspaper stand.

'Steady on, Missus, you nearly dropped your baby,' the news vendor told her as he grasped her by the arm. 'Want a paper, do you?'

Patsy shook her head. 'I've no money,' she mumbled. 'Can you tell me the name of the man who's been injured?'

'Think you know him do you, Missus?' His beady black eyes were curious.

'I'm not sure.'

'Nor is anyone else, luv,' he guffawed. 'Squashed flat he was by that great horse. I think they had to put the horse down, but they took the fella off to the Liverpool General. Look, there's a picture of it all on the front page.'

Patsy stared at the black-and-white picture and a lump came into her throat. There was no mistaking that the horse was Samson. He was lying on his side and the cart was overturned nearby.

So that meant the man involved, the man who'd been badly injured and taken to Liverpool General Hospital, must be Billy, she told herself numbly.

Chapter Twenty-Three

Tears streaming down her face, Liam held tightly in her arms, Patsy headed instinctively towards her home in Paradise Place.

As she trudged through the darkening streets she no longer worried about who saw her with the baby; there were other more important matters to be dealt with now. Her mind was filled with memories of Billy.

She recalled the days before he left school when he'd first worked for her dad cleaning out Samson's stable every Saturday morning. He'd been a sturdy lad in short trousers and a brown pullover that his mam had knitted for him. He had been so eager to please, and so fond of the horse, that in next to no time he was helping to feed and groom Samson every evening as well as before school in the morning. The minute he was old enough to leave school her dad had taken him on full time.

How proud Billy had been the first time her dad had let him handle the reins! His solemn face was transformed by a beaming smile that had made his light blue eyes shine as brilliantly as the sky on a cloudless summer day.

She loved it when Billy smiled, especially when he smiled at her. His smile was so warm and friendly, as if he really was pleased to see you, not a polite cold gesture like so many people gave you. Billy's smile not only lit up his eyes and his whole face, but it made you feel good. It was as if the world was suddenly a nicer place.

He was considerate of other people's feelings, too. She had never heard him say anything unkind about anyone. And he was always polite and helpful. Even the grumpiest of men down at the docks seemed pleased to see him and exchanged a comradely word with him. No matter how difficult to handle the load might be, or how heavy, Billy never grumbled. He simply got on with the job in hand whatever it might be and she knew this impressed the dockers, as well as the bosses they came into contact with when they were making deliveries.

He didn't talk a lot, but he watched and took an interest in all that was going on around him. He learned very quickly. She recalled her dad saying he only had to tell Billy once, or show him how to do something once, and after that he remembered.

Her dad had always been praising him. He would have been full of praise for the way the two of them had taken over the business and expanded it after he'd died, she thought proudly.

A shudder went through her. Her dad had died on the dock road and now the same thing had happened to Billy. Only Billy wasn't dead, she reminded herself. He was hurt, very badly hurt, but he wasn't dead. It was important that she remembered that. It was the one thing she had to hold on to now.

Patsy's steps took her home. The door was locked. She slipped her hand in the letterbox automatically searching for the piece of string with the key on it, but it seemed to be missing. Impatiently she banged on the door and called out through the letterbox, 'It's me, Mam. Let me in, I can't find the key.'

There was no answering call, but when she hammered again even harder on the door she heard footsteps coming down the hallway. The door swung open and a grey-haired woman wearing a bright red cotton apron over a grey dress stood there glaring at her angrily.

'Do you have to hammer the bloody door down, luv? I was out the back in the lavvy. What is it you want anyway?' Patsy stared back at the woman blankly. 'Who are you? What are you doing in me mam's house?'

'I'm not in your mam's house. This is my place.'

Patsy shook her head. 'You're wrong. Mrs Callaghan lives here! Maeve Callaghan. I'm her daughter, Patsy.'

'She might have lived here once, but she don't no longer,' the woman snapped. 'The last I heard of her she'd scarpered off to Blackpool.'

As she started to close the door Patsy put out a hand to stop her. 'Stop kidding me, Missus. I want me mam, she lives here and so do I if it comes to that.'

'Bugger off, there's no Callaghans living here. Go on!' The woman pushed hard at the door. 'Bugger off before I call the scuffers.'

Patsy watched perplexed as the door was

slammed in her face. She took a step back, staring up at the bedroom windows. When she saw the woman peering out from behind the front room curtains, as if to make sure she was going, she moved away.

Slowly it came back to her fuddled mind that Billy had told her he hadn't been able to find her mam when he'd gone to the Grafton. He'd said something about her going away, but not that she'd moved out of Paradise Place for good.

She wondered if she went back and explained all this to the woman who was living in their house now if it would help at all, but decided that it would probably be a waste of time. The woman probably wouldn't believe her.

She leaned against a lamppost wondering what to do next. Perhaps if she went along to the Grafton someone there might be able to tell her where her mam had gone. If she'd moved right away from Paradise Place, though, what good would that do? She had no money to go looking for her.

Liam squirmed uncomfortably in his cocoon of shawls and began to cry. He sounded far from well. He was probably ready for another feed, Patsy thought listlessly. A keen wind had sprung up and she shivered with cold. She'd have to find somewhere sheltered where she could sit and feed him.

He probably needed changing as well, but his clean nappy was back in the stable and she couldn't get in there because it was all locked up.

As she stood there shivering in the cold and

darkness she realised that there was only one place left where she could go and that was to Billy Grant's house.

Billy's mother answered the door. 'Patsy? What are you doing here?' she exclaimed, a startled look on her plump face as if she was seeing a ghost.

'Weren't you on the cart then when Billy had the accident?' she asked in surprise. 'The police came and said that Billy's in hospital, but then you must know that! My Joe's gone to the hospital. I thought it was him back, though he wouldn't be knocking, now would he. Oh, look, come on in and I'll make us both a cup of tea, you look in nearly as bad a state as I am,' she gabbled.

It wasn't until Patsy was in Mrs Grant's neat but overcrowded living room that she seemed to realise what Patsy was carrying in her arms.

Elaine Grant's motherly face registered shock and disquiet. 'This isn't yours, is it?' she asked coming closer and peeping inside the shawl. 'Is it a girl or a boy, luv?'

'It's a little boy. Liam.'

As Patsy peeled back the damp shawl so that Elaine could see him better, Liam gave a sharp dry cough and Elaine was immediately all concern.

'Poor little mite, it sounds to me as though he's got a touch of bronchitis. Have you taken him to the doctor?'

'No.' Patsy looked at her guiltily. 'No, not yet.'

Elaine looked anxious. 'The poor little soul is soaked right through, luv. Have you got a change of clothes we can put on him?'

Patsy shook her head dolefully.

'Here, give him to me, you look all in, Patsy. Sit down by the fire while I see to him and then I'll make a cup of tea for us both.'

Patsy watched in grateful silence as Elaine Grant stripped off Liam's soaking wet nappy and saturated clothes.

'How old is he, Patsy?' Elaine asked sharply as she wrapped the tiny body in a warm thick towel.

'Just over a week.'

Elaine was silent for a few seconds, her mind racing as she tried to sum up the situation.

'Stay there by the fire,' she said, handing the baby to Patsy, 'and I'll go and see what I can find to wrap him in while I wash and dry his clothes.'

She came back a few minutes later with some pieces of old sheet, a thick towel, and one of Joe's woollen vests.

'I'm sure we can make something out of these,' she said, taking a pair of scissors from the side-board drawer and starting to cut up the sheet into squares.

'When I've done this I'll rub his little chest with some camphorated oil before I wrap him up. That'll help to soften his cough. I bet that's what your mam used to do for you when you were a bit chesty?'

'I can't find me mam,' Patsy said wearily. 'Do you know where she might be, Mrs Grant?'

Elaine Grant shook her head. 'I heard she'd gone away. There was a rumour going around that you'd left home and that she'd gone as well. It was a couple of weeks or more ago when I first heard it.'

Patsy nodded absently. 'I seem to remember

244

Billy said something like that.'

'You mean you haven't been home since . . . since you had the baby, luv?'

Patsy shook her head. 'Not until today. I was worried when it started to get dark and Billy hadn't come back.'

Elaine stared at her bemused. 'Has there been anything wrong with Samson over the last few weeks?' she asked in a bewildered voice. 'I thought Billy said he wasn't well, perhaps I misunderstood him.'

Patsy's face clouded. She wasn't sure exactly what Billy had told his mam to cover for the time he'd spent with her. She'd probably made a mistake coming to Elaine's but she felt so befuddled that she didn't know what else to do.

'Samson's dead, isn't he,' she said in an attempt to avoid Elaine's question. 'Do you know how the accident happened?'

'No, luv!' Elaine patted her shoulder. 'My Joe will be able to tell us when he gets home. He shouldn't be much longer now.'

'Will Billy be with him?'

'No, I shouldn't think so. He's been badly hurt, remember. They'll probably decide to keep him in hospital for a quite a while.'

'So what am I going to do? He's got the key,' Patsy exclaimed agitatedly. 'I can't get back into the stable without it and I can't go back down that long tunnel again, there's rats there!'

'Are you saying that you've been living there?' Elaine asked incredulously. 'Was your baby born there?'

Patsy nodded. 'Yes, just over a week ago.'

Elaine's mind raced as she wrapped the baby up in a makeshift shawl and handed him back to Patsy. She couldn't believe what she was hearing, she didn't even want to, yet she felt she had to know the facts.

'Patsy,' she asked very gently, 'who was with you when the baby was born, who helped you? Was it my Billy?'

Patsy nodded again, but avoided meeting Elaine's eyes and concentrated on suckling the baby.

Elaine thought back over what had been happening over the past two weeks, ever since Billy had told her that Samson wasn't well and that he had to stay on in the stable to keep an eye on him. She knew now that it hadn't been Samson at all, but Patsy and her baby that Billy had been looking after. She remembered all the food, the soups and stews that she had given him.

At the time it had struck her that his appetite was bigger than usual, but she'd said nothing because she'd seen how upset he was. Now she could understand why, as well as the reason for him needing almost twice the food he normally ate. And if there had only been him there when Patsy's baby was born then no wonder he'd been worried.

Why on earth didn't he come and fetch me if he couldn't find Patsy's mother? she thought angrily. Helping out at childbirth was a woman's job, certainly not something a young lad should be doing. No wonder he looked as though he had the cares of the world on his shoulders: he probably wasn't even sure that he'd done everything properly. Even if they hadn't sent for a doctor when the baby was born then Patsy should have seen one right away afterwards, but it didn't sound as though she had.

Elaine looked across at the baby now sleeping soundly in Patsy's arms. He was such a tiny little scrap and if he'd had to start his life in nothing better than a stable it was no wonder he had bronchitis.

First thing tomorrow morning she'd get the doctor in to have a look at him, she resolved. It wouldn't do any harm and it would set her own mind at rest to know that it wasn't Billy's fault the child wasn't well.

Her mind went back to Billy and she longed for Joe to come home from the hospital and let her know he was going to be all right. Everything seemed to be happening at once. First the accident and now this.

She didn't understand why Patsy had been living in the stable or what she meant about not being able to get back in there because Billy had taken the key with him. She sighed. It didn't really matter, of course. She couldn't let her go back there even if they could find a way of getting in.

'While we're waiting for my Joe to come home I'll go and sort out where you and the baby can sleep,' she told Patsy. 'You'd better have our Janie's room for tonight and she can come down here and sleep . . .'

'No . . . no, Mrs Grant. I can't do that. I can't

turn your Janie out of her bed,' Patsy protested.

'Gracious, why ever not? It won't hurt her to sleep on the sofa for one night!'

'No, please. I don't want to do that,' Patsy said awkwardly, colour rushing to her cheeks.

She and Janie had never got on very well when they'd been at school, but she didn't want to tell Mrs Grant that. Janie had always teased her about Billy and made fun of her for paying so much attention to Samson.

'It wouldn't be fair to disturb her. Janie has to get up and go to work in the morning,' she added lamely.

'Very well. Then you can have young Freddie's bed. He'll be glad of the excuse that he had to sleep on the sofa when he nods off in school tomorrow,' she smiled.

'I'm really sorry to put you out like this, Mrs Grant.'

'It's no trouble, no trouble at all,' Elaine Grant assured her. 'In fact,' she said suddenly, her face brightening, 'there's no need to disturb Freddie, you can have our Billy's bed. He won't be needing it if he's in hospital overnight, now will he? You sleep in our Billy's bed and we'll sort things out better tomorrow.'

Patsy looked apprehensive. 'Are you quite sure?'

'Of course I am. Anyway, it's what our Billy would want and it will put his mind at rest to know you and the baby are safe and sound,' she said firmly. 'While you finish feeding little Liam I'll go upstairs and empty one of the drawers in

248

my chest-of-drawers and then I'll make up a bed for the baby in it. I'll put it right alongside your bed, Patsy, and then it will be easy for you to pick him up if he cries in the night.'

With Liam fed and comfortably settled, Elaine made a pot of tea and a plate of ham sandwiches for herself and Patsy as they waited for Joe to return with news of Billy.

Chapter Twenty-Four

Billy Grant had no idea where he was or even what his name was when he first regained consciousness. Hour after hour he stared at the white ceiling and the green walls, his handsome face expressionless.

For three days he lay cocooned in a blank world that was punctuated only by the routine of mealtimes when he was fed liquids from a cup, and periodic visits by doctors who studied the medical charts clipped to the foot of his hospital bed. They then examined him and conferred with colleagues, with grave faces and much shaking of their heads.

Billy could hear the sound of their voices as they congregated around his bedside, but the words had no meaning for him.

Even the discomfort of having his right leg suspended high in the air by means of ropes and pulleys, or of having the many lacerations on his face and head dressed with antiseptic fluids and lotions, failed to penetrate his mind or concern him at all.

It was only on the third day, when he was subjected to the torture of having his broken ribs strapped up, that he regained a degree of consciousness. It was as if the hideous pain that was inflicted on him cleared some of the mists from his mind.

As he lay gasping in agony from the nurses' ministrations he started to question what they were doing to him. Where was he? What had happened to him? He couldn't remember, and he felt not only confused but apprehensive because from the nature of his injuries he knew it had been something serious.

The poker-faced nurses in their dark blue dresses, stiffly starched white aprons and crisp white caps were noncommittal. They admitted that he had been brought in by ambulance three days ago, but told him he must wait and talk to one of the doctors, as there was nothing else they could tell him.

He questioned the orderlies who washed him and shaved him and combed his thick brown hair, but they were too busy to tell him any details. When they brought him drinks of water or cups of tea and made a point of asking him how he was feeling, or made conversation about the weather, he didn't bother to answer them: it was all so unimportant.

Billy begged to see the doctor or anyone who could tell him the details of what had happened to him. He knew he must have been in an accident or he wouldn't have been brought into hospital, but where had it happened and what sort of accident had it been?

It was left to his father eventually to tell him the details.

Joe Grant hated the smell of disinfectant and

the sterile atmosphere of the hospital ward, but he refused to go home. He had been at Billy's bedside every day since the police had come to his house to tell him son was injured.

As soon as Billy regained consciousness and started asking questions Joe did his best to give him the answers, but in as circumspect a way as possible so as not to cause him any more trauma.

'Yes, lad, you were in an accident,' he said quietly. 'A pretty bad one at that.'

'Was I knocked down?'

'No, not exactly, not in the way you mean.'

'Then why are my ribs all bust and my leg broken?'

'That's because you were crushed, lad.' He hesitated, not wanting to distress his son, but Billy was not satisfied, he was determined to hear the whole story. He insisted on knowing where and when.

'It happened while you were leading Samson. He fell over on you,' Joe told him hesitantly.

'Samson did? What happened?' Billy looked alarmed. 'Is he all right?'

Joe shook his head. 'Samson's dead, I'm afraid.' He gripped Billy's hand. 'I'm sorry, lad, I know how fond you were of that horse.'

Billy took a deep breath and stared at his father in disbelief. 'How did it happen?' he asked weakly.

'The vet said that poor old Samson had some sort of heart attack. He keeled over without any warning. You'd just come back from the Wirral on the ferryboat with a very heavy load. You'd reached the top of the floating roadway, unhitched the spare horse that had helped to pull the cart up the slipway, and then it happened. You had hold of Samson's bridle and you were about to lead him on to the roadway when he buckled up. He collapsed and fell over sideways and landed on you. You were trapped underneath him and the cart.'

'And Samson was dead? Just like that?' Billy's voice was thick with disbelief.

'Dead as a doornail, lad. His heart gave out, so the police vet said. He wouldn't have felt a thing so there's no cause for you to take on.'

Billy ran his hand through his hair. 'Samson dead? I can't take it in,' he muttered.

'It was you that took the brunt of his fall. Squashed, you were,' Joe Grant went on. 'Tidy weight that old horse and to fall full on you like he did it's lucky you're still alive.'

Billy shook his head. 'I don't know about that, I feel half dead.'

'Well you would, lad. You've got three crushed ribs, a broken leg, lacerations to your face and head and you've been unconscious for almost three days.'

'Do you know when I'm going to get out of here?'

'Not for a while, I shouldn't think. Your ribs have got to knit together for a start and then there's your leg. It's broken in I don't know how many places so it will take some time.'

Billy became agitated. 'I've got to get back to work. Have you any idea what happened to the load I was carrying?'

'Nothing to worry about there. The dockers who were standing by waiting for you to bring the stuff alongside turned to and unloaded the cart. They took everything straight on to the ship. As for getting back to work, well you'd have a job to do that in your present state now, wouldn't you? What's more, the cart was smashed to smithereens and you have no horse so lie still and get yourself better.'

'You don't understand, Dad, I've got to work. Patsy needs money to live on.' A shadow passed over his face. 'Was Patsy hurt when Samson collapsed and the cart turned over?' He grabbed at Joe's hand. His voice sank to a strained whisper. 'Patsy wasn't killed, was she?' he asked hoarsely.

'Of course she wasn't,' Joe said firmly. 'She wasn't even with you!'

'She must have been, she always comes out with me,' Billy persisted.

'Well, she wasn't with you this time. You were on your own.'

Billy shook his head from side to side as if doubting what his father was telling him.

'Don't you worry your head about Patsy,' Joe said firmly. 'There's nothing at all wrong with her and she's well taken care of because she's moved into our place. Your mam's letting her sleep in your bed and that's where she'll stay until you come out of here. She's all right and so is the baby.'

'Baby? What baby?' Billy asked in a puzzled voice.

'Patsy's new baby, of course. Don't tell me you've forgotten about it?'

Billy rubbed his hand over his eyes as if to clear a mist from them and then pushed his fingers through his thick mat of hair. Slowly the blankness disappeared from his blue eyes and was replaced by a look of dawning enlightenment.

'Of course, the baby!' he muttered. 'Little Liam! Yes, you're right, I'd forgotten about him.' He grinned up at his father. 'It must have been some almighty bump I had on my head for me to forget about that!'

Joe Grant waited expectantly. Like his wife he was anxious to know if it was Billy's child, but Patsy had not said a word and because of her distressed state neither of them liked to question her. Janie had tried several times to draw her out, but Patsy had kept her own counsel.

The smile suddenly vanished from Billy's face. 'Where did you say Patsy was?'

'She's living with us. Sleeping in your bed for the moment,' his father repeated.

'How did she get out of the stable? I left her locked in and I took the key along with me. Did someone find it and let her out?'

'No, I don't think so.' Joe looked puzzled. 'They couldn't have done! When she turned up on our doorstep both Patsy and the little one were soaking wet and she told your mam she couldn't get into the stable to get dry clothes. Your mam had to cut up some sheets and towels and wrap the baby in one of my old woollen vests for warmth.'

'How did she get out of the stable, then?' Billy asked in bewilderment.

'She said something about a tunnel, but we didn't take too much notice at the time. Your mam thought that perhaps Patsy was rambling because she'd heard about your accident and was out her mind with worry.'

Billy looked perplexed. 'I don't understand how she could have heard about it if she was locked in the stable.'

'She told your mam that she'd seen it on a newspaper placard when she came out of the tunnel, but that didn't make much sense to us.'

Billy stared at Joe transfixed. 'She must have found those old tunnels, Dad.'

It was Joe's turn to look bemused. 'What bloody tunnels are you talking about, lad?'

'Some docker told us a tale about there being tunnels under the city. It seems they were dug out over a hundred years or more ago, just after the Napoleonic wars in fact. This fella said there was an entrance in a stable somewhere. It must have been our stable he was talking about and Patsy must have found it.'

Joe shook his head. 'You've lost me, lad. Anyway, the main thing is she's safe and well and so is the baby. He had a touch of bronchitis, but your mam knew how to deal with that. She rubbed his little chest with camphorated oil and he's as right as rain now. Bonny little fellow even though he's a bit on the thin side.'

Billy nodded but said nothing. His mind was racing. It was all coming back to him. Patsy's mother throwing her out because she was pregnant, his futile attempt to find Bruno, and Patsy saying she'd have to move into the stable because she had nowhere else to stay.

He'd wanted her to come back to his home and let his mam help her, but she'd refused. She hadn't wanted anyone to know that she was pregnant. Then before they could decide what she ought to do she'd gone into labour.

He closed his eyes, wanting to shut out all memory of what had happened next. He'd felt so inept, so completely useless. Seeing Patsy in such terrible pain and distress and not knowing what to do had been so frightening. He'd done his best to help her, but had it been enough? If only she had let him fetch his mother, or Mrs Murphy, or a doctor. But he'd been afraid to provoke or vex her. Anyway, he couldn't have left her alone, not while she was in that state.

After the baby had been born she still wouldn't let him tell anyone. He'd done the best he could. He'd fitted the stable up with a Valor oil stove so that there was some heating and a Primus stove to warm up their food and to heat up water to bath the baby. It had been a rough and ready arrangement, but it was what she wanted.

Telling his mother that Samson was ill was the only way he could think of absenting himself from home so that he could stay with her. Now Samson was dead. It was almost like a punishment, he thought guiltily.

Samson wasn't a young horse and keeping him shut up for well over a week probably hadn't done him any good. Taking him out and expecting him to pull an extra-heavy load when he'd been idle for such a long spell had been too much for the poor beast. That's why his heart had given out so suddenly.

As he sat by Billy's bedside, Joe Grant questioned if he had done right to remind Billy of all this. He wondered why Billy had never told them about his feelings for Patsy or about the baby. For the baby to be born in such primitive conditions as a ramshackle old stable was unbelievable. There wasn't even any water or lighting there and certainly no heating. He and Patsy must have had a reason for carrying on like that and he wondered if Maeve Callaghan was against them marrying.

'Do you want Patsy to come in and see you tomorrow, lad?'

'Yeah,' Billy nodded, 'and me mam.'

'Right then I'll tell them. I wouldn't think they'd let the baby in so they probably won't be able to come together. If your mam comes in to see you tomorrow then she can mind the baby the day after while Patsy visits you.'

'Yeah, that'll do fine.'

'If Patsy comes on her own it will give the two of you a chance to make arrangements about what you want to do,' Joe added with heavy meaning.

Billy sighed. 'Yes, I suppose so. Neither of us have a job now if Samson's gone. Anyway,' he gave a mirthless grin, 'I'm not likely to be walking or able to do anything useful for quite a while, am I?'

'No, but there's still the baby to consider,' Joe reminded him.

'Right mess we're both in, aren't we,' Billy said grimly.

'There's no need for you to worry, lad,' Joe told him gruffly. 'Like I told you, Patsy has moved in with us and your mam'll keep an eye on her and the baby so you've nothing to worry about.'

'It's the future I'm worried about,' Billy told him. 'Where's Patsy and the baby going to live after I get out of hospital? They can't go back to living in the stable now, can they?'

'She'll have to stay with us then,' Joe told him.

'There isn't room! Not unless I move in with young Freddie and that wouldn't work because his room is so small he can hardly turn round in it.'

Joe didn't know what to say. He'd assumed that the baby was Billy's and that he and Patsy would get married as soon as Billy came out of hospital. From the way Billy was talking, though, that was the last thing he was planning. He didn't understand it. 'We'll manage somehow, lad, so don't you worry,' he muttered. 'You just get better and things will sort themselves out, you'll see.'

Seeing Billy lying there so helpless, his leg supported in a cradle, his head bandaged, his face a mass of cuts and grazes, tugged at Joe Grant's heart.

Billy was a chip off the old block. Perhaps it was because Billy was his first-born that he felt there was a stronger bond between them than he had with either of his other two children.

He'd looked just like Billy when he'd been in his twenties. He passed a hand over his bald head;

his hair had been as thick and brown as Billy's was when he'd first started going out with Elaine. A lot of water under the bridge since then, he reflected. He wondered if Billy would be as bald as he was in twenty years' time. He was certainly taking on his share of responsibilities!

He didn't understand what was going on between Billy and Patsy, nor could he work out why Maeve Callaghan hadn't taken care of her when the baby was born. The whole thing was a complete mystery to him.

When he'd asked Elaine why Patsy couldn't go and stay with her mother she'd said that Maeve Callaghan was gone, she'd left Paradise Place and a Mrs Blackwood was living in her house.

None of it made any sense as far as he was concerned, Joe thought, but he supposed the truth would come out in the end and all the pieces would fall into place. At the moment, all he wanted was for Billy to get better.

Chapter Twenty-Five

The night before Billy Grant came home from hospital, Patsy hardly slept a wink. She tossed and turned: so many conflicting thoughts were going through her mind. She wished she could get up and make herself a cup of tea or walk around, but she dare not do that because it might disturb everyone else.

The bed was comfortable, in fact from the very first night at the Grants' it had felt like the height of luxury to her. Yet she couldn't settle and it wasn't because Liam was restless.

He slept soundly. The poultice of brown paper, camphorated oil and grease that Elaine had put on his little chest that first night had made his breathing easier and after a couple of days he seemed to be quite recovered.

Elaine Grant had put a feather pillow in the drawer for him. The high sides protected Liam from any draught and he was covered over with a cut-down sheet and a white shawl so that he was both safe and snug.

Patsy tried to blame her sleeplessness on the strangeness of the situation she found herself in. Even now, after three months, she simply couldn't get used to being in Billy's home and sleeping in his bed.

Although she'd known Billy since even before they'd started school she had seldom been inside his home. Once or twice she had called for his younger sister Janie who'd been in her class at school.

Even then she had waited on the doorstep while whoever opened the door called out to Janie to let her know that Patsy was there. The only exception had been when Janie had hurt her ankle and couldn't go to school and she'd brought some homework that Janie was supposed to do. Janie had been lying on the sofa and Mrs Grant had asked Patsy if she'd like a biscuit and a glass of milk. She'd refused because the room had looked so spick and span and well polished that she'd been afraid she might make crumbs or spill the milk.

Now here she was, in the Grants' house, lying in Billy's bed with her own baby on the floor beside her. It all seemed so unreal and so different from when she'd been sleeping on a makeshift bed of straw in the stable.

She couldn't get over how loyal Billy had been and the way he had let his mother believe that he was staying at the stable all night because Samson wasn't well. She kept wondering what Elaine Grant had thought when she'd found out that it had been a lie. Yet she's never said anything about it the whole time I've been staying here, Patsy mused. In fact, none of them had asked any awkward questions about her and Billy, or about the baby.

From the moment she had arrived, Patsy felt

she owed it to Billy's mother to tell her that the baby wasn't his. Several times she'd been about to confide in Janie but she kept putting it off because she was afraid that if they knew the truth then Mrs Grant mightn't let her stay there and she had nowhere else to go.

It had been a shock to find that her mam had cleared off and that no one knew where she'd gone. When Billy had said that her mam had gone away she'd thought he meant that Maeve had cleared off with one of her fancy men. Patsy hadn't been too concerned because she'd thought that her mam would be back again the moment she was tired of him, or he'd had enough of her. She didn't for one moment think it meant that her mam had given up their house.

No doubt that was what she was planning to do when she kicked me out and threw all my things after me, Patsy reasoned.

She turned restlessly, her brain racing like a clockwork car. Why did other people's mams stay put and seem content with their lot? Her mam never had. All those horrible 'uncles' in the days when her dad was away at sea. All the rows between her mam and her dad when he'd decided to find a job ashore because she said she'd have no freedom if he did that.

For the first few weeks after her dad returned her mam had promised that from now on they'd look after each other and be really good friends.

And I really believed she meant it, Patsy thought sadly.

The business had been bringing them in a

comfortable living. Too comfortable, probably, she thought bitterly. There was always plenty of money available for her mam to spend in the Grafton. She'd started propping up the bar every night, and treating all and sundry to drinks, so she'd quickly made a whole host of new friends. It was probably one of these new fellas she'd gone off with. This time it must be serious if she's given up the house! Patsy thumped her pillow angrily.

Thinking about her mam and her new boyfriend didn't help her any, Patsy thought despairingly. She'd be better off thinking about her own future, especially now she'd got the baby to look after as well as herself.

Billy's mother seemed to think it would be months before Billy was going to be able to work again. And with Samson dead, their business venture was finished since neither of them had enough money to buy a new horse.

She finally fell asleep thinking about what sort of work she could do and dreamed that Bruno had come back and was so happy about the baby that he couldn't wait to take them both back to Spain.

Her dream was so real that when Liam's hungry cry wakened her she half expected to find Bruno there.

She put Liam back into his cot after she'd fed him, then snuggled back down into Billy's bed and pulled the covers up to her chin. She couldn't get back to sleep again, though, because all her doubts and worries had come rushing back.

She heard the day's routine start. First it was Joe Grant's heavy tread as he went downstairs and then the front door slamming behind him as he left the house. Next came the scuttle of Janie's feet on the stairs as she dashed up and down getting ready for work. Finally there was Freddie, who was now in his last few days at school, banging down the stairs calling out to ask what was for breakfast. Ten minutes later he slammed the front door behind him and Patsy heard the sound of his feet running down the street.

The tap on the bedroom door startled her. Today of all days, knowing that Billy was coming home from hospital, she should have got dressed straight after feeding Liam instead of settling down in bed again, she thought guiltily.

'I've brought you up a cuppa,' Elaine announced as she came into the room.

Patsy smiled gratefully. 'I . . . I was just about to get up,' she told her. 'I thought it was best for me to stay here as usual so as not to be in every-one's way while they were getting ready for work.'

'Quite right,' Elaine agreed as she bent over the makeshift cot and smiled down at Liam.

She was not only up and dressed, with a clean flowered apron covering her light blue cotton dress, but even her brown hair was neatly combed, Patsy noticed.

'There's no point in rushing,' Elaine went on as she picked Liam up. 'They won't be bringing Billy home until midday so we've got plenty of time to get things ready for him. He's going to see a great change in this little fella, isn't he?'

'Yes, three months has made a big difference,' Patsy agreed.

'He looked like a little skinned rabbit the night you turned up with him, the night of our Billy's accident,' Elaine went on.

Patsy nodded. She knew Elaine was waiting for her to say something more, perhaps tell her that Liam was Billy's baby. Despite her earlier resolution Patsy felt that now it was up to Billy to tell his mother whatever he thought fit so she remained quiet.

'Don't you think Billy would be happier to be back in his own bed rather than having to sleep downstairs on the couch?' she asked. 'I'm sure he'd be much more comfortable with all his own things around him.'

'No,' Elaine shook her head. 'It's better for Billy to be down there. If he's stuck away up here he'll feel like an invalid instead of being one of the family again.'

Patsy nodded. 'I suppose he would find it difficult to get up and down the stairs using crutches and with that metal calliper on his leg.'

'That's right, and don't forget the doctor said he mustn't bend his leg at all. Anyway, being downstairs will be handier for the nurse when she comes in twice a week to change the dressings.'

'How long does the doctor think the calliper will have to stay on?'

'Goodness only knows! When it does come off he's going to have to learn to walk again. The doctor said he'll probably always have problems with the leg and that he may have a permanent limp.'

'Well at least his ribs have healed and most of

the scars have gone from his face,' Patsy said brightly.

'Yeah! I suppose we should be grateful for small mercies,' Elaine Grant sighed. 'I've no doubt he'll be glad to get out of that hospital and be back home with us all, even if he's on crutches for months to come.'

The thought of Billy not being able to work for the foreseeable future worried Patsy a great deal. It meant that as well as providing for her and Liam, Joe and Elaine Grant would also have to keep Billy.

Joe Grant might earn good money, but it wouldn't stretch endlessly. He and Elaine had been very kind to let her stay there all this time. She couldn't expect them to let her go on living with them for ever, though, not unless she was able to contribute her fair share of the household expenses.

The trouble was that she had nothing to offer, Patsy thought unhappily. Although her mother had paid Billy a proper wage when he'd taken over the running of her dad's business she'd only ever given Patsy a few shillings a week pocket money.

'You don't need to worry,' her mam had said, 'I'll buy you all the new clothes you want as well as everything else. You won't go short of anything. As long as you've got some money in your pocket for the flicks that's all you need.'

Maeve never had bought her any new clothes, though. All the money that Billy handed over from the business her mam had kept for herself and spent it at the Grafton as fast as Billy earned it.

She hadn't even paid some of the bills. Several times they'd had a visit from the man who owned the stable pointing out that rent was well overdue and if they didn't pay up right away then they were out.

Now, if Billy was to be on crutches for months to come, even if they could get hold of another horse he wouldn't be able to manage to take it out on his own. Nor would he be able to cope with loading up the cart. And since she had the baby to look after she wouldn't be able to help him out on the cart either, not unless his mam would take care of Liam while they worked.

It hadn't seemed fair to worry Billy about such matters while he was so ill in hospital, but as soon as he was back at home, and settled in, Patsy knew she would have to discuss it with him and they'd have to try and work something out.

Perhaps the best thing they could do, Patsy thought sadly, would be to clear out whatever remained in the stable and call it a day. There might be a few bits and pieces that they could sell, like Samson's harness and tack and whatever remained of the feed and straw.

As for the immediate future, well once Billy was used to moving about perhaps he would be able to look after Liam for a couple of hours each day and she could go out to work. It would only be for a very short time because once Bruno came back, and she was able to tell him about the baby, then she hoped they would be married and off to Spain as soon as it could all be arranged.

It all seemed so very unsatisfactory and such a muddle that Patsy's mind was in turmoil. She wasn't at all sure how the Grants would feel about her and Liam staying on any longer. If, as she suspected, they were only making a home for her because they thought the baby was Billy's then once they knew the truth they might feel very different about having her there.

They had been kindness itself, Patsy thought gratefully. She'd never be able to repay Elaine for the way she had looked after Liam during those first couple of weeks when they'd first arrived on their doorstep. It had been Elaine who had nursed Liam back to health, found clothes for him and cared for them both. Apart from feeding him I was too ill to do very much for him, she thought.

Janie and Freddie had both been so good, too, helping to look after the baby so that she could go with Elaine to visit Billy in hospital.

Living with the Grants had been an eye-opener. It had shown her what a happy home life could be like. The more she witnessed the warmth and support they gave each other, the more she dreamed that one day she and Bruno would have a home life exactly like that.

Patsy constantly went over in her mind all the wonderful things Bruno had told her about his home in Spain. He said how friendly all the people were and that his family would love her. She could almost feel the warm sun and see the golden sands. She could visualise the people dancing, hear the music, and the happy laughter.

She dreamed of the day when Bruno would be

back in New Brighton and reunited with her and baby Liam. She could hardly wait for them to be together so that they could start making plans to go to his home in Spain as soon as the season ended.

She felt bitter. It was hard to understand why Bruno hadn't let her know that he was leaving New Brighton or told her where he was going. It wasn't as though they'd had a row. She knew he'd been frustrated because there was nowhere they could go in the cold weather so that they could be on their own. Perhaps she should have taken him home, but after what had happened on her sixteenth birthday how could she?

Perhaps Bruno had tried to get in touch with her and been unable to find her because she'd been living in the stable, she thought hopefully.

If he'd gone to her house after her mam had left he would have either found it empty or Mrs Blackwood living there and she wouldn't have been very helpful. She'd have said that me mam had gone and Bruno might think I'd gone with her.

Chapter Twenty-Six

Having Billy at home seemed to create problems no one had anticipated. For the first couple of days everyone was in a state of euphoria, dashing around waiting on him hand and foot. Once the novelty wore off, however, they all began to understand the full impact of what having an invalid to care for involved.

The bulk of the extra work fell on Elaine, but this was partly her own fault. When Patsy offered to help Billy to wash and dress each morning she was aghast.

'You can't do that!' she exclaimed in shocked tones. 'It wouldn't be right for you to see him without any clothes on when you're not married.'

Billy was not a good patient. Far from it. He was impatient, demanding and irritable. Because of his good looks and warm smile he had been a favourite with most of the nurses and as a result they had danced attendance on him more than was normal.

While he'd been in hospital he'd been longing to get home; now that he was at home he missed not only the nurses, but also the companionship of the other patients in the ward. 'Being in hospital was like being in a different world,' he told his mother and Patsy. 'There was always something new happening on the ward with people leaving or new patients being brought in.'

Even though he'd been confined to bed, and had been lying prone for most of the time, he hadn't been bored.

'There was so much going on I didn't have time to think,' he told them. 'Mealtimes, medicine rounds, bed-making and all the rest of it took up every hour of the day. All day long there were doctors or specialists coming into the ward to visit one or other of the patients. And each morning there was a tour of inspection by Matron and her sisters and nurses. Before she came round the place was full of cleaners and orderlies making sure everything was spick and span. Then the nurses would come round to check that all our beds were tidy. Everything had to be exactly right for Matron – even a creased bedcover would bring a stinging reprimand.'

Billy missed the muted noise and orderly bustle. His mother took him his breakfast and insisted that he should stay where he was.

'You rest that leg of yours and I'll come and give you a hand to wash and dress as soon as I've finished clearing up and done the shopping,' she would promise.

There was so much for her to do that often it was almost midday before she managed to find time to see to him.

Realising the pressure Elaine was under, Patsy did her best to help with tidying Billy's room and the rest of the house after she'd fed and bathed Liam.

The trouble was Liam always seemed to wake up when she was halfway through a cleaning job and the baby's crying irritated Billy. He only liked the baby when it was asleep or had just been fed and changed and was gurgling and contented.

Patsy tried hard to keep them both happy, but it was not always very successful. When the baby wasn't grizzling then Billy was complaining about something or other. A further problem was that Elaine, too, was becoming more and more tight-lipped and irritable.

In her case it was a combination of being over-worked and the fact that now Billy was at home, as well as Patsy and Liam living there, she was finding it difficult to stretch the weekly house-keeping money to cover all the food and other things that were needed.

'I was wondering about taking a part-time job now that I've started weaning Liam,' Patsy suggested tentatively. It was something that had been in her mind for quite a while, but she wasn't sure how Elaine would react to the idea.

Elaine sighed. 'It's a great thought, luv, but what about Liam? I'd look after him like a shot, but I've got me hands full as it is what with housework and shopping and looking after our Billy.'

'I thought that perhaps Billy could keep an eye on Liam,' she mused.

'Billy!' Elaine's eyes widened. 'How can Billy look after a young baby? He can't do much for himself let alone tend a baby.'

'Not right at this moment, perhaps,' Patsy conceded, 'but in a few weeks, when he's more used to getting about on his crutches. I thought he might enjoy it,' she said lamely.

'Well, you could ask him what he thinks about it, I suppose,' Elaine agreed reluctantly.

'Me carry a baby around, when I can't even balance on my bloody crutches?' he said bitterly. 'If I dropped him I wouldn't be able to pick him up!'

'Well I didn't mean right this moment,' Patsy said quickly. 'I meant later on, when you can balance or when you no longer have to use your crutches.'

'And when will that be?' he asked cynically.

'As soon as you stop feeling sorry for yourself and make yourself walk,' Patsy snapped, a look of exasperation on her face.

Billy stared at her in disbelief then for the first time since he'd come home from hospital he laughed.

'Still the same old slave driver, aren't you,' he guffawed. 'I'm not Samson so don't get the whip to me, just because I'm not moving quickly enough for you, luv.'

'I won't,' she promised, 'but I can't stand seeing you simply lying there accepting what's happened and not putting up a fight. One of us has got to work and help your mam with the housekeeping money.'

He looked at her blankly as though he didn't understand what she was talking about.

'I've been living here for months and I've not tipped up a penny piece,' Patsy pointed out. 'All I've done is take, take, and take. Food, things for

Liam and even clothes for me. Your mam's provided them all from the housekeeping money your dad hands over on a Friday night. It's not fair on either of them.'

Suddenly the old Billy was grinning back at her. The kind, considerate partner she'd known since she was a young girl. It was almost as though, because of his long stay in hospital, he'd forgotten about the need to earn money for food and home comforts. Now he was as anxious as she was to pay his way.

He ran a hand through his hair. 'No, you're right, but what can we do? You have the baby to look after and I'm pretty helpless no matter what you say.'

'We could clear out the stuff in the stable for a start,' she told him. 'The rent hasn't been paid and the owner is threatening to kick us out anyway. There's Samson's spare harness in there and there must also be straw and hay and perhaps some feed that we could sell.'

'How am I going to manage to sort that lot out when I'm on crutches?'

'I bet your dad would help if you asked him and Freddie would give a hand.'

'You're on, luv,' Billy grinned. 'We'll give it a go on Sunday.'

Elaine agreed to keep an eye on Liam while Patsy went to the stable with Billy, Joe and Freddie.

'Bloody hell, it stinks in here!' Joe exclaimed as they opened the door and the strong odour of horse manure that had been left untouched for about three months hit them. 'Have to clean this lot up and air the place before the landlord sees it.'

'It's a stable, Dad, not a palace,' Billy told him.

'Bloody stinking one too. Look at the state of the place. Look at that bloody wall over there! It's falling apart!'

'I can explain that,' Patsy said quickly. 'I knocked that hole in it when I was trying to get out. That's the tunnel I was telling you about, the one I escaped through.'

Billy looked puzzled. 'Escaped? What are you on about?'

'The day you had your accident, Billy,' she reminded him, 'you'd left me locked in here and you'd taken the key with you, do you remember?'

Billy nodded. 'I'd forgotten all about that. You said something about the tunnel when I was in hospital. What's it got to do with this mess though?' he asked, indicating the crumbling wall.

'It's where I broke out,' she grinned. 'The tunnel is on the other side of it.'

'Can I go and look?' Freddie asked eagerly.

'Look yes, but don't try walking along the bloody thing. It might fall in on your head and one bugger on crutches is enough,' his father told him.

'No, it's safe enough structurally,' Patsy assured them. 'I walked miles through it, all the way into town, and it was fine apart from the dampness and slimy walls. Oh, and all the rubbish that had been tipped down into it, especially at the other end where it comes out behind the market. Masses of stinking fruit and vegetables and soggy cardboard boxes,' she added with a shudder.

While Freddie and Joe explored the tunnel, Billy and Patsy took stock of what there was in the stable that might be saleable.

As they were finishing Elaine appeared with Liam in her arms, looking for Patsy.

'This baby needs a feed,' she announced, 'and the rest of you can pack up and come home because I've got a meal ready for you.'

While they tucked into generous helpings of scouse, they talked non-stop about the tunnel. Joe agreed that he and Freddie would walk the full length of it before Joe repaired the broken wall. He reluctantly admitted that he too had heard rumours about the tunnels that had been built by engineers returning from the Napoleonic wars.

'I always thought it was a load of bunkum,' he told them. 'Now I've got the chance to see for myself I'm going to do so.'

'And me as well,' Freddie put in quickly, his boyish face full of excitement.

'It might be dangerous,' Elaine protested. 'If it's as old as you say then the roof could cave in at any moment.'

'I'm sure it's safe,' Patsy told her. 'The roof is sound and quite high so they won't have to crawl or anything. I walked upright the whole way and I'm as tall as Freddie.'

'Then Freddie and me will go and do it while you have a rest for an hour or so, Billy,' Joe said, pushing back his chair.

'Yes and then you and Patsy can go back and sort things out at the stable after she's fed Liam,'

Elaine said quickly when she saw that Billy was about to protest.

By the end of Sunday they had stacked up anything that they thought they could sell in the middle of the stable floor and cleaned the place up. Joe had even managed to fix the bricks back into the alcove wall.

The following week, with Joe's help, they found someone willing to buy the tack. When the man came to take it away he agreed to take the feed and hay as well as long as they agreed a knock-down price.

It seemed pointless to argue. They needed to get rid of it before the landlord turned them out and even the meagre sum they were being offered was better than nothing.

'Please take it,' Patsy insisted when they handed the money over to Elaine. 'You've done so much for me over the last months I know it's only a fraction of what I owe you. Apart from giving me somewhere to sleep and feeding me, everything I've got on you and Janie have given me. You've even cut up your sheets and towels and blankets for the baby, as well as buying him clothes.'

Cleaning out the stable seemed to clear the fog that had temporarily blurred Billy's mind and blotted out so much from the past.

'Have you heard from your mam?' he asked Patsy.

She shook her head. 'I don't know where she is. There's a Mrs Blackwood living in our house now.'

Billy frowned. 'Doesn't anyone know where your mam's gone?'

'No!' Patsy's face clouded. 'Mam doesn't even know that Liam's been born and he's over four months old now.'

'And what about Bruno?'

Patsy shook her head. 'I've not heard from him either.'

'So you haven't been over to New Brighton to tell him?'

Her mouth tightened. 'I thought of doing so hundreds of times, but I hadn't the money for the ferryboat and I couldn't bring myself to ask your mam for it. She'd want to know why I was gadding off to New Brighton, wouldn't she, and neither of us have ever said anything to her about Bruno. Anyway, I thought that he'd come looking for me before now.'

'It's probably best to leave things like that,' Billy admitted. 'Don't start rocking the boat, not when my mam's so taken with Liam.'

'She'll have to know one day, Billy! Supposing Bruno comes looking for me and finds strangers living where I used to and they tell him to try your house?'

'The season will be finished in another few weeks and he'll probably be off back to Spain so you may never see him again.'

Patsy shrugged, but her face softened as she looked down at the baby in her arms. 'I suppose he ought to know about Liam.'

'Then you'd better go over there and tell him!' He fished in his pockets and held out some coins. 'Here, me dad gave me this when I was in hospital. He insisted I have a few bob in case I needed to buy a paper or soap or anything.'

Patsy looked at the money Billy was holding out and shook her head.

'Go on, take it,' he insisted. 'Go over and see Bruno and clear the air so that we all know where we stand one way or the other.'

Chapter Twenty-Seven

It took Patsy three days to pluck up the courage to go across to New Brighton and face Bruno Alvarez.

She hadn't been anywhere since Liam had been born, except when Elaine asked her to go to the nearby corner shop to buy groceries, and she found the thought of going that far on her own quite daunting.

She wished Billy was well enough to go with her, but he could still only walk very short distances on his crutches.

She could always ask Maureen Murphy, she supposed, but that would mean waiting until the weekend when Maureen wasn't at work and she wasn't sure if Maureen would come with her or not. They didn't have much to do with each other these days. They'd quarrelled the day she'd gone round to ask Mrs Murphy if she knew where her mam might have gone.

Mrs Murphy had told her that she had no idea at all. Maureen had insisted on taking a look at the baby and then she'd refused to believe it was Bruno's.

'It wouldn't have such light-coloured skin and fuzzy red hair if it was his,' she pronounced.

'Rubbish!' Patsy defended. 'Liam takes after my

side of the family. He looks like my dad. Anyway, he will probably change as he gets older. Babies often lose all their hair and the new lot is quite different to what they were born with.'

'And what about the colour of his eyes, then?'

'All babies' eyes are blue when they're born, everyone knows that!'

'His aren't!' Maureen exclaimed triumphantly. 'If you look closely they're a funny shade of green or hazel, I can't tell which.'

'They're blue,' Patsy insisted. It's the light in here, you can't see them properly.'

Maureen was not convinced. 'He's a lovely little thing, but he's not a bit like Bruno,' she'd insisted stubbornly.

Since then, on the few occasions when she'd seen Maureen in the street, Patsy had tried to avoid her. She'd often wondered herself why Liam had not the slightest trace of Bruno's Latin swarthiness and build, but she didn't want to listen to Maureen telling her so.

Each morning Patsy found some reason to put off her trip to New Brighton. One day it was because it was too wet, the next because it was too hot.

When Billy became increasingly irritable with the way she was prevaricating she finally forced herself to go. She dressed Liam in a white cotton romper suit that Elaine had bought for him and laid out her blue-and-white spotted voile dress that her dad had bought her. She hadn't worn it since Liam was born and she hoped she would be able to get into it.

Tears came to her eyes as she dressed. Her dad's birthday had been such a momentous night, she thought sadly. So many things had happened since then; things that she struggled daily to push to the back of her mind.

Much to her surprise Patsy found that she enjoyed the journey over to New Brighton. It was mid-morning so the trams were not very busy and no one was pushing or shoving. When she reached the Pier Head, though, it was a different story. The *Royal Iris* was at the landing stage and it was packed with day-trippers making the most of the last few days of late summer sunshine.

The Mersey was as calm as a millpond. Patsy managed to find a seat on deck and sat there in the warm sunshine, holding Liam in her arms, watching the boats moored alongside and the white gulls soaring and screeching around them.

As she gazed out over the blue-grey water to where New Brighton Tower rose high against a clear blue sky her heart began to pound at the thought of seeing Bruno again.

It was almost six months since she'd last seen him, before Liam had been born, even. It seemed a lifetime ago since they had strolled along the promenade and made love in the sandhills. She still felt bitter because he had never made any attempt to find her.

You don't know that for sure, she reminded herself. He'd known where she lived so he might have come looking for her and not been able to find her. After all, Billy had once gone across to New Brighton looking for him and not found him.

As the *Royal Iris* grated alongside the landing stage she joined the throng of people who were making their way on to the pier and along the promenade to the Tower Fairground.

She stood for a moment taking in the busy scene. The roundabouts, dodgem cars, and the variety of stalls selling everything from ice-cream and candyfloss to funny hats and trinkets were all busy. There were crowds at the hoop-la booths and at all the other sideshows; even a queue outside the fortune teller's tent.

She looked for the spot where the menagarie was normally housed, but couldn't see the huge green-and-white awning anywhere. In the end, because Liam was so heavy to carry around in such a crowded place, she asked one of the stall holders where it was.

'There's no menagerie here this year, luv,' he told her.

'No animals here at all? What about the lions and tigers?'

He shook his head. 'No, there's no circus this year.'

'Why is that? What's happened?'

The stall holder shrugged. 'Don't really know, luv. They never came back. I did hear the trainer had gone to Rhyl, or some other Welsh seaside place with the animals this year. Wanted a change, I suppose. Not such a bad idea really. Might try Margate or Southend myself next year. You get fed up with being in one place all the time, gorra try and see a bit of the world, haven't you?'

Patsy smiled and thanked him, but she still

wasn't satisfied so she crossed to another part of the fairground to see if she could find out anything more.

No matter whom she asked the answer was always the same. Bruno Alvarez had not been there that season. No one was quite sure where he was, but they didn't think he had gone back to Spain. Everyone seemed to know that he'd been at Blackpool during the winter. Some of them even told her that he had come back to New Brighton to put on a show over Christmas, but after that they had no idea where he'd gone.

Dispirited and disappointed, Patsy decided that since her trip had been a complete waste of time she might as well go straight back to Liverpool. The *Royal Iris* pulled away seconds before she reached the landing stage. Her heart sank as she stood there watching it sail into midstream and head for Liverpool. It would be another hour before there was another boat.

She was in no mood to walk along the crowded promenade. She wondered whether to wait for the next boat or take a bus to Seacombe and pick up the *Royal Daffodil* from there. The day had become oppressively hot and as she saw the dark clouds building over the Welsh mountains in the far distance she thought there might be a thunderstorm brewing up. If there was, then the sooner she was back in Liverpool the better.

She felt utterly drained. She'd been so tensed up about seeing Bruno again after all this time that now she felt bewildered and out of her depth. It was like having a door slammed in her face.

All the way back to Liverpool she wondered what she should tell Billy. He'd want to know how she got on, so how would he react when she told him the truth?

'I'm as disappointed as you are,' he scowled. 'I was hoping this trip would clear the air between you and Bruno for good and then the rest of us could get on with our lives.'

She stared at him nonplussed. She realised that getting rid of the stable had been a turning point for Billy. His apathy about life and the future had disappeared and understandably he wanted her to come to some decision about her future. The trouble was, she was pretty sure he meant *their* future.

She waited for Billy to speak out, to elaborate, but he said no more. There was an uneasy air of tension between them. She turned away quickly: from the look on his face Patsy was sure he was waiting for her to say she was going to forget all about Bruno now that she knew he was gone.

How could she do that when every fibre of her being cried out for the handsome Spaniard? He was not only the father of her child, he was her only love. How could she go into another man's arms when Bruno possessed her heart?

She was so fond of Billy that she couldn't bear to hurt him by telling him this. If only he *was* her brother! She'd wanted him to be that from the very first day he'd come to work for her dad, when she'd been little more than a child herself.

For the next few days Billy stayed morose and brooding, but he kept his own counsel about Bruno. Now that he realised that there was no longer a business waiting for him, even when he was well enough to pick up the reins again, he seemed anxious to start making plans.

He began to strive to walk further and further each day without crutches. Although it caused him considerable pain he insisted on trying to walk up the stairs and his look of triumph when he managed it brought a lump to Patsy's throat.

She had hated to see him so helpless. It was terrible that a man who was so well built and who had been so fit should be reduced to shambling around on crutches. Now, as each day he managed to walk a little bit further without them, she felt as pleased about his progress as he did.

'It's still going to be a long time before I'm fit enough to work again,' he said gloomily. 'No one will want to employ a cripple. What can I do? I can't lift anything and I can't walk very far or very fast. Even a job as a doorman is beyond me since they're expected to carry the guests' luggage up to their rooms.'

'You might manage to get a job as a night-watchman.'

'Not a chance! Once the burglars found out that I couldn't run after them they'd be breaking in every night of the week.'

Patsy chewed her lip thoughtfully. Perhaps this was the right time to suggest again that Billy should look after Liam and she should be the one to find a job.

'What sort of job were you thinking about?' he asked dubiously.

'I don't know really. Perhaps working in a shop

or something. Only part time,' she assured him quickly.

'And there's a lot of that sort of work around, is there?'

She shrugged. 'No, probably not. Perhaps I could get some work cleaning, then.'

'Charring? You? The girl who was a partner in her own business?'

'Well we haven't got a business now, have we,' she snapped. 'I don't want to go as a char, cleaning up other people's messes and I don't particularly want to work in a shop pandering to the whims of people who can afford to buy things that I can't, but what else is there for me to do? Tell me that, Billy Grant.'

'Wow! Temper, temper, Patsy Callaghan. It must be right what they say about red hair,' Billy laughed. 'Well, I'll tell you what you could do – you could become a nurse in a hospital.'

Patsy stared at him in disbelief. 'Are you mad, Billy? Do you know what I'd have to do to become a nurse?'

'Yes, you'd have to enrol for training. It's like an apprenticeship and it's hard work, but you're used to that so you'd manage.'

'So where would I go to train?'

'A hospital, of course. It takes about three years to become properly qualified and you'd have to live in the hospital.'

'You know all about this, do you?'

'Yes, I do,' he told her smugly. 'The nurses talked to me a lot, especially the night nurses when I couldn't sleep. They told me about how they had trained and all the rest of it.'

'And did they tell you what I'd do with a baby while I was training?'

Billy's face clouded. 'I'd forgotten about Liam.'

'Yes, well you may have managed to do so, but I can't.'

'Now he's weaned you could leave him with someone, couldn't you?' Billy asked mildly.

'That's what I was planning on doing when I said I'd get a job. I was planning to leave him with you! Only for a few hours each day, though,' she added swiftly.

'If you were training to be a nurse and earning some money then you could pay someone to look after Liam for you permanently.'

Patsy shook her head. 'I know it seems a good idea, Billy, but I couldn't bring myself to do that. Look at him!' She gazed down at the baby who was lying on a rug by her feet, kicking his legs and waving a rattle in the air. 'He's far too precious for me to hand over to anyone else to look after permanently.'

'Not if it was someone you knew really well, someone who'd loved him as much as you do,' he persisted.

She stared at him, puzzled. 'I don't follow. When I suggested that you should look after him for a few hours each day you didn't seem to like the idea.'

'No, not me! I'd be no good at looking after him. I mean my mam, of course! Liam would be perfectly safe with her so you'd have no worries about him at all.'

'I couldn't expect her to take on a young baby!' Patsy exclaimed, aghast. 'Think of all the work that's involved, Billy! Your mam's brought up one family. She probably can't wait for the day when I leave and she can have her home free of nappies airing on the fireguard and baby clothes all over the place.'

Chapter Twenty-Eight

Patsy kept toying with Billy's suggestion that she should train as a nurse. In many ways she liked the idea, because it would mean that she would be doing something worthwhile.

It would also make life easier for the Grants if she wasn't living there, she told herself. Now that Billy could manage to get up and down stairs he could have his bedroom back instead of having to sleep on the sofa.

The really big problem was Liam. Could she bear to leave him in someone else's care even if Elaine agreed to look after him?

He was now almost six months old and he was becoming aware of all that went on around him. He wasn't a robust child, but he was certainly very active and Patsy wondered if it would be asking too much of Elaine to have him all the time.

Liam reminded her so much of her own father with his light blue eyes and long thin build. He had her red curls, though, and freckles right across the bridge of his nose the same as she had. There seemed to be nothing at all of Bruno in either his colouring or features. Bruno's skin had been a warm olive brown that made his teeth look brilliantly white when he smiled. His eyes were as dark as chocolate under his heavy dark brows.

She wondered what Bruno would have thought of Liam if she'd been able to find him. There must be a reason why she hadn't heard a word from him in all this time. After all, he knew where she lived.

She pondered over all the advantages and drawbacks of having to leave Liam while she trained to be a nurse. Finally, she made her decision and plucked up the courage to mention the matter to Elaine.

'Billy has already asked me and I said I would,' Elaine smiled.

'It will be an awful lot of extra work for you to take on,' Patsy pointed out. 'Liam will be crawling any day now and once he starts toddling then you really will have your hands full.'

'I know all about that, luv! I've brought up three of my own, remember. Anyway,' she added, a wide smile on her plump face, 'if I can't look after my grandson then who else can?'

Patsy bit her lip. Her grandson? So Elaine still thought Liam was Billy's baby!

She opened her mouth to deny it then shut it again quickly, remembering Billy's warning that if they told Elaine that Bruno was Liam's father she certainly wouldn't want to look after him. She might even tell Patsy to get out right away and take her baby with her.

She wondered if Billy also still thought that the baby was his. Was that why he was trying to be so helpful and why he was suggesting that his mother would look after Liam for her?

But he couldn't be, she reasoned. She and Billy

had only ever made love once and she had been meeting Bruno every Sunday all through last summer. Anyway, Liam with his red hair wasn't a bit like Billy. He wasn't like Bruno either, she reminded herself.

The more she thought about becoming a nurse the more the idea appealed to her. She asked Billy if he knew the name of any of the nurses he'd talked to when he'd been in hospital so that she could go and ask them how she went about it.

'Go to the Labour Exchange and ask there,' he told her. 'They're sure to have all the details.'

Patsy followed his advice and a week later, full of nervous trepidation, she was on her way for an interview at Liverpool General Hospital.

When, two weeks later, a letter arrived telling her to report for her initial training, Patsy felt so nervous that she almost had second thoughts about what she was doing. Thinking about leaving Liam in Elaine's care was one thing; walking out of the house and leaving him there with her was another.

'After the first month of your training you'll be able to come home on your day off each week,' Billy reminded her.

'Maybe, but right now it's the first month I'm worried about. That's four whole weeks! How am I going to last that long without seeing Liam?'

'It will be over in no time at all,' he told her confidently.

'That's rubbish and you know it, Billy,' she told him angrily.

'No it's not and I do know what I'm talking

about. I was in hospital for months and it seemed like no time at all.'

'You hadn't left your baby behind though, had you?'

He didn't answer, but the look he gave her sent a *frisson* of fear through her and she felt herself colour up in embarrassment.

She tried to laugh it off. 'Well, you know what I mean, don't you!'

When he still remained silent Patsy said awkwardly, 'I'd better go and tell Elaine the news and see if she's still happy about our arrangement.'

The next two weeks were chaotic. Patsy spent every moment she could with Liam. Sometimes she felt like a drowning man clutching at the only thing that could save her life; at others like a protective lioness with her only cub. She couldn't bear to let Liam out of her sight or out of her arms.

'He'll still be here when you come home in a month's time,' Billy told her, when he saw Patsy sitting down nursing Liam instead of putting him into his cot to sleep.

'Yes, and by then he might be too big to want cuddling. Babies can change quite a lot in a month, you know.'

'Not him! He likes being cuddled too much, and I'll be cuddling him every day while you're away, and so will me mam and Janie and even young Freddie.'

Patsy buried her face in Liam's red curls. She didn't want Billy to see the tears in her eyes, not when they were all rallying round to help her.

The hospital was a grim and unfriendly red-brick building with five storeys of long narrow windows. She always thought that from the outside it resembled a prison as much as a hospital.

And that's what it is going to be for me for the next four weeks, Patsy thought miserably as she made her way inside. It was all very well Billy saying the time would fly by because she'd be so busy and there would be so many new people and new experiences, but already there was an ache in her heart.

By the end of the second day, Patsy really did feel like a prisoner. She'd been assigned a narrow, cell-like bedroom and issued with a uniform. The light blue dress was of stiff scratchy cotton and there was a heavily starched white apron to wear over it, as well as an equally crisply starched white cap to cover up her red curls.

There were so many rules that she was sure she would never remember half of them. Nurses must not behave in a frivolous manner; they must not wear jewellery, they must never eat while on the wards, they must never run no matter if it was an emergency.

Most important of all was the code about how they must address all those who were senior to them. Patsy could understand this and recognised that doctors wore white coats and that the matron was dressed in black with a snow white flowing head-dress. She found it difficult to work out what all the differently coloured uniforms and armbands worn by the nurses meant, though.

The six o'clock call in the morning didn't worry Patsy at all since she was used to getting up early. It was after breakfast, which was eaten in the enormous dining room along with about fifty other nurses, when she found she was going to spend most of the morning in a classroom, that was disconcerting.

She'd thought that being a nurse was looking after sick people, not having lessons as though she was still at school.

'How can we look after patients if we don't know anything about their illnesses or how to treat them?' one of her classmates commented in a withering tone.

'I thought we'd learn as we went along.'

'Well we will, but they teach us the basics first before they let us loose on the wards.'

In the afternoon, however, she was sent to a ward where she helped trained nurses and orderlies with bed-making, carrying in cups of tea and trays of food from the ward kitchen, and general tidying up.

After their last meal of the day in the staff dining room all probationers had to report back to the classroom for another two hours' study. When that ended they were allowed to collect a mug of hot cocoa from the dining room and then told to go straight to their rooms and that lights out would be in half an hour.

On her first night, as she lay there in the darkness, all the events of the day jostled in her mind. So many new experiences, so many rules and regulations. She remembered how difficult some of the patients had been, how sharply some of the older nurses had spoken to her, and all the countless things she was supposed to learn.

She'd thought looking after baby Liam had been difficult at times when he was peevish, but that had been easy compared to dealing with some of the women she'd encountered that afternoon. She knew they were sick, and probably in pain, but did they have to complain quite so much?

She fell asleep wondering if it would be any easier the next day when, according to the rota she'd been given, she would be on the men's ward.

Slowly a pattern of bed, study, nursing and then study again before bed began to emerge and the days blended one into the other.

Her longing to see Liam was always uppermost in her mind. She knew Elaine was capable and would take every care of him, but being separated from him was tearing Patsy apart. She longed to feel his little arms around her neck, his wet lips planted in a noisy kiss on her cheek. She missed the smell of him when he was warm from his bath, holding him in her arms and watching his eyelids droop as sleep claimed him.

She kept a piece of paper under her pillow with the days marked down on it and every night she crossed another one off.

By her third week at Liverpool General she was well into the routine and she particularly enjoyed carrying trays of food or drink to the patients. Now that she was feeling more confident she even exchanged chitchat with them and this made each day pass so much more quickly.

She was also being encouraged by the staff nurse to practise on the ward some of the things that she'd been taught in the classroom. It started with making beds, progressed to bedbaths and then to taking temperatures all under the eagle eye of the senior nurse or ward sister.

The day before her month's probation ended, Patsy went along to the Training School Office to ask for official permission to go home the following day.

Although permission was granted, Patsy had to listen to a lecture on behaviour. She must not go out into the street wearing her uniform or her cap, she was told, and when she returned she must not go into a ward while still wearing her outdoor clothes.

Patsy smiled to herself. Whatever made them think she would want to wear her uniform to go home in? Not having to put on the stiff uncomfortable dress and starched white apron would be wonderful.

Patsy was up long before the early morning bell sounded. She didn't stop to eat breakfast, but shot out the doors as soon as it was permissible for her to do so. On the tram all the way back to Paradise Place she was singing softly to herself, she felt so happy. A few more minutes and she would be holding Liam in her arms again.

When she burst into the house she found Billy nursing Liam, who'd been fed and dressed all ready to greet her. As she went to take him from Billy's arms, Liam drew back and his tiny face puckered up as if he was about to cry. Patsy felt mortified.

'He doesn't know me! He's forgotten me already!' Tears spilled down her cheeks as she looked from Elaine to Billy in distress.

'He'll be all right in a minute or two,' Billy assured her. 'A month is a long time for a little chap like him.'

'Come and sit down, luv. I've got some breakfast all ready for you. Sit down and eat that and let him get used to you being here,' Elaine added tactfully.

Patsy did as she was asked, but it almost choked her to swallow even the cup of tea Elaine poured out for her. She'd so looked forward to holding Liam. She'd expected him to hold out his little arms to her; instead he had drawn back as if she was a stranger.

Billy bounced the baby up and down on his knee, pointing to Patsy and talking to Liam softly. Within a few minutes the baby was gurgling noisily and went to Patsy quite happily.

She spent every moment of her time at home either nursing Liam, playing with him or sitting by his cot watching him sleep. Billy sensed that she wasn't at all sure that she'd be able to bring herself to go back to the hospital.

'The worst part is over now,' he reminded her. 'From now on you will have a day off every week.'

Patsy sighed. 'Even a week is a long time for Liam to remember who I am,' she pointed out.

Billy shook his head. 'He soon remembered you this time, now didn't he?'

'Yes, but if I'm always away, except for one day a week, he'll think your mother is his mam, not me.'

Billy looked taken aback. 'You're wrong, Patsy. My mother would never let him think that.'

'How can she stop him from thinking that?' she asked, tears spilling down her cheeks.

'There must be some way to prevent that happening,' Billy stated, anxious to put her mind at rest. 'I'll have a word with her and see if she can think of anything we can do.'

'Why don't you go into Jerome's, the photographers in Lord Street, and get a picture of yourself taken, Patsy?' Elaine suggested.

'Great idea,' Billy enthused. 'We can show it to Liam every morning when he wakes up and again every night before he's put to bed.'

'And we'll teach him to say "Mam" every time he sees it,' Elaine promised. 'That way you won't be a stranger to him. He'll know exactly who you are when you come home on your day off.'

Chapter Twenty-Nine

Gradually Patsy found herself settling into the long days of busy hospital routine and of being at home only one day each week. Billy made quite sure that there was no recurrence of the upsetting incident of little Liam not recognising her. As soon as Patsy brought home the framed photograph she'd had taken at Jerome's Studios it was placed in a prominent position on the mantelpiece.

Billy showed it to Liam last thing every night and first thing every morning. As Liam grew older, Billy taught him to point to the picture and say 'Mam' and encouraged him to kiss it each night before he went to bed.

Elaine was equally co-operative. She made sure right from the start that Liam called her 'Nana' so that there was no fear of confusion in the child's mind.

Although Patsy knew how lucky she was to have such a wonderful show of unity she still longed to spend more time with Liam. Each week, he seemed to have accomplished something new and she hadn't been there to see him doing it.

Liam had barely been crawling when she started training as a nurse yet in no time at all he had managed to pull himself up on to his feet. Then she found he was toddling around, grabbing at Elaine's skirt or Billy's leg or a piece of furniture to balance himself. A few weeks later when she came home he was toddling around unaided.

It was the same when he started to talk. She had been so proud the first time he had managed to say 'Mam' that she wanted the whole world to know. Yet, she felt heartbroken when on a subsequent visit he pointed to various familiar objects and called them all by their right name. She felt she had been cheated. She should have been the one there encouraging him to talk.

The only thing she could feel happy about, she thought, was that she was earning enough money to pay for everything he might need.

She gave Elaine the bulk of her wages. When Elaine protested, saying that she should be saving it towards the future, Patsy insisted that she still had a lot of paying back to do first before she started saving.

She knew Elaine appreciated what she was doing. Billy had still not found a job although he was now a great deal better and no longer needed crutches. In the house he simply held on to the furniture as he moved around. When he went out he used a walking stick. He moved very slowly and his limp was quite pronounced, but it was progress.

'Not many openings for a limp layabout,' he joked whenever Patsy asked him if he'd had any luck in finding a job.

'He does his share about the place, believe me,' Elaine would tell her. 'If our Billy found a job then

I'd have to find a playmate for Liam. The two of them get on like a house on fire, never out of each other's sight.'

As Elaine spoke Patsy was aware that she was looking at her speculatively and her heart pounded uneasily. For one moment she wondered whether she was going to start asking questions about the relationship between her and Billy.

She and Billy were still the best of friends, but that was all, and Patsy knew it puzzled Elaine and that she wanted to ask her about it, but so far she'd avoided her questions. Patsy knew that deep down she still thought of Liam as her grandson.

Patsy could never understand why Billy hadn't explained the situation to her himself. After all this time it was unlikely that Elaine would turn her and Liam out. She wondered if Billy was fondly harbouring the same idea as his mother did about Liam. If so, she was grateful that he had never tried to teach Liam to call him 'Dad'.

Some day Liam would have to be told the truth, but she still hoped that by then Bruno would have returned and would take his rightful place in their lives. Her feelings for him were still the same. She dreamed of him often, recalling every detail of his good looks, Mediterranean charm and fine physique.

Her feelings for Billy were on a different level. She would do anything she could to help him and she knew he would do the same for her. Their time spent working together when her father had been alive had been the happiest of her life. And her close affinity with Billy had remained when there was only the two of them running the business.

His accident had been a terrible blow to her as well as to him and his family. His mother's generosity was a debt she would never be able to repay. Even Joe, who was such a rough and ready character, had shown nothing but kindness to her, and Janie and Freddie had been as warm and loving as if they were her own brother and sister.

Patsy knew she had a great deal to be thankful for: without the help of the Grants she and Liam would have been in dire straits after her mam had disappeared.

Even her life at the hospital, strenuous though it could be, was enjoyable in a great many ways, Patsy thought. There was so much variety. Patients rarely stayed for more than a week or two. There were constantly fresh faces, different ailments to be dealt with, and varied treatments. As well as frequent changes of nursing staff and doctors, her own duties meant that she was often transferred to a different ward without any warning.

Whether she was nursing men, women or children, Patsy found she was learning something new all the time. Most important of all, she felt she was doing something worthwhile.

She had made a number of friends amongst the other nurses. She always took care, though, not to become too close to any of them because she didn't want details of her home life, especially information about Liam, to be known. The nursing authorities didn't look favourably on employing married women and certainly not those who had children to care for. As far as they were aware she was a single girl with no family ties.

Occasionally, on one of her days off, Patsy was tempted to go over to New Brighton and see if there was any news of Bruno, but something always stopped her. Usually it was her longing to spend every minute she could with Liam.

She told herself that next summer she'd definitely take Liam there. Bruno and the animals would be back by then, she felt sure, and she could imagine how excited Liam would be when he saw the ferocious lions and the tigers being trained. She wondered what Bruno would say when he saw Liam for the first time and she went hot all over as she imagined the astonished pride on his face.

She never did make the journey. In fact, when Billy suggested taking Liam on the ferryboat for a day trip she vetoed the idea. Common sense told her that Bruno knew where she lived if he wanted to see her again. Since he'd never done so it was much better, she decided, to keep her dreams and illusions rather than have them shattered.

Patsy never managed to find out where her mother had gone either. She had not heard a word from her mam since the day she had turned her out with her belongings stuffed inside an old canvas sack. No one in Paradise Place ever mentioned her name. It was as if Maeve Callaghan had never existed.

Patsy often asked herself how long her present settled and relatively happy state could last. Liam was now three years old and very active. He wanted to be doing something, or going somewhere with Billy, every minute of the day. When Billy was not around he pestered Elaine to take him out. He loved going to the shops, but most of all he liked to visit St John's Market, which was noisy and packed with a medley of stalls.

Each time she saw him Patsy was aware that he seemed to be growing more and more like her dad. Liam had her red curly hair, but his eyes were a pale hazel shade, and looked huge in his small pointed face. He had pale skin and the sprinkling of freckles over the bridge of his nose matched hers exactly.

He would never be a very robust child, but he was wiry and full of energy. His curiosity about everything going on around him was tremendous and even Billy sometimes tired of his constant barrage of questions.

On her day at home she always tried to take Liam out somewhere so as to give Elaine a chance to have some time on her own. She knew it was the only real rest she got from him, except at the weekends when either Joe or Freddie would take him to the park.

Janie loved him dearly, but now that she had a regular boyfriend the amount of time she wanted to spend with Liam was limited. Once Freddie had left school and become an assistant in an ironmongers he had to work all day on a Saturday, so Sunday was the only time he had for Liam.

Patsy's bubble of contentment burst suddenly a week after Liam's fourth birthday.

When she was told to report immediately to Matron's office she tried to think of anything she might have done wrong or any rule she might have contravened.

The news she was given was far worse than any chastisement for a minor infringement of rules.

'I have received a request from a Mrs Grant asking if you can be allowed home immediately,' Matron told her. She stared hard at Patsy from over the top of her gold-rimmed glasses. 'Who is this Mrs Grant?'

'She's . . . she's the lady I live with,' Patsy told her.

'A relation?'

'No, not exactly. I have lived with her ever since I was a child, though,' she mumbled.

'So do you know why she should need you at home so urgently?'

Patsy shook her head. Her mind was racing. She was sure something awful must have happened for Elaine to send for her. She wondered if Billy had met with another accident. She prayed it was nothing to do with Liam. He had seemed well enough when she'd been home three days ago. If he'd a bad cold, or even fallen over, Elaine would have dealt with it like she always did without sending for her to come home. Unless Elaine was ill? If she couldn't look after Liam then Billy would be able to see to him.

'So you have no idea why she has sent for you?'

Matron persisted, cutting into the thoughts that were jumbling around in Patsy's head.

'No, Ma'am. No idea at all.'

Matron frowned and studied the duty rota lying on her desk. 'It is very inconvenient for you to expect time off without due notice, Nurse Callaghan. You may take two hours off in the middle of your shift, but I rely on you to report back for work on time.'

Reluctantly, Patsy went back to the ward, but her mind was not on her work. She couldn't settle. She felt certain that Elaine asking for her to come home had something to do with Liam.

Because she was not concentrating on what she was doing, Patsy made several silly mistakes. When she apologised to Sister Pringle who was in charge of the ward, and explained about the message, Sister Pringle decided that it might be better if she went home right away before she made some serious error.

'It's two o'clock now, so I'll expect you back on duty at five o'clock, remember.'

Patsy wasted no time. She dashed up to her room, tore off her apron and cap and stuffed them in her locker. She knew it was against hospital rules to go out in uniform, but she didn't stop to change out of her blue dress. She just fastened her topcoat over it and hoped no one would notice.

All the way back to Paradise Place, Patsy kept telling herself that she mustn't panic. In her heart though she knew that Elaine would not have sent for her unless it was something very serious.

'Thank God you've managed to get away,'

Elaine greeted her the moment she entered the house. She looked hollow-eyed with worry.

'It's little Liam, isn't it?' Patsy asked.

Elaine nodded. 'We're not sure what's wrong with him, luv. He's had a bit of a cough and this morning he brought up some blood so I sent for the doctor . . .'

'Blood! How is he now?' Patsy demanded anxiously, looking round the room, expecting to see Billy sitting there nursing him.

'He's in hospital, luv. Billy's staying there with him. I wanted to be here to tell you myself or I wouldn't have left his bedside, either.'

'Can I go and see him?'

'Of course. Do you want to go right away or would you like a cup of tea first?'

'Right away. I only have a couple of hours off and then I'm due back on duty.'

Elaine looked shocked. 'Must you go back so soon? I thought you would want to be with Liam.'

'I do want to be with him more than anything in the world,' Patsy answered sharply, 'but this is all the time I can get off.'

When she saw Liam lying listlessly in the hospital bed, every vestige of colour drained from his cheeks, all thought of getting back to her own hospital on time went from Patsy's mind.

'I'm not leaving until I've seen a doctor and found out exactly what's wrong with him,' she insisted.

'There won't be a doctor on the ward again until tomorrow morning,' the sister in charge warned her.

'Wouldn't it be best if you went back and explained the situation and then asked if you could have more time off?' Billy suggested. 'I'll stay here with Liam until you manage to get back, even if it takes you until tomorrow.'

Patsy shook her head. 'I really don't know, Billy. No one there knows about Liam, I never said anything about him when I applied to become a nurse because I knew they wouldn't take me on if they knew I had a young child. And I've never mentioned him to anyone since.'

'Billy is right, though, luv. You should ask for time off. It's the best thing you can do,' Elaine urged.

Patsy felt in a complete daze as she went back to the Liverpool General. She knew she was going to be late, but it didn't seem to matter since she intended leaving again right away.

Nevertheless, she put her starched white apron and cap back on, deciding it would create a better impression than if she went straight on to the ward in outdoor clothes, which was strictly forbidden.

As she pinned her cap into place on her unruly curls, she couldn't put the sight of Liam lying there so wan and listless out of her mind. It had all happened so quickly. Only a few days ago, when she'd last been home, he had been running around so full of life that it didn't seem possible that he could be so ill.

Sister Pringle tapped her watch irritably when Patsy appeared on the ward and could hardly control her anger when Patsy told her that she needed more time off. 'Really, Nurse Callaghan, this is most inconvenient,' she said sharply. 'You'd better go and ask the duty sister and see what she has to say. She's the one who has overall responsibility for all the nurses at the hospital.'

'It's not up to me, you'll have to ask Matron,' the duty sister snapped after Patsy had explained the situation. 'Wait here and I'll go and find out if she will see you.'

Patsy thought the duty sister was never going to come back, but when she did it was to tell her that Matron would see her as soon as she was free.

'Go and take a seat in the corridor outside Matron's office and wait until you are called,' she told her. 'You'd better go and put a clean apron on first, that one looks rather creased,' she remarked, looking Patsy up and down critically.

It was almost an hour before Matron summoned her into her room and it seemed like eternity to Patsy. Several times she was on the point of walking out of the hospital and rushing back to Liam's bedside. When she was finally called into Matron's office she felt numb with anxiety.

She knew she was telling her story badly, but she was so worried about Liam that her brain refused to function properly.

'This is all very irregular, Nurse Callaghan,' Matron told her. She gave her a steely glare and drummed on the desk with her pen. 'Have you taken your annual holiday yet?' she barked.

Patsy shook her head.

'Very well, then I think the best thing you can

do is to take it now,' she pronounced. 'In your absence I will consider your situation very carefully and let you have my decision as to whether we wish to retain you as a nurse here or not.'

Chapter Thirty

Every day Patsy visited Liam at the Liverpool Children's Hospital and stayed by his bedside for as long as the hospital staff would permit her to do so. She watched anxiously as different doctors were brought in to examine him and carry out various tests, but no one would say what was the matter with him.

The diagnosis when it finally came was a tremendous blow both to Patsy and to the Grants. Liam, they were told, had tuberculosis.

Once the hospital had decided on the nature of his illness Liam was taken off the danger list and all special visiting privileges were withdrawn. To their dismay they found they were only allowed to see him for one hour each day and only two people were allowed at his bedside at any one time.

Patsy knew this was standard hospital practice, but she still couldn't reconcile herself to it. She wanted to be with him all the time, night and day. She wanted to be the one to feed him, amuse him, hold his hand or stroke his forehead when he wasn't feeling well.

'This child needs rest, not constant attention and stimulation,' the ward sister told Patsy briskly when she begged to be allowed to stay a little longer.

Billy and Elaine were also upset by the curtailment of the visiting hours. Realising that Patsy wanted to stay with him for the whole of the hour, when they were allowed into the ward they were forced to take it in turns to be at his bedside.

They all tried their best to appear bright and cheerful when they visited Liam. But although they assured him that he would soon be back home again, they were filled with a sense of unease as he seemed to grow paler and thinner and weaker each time they saw him.

Elaine was beside herself with distress. In her eyes, having tuberculosis was as bad as having the plague. She refused to believe that there was any cure and she was suspicious and critical of everything the hospital was doing for Liam.

'I can't think how this has happened,' she said over and over again as they left the hospital and made their way back to Paradise Place. 'I've taken the greatest care of him, Patsy. He's never been allowed out without a coat, his feet have always been kept dry . . .'

'You make him sound like a horse, not a little child,' Billy snapped. He felt terrible that such a thing should have happened while Liam was entrusted to their care. Having to walk away and leave him lying there in hospital made his senses spin and he became tense and angry at the slightest thing.

'I know you've looked after Liam,' Patsy told Elaine, putting her arms round the plump motherly figure and hugging her. 'No one could have cared for him better.'

Elaine was inconsolable though and nothing Patsy said seemed to make any difference. Every night after they returned from the hospital they would sit drinking tea and going over and over the situation. It was as if talking out loud about the child helped to ease the concern they were all feeling.

Deep in her heart Patsy felt it was her fault. She should never have left him to be brought up by someone else, no matter how kind and considerate they might be. Liam was her responsibility and she should have been there looking out for him.

'Might be the bloody bad start he had in life,' Joe Grant said. His bony face was drawn and grey with worry.

'Joe!' Elaine frowned and shook her head, signalling him to be silent.

'It's all right,' Patsy said dully. 'I've been wondering the same thing. An old stable wasn't the ideal place for a newborn baby.'

'It was probably something I didn't do right when he was born,' Billy muttered.

Patsy grabbed hold of his hand and squeezed it. 'You were wonderful, Billy, no one could have done any better.'

'Perhaps we ought to tell the doctors about the hardships he suffered at birth,' Elaine said worriedly. 'They did ask if he'd had any health problems, or whether there were any unusual circumstances, or if he had been in contact with anyone who had TB.'

Patsy shrugged. 'Tell them if you like. But I'm quite sure that Billy did everything right at the time and that where Liam was born has nothing at all to do with him being ill now.'

'Well, he hasn't been in touch with anyone who has TB. None of us have,' Elaine pointed out.

'Gerraway! You don't know who the hell you're rubbing shoulders with when you take him to the shops or down the bloody market,' Joe told her.

'I take him to the swings in the park and he sometimes plays around with the other kids who are there. Any one of them could have TB,' Billy added.

'Then there's that bloody hospital where you work, Patsy. You come straight home from there and the first thing you do when you get in the bloody house is pick Liam up and kiss him,' Joe pointed out.

Patsy shook her head. 'I don't think there is any chance of me bringing germs home. I always change out of my uniform before I leave the hospital. I have to, it's one of the rules.'

'It's no good us sitting around blaming each other,' Billy said quietly. 'What we've got to do now is decide what steps we're going to take to get him better.'

'Not much bloody choice, is there,' Joe said irritably. 'They say he's got to go into an isolation hospital so that's that! It's out of our hands once they cart him off to one of those places.'

Elaine sighed. 'They haven't told us which hospital it will be yet. I hope they don't send him too far away because it will be so difficult to visit him if they do.'

'They probably won't allow much visiting,'

Patsy warned. 'The treatment is very tiring for the patient, especially for one as small as he is, so they'll want him to be kept as quiet as possible.'

'Oh, I suppose you know all about that. So what is the treatment then? Come on, give us the griff,' Joe demanded.'

'It depends on how bad he is. I looked it all up in the medical books. In some cases they collapse the lungs to give them a chance to heal.'

'What, both the buggers?' Joe looked aghast. 'How do you bloody well breathe if they does that?'

'Not both lungs at once! They do it one at a time, that's why the treatment takes such a long time.'

Billy frowned. 'How do they collapse a lung, Patsy?'

'They pump air into the chest cavity and surround the lung with it. The air gradually seeps out so they repeat it every week or ten days and gradually the lung repairs itself.'

'Would they do that to a tiny little mite like Liam?' Elaine asked.

'I'm not sure. We'll have to wait and see.'

'First things first,' Billy told them. 'Let's find out where Liam is being sent.'

It was another two days before they were informed where he was to be treated and when they were told all of them were shocked.

'Wallasey Isolation Hospital! That's the other side of the bloody Mersey,' Joe ranted. 'That could mean a journey of well over an hour each sodding way!'

'All that way and we'll only be able to stay half

317

an hour!' Elaine agreed, shaking her head sadly.

'And we can only visit on a Wednesday or Sunday afternoon,' Billy added, reading from the sheet of instruction they'd been handed.

'It says only two visitors at a time,' Elaine reminded them.

When her leave was over Patsy reported back for duty at Liverpool General, but her mind was not really on her work. She wanted to be with Liam. To be at his bedside, to comfort him when he cried, to try and explain the procedures to him when they began his treatment so that he wouldn't be frightened.

He was little more than a toddler; he'd been well loved and cosseted all his life. He was the centre of a warm, loving family, even if they weren't strictly blood relations, and now he was going to have to face this ordeal on his own.

For all his rough and ready ways Joe loved him dearly and Janie and Freddie treated him as they would a little brother. Janie was forever bringing home toys and colouring books for him. Freddie always bought him some sweets or a bar of chocolate when he got his pay packet on a Friday night and sometimes played a game of some kind with him.

Elaine was like a second mother to Liam. She'd fed him, clothed him, played with him, taught him to talk and how to behave. She's done more for him than I have, Patsy thought guiltily.

Was this her punishment for not being a real mother to Liam? Was God punishing her for her sins? She'd never even had Liam christened, but that wasn't because she didn't believe in God, but because she couldn't face Father O'Brian. He'd want to know why she'd neglected her faith and lecture her about falling from a state of Grace.

Going to Mass had been the last thing on Patsy's mind after her dad had died. It had been Billy, not God, who'd come to her aid and made her see sense. It had been sheer hard work, not prayers, that had helped her to pull through and get back on her feet.

If God was all-seeing, as he was supposed to be, then he must know all about that. Anyway, she reminded herself, Jesus had been born in a stable, the same as Liam, so surely he would understand the plight she'd been in.

The Grants weren't Catholics, in fact they didn't seem to go to any sort of church, so how could she expect them to take Liam to Mass every Sunday when she was working?

Even now, with Liam's life in the balance, she didn't feel that prayers would do any good. The right diagnosis, the skill of the doctor who was in charge of his treatment, and the care and ministrations of the nurses looking after him were what would pull him through.

She only wished she could be one of those nurses. The moment the thought came into her head, Patsy wondered if it was at all possible. She said nothing to anyone, but the idea haunted her and went over and over in her mind so often that she decided she would make some enquiries.

She started her quest by finding out as much as she possibly could about the hospital where

Liam had been sent. When she had all the details, and was completely sure about what she intended to do, she told Billy that she was going to find out if she could work as a nurse at the isolation hospital.

His face lit up. 'That's a wonderful idea, Patsy,' he enthused. 'Poor kid, he'll think we've all deserted him. When you're his age, seeing someone for half an hour twice a week is no good. Anyway, waiting from Wednesday to the following Sunday is far too long.'

'Well don't say anything to your mam yet,' she cautioned. 'It may not come off. I've got to find out first if they want any nurses there.'

'It's worth a try. What are you going to do – go over to the hospital and ask?'

'I don't know, I haven't thought that far,' she admitted.

'I'll come over with you, if you like.'

'Thanks, Billy. You might have to wait around for a long time though. The matron, or whoever takes on new staff, mightn't even see me. I might have to go back again another day.'

'That's all right by me. I don't mind waiting. I'm good at it, I've had plenty of practice of hanging around doing nothing,' he added with a wry smile.

Patsy's eyes filled with tears. 'Oh, Billy. I feel awful saddling you and your mam and family with all this trouble.'

'Hey, that will do!' Gently he brushed her tears away then wrapped his arms round her, holding her so close that she could feel the heat of his body.

'No more crying, luv. Right?'

She buried her face against the comforting warmth of his broad shoulder. 'I'm listening and I would like you to come with me. I promise not to break down and cry if they turn me down and send me packing.'

'I wouldn't think they'd do that, not when they know you're a fully trained nurse. You never know, you might be able to arrange for a transfer from the Liverpool General to the Wallasey Isolation Hospital without any trouble at all.'

'Always the optimist, aren't you, Billy?' Patsy said with a smile. 'I don't know where I would be without you!' She kissed his cheek before gently pulling away from him.

'Why don't you start making some enquiries at the isolation hospital when you go over on your first visit there to see Liam next Wednesday?'

'You'll come as well?'

'I've already said so, haven't I? Yes, of course I'll come with you.'

Travelling across on the ferryboat brought back bittersweet memories for both of them. Patsy clutched Billy's hand tightly as they reached the spot on the floating roadway where he had met with his accident.

She was glad they were going to Seacombe and not New Brighton and would be getting a bus from there into the centre of Wallasey where the hospital was.

When they reached mid-river she was unable to resist studying the New Brighton coastline and picking out the familiar landmarks. As she surveyed the huge Tower Building she couldn't help wondering if there was still a circus in the fairground that surrounded it.

She was shaking with nerves by the time they arrived at the hospital.

'Come on, let's visit Liam first and then we'll deal with the other matter afterwards,' Billy told her.

Liam was in a long narrow ward with ground-to-ceiling glass doors that opened on to a stretch of green grass. Although there was quite a keen breeze the doors were wide open.

'He'll catch his death of cold in this place,' Billy commented as he turned up his jacket collar.

'Fresh air is all part of the treatment,' Patsy assured him.

'What, even in winter?'

'So I understand. We'll have to bring him in a woolly hat and some gloves when it gets colder.'

Billy shot her a sideways glance to see if she was smiling and then frowned heavily when he saw she was quite serious.

Liam was so pleased to see them that it brought a lump into Patsy's throat. She made a pretence of putting some of the things she had brought for him into the locker by his bedside so that he wouldn't see the tears in her eyes.

Patsy's heart sank as she looked at his thin little legs and arms. He had always been on the skinny side, but now they were like matchsticks. She found herself wondering why she had never suspected that something was wrong with him when he didn't fill out. He'd been a very small baby, but with all the food Elaine gave him he should have been quite tubby when he reached the toddler stage.

Patsy sighed. She'd always told herself that he was going to be tall and lean like her dad, but she should have known that those characteristics wouldn't have developed until he was entering manhood.

It was no good dwelling on the past, she thought, swallowing back her tears. If she'd made mistakes then she must try and rectify them.

It made her all the more determined to work at the hospital he was in. As a nurse, even if it wasn't on his ward, she would be able to find a way to monitor his progress first hand and to be there to comfort and reassure him while he was undergoing treatment.

Chapter Thirty-One

Patsy found it much easier to transfer from one hospital to the other than she had thought possible.

Not everyone liked the idea of nursing TB patients because of the fear of catching the disease, or infecting someone in their own family, so the isolation hospital was always ready to consider suitable applicants.

A further point that made the transition easy was the fact that the matron at Liverpool General Hospital was not very pleased with the way Nurse Callaghan had been acting over the last few months and was quite relieved to see her go. First of all there had been the summons for Nurse Callaghan to go home in the middle of the day because of a family crisis, followed almost immediately by the necessity of taking her leave early.

According to Sister Pringle, when eventually Nurse Callaghan did return to duty she seemed to have her mind on other things and her work on the ward had suffered because of this. It was only the inconvenience of being short-staffed that had stopped Matron dismissing her right away.

Patsy settled in quickly at the new hospital. She was not working on the children's ward, but hoped that perhaps she would be transferred in the near future. But she managed to see Liam most days, even though sometimes it was from a distance.

She had told no one in the hospital that she was his mother, but being under the same roof as him was comforting even when she wasn't able to sit with him or even speak to him.

Patsy tried to be as discreet as possible, but she suspected that the nurses on the children's ward wondered why she was always pausing by the door. On the first two or three occasions she had explained that she was new to the hospital and had lost her way, but she knew she couldn't go on making such an excuse for ever.

The truth emerged the night after Liam underwent his first major treatment. She had slipped along to his ward late in the evening, at a time when she knew the night staff would have completed their rounds and would be in the staff room, to check if he was all right.

Her heart ached as she saw him lying there awake, and in obvious distress. Before she could help herself she was kneeling at his bedside, stroking his damp hair back from his brow and murmuring words of comfort.

When she tried to leave he clung on to her, sobbing so loudly that the duty nurse came hurrying in to see what was wrong. When she found Patsy at Liam's bedside she demanded to know what was going on. She listened in obvious disbelief as Patsy explained she was Liam's mother. She then insisted that Patsy must leave the ward and said she would have to report the incident to Sister.

Patsy didn't sleep a wink that night. She knew she had broken hospital rules and that there would be trouble the next day. It was no surprise at all when around mid-morning the staff nurse on the ward where she was working told her to report immediately to Matron.

Outside the door to Matron's office, Patsy smoothed down her starched white apron, straightened her white cap and took a deep breath to steady her nerves before she knocked. As she waited nervously for the summons to enter, Patsy braced herself for an onslaught.

She had gone over and over in her mind what she should say and had decided that the truth would carry more weight than any excuses. She was sure that once Matron knew that Liam was her child she would understand her fears and anxiety and why she was constantly hovering near his bedside.

She was quite wrong. Matron was completely unsympathetic.

'You have been trained to look after people who are sick, Nurse Callaghan, not your relations,' she said icily. 'What you have been doing not only transgresses the trust I have placed in you, but is highly unprofessional.'

'Liam is my son, I am terribly concerned about him,' Patsy responded heatedly. 'He is not yet five years old and this is the first time he has been away from his home. I'm not interfering in his treatment in any way.'

'That will do, Nurse Callaghan! I do not consider these to be mitigating circumstances and

I will not enter into any further discussion of the matter. Do you understand?' she added sternly.

Patsy tried to bite back the angry retort that rose to her lips but the words gushed out like a jet of scalding hot water.

'You can't do this, you can't stop me seeing him!' she raged. 'He needs me at his bedside, he needs my reassurance.'

'Nurse Callaghan!' Matron's face was red with anger. 'How dare you dispute my judgement!'

'Liam is a desperately sick little boy and he needs to know that his mother is there near him,' Patsy repeated stubbornly.

'Why should one child receive different treatment from all the others? Have you stopped and considered what it is doing to the other patients to see one small boy getting preferential treatment?'

Too choked to answer, Patsy looked down at her shoes.

'I'm waiting for your answer, Nurse Callaghan,' Matron snapped.

Patsy knew she was defeated. 'I'm sorry, Matron. I won't do it again,' she said meekly.

'You most certainly won't, Nurse Callaghan,' Matron said frostily. 'You are dismissed. I want you off the hospital premises within the hour. Do you understand?'

The colour drained from Patsy's face. 'You can't mean that,' she gasped.

Matron gave her a withering look. 'You should have thought about the consequences before you behaved in such an unprofessional way. Kindly close the door as you leave.'

Patsy went straight from Matron's office to the ward where Liam was. Without asking anyone's permission she walked over to his bed and gave him a big hug.

'Look, luv, I won't be able to see you again until visiting day,' she told him.

He looked crestfallen. 'You said you'd come and kiss me good-night every night while I was in here,' he reminded her.

'I know, pet, but things have changed. I'm not working at this hospital any more. I'll be in to see you on Wednesday though. Who shall I bring with me?'

'Nana said she'd come, and Billy was going to come as well,' he pouted.

'Well so they can.'

'If they come then you won't come.'

'We'll all come,' she promised. 'Billy can pop in for a few minutes and then he'll wait outside while Nana comes in to see you and I'll be here the whole time. How about that?'

Liam's pallid face brightened. 'And will you all bring me something?'

'You'll have to wait and see, won't you,' Patsy smiled, as she hugged and kissed him again.

'Nurse Callaghan, what are you doing here? Matron said you were not to be allowed on this ward except at normal visiting times so will you please leave immediately.'

'I've got to go now, Liam,' Patsy told him, tears trickling down her cheeks. 'I'll see you on Wednesday, I promise.'

When she left the isolation hospital she couldn't bring herself to go back to Paradise Place. How was she to explain to Elaine and Billy what a mess she had made of things?

She walked slowly up Mill Lane to Liscard Road and walked round for almost half an hour staring unseeingly into the shop windows. What was she going to do now? She was out of work at a time when they needed as much money as possible for Liam. When he came out of hospital he would need plenty of nourishing food to build up his strength and she could hardly ask to go back to Liverpool General.

Her feeling of gloom deepened. Perhaps Liam never would come out of hospital. So few children recovered, because they hadn't the stamina to fight the disease or stand up to the long, arduous treatment.

The thought that he might die filled her with even deeper fear. He'd never even met his father! Bruno didn't even know he existed.

She had to do something about that and there was no better time than the present, she decided. She was in Wallasey so she was only a bus ride away from New Brighton. She'd go to the fairground again and this time she would definitely find out what had happened to Bruno. Someone there must know.

The fairground was thronged with people and everything seemed to have changed from when she had last been there. There were far more swings and roundabouts and a great many new sideshows, but there was still no circus.

'Bruno Alvarez? Yes, I remember him,' one of the stall holders told her. 'Tall, dark-haired chap, came from Spain or one of those Mediterranean places. He used to train the lions and big cats. Is that the fellow?'

'Yes,' Patsy agreed eagerly. 'That sounds like Bruno. Can you tell me where I can find him?'

The man pushed his hat back and scratched his head. 'No, not really. He left a few years back, took his animals with him and hasn't been back since.'

'You must know where he went?'

The man scratched his head again. 'Can't say I do, really. There were rumours that he'd gone to Blackpool and then someone said Rhyl and someone else said Morecambe. There's any number of seaside places up and down the coast so he could be at any of them.'

'Thanks.'

'Hold on,' the man said as Patsy turned away. 'There was something that happened the day before he left that might interest you.'

'Go on.'

'Some woman, quite a bit older than him, came here looking for him. She was quite a looker and she had lovely hair. Reddish blonde it was. Bruno seemed a bit surprised to see her, but she grabbed hold of him and began hugging and kissing him and a couple of minutes later he had his arm round her waist and they went off towards his van.'

'Is that all?'

'Well yes. Except that next morning Bruno packed up all his belongings and he and the woman and the animals took off. Like I said, no one's seen or heard of them since.'

'Thanks!' It wasn't what she'd wanted to hear. From the man's description there was very little doubt in her mind who the woman had been.

Patsy felt numb as she left the fairground, wandered out on to the promenade and made her way across to the pier. Leaning on the railings she stared out unseeingly across the choppy waters of the Mersey.

The disappearance of her mother from their house in Paradise Place, and of Bruno from the fairground, had happened about the same time. Linked to what she had just been told the pieces fitted together like a jigsaw. I should have known from the way mam carried on with Bruno when she met him on my sixteenth birthday that she was involved, Patsy thought bitterly.

She had tried to forget about finding them in bed together the next morning. Or the way Bruno had seemed to change towards her immediately afterwards.

She knew now why her mam had given up the house.

Yet, when Mam found out that I was pregnant I told her that it was Bruno's baby, she thought angrily. Even though she knew that she still went away with him. She abandoned me and pinched my boyfriend, knowing I was going to need help from both of them. If it hadn't been for Billy and his family looking after me I would have had no one.

Patsy thought of the countless times he had taken her in his arms and comforted her, and the look in his eyes whenever he'd done so. Above all she remembered his tenderness on the one and only occasion when they'd made love. The more she thought about the way Billy had behaved, his kindness, his steadfastness throughout all her troubles, the more incredible it seemed that he still felt the same way about her.

Billy really must love me a great deal, she thought with astonishment. His feelings for her had withstood the countless difficulties they'd gone through together.

She'd taken him so much for granted. She hadn't treated him anywhere near as well as she should have done. It was something she would always regret, but it wasn't too late to do something about it.

The time had come to admit to him and to herself just how much she cared for him, to openly acknowledge that she loved him.

Filled with a mixture of relief, joy and hope for the future she headed for the nearest bus that would take her back to Seacombe ferry. It would make her journey longer, but she didn't want to catch a boat from New Brighton: the crossing would bring back too many sad memories.

Anyway, there was no immediate hurry. As far as Billy and Elaine knew, she was at work so they wouldn't be expecting her. The longer the journey took, the more time she had to decide what she was going to tell them about losing her job.

The only good thing that she could see coming out of all this was that she would be able to visit Liam regularly every Wednesday and Sunday.

Chapter Thirty-Two

Patsy was so immersed in her misery as she stood leaning on the rail of the ferryboat as it pulled alongside at Liverpool that she didn't notice the young man in grey flannels, brown tweed jacket and brown cap patiently waiting on the slipway.

The gangplank was lowered and she was making her way on to the floating roadway when she was startled by him limping towards her. He grasped her by the arm.

'Where the hell have you been, Patsy? I've met every boat from New Brighton and Seacombe for the past two hours. I thought I must have missed you. I even rushed back to Paradise Place and left messages with everyone I could find to tell you to get back to the hospital as quickly as you could. Then I came back here to the Pier Head to check if you were on any of the boats as they arrived.'

'Billy! What are you doing here? How did you know I was on the way home?'

'We had a policeman call at the house to say they'd had a phone message from the Wallasey Hospital, that's why I'm here. We've been at our wits' end trying to find you.'

Patsy turned a brick red, her green eyes flaming. 'They had no right to do that! My quarrel with the matron was nothing at all to do with you. Why send the police, anyway? What I did wasn't criminal!'

'I don't know what the devil you're on about,' Billy frowned. 'The police came with a message about Liam. They said we ought to go over there right away. When me mam and me got there we couldn't find you and we were told that you had left the hospital.'

'What's happened to him?' she asked anxiously.

'He's much worse. They want us to be with him. Come on.' He turned her round and hurried her back on to the boat she'd just arrived on, which was already preparing to cast off again for a return journey to Seacombe.

Patsy felt numb and then guilty as she listened to Billy's account of what he and Elaine had been told when they reached the hospital.

'They said there had been some sort of disturbance on the ward this morning and that as a result Liam was very upset. It seems he cried so much that it brought on a severe bout of coughing that wouldn't stop. In the end he was coughing up so much blood that they had to take emergency measures.'

'Oh my God!' The colour drained from Patsy's face.

Bill looked puzzled. 'Mam thought you were there at the hospital with him and that you'd been the one to send for us.' He frowned. 'You should have been there. Where were you?'

Patsy ignored his question. 'Liam is going to be all right, isn't he?' she asked anxiously.

'I'm sure he is.' Billy put an arm round her shoulder and hugged her close to him. 'Don't worry, they're doing everything they can for him,' he said confidently, planting a reassuring kiss on the top of her red curls.

Patsy flinched and pulled away. 'I should have been there. He needs me.' She sniffed and dabbed at her eyes. 'Oh, Billy, why does everything always go wrong for me?'

'Don't worry, me mam's there with him,' he reminded her. 'She'll do all she can to comfort him.'

'That's not the point. I'm the one who should be there, I'm his mother,' Patsy insisted angrily. 'What if they told him I was coming to see him and he's been expecting me? He won't understand why I'm not there and he'll be breaking his little heart.'

'Well, there's nothing you can do about it now, Patsy. Neither of us can turn the clock back. What on earth made you leave the hospital in the middle of the morning, anyway? You still haven't told me.'

'I was ordered to leave. I broke the rules. I was caught cuddling Liam when I shouldn't have been anywhere near the ward he's in. I was sent to Matron and when I tried to explain that Liam was my child she dismissed me on the spot and told me to be off the premises within an hour. She said I'd been trained to nurse the sick, not my own family,' she added bitterly.

'What a right cow!' Billy exclaimed indignantly. 'Liam is sick and if he's in hospital then he's a patient, isn't he! And she made you leave right away?'

335

'I was supposed to, but I went back to say goodbye to Liam. I couldn't disappear without trying to explain to him why I wouldn't be seeing him again until Wednesday afternoon.'

'Do you think that's what upset him?'

'I suppose so, but I had no choice, Billy. Sister Beasley who's in charge of that ward insisted I leave immediately. She ranted on and on, saying that I had no right to be there. I know she was only doing what she was told to do,' she added quickly as she saw the anger in Billy's eyes.

'Be that as it may, she could have let you have a few minutes to explain things to him.'

Patsy looked embarrassed. 'I suppose it was my fault for breaking the rules. Liam was awfully upset, though, when I left, poor little luv. That's probably why he was crying so much.'

Billy shook his head in disbelief. He still didn't agree with the treatment that had been meted out to Patsy.

'If you left the hospital before midday why has it taken you three hours to get home?' he asked, frowning.

Patsy shot a sideways glance at Billy, wondering how he'd react if she told him the truth.

'Well?'

'I went to New Brighton to see if I could find any trace of Bruno,' she muttered. 'I thought that since Liam was so ill Bruno ought to know about him. I thought he might even want to come and see Liam.'

Billy's face darkened and his jaw tightened, but he said nothing.

'I didn't find him,' Patsy went on. 'I did manage to get some news about what had happened to him, though.'

'Go on!'

Patsy shook her head. 'I don't want to talk about it.'

'Well I do,' Billy said grimly. 'Now you've told me this much you might as well tell me the rest.'

'He's gone, no one is quite sure where, but . . . he went off with a woman who was older than him. From the description I was given there's no doubt in my mind who it was.'

Billy stared at her, astounded. 'Surely you don't mean . . .'

'Yes, I mean my mam,' she admitted dully. 'I'm not really surprised. In fact, I think I've suspected something like that all along, but I couldn't bring myself to admit it.'

Billy gave a soundless whistle. 'Well, she certainly paid plenty of attention to Bruno the night you brought him over to meet her,' he admitted.

'He stayed the night. I told you that,' Patsy said bitterly. 'He was supposed to be sleeping on the sofa, but I found them in bed together next morning. That must have been the start of it.'

'So that's why she cleared out of the house without a word to anyone!'

Patsy nodded. 'They both did a disappearing act at about the same time.'

Billy placed an arm around Patsy's shoulder. 'That's the end of it then, luv. No more nonsense or dreams about going to live in Spain. The best thing you can do is put all that out of your head and make the most of what you've got here.'

'I know,' Patsy sniffed. 'I've been an idiot, haven't I, Billy?'

'We all have our dreams, Patsy. That's what keeps us going most of the time,' he said stiffly.

She looked up at him questioningly. His face was impassive, but there was such grim sadness registered there that it made her feel guilty about the way she'd treated him over the years.

'You know, Billy, you're really the only true friend I've ever had,' she said thoughtfully. She slipped her hand into his and squeezed it, aware that she would be needing all the warmth and friendship he could offer over the next few days.

When this was all over and Liam was safe and well, she'd do her best to make up to Billy for the way she'd treated him in the past, she resolved. He'd been through so much, especially since his accident, yet he rarely grumbled or complained and he put her and Liam's needs first all the time.

When they arrived at the hospital they were not allowed to go straight to Liam's bedside, but were kept waiting in the reception area. Patsy fretted over the delay and wondered if it was because of what had happened between her and Sister Beasley earlier in the day.

She paced up and down, ignoring Billy's advice to try and be patient for a little longer. She couldn't sit still knowing that Liam was lying so desperately ill somewhere in the building. She wanted to be with him, to do whatever she could to alleviate his pain and misery.

When finally they were told to go to Matron's office instead of to the ward, Patsy felt ready to explode with indignation and frustration. She stalked down the corridor, her head high, anger flaring in her green eyes. Inwardly she was trembling, fear in her heart in case Matron was going to exert her power and not allow her to see Liam after all.

When they entered Matron's office she was surprised to see Elaine was already there. Billy had told her that his mam was with Liam, that he had left her at the bedside.

Patsy's fear escalated. Did this mean that Liam was worse and that he wasn't being allowed visitors at all? Or did it mean they had found it necessary to operate on him and Matron had undertaken personally to explain all this to them?

Patsy looked from Elaine to Matron and back again. Elaine's face was white and drawn, her eyes red-rimmed as though she had been crying copiously. The moment she saw Patsy she burst into choking sobs.

Patsy reached out to take her hand, but Elaine pushed her away. 'Why couldn't you have been here?' she said hoarsely. 'You should have been the one with poor little Liam, not me.'

Stunned by the anger in Elaine's voice, Patsy drew back and looked questioningly at Matron.

Matron, her face expressionless, looked first at Patsy and then at Billy. 'I'm afraid Liam is dead,' she told them crisply.

'Dead?' Patsy shook her head in disbelief. 'He was perfectly all right when I left here this morning,' she said accusingly. 'He was a very sick child, but he wasn't about to die.'

'Liam was very upset, Miss Callaghan, by whatever it was you had said to him when you left. He started crying, which resulted in a severe bout of coughing. In spite of all Sister Beasley and the rest of my staff could do his condition deteriorated rapidly. We sent for you immediately,' she added stiffly.

'He brought up so much blood, Patsy, it was really terrible,' Elaine shuddered. 'There was blood everywhere! His nightclothes and his bedding were soaked in it. I've never seen so much blood in my life.'

Patsy shook her head in disbelief. 'No, it can't be true!' She looked round her wildly. 'Where is he? I want to see my baby!'

'Please calm down, Miss Callaghan. You will be allowed to see him before you leave,' Matron told her coldly.

'It's all your fault that this happened!' Patsy flared up accusingly.

Matron didn't deign to answer. She stretched out a hand and pressed a buzzer on her desk. 'Someone is coming to take you along right now,' she told Patsy calmly. She turned to Elaine. 'Do you wish to see the body again?'

Elaine shook her head; she was trembling so much she couldn't speak.

'Then someone will take you back to reception and you can wait there until the rest of your family have seen the child's body and are ready to leave,' she said dismissively.

Patsy stumbled from the room too numb to make any reply. The words 'see the body' echoed over and over in her head. She couldn't believe that those cold, impersonal words meant Liam. When she'd left the hospital at mid-morning he'd been alive and expressing his love for her with hugs and kisses. She could still feel his warm little body in her arms as she'd held him close.

Now she would never see him again. Never be able to kiss and cuddle him or tell him how much she loved him and how precious he was to her, she thought, distraught, as she and Billy were taken into a small side ward where he was lying. She gazed down at him through a haze of tears. He was so still and white, and his face was so serene, that he looked almost like a china doll.

As Patsy bent to pick him up Sister Beasley placed a restraining hand on her arm and stopped her.

'You may kiss him goodbye, but you know you must not move him,' she reminded her gravely.

Patsy shook her hand away. 'He's still mine, even if you have killed him,' she said bitterly.

'Kiss him goodbye, Patsy, that's all you can do now,' Billy whispered, putting a comforting arm around her shoulders. He leaned forward and placed his own lips against the child's icy brow and then pulled back and waited until Patsy had done the same.

Silently she turned away and Billy led her from the room, back to where Elaine was waiting for them.

Chapter Thirty-Three

Patsy tried desperately to block out all memories of Liam's death and funeral from her mind, but it was impossible. Throughout the day, as well as the moment she closed her eyes at night, she saw again the tiny white coffin with its gleaming brass handles being carried on the shoulders of Billy and Joe Grant to its final resting place.

She had been so distraught over Liam's death that she'd left Billy and his family to arrange the funeral. She couldn't face Father O'Brian knowing how greatly she had sinned. She hadn't been to Mass or even inside his church since Liam was born so she felt it would be hypocritical to ask him to officiate at her child's funeral.

Billy and Joe had done everything and because they weren't Catholics themselves they had gone along with Elaine's suggestion that Liam should be buried in the same plot as her own mother and father. Patsy hadn't argued. She'd felt so numb with pain that she couldn't focus her thoughts to make any decisions. Afterwards she'd felt both sad and guilty because she knew Liam should have been laid to rest alongside her own dad.

It had been a very quiet funeral. Apart from the Grants, no one else attended. Maureen and Megan Murphy and their mother refused to come. They denounced what was happening as blasphemous and told Patsy that Father O'Brian would be horrified when he found out and probably excommunicate her.

The threat of damnation did nothing to ease the bitter sting of Liam's death. As the tiny white coffin was lowered into the ground she had stood there shrinking back into the past, knowing she would never be able to forget that she had been the cause of the upset that had brought about Liam's death. Even worse, she should have been there to hold and comfort him in his final hour, not Elaine.

If she hadn't sneaked in to talk to him none of this might have happened. Liam might still be alive, she told herself over and over again. He would probably still be seriously ill and needing treatment for tuberculosis. It might have taken years of careful nursing before he was completely well, but he would still have been alive.

Afterwards, she lost all track of time, she was so consumed by guilt.

It also troubled her that she had been culpable of negligence when he'd been born because of her own pig-headedness. This, as much as anything else, had probably contributed to the fact that he had always been underweight and small for his age.

If only Liam had been born at home or in a hospital with a midwife, where he would have had the right sort of attention. For him to have been born in a stable with only Billy there to help her had been asking for trouble.

One of the first things she had been taught when she began her training to be a nurse was the need for scrupulous cleanliness. Billy hadn't even been able to wash his hands before he helped to deliver Liam. There had been no fresh water available and not even a clean sheet to wrap the baby in.

If Liam had been taken from the stable into normal surroundings right away he might have stood a better chance. His earliest days, when he was most vulnerable to infection, had been spent lying in a makeshift cot with only a Valor oil stove for heating and with Samson standing in a corner breathing the same air as him.

She kept the guilt and misgivings to herself, constantly mulling them over, knowing she was the one who must shoulder the blame. To talk about them to Billy or Elaine would be to heap recriminations on them and that would be unjust. Billy would feel he should have done more when Liam had been born. Elaine might think that she hadn't looked after Liam as well as she might have done while he was in her care.

Patsy didn't want either of them to think that these things were true. The blame, and she felt there was plenty of it, lay on her shoulders. She was the one who was at fault, not them. All the Grants, even Joe, had done their utmost for Liam, certainly far more than her own mam had done.

Thinking about her mam made Patsy's blood boil and resentment rise up inside her. How could her mother have been so callous as to turn her out into the street when she found out she was pregnant? Even after all this time it seemed unbelievably harsh.

Patsy still found it hard to accept that her own mam should connive to steal Bruno away from her, especially after she'd told her that Bruno was the father of the baby she was carrying. I'd even told her that Bruno was going to marry me and that when the season ended we were going back to his home in Spain together, she thought bitterly.

She was glad her mam had left Paradise Place and hoped she would never have to face her again.

Perhaps she had done the right thing, Patsy reflected. Paradise Place had not brought either of them any great happiness or contentment. Maybe I should do the same, she thought wryly. Leave Paradise Place and all its bittersweet memories behind and go somewhere where I'm not known and start afresh.

She was a trained nurse so surely she would find it easy enough to find work somewhere away from Liverpool and make a completely new life for herself?

There was only one thing which made her hesitate to take such a radical step and that was leaving Billy behind. He had been so good to her, so caring, the greatest friend she'd had throughout all her troubles. Now, when he had problems of his own it seemed heartless to walk away and leave him.

Since his accident he had not found any kind of permanent work. He was still young and good looking, but his damaged leg was a tremendous handicap. He would always have a limp and when he was tired or not feeling very well the limp became much more pronounced.

Patsy walked round for days in a complete daze trying to decide about her future. She longed to discuss it, to talk her ideas through with someone, but she didn't feel there was anyone she could confide in.

Elaine was as heartbroken as she was. Patsy knew she'd have loved to have been able to openly claim Liam as her grandson. Several times she had pointed out that he had a tiny birthmark at the base of his spine and that Billy had one in exactly the same place, as though that might prove he was Billy's child.

Elaine's grieving took the form of cleaning the house from top to bottom and washing everything in sight. She seemed to resent anyone at all being in the house so Patsy had taken to wandering round the town, staring unseeingly into shop windows.

She missed Samson. She'd found him a wonderful source of comfort when she had problems. She had always talked to him while she groomed him and his companionable snorts, or friendly head butts, had so often inspired the resolution of any uncertainties she had.

She knew Billy was grieving over Liam yet neither of them could talk about it to each other. It had become a taboo subject. After the funeral Billy went his way and she went hers. It was almost as if they were deliberately avoiding each other. The only time they were in the same room together was at mealtimes and more often than not Billy was absent from these. Elaine would cover his dinner over with a plate and leave it in the oven to keep warm so that he could have it whenever he came home.

Patsy had no idea where he went; nor did anyone else. He looked so haggard and had lost so much weight that she felt concerned about his health.

Joe still dropped into the Grafton on his way home, and very often he and Billy met up in there and came home together.

The fact that Billy seemed to be going for a beer regularly worried Patsy because he never had been much of a drinker. In moderation having a beer didn't matter, but Patsy was concerned in case drinking was becoming his way of coping with his grief.

Janie and Freddie were upset by what had happened. They had both been very fond of Liam too. They were young and leading full and busy lives, though, so the bonds between them and Liam were nowhere near as strong or as binding.

Patsy felt that perhaps if they all talked about Liam more, instead of shying away from even mentioning his name, then she and Billy as well as Elaine and Joe would come to terms with their loss much better.

Perhaps she was the one who must act first, Patsy thought. She wondered if she went to Liam's graveside and spent some time there whether she would find peace. She hadn't been near his grave since the day of the funeral because it was in the graveyard of a Protestant church, which she'd been brought up to think of as a place she mustn't go.

Now, as she made her way there, and walked between the long rows of gravestones to the spot where Liam had been buried, she thought how stupid it was to have let such a trivial reason prevent her from coming before.

When she reached the newly formed grave she was surprised to see that a little headstone had been erected and that the ground around the grave had been carefully tended.

Even on this point, I've failed him, she thought bitterly as she knelt down beside the mound of freshly raked earth. Someone else has done what I should have been doing and they've cared for him in death more than I have.

The tears which seemed to have dried up since the day of the funeral flowed down her cheeks. She made no attempt to stop them, for they brought such a wonderful feeling of relief.

As she placed on the grave the carousel her father had bought for her when she'd been only a child herself she told herself that this was to be her final farewell both to Liam and to everything that had ever happened before in her life.

It was time to move on, perhaps to leave Paradise Place for ever.

Chapter Thirty-Four

Patsy was still kneeling at the side of Liam's grave, tears trickling unchecked down her cheeks, when Billy found her.

'I've been looking for you. I thought I might find you here,' he said gently, crouching down beside her and placing his arm around her shoulders.

Patsy half turned and buried her face against his shoulder. 'I sometimes think you must be my guardian angel,' she sobbed. 'You're always around when I need you most.'

He held her in silence for a few moments, until her sobs quietened. Then very gently he pulled away and dabbed at her eyes with his handkerchief.

'Come on, let's take a little walk, shall we? It's sometimes easier to talk when you are on the move. There's a great deal I want to say to you, Patsy.'

Stiffly she rose to her feet, her eyes still on the tiny grave.

'Where did I go wrong, Billy?' she pleaded, looking up into his face.

'I don't think you went wrong, it was the way things happened,' he said gently.

She shook her head. 'It's more than that. Things

349

don't simply happen. You do things that make them come about and if you make the wrong decision, go down the wrong path, then that's when things start to go wrong.'

He looked at her despairingly, shaking his head in protest.

'You couldn't have done anything any different, Patsy,' he told her gravely. 'It wasn't your fault that your dad had an accident, it wasn't even his. The weather that day was treacherous and as a result there was a mishap.'

'And your accident? That was my fault now, wasn't it?' she asked sadly.

'No, of course it wasn't. How could it be your fault that poor old Samson had a heart attack? If anything, it was mine for overloading the cart.'

'You wouldn't have done that if I'd been there. You were working on your own and struggling to save time by trying to carry two loads in one journey.'

Billy shook his head. 'I don't think that was the problem at all. You might just as well say that the relief horse I hitched on to help Samson up the slipway didn't pull as well as he should and that Samson had to take the full brunt of the load and that was what did his heart in.'

Patsy sighed. 'Yes, Samson wasn't at his peak, was he?' she said thoughtfully. 'And that *was* my fault,' she added stubbornly. 'He hadn't been exercised or taken out of the stable for a week and he was used to going out every day except Sunday.'

'Think that if you like,' Billy said, 'but it's a load of nonsense. He was getting on in years. He had to die some time, we all do. It was just bad luck that he fell over sideways and I was trapped underneath.'

'If I'd been on the run with you that day, as I usually was, then I would have been the one leading him, not you,' Patsy pointed out.

Billy gave a forced laugh. 'Yes, you might have been! So think yourself lucky that it wasn't you!'

'Don't you understand, I can't think like that?' Patsy fumed. 'I feel guilty because in a way it was my fault. If I'd been there you wouldn't have been injured.'

Billy shrugged his shoulders dismissively. 'Well, that's the luck of the draw now, isn't it. Call it Fate or what you will, it's something we have no control over so there's no point in worrying about it.'

'I can't help worrying because as a result of what happened you're lame in one leg and you've been out of work ever since.'

'I earn a crust now and again,' he joked. 'Anyway, in the last few years you've stumped up more than your fair share towards the house-keeping, Patsy. All the money handed over to my mam goes into the same pot, you know.'

'You, your mam and your entire family have been so good to me, Billy, that I'll never be able to repay you all. The way you helped to look after little Liam was wonderful.'

Billy's face clouded. 'My mam is taking it pretty hard not having Liam around, you know. She doesn't say very much about it, but I know it's cut her to the quick. Having a baby in the house to look after gave her a new lease of life.'

'I don't think she'd have been able to cope with him though if you hadn't been there to help keep an eye on him,' Patsy said thoughtfully. 'Once he started walking he was quite a handful, wasn't he?'

'That's true enough,' Billy smiled. 'He could move like greased lightning. I'm going to miss him as well. I'll have to find another way of filling in my time now.'

'So have you any plans about what you are going to do in the future, Billy? Is it worth trying to start up the haulage business again?'

He shrugged. 'I don't know. Times are changing so rapidly that there's not much point in buying another horse. That sort of transport is finished. Whenever I go down to the docks it seems to me that more and more of the haulage firms are using lorries.'

'I suppose you could get a job driving one of those?' Patsy said tentatively.

'No!' Billy said firmly. 'I have thought about it, but I can't face up to learning to drive a lorry. I don't think I'd make a very good job of it with my gammy leg.'

'You don't know until you give it a try.'

He grinned dismissively. 'That's enough about me, what about you? Are you going to carry on nursing?'

'I don't know. Some days when I remember how much I enjoyed working at the Liverpool General I can't wait to be back nursing. Then, when I think about Liam dying, I never want to go inside a hospital ever again. I think I'd be much better off packing it all in and doing something completely different.'

'I can understand you having doubts,' Billy agreed, 'only it seems a pity to throw away all that training, doesn't it?'

'I don't know, Billy.' Patsy's voice wobbled and tears once more began to trickle down her cheeks. 'If only I didn't feel so guilty about Liam it would be easier to make my mind up, perhaps. I keep wondering if I should leave Paradise Place, go right away from Liverpool like my mother's done, and start afresh. If I did that then I might manage to shake off all the bad luck I seem to be having.'

'You haven't really had all that much bad luck,' Billy protested.

She looked sceptical. 'I haven't?'

'No more than most people,' he muttered.

'How can you say that? Unless, of course, you agree that all the bad things that have happened to me are my own fault.'

'No, I'm not saying that, but it's too late to change anything that's happened. Life's too short to worry about the past. You're young and healthy so think of the future.'

'At the moment I can only think about the past,' Patsy said ruefully. 'Every minute of the day and night I blame myself for Liam's death.'

Billy looked angry. A muscle twitched at the side of his face. 'That's absolutely ridiculous!' he fumed.

She shook her head emphatically. 'No, it's not. If Liam hadn't been born in a stable, if I hadn't refused to let you fetch a doctor, if I had done something about moving him into a proper house instead of insisting upon hiding out in the stable after he was born . . .'

'Hey, stop it!' Billy exclaimed in alarm. 'You did what you thought was right at the time, remember! We both did. Bear in mind that I went along with your decisions. If you think for one minute that you are responsible for what happened to Liam then I'm just as guilty and I refuse to accept that.'

'Oh, Billy!' Patsy stopped walking and turned towards him imploringly, a haunted look in her green eyes. 'What would I do without you?'

'Hey! Steady on, you know I'm always around if you want a friendly shoulder to lean on.'

'I want more than that,' she whispered contritely.

'What do you mean?'

'Oh, Billy! I've been such a fool. All the heartache I must have caused you because I've always refused to recognise my feelings for you.' She held up a hand as he made to speak. 'Let me finish,' she begged softly. 'I want you to know that I do love you very, very deeply. I think I always have, but I wouldn't admit it even to myself. I was infatuated by Bruno, but I know now that was all it was. He was larger than life with his foreign charm and glamorous uniform and job. I was just a fling for him, but pride wouldn't let me admit that. What I feel for you, Billy, is something quite different. It's a deep, tender feeling that grows stronger every day.'

Billy drew her into his arms, burying his face in her bright red curls. 'What would we do without each other, Patsy?' He sighed. 'You didn't really mean it when you said you were thinking of leaving Paradise Place, did you?'

'I certainly have thought about it a number of times,' she admitted. 'Some day, I suppose, I might find the courage to move away from Paradise Place and all its harowing memories, but I'm not sure I'd have the guts to do it on my own. Would you come with me?'

Billy's eyes were thoughtful as they held hers in a long, steady gaze. 'I think you should remember, Patsy, that Paradise Place has made both of us what we are and we belong here,' he told her solemnly.

'Maybe, but what sort of a life is it going to provide us with in the future?' she asked bleakly.

He looked at her earnestly. 'If you promise to stick around then I'll tell you about the plan I've been mulling over,' he offered.

Her face brightened. 'Go on! I'll tell you if I'll stay when I hear what your plan is, so it had better be something special.'

He pushed back his cap and ran his hand over his thick hair. 'I don't really know how to start,' he admitted.

'I'm waiting! It had better be good. And don't forget, I haven't made that promise yet,' she said teasingly.

'Right!' He hesitated as if searching for the right words. 'Well, I'm thinking of opening a shop in Paradise Place. The sort of place that sells all sorts of household item. Everything from coal and firewood to pots and pans, from cutlery to ladders and paint, even tools like hammers and saws . . .'

'You mean a hardware shop and chandlers combined?' Patsy interrupted.

'Yeah! Something like that. A place where local people can buy anything and everything they might need for their home. What do you think of the idea?'

'The idea's great. Do you think you'd be able to manage to run it on your own?'

Billy ran his hand through his hair again. 'That might be a problem. I'd probably need someone to help me,' he admitted.

Patsy nodded. 'It would need to be someone that you know you can work side by side with,' she said with a knowing smirk.

'You think so? Well, do you know anyone at all who might be suitable for the job?' he asked, trying not to smile.

'I do, but only if it was a proper partnership you were offering. It would have to be legally binding, not simply a handshake.'

He looked at her, bewildered, then his eyes blazed with anticipation. 'Do you mean what I think you mean?' he asked cautiously.

'Depends what you think that is.'

'That you're interested not only in the business proposition, but that you're willing to marry me?'

Patsy gave an emphatic nod. 'If it can be arranged?'

He grabbed hold of her, smiling, hugging her enthusiastically. 'Oh, Patsy! My darling Patsy. You have no idea how often I've wanted to ask you to marry me. I've loved you ever since the first day

I came to work for your dad. I watched you grow up, more beautiful every day and I vowed that one day, when you were old enough, I would ask you to marry me.'

'So why didn't you?' she said wistfully.

'I was afraid to ask in case you refused me.'

'I suppose there was a time when I might have done so,' she admitted, 'but that was in the distant past.'

'So what changed your mind? Has it anything to do with the fact that you know Bruno will never come back?' he asked in a grim voice.

She shook her head. 'No, it's because at long last I have grown up. I have always realised that you are the most wonderful person I've ever known,' she added with a warm smile.

He held her face between his hands and kissed her tenderly. 'My sweet, precious Patsy. You are all I've ever wanted and now that I know that wish has come true I'm the happiest man alive.'

'So we can both make our fresh start right here in Paradise Place,' she smiled. 'We know we can work well together so you can open your shop and we'll work in it side by side.'

'Oh, Patsy, you've made me so happy. It's more than I dared to dream about!'

'It will be a joint venture,' she agreed softly.

'And a success because of my wonderful, beautiful partner,' Billy told her.

Patsy sighed. It would be a fresh start for both of them, but especially for her, she thought contentedly.

As they went to tell Elaine and Joe Grant of

their plans, Patsy felt an almost unbearable excitement about their hopes.

Yet, even though she and Billy were to be married and some day, in the not too distant future, there would be another baby, she would never forget baby Liam or stop grieving for him, she thought wistfully. Liam would always have a very special corner in her heart.

If you enjoyed *Patsy of Paradise Place* why not try Rosie Harris's gripping new novel . . .

ONE STEP FORWARD

Ever since she was eight years old, Katie Roberts has dreamed of getting away from the Cardiff slums where she lives.

When she is only a girl, her handsome but wicked father, Lewis, is imprisoned for theft leaving Katie and her mother homeless and penniless. Life is hard for Katie – not only because of their poverty but also because of the stigma of her father's shame.

When Lewis is released years later, it seems that life must improve. But to Katie's horror, it becomes worse than she has ever known it. When she and her father are left alone together, Katie seeks happiness and love elsewhere but, as she struggles to make a new life for herself, there is difficulty and danger at every turn . . .

Read on for an extract . . .

Chapter One

Eight-year-old Katie Roberts struggled to her feet and wiped away the tears streaming from her big grey eyes with the back of her hand. She would remember September 1926, and starting school in Tiger Bay, for the rest of her life.

Her long fair hair was caked with mud and there was a cut on one cheek of her heart-shaped face. Her white pinny was stained with grass and mud, her blue cotton dress was torn and there were angry red patches on her arms where the other three children had seized hold of her and forced her face down onto the ground.

Around her mouth were cuts and grazes where one of the boys had forced a handful of grass, flower heads and mud between her lips.

'Don't cry, you're all right now!'

Although her lip was bleeding she tried to smile as she looked gratefully at Aled Phillips, the gangly older boy who had rescued her from her tormentors.

Inwardly she was shaking with fear. Ever since she and her mother had come to live in Tiger Bay a month ago her whole life had changed and most of the time she felt lost and forlorn.

She thought back with deep longing to the time when her entire universe had been her home in

Catherine Street, where she and her mam and dad had lived with her nana, Sian Roberts.

In those halcyon days, life had revolved around Katie's needs, her likes and dislikes. Nana Roberts had always been petting her, asking her what she wanted to do, or what she would like to eat. She had cared for her, cuddled her, taken her out to the park or to the shops, read stories to her and sung her to sleep at night for as long as Katie could remember.

There had never been any loud voices or harsh words when she'd lived in Catherine Street, not until the day the police had come and taken her father away.

That was when everything had started to change.

They claimed that Lewis Roberts had been stealing but Nana Roberts declared that was nonsense. Why should he steal when he had everything he wanted?

Sometimes Katie found it hard to remember exactly what he looked like. At other times she could see him clearly, as if he was standing right beside her; a handsome, stocky-built man with grey eyes and a square chin, a glass of beer in one hand and a cigarette in the other.

When she'd been very small he used to carry her on his wide shoulders all the way from Catherine Street to Roath Park. She remembered how she used to cling onto his shock of black hair, scared she was going to fall off because he walked so fast.

She hadn't seen him since the two policemen

came hammering on the front door, but Nana Roberts told her he'd been sent to prison and wouldn't be coming home again for ages and ages.

Her mam had cried for days, bringing out huge blotchy red lumps on her face. She kept saying she really hated him for the disgrace he'd brought down on their heads, and that she would never be able to show her face outside again.

Nana Roberts had tut-tutted a lot as if she was going over and over everything in her head. Sometimes her lined face had looked so sad that Katie had cried as well. Not harsh, ugly, choking sobs like her mam made, but snuffly mewing sounds just to show how much she cared.

She'd expected Nana Roberts to pick her up and cuddle her and feed her sweets to make everything better, but she'd simply ignored her. Then, a few weeks after her dada had been taken away, Nana Roberts had gone upstairs and shut herself in her bedroom.

Hours later, when her mother told her to go and tell nana to come down and have a cup of tea she'd found her sprawled on the bed, her face a funny grey colour. She'd tried to waken her, but even though she'd shaken her arm and tugged at her black skirt, Nana Roberts had gone on sleeping.

Katie knew something was wrong so she'd gone back downstairs and tried to tell her mam, but Rachael had been too immersed in her own grief to take any notice. It was almost dark before Katie managed to get her mam to go upstairs to see what was wrong with Nana Roberts. And by then it was too late.

Her mam started screaming, rushed down the stairs and banged on the front door of the house next door, gabbling so hysterically that Stan Parsons couldn't make head or tail of what she was saying. He'd called out to his wife, Mona, and the pair of them went upstairs to Nana Roberts's bedroom to find out for themselves what had happened.

Katie watched in terrified silence as Mona held the hand mirror to Nana Roberts's mouth and then shook her head sadly when nothing happened. Not a single blur appeared on the shining surface, only a reflection of Nana Roberts's small round face with her eyes tight shut and her grey hair drawn back into a tight bun on top of her head.

Stan Parsons went for an ambulance, but when it arrived the men didn't even bother to carry Nana Roberts downstairs and put her into it.

'She's dead, mun! Looks like a heart attack. Been gone for hours, I'd say. Left it a bit late, like, to send for us, didn't you?'

Katie's mam had looked bewildered. 'I . . . I didn't know there was anything wrong,' she whispered.

'Not been having a barney, the two of you, then?'

Her mam had shaken her head. 'No, nothing like that. She did have something of an upset a couple of weeks back, mind.'

'Oh yes?' The ambulance man looked at her questioningly.

'Bit of bad news, like, about her son,' Rachael said evasively. 'Upset her a lot, there's no doubt about that.'

'Better send for your doctor,' the ambulance man advised. 'No point in us taking the old lady to hospital when she's been dead for hours now, is there?'

That was when everything seemed to get really bad. There were people coming and going to the house for several days after that, Katie remembered.

The doctor had come right away with his black bag, and a stethoscope dangling around his neck like a necklace. He hurried upstairs with her mam and they'd shut the door, so she could only sit on the stairs and wait and wonder what was going on.

A little while later Father Patrick came, rosary beads in hand and an elaborate stole draped over his black vestments. She and her mam followed him upstairs and they'd all spent a long time in Nana Roberts's room saying prayers, mostly *Our Father* and *Hail Mary* over and over again.

The next day, two men in black brought a shiny wooden box and stood it on the big table in the best room. Her mam said it was a coffin and that they were going to put Nana Roberts in it so that she could go on sleeping peacefully for as long as she liked.

Later in the week, a horse wearing black feathers on its head and pulling a long carriage with glass sides stopped outside the house. Her mam said it was the hearse and that it had come to take Nana Roberts, and all the flowers that friends and neighbours had brought along, to the church for Nana Roberts's funeral.

Katie didn't like that part at all. Even though it was a warm summer day she'd had to wear a black dress, shiny black shoes and long white socks, and her long fair hair had been tied back with a black ribbon.

Her mam had been wearing black as well. With her shining fair hair and slim figure she'd looked lovely, even though her face had been sad and there were tears in her eyes. They'd sat in the front pew in church, which was full of Nana's friends and people who lived nearby. Father Patrick said special prayers and lots of things about Nana Roberts that she didn't understand.

Then they'd all gone along to the cemetery and Father Patrick had said more prayers as the men who were carrying her nana's coffin lowered it down into a big hole.

Her mam had thrown some earth down onto the coffin and she'd been told to do the same. She had shaken her head and hidden behind her mam. She didn't want to throw dirt down onto it because she knew Nana Roberts wouldn't have liked that one little bit! She felt angry that her mam had done it, even though Father Patrick had done the same.

Nana Roberts always liked things to be spick and span. She hated dust, cobwebs and dirt of any kind. She liked everywhere to be scrubbed spotless and polished until you could see your face in it. She always put old newspapers down on the floors when it was raining so that no dirt was walked indoors.

Katie hadn't wanted to come away and leave Nana Roberts there. She'd be so lonely all on her own, she reasoned. Anyway, how were they going to manage without her? She was always in charge of everything at home. She was the one who laid down the law and made all the rules. It was Nana Roberts, not her mam, who did all the cooking and the baking. It was Nana Roberts she turned to when she wanted something, so she knew she was going to miss her something terrible.

They'd left all the lovely flowers and wreaths behind in the cemetery. Her mam said that after the men had filled in the grave they'd pile them all on top of it. Her mam promised they'd both come back the next day and make sure they were arranged properly.

Katie had thought that meant things would go back to normal after they'd made sure the flowers were all in the right place. She knew the house would seem empty without Nana Roberts bustling around with her duster and polish, but she thought that perhaps her mam would do all those sort of things instead.

It hadn't been like that at all. Next morning her mam had said they had to start packing. At first she'd been quite excited because she thought they were going on holiday. She remembered when Nana Roberts had taken her to Swansea and they'd stayed in a boarding house for a whole week. It had been wonderful! She'd been able to play on the sand, building sandcastles with her bucket and spade, and she had gone paddling in the sea until the water came right up over her knees.

It wasn't going to be like that at all this time.

She couldn't believe it when her mam said they were packing because they were leaving Catherine Street and never coming back.

'Where are we going, then?'

'I'm not sure yet, cariad. We have to find somewhere cheaper to live. This was Nana Roberts's house, see, and now the landlord wants us out.'

'Why?'

'Someone else is coming to live here.'

Katie felt bewildered. 'Why don't we want to live here anymore?' she asked.

Her mam hugged her. 'We do, cariad, but we can't afford the rent. Your poor mam hasn't any money. Nana Roberts was the one who paid all the bills, even before your dada went to prison. Now we've got no money coming in at all, not even money to buy food. That's why we'll have to move out of this lovely house and find a cheap room somewhere. I'm going to have to get a job, cariad.'

As she piled all her clothes, dolls and toys into one of Nana Roberts's big suitcases, Katie pursed her little rosebud mouth and frowned. It didn't make any sense at all to her. Why did they have to move? If her mam was going to go out to work then why couldn't they pay rent like Nana Roberts had done and stay where they were?

She tried to ask her mam about this, but Rachael was too worried to listen, let alone give her an answer.

'You go and pack your dolls. I'll explain everything to you later, I've far too much to do now,' she said rather crossly. 'There's a man coming here later on this morning to tell me how much he will give me for Nana Roberts's furniture and I want to make sure everything is ready for him.'

'I've already done that!' Katie told her. She sat on the windowsill and watched as her mother emptied out all Nana Roberts's clothes from the big mahogany chest of drawers and from the cupboards and drawers in the matching dressing table.

'Can I look at Nana's jewels?' she asked plaintively.

'Yes, if you want to. Make sure you don't drop any of them on the floor, though, or put them down anywhere and forget them. I'm taking those to the pawnbroker later on to see what he will give me for them.'

Katie picked up the handsome walnut box with its elaborate gold leaf decoration that had been Nana Roberts's pride and joy, and scrambled up onto the bed with it. Carefully she turned the little gold key. As she opened back the lid, displaying the assortment of rings, brooches and necklaces inside, she looked at her mam accusingly. 'Are you going to sell all of Nana Roberts's jewels?' she frowned.

Rachael pushed her straggling blonde hair back behind her ears and her hazel eyes were clouded with unhappiness as she nodded. 'Yes, cariad,' she sighed. 'We'll need every penny to get by on for the next few weeks until I find some work, so I'm afraid they'll have to go.'

'Every single one of them?' Katie persisted.

Rachael nodded, then hesitated. 'Well, perhaps

you could keep just one piece. You decide which one you like the best.'

'They're all lovely!'

'I know that, but we need the money. No more arguing. If you can't decide which piece you want then I shall sell them all.'

While her mother polished the furniture to make sure it was looking its very best, Katie spread out all the pieces of jewellery and looked at each one of them very carefully, trying to make up her mind which one she liked the most.

She was still sitting on the windowsill doing this when the man who was to buy the furniture arrived. She felt the tears in her eyes as she saw the horse and cart with two men on it stop outside. A rough looking man in brown cord trousers, brown tweed jacket and wearing a greasy brown cap, jumped down and walked to their door.

He knocked so loudly that Rachael almost jumped out of her skin. Then she smoothed back her untidy hair, straightened her apron and went to open the door.

Jake Adcock was a burly man with small sharp eyes and a heavy moustache, which he kept stroking as if it helped him to think. He pawed over the furniture, sniffing and stroking his moustache, and pushing his cap back on his head as if he couldn't make up his mind whether to buy the pieces or not.

Rachael followed him from room to room, nervously rolling the edge of her apron between her fingers. She kept opening her mouth to speak, then closing it again and chewing on her lower lip as if afraid she might say something to upset him or put him off the deal.

'Look yer, missus, it's a load of terribly old stuff you got here,' Jake Adcock told her. 'Worn out most of it! Not sure if I want to take it off your hands or not.'

'It's been very well looked after,' Rachael told him timidly. 'And it was top quality when my mother-in-law bought it.'

He pushed his cap back and scratched his head. 'That was a long time ago though, wasn't it, missus?'

Rachael nodded but didn't answer.

'Tell yer what, I'll give you twenty pounds for the lot, and I won't charge yer anything for taking it all away. How's that?'

Rachael looked shocked. Her thin downturned mouth quivered and she looked so worried that Katie jumped down off the windowsill and went over and clung to her arm.

Rachael looked down at her and then hugged her close.

'I was expecting a lot more than that,' she told Jake Adcock in a strained voice. 'It's all me and my little girl will have to live on until I can find work.'

Jake Adcock pulled at the ends of his droopy moustache. 'I'm being generous, missus, but if yer want to try someone else then it's up to you.'

Rachael felt undecided about what to do. She knew he was cheating her. She was sure that if Lewis had been there he would have managed to get twice that amount for his mother's belongings.

Katie sidled away and went back to the

windowsill. She didn't like this man one little bit and she certainly didn't like the horrible things he was saying about Nana Roberts's furniture.

Jake Adcock's eyes followed her as she began picking up the rings and brooches she'd been looking at and putting them back into the jewellery box.

"Course, if you've got anything else yer want to sell, missus, then I might be able to do yer a better deal.'

Rachael shook her head. 'That is everything she left. Except her clothes.'

'I suppose I could give yer a few bob for those,' he said reluctantly, 'though if they're anything like the furniture they'll only be good for the rag and bone man. Isn't there any jewellery? Rings, and bits and bobs of that sort?'

Katie tried to push the rings and brooches she was sorting through under her skirt out of sight, but he'd already seen them and his eyes were glistening greedily.

'There's a few pieces, but I didn't think you'd be interested in things of that sort. I . . . was going to keep them, or perhaps sell them later on.'

Jake Adcock shrugged. 'It's up to you, missus, but if it's now yer wanting money then I'd do yer a better deal than old Manny the pawnbroker, mind. Right twisting old tyke he is and no mistake. Shall I take a look and see what you've got to offer?'

Rachael shivered. She felt so completely out of control. She needed money now, enough to pay for a room for the two of them and keep them in food for at least a couple of weeks until she could find herself a job.

'Yes, I suppose you could look at them,' she agreed cautiously. She took a deep breath and looked Adcock straight in the eye. 'They're good pieces, all of them, mind. I won't be selling unless you make me a decent offer.'

Adcock placed his hand on his wide barrel chest. 'Cross my heart, missus, I'll be as generous as a man can be.'

'Katie, bring that box of nana's things over here,' Rachael told her.

'Yes, Mam.' Katie hesitated for a moment then scrabbled all the pieces she'd been looking at together and pushed them into the box higgledy-piggledy. She didn't stop to lay each one in its own little velvet nest because she didn't want them to look nice, she didn't want this horrible man to take them away.

Jake Adcock's eyes gleamed avariciously as he sorted through the contents of the jewellery box, but when he looked up his face was dour and he was pulling at the ends of his moustache as if he wasn't sure what to do.

'Another fiver for the clothes and bedding and another fiver for this lot, how about that?'

'No!' cried Katie. 'They're worth tons more than that! They're worth a fortune! My nana called them her Crown Jewels.'

Jake Adcock scowled at Katie, frightening her so much that she felt tears stinging her eyes.

'Mrs Roberts always did say they were all valuable pieces,' Rachael agreed.

'Duw anwyl! Yer a hard woman to deal with,' Jake Adcock muttered. 'Tell you what, missus. Seeing as how I'm kind-hearted and can see you're in a spot of trouble, I'll make my offer up to fifty pounds. That's my final offer, mind. Fifty pounds and that includes everything in the house!' He gave a deep belly laugh. 'No wonder they call me generous Jake. Fool to myself, I am.'

'Very well then.' Rachael made her voice casual.

Fifty pounds! It seemed like a fortune and far more than she had expected. With fifty pounds she'd not only be able to pay a month's rent in advance on a cheap furnished room, but she'd have enough left over to feed them for three or four weeks as well. By then she would have found a job and they'd have no worries.

Katie watched wide-eyed as the man called out to the lad he'd left outside holding the horse and the two of them began moving the furniture out and piling it on the cart.

He left the jewellery box until last and he tucked this under his arm after he'd counted out a pile of dirty notes and handed them to Rachael.

'Right, that's it then. Good luck to yer, missus.' He doffed his cap and made for the door before Rachael could even count her money.

Katie looked around the bare rooms. Every step she took echoed and she wondered where they would be sleeping that night now that all the beds and blankets had gone. There wasn't even a kettle left on the hob or a cup in the kitchen cupboards. Jake Adcock had stripped the house bare.

'Come on, Katie,' Rachael held out Katie's coat for her to put on. 'We'd best be going.'

'Yes, Mam.' Katie fastened up her coat then stooped down and opened up one of the suitcases.

'Come on, girl, what do you think you are doing? If we go now, before the rent man comes, that will be one less thing to pay out for and he'll never find us once we've left Catherine Street.'

'I want to put these in my suitcase, Mam,' she giggled, as she fished a ring and two brooches out of her knicker leg, 'they're scratching my botty.'

'Katie! Where did those come from, they're out of Nana Roberts's jewellery box!' Rachael exclaimed in shocked tones.

'You said I could keep whichever one I liked best. And I liked all of these.'

Rachael regarded her severely for a minute then she burst out laughing.

'Fair-dos', I suppose,' she said as she shrugged on her coat and pulled her blue cloche hat well down on her ears. 'What Jake Adcock didn't see and doesn't know about he'll never miss, will he!'

Looking for Love

For Pamela, Jenny and Jill

Acknowledgements

My sincere thanks to Caroline Sheldon, Georgina Hawtrey-Woore, Justine Taylor, Sara Walsh and everyone else at Random House who have been so helpful and supportive.

Chapter One

Abbie Martin knew she ought to be in bed and asleep, but tomorrow, Sunday, would be the 18th July 1926, and it would be her eleventh birthday, and she couldn't sleep for worrying about whether or not she would be getting the wooden hoop she'd set her heart on. If she didn't get one this year then she'd be too old to have one at all.

Her friend Sandra Lewis, who lived in the same street, had a lovely red hoop, and Abbie had begged her mammy to buy her a blue one. Then, when they played together, they wouldn't have to take it in turns to share Sandra's. They'd be able to run races or bowl them along side by side and pretend they were riding bikes or that they were sitting alongside one another in a posh motor car.

'You can think yourself lucky if you get a new pair of shoes for your birthday,' her mammy had said caustically. 'We've not got money to waste on rubbish like hoops. It's all right for Sandra, her dad's in regular work and so is her mam.'

'I wish my dad would come home,' Abbie murmured wistfully.

'What dad?' Ellen Martin snapped. 'You never even knew the bugger. One look at you and he was off! He skedaddled when you were only a couple of days old. He said he was off to join the

1

Army and that was the last any of us ever heard of him.'

'Father Patrick said he still might come back one day, if we all pray hard enough,' Abbie said, her lower lip trembling.

'Shurrup with your daft talk!' Ellen's mouth tightened and the wrinkles around her dull brown eyes increased. 'He's gone for good, and after all this time I wouldn't even give him house room if he came home and stood on the doorstep and begged me to take him in.'

Abbie looked at her mother, wide-eyed. How could she say that, she wondered. If her dad ever did come back then she was sure her mammy would be happy again. She might even kiss and cuddle Abbie like Sandra's mammy cuddled Sandra. And if her dad came back she was sure he would take her on his knee and kiss her and tell her how much he loved her, because that was what Sandra's dad was always doing; it was what dads did.

Abbie's dad would buy her a hoop, too, even though she was almost too old for such a plaything, she was sure of that. Hoops and tops and dolls were really only for little kids. When she went back to school in September it would be skipping-ropes, roller skates if you were lucky enough to be able to afford them, and swopping cigarette cards and comics.

Abbie was so desperate to have her own hoop that she'd even plucked up the courage to ask Billy, her eldest brother, who was twenty-six and worked down at the Docks helping to unload cargo from the boats, if he'd buy her one. He'd not even bothered to reply, simply cuffed her around the ears, told her to grow up, and then shoved her out of the back door into the dark jowler, which separated their house in Bostock Street from the houses in Kew Street, with the toe of his boot.

Only her other brother Sam, who was almost three years older than her and would be fourteen next January, seemed to understand how much she wanted a blue hoop. Even though he had started working on Saturdays as a delivery boy for the ironmonger in Scotland Road, he still hadn't got enough money saved up to buy her one.

'It will soon be the school holidays and I'll be working every day in August, so if you don't get a hoop for your birthday then I might be able to manage to buy you one – if Mam doesn't take all my money off me,' he promised.

Abbie moved away from the window the moment she saw her brother Billy and her mother come staggering down the street, their arms linked as they swayed drunkenly from side to side.

They were an odd-looking couple. Billy was short and as skinny as a beanpole, while her mammy was twice his size. They looked alike, though, because they both had lank brown hair that was so thin that in places you could see the shiny pink of their scalps through it. Sam had the same colour hair as them, but his was as thick as a brush, and short and shiny.

Abbie's own hair was quite different. It was jet black, very thick and very straight with a heavy fringe. When it grew too long her mammy used to

3

stick a pudding basin on her head and then chop off any hair sticking out beneath the rim.

In the twilight, with her broad shoulders, stout legs, muscular arms, and a greasy old cap on her head the same as Billy's, her mammy looked like a big strong man. She drank like a man, too, Abbie thought with a shudder.

Every Friday night, as soon as they were paid, both her mammy and Billy went drinking, trailing from one pub to the next in Scotland Road and Great Homer Street until closing time. And they were back in the pubs again on Saturday night, if there was any money left after they'd been to the pawnshop to get their Sunday-best clothes out.

On Sunday they went to Mass if they'd sobered up enough. Her mammy would be dressed up in her best brown coat, brown felt cloche hat and brown lace-up shoes, whatever the weather, and Billy would be wearing his shiny navy suit with a white shirt and spotted red tie.

They'd all be on their knees, praying for their souls, and her mammy and Billy kowtowing to Father Patrick by slipping a shiny bright tanner into the collection plate, even if there was nothing at home for Sunday dinner. And her mammy always lit a penny candle to the memory of her daughter, Audrey, who'd been a year younger than Billy, but who'd been dead now for about eleven years.

By the following Wednesday all their finery would be back in Solly Greenberg's pawnshop. Abbie's mammy needed the money to buy some scrag-end of mutton from Bank's meat shop, and some potatoes, onions and carrots from the market, to make a pot of scouse that had to last them all until payday came round again.

On payday they always redeemed their clothes, ready for Sunday, and then started all over again.

Abbie couldn't understand why Billy didn't find himself a girlfriend and get married instead of going out drinking with their mam all the time. She'd talked about it to her friend Sandra.

'He's like Michael Ryan,' Sandra told her solemnly. 'He's about the same age as your Billy and he doesn't have a girlfriend either.'

'But he doesn't go out drinking with his mam, does he!'

'No, he goes drinking on his own or with his dad whenever Paddy Ryan's ship is in dock.' Sandra giggled, 'I think Michael Ryan's ever so handsome, don't you?'

Abbie shrugged. 'He's old, like our Billy,' she said dismissively.

'Your Sam isn't old, though,' Sandra grinned.

Abbie didn't answer. Sam was special, and she didn't want to talk about him or share her thoughts about him with anyone.

If it had been anyone else but Sam she would have been happy to talk about him, and tease Sandra about having a crush on him, but not when it was Sam. She wanted to keep him all to herself. He was the only person who really loved her, who cuddled her and comforted her when she was lonely or sad.

Sandra was her very best friend and Sam's pal, Peter Ryan, was a good friend as well. She liked it when the four of them played together, but they didn't understand her or love her like Sam did.

Although it was very late it still wasn't properly dark, and the July night was so warm that the poky little back-bedroom in the small terraced house in Bostock Street was stuffy and airless.

Knowing her mother would be home at any minute, Abbie quickly got ready for bed. She removed her flowered cotton skirt and the shrunken jumper that had once belonged to her brother Sam, and put them over the bedrail. Gingerly, she took off the rubber-soled plimsolls that had also been his until he'd outgrown them. His big toe had gone right through the canvas upper leaving a frayed jagged hole, and sometimes her big toenail caught on it and made her yelp with pain. She had no socks and the plimsolls chafed her ankles because they were too big, and her heels felt sore where they had been rubbed raw.

She still felt hot and sticky, even though she was wearing only her grubby cotton knickers as she scrambled into bed. She pulled the grimy sheet up over her head to try and shut out the sound of raucous voices, as her mammy and Billy came into the house and stumbled into the table in the living room, knocking over a couple of chairs. They'd been out drinking all evening and spent enough money on beer and cigarettes to buy a dozen hoops, she thought sadly.

Abbie trembled as the noise from downstairs became louder, and she burrowed deeper into the bed, but it was no good, she couldn't shut out the racket they were making and she knew it would go on for another hour at least. At present they were only singing and joking, but any moment now they would start argy-bargying with each other, and that's when one or both of them could turn nasty.

Her mammy had a terrible temper when she was riled, and if she came upstairs and found Abbie still awake, even though it was her birthday the next day, she'd still wallop her. Yet how could she sleep when they were kicking up such a din, she thought peevishly.

Sneaking out of bed, she padded across the bare boards to the door. 'Sam, Sam, are you still awake?' she called in a sibilant whisper. 'Can I come in your bed with you?'

'You know you can't! What would happen if our Billy found you in here? Stay in your own bed and curl up and go to sleep before they come upstairs and find you still awake, Abbie,' Sam called back from the room along the passage.

'I can't sleep, Sam!' A sob shook her voice. 'I'm so frightened.'

She knew she was lucky to have a bedroom all to herself, even if it wasn't much bigger than a cupboard. It was at the back of the house, a tiny room built over the scullery, and she felt cut off from the two main bedrooms. She heard Sam's bed-springs creak and the next minute he was padding along the landing towards her room.

'You'd better get back into bed before they come upstairs,' he warned again.

7

'Will you stay with me then? Please, Sam,' she pleaded.

'For a few minutes, but only if you promise to go to sleep.'

'If you cuddle me, then perhaps I might be able to,' she agreed plaintively.

'You'll get me into trouble if Mam or Billy catch me in here so hurry up and go to sleep,' he murmured as he climbed into her bed.

'I will try, Sam.' Abbie's huge blue eyes filled with tears and her mouth trembled as she snuggled into him. 'No one else but you loves me or ever cuddles me.'

He curled up beside her on the narrow iron bedstead, whispering words of comfort as the noise from downstairs became even louder. One minute their mother and Billy were singing at the top of their voices, the next they were viciously cursing each other.

Sam had intended to slip out of Abbie's bed and creep back into his own room before Billy came up to bed, but he was so tired that even though he didn't mean to do so, he dozed off. The next thing he knew, Billy was in the room, hauling him out of the bed by the scruff of his neck and booting him along the passage to the bedroom they shared.

'I've told you before, you little bugger, about running in to that little bitch every time she whimpers. Encourage her, you do. She's always whingeing or whining about something,' he snarled as he stumbled after Sam into their own room.

'You and Mam woke her up with all the noise

8

you were making when you came home and she was frightened,' Sam protested.

'Don't you bloody well answer me back!' Picking up the boot he had just taken off, Billy hurled it in Sam's direction.

Sam ducked and the heavy steel-tipped boot smashed into the window, and there was the sound of breaking glass.

'Now look what you've done, you stupid sod!' Billy grunted.

'What the hell's going on?' Ellen Martin stumbled into the room. Her eyes were bleary, her hair was straggling round her face and there were beer stains down the front of her red cotton blouse and black skirt. 'Was that glass breaking?'

'It's this silly young bugger's fault,' Billy muttered, making a grab at Sam and missing.

'You broke the window when you threw your boot at me,' Sam argued.

Ellen glared at Sam. 'I don't care whose fault it is, you can sodding well mend it and pay for the glass. That will take care of most of the money you earn during your school holiday,' she told him sharply.

'Oh, come on Mam, that's not fair ...'

'Any more lip and you'll feel my hand round your face,' Billy growled menacingly.

'Shut up, the pair of you,' Ellen bellowed. 'I've had a skinful and I've got a head on me like a bucket, and I need some kip.'

Reeling drunkenly she made her way to her own bedroom at the front of the house, slamming the door shut with such force that the whole place shook.

Belching and reeking of beer, Billy collapsed on the bed fully dressed and still wearing one boot. In a befuddled, drunken stupor he began snoring noisily almost at once.

Sam could hear Abbie sobbing and started to creep out of the room to make sure she was all right, but Billy suddenly snorted violently and sat up. Sam kept perfectly still, clinging on to the edge of the bed as far away from Billy as possible, holding his breath, waiting for him to pass out again.

As soon as he did, Sam made his way back into his sister's bedroom. 'Ssh!' he warned as her sobbing grew louder. 'If Mam hears you then you'll be in for a hiding. Now go to sleep or you won't be able to get up in time for Mass in the morning, and then you'll be in even more trouble.'

Abbie's eleventh birthday started out as one of the most miserable days of her life.

She woke early, dying to find out if her mammy had bought her a hoop after all, but when it was time for Abbie to leave for church, Ellen was still in bed, sleeping off her excesses from the night before.

Abbie didn't know what to do. She couldn't possibly wait until she came home again, so she crept into her mother's bedroom to see if she could waken her. Gently, she kissed her mother's raddled face.

Ellen's hand came up and slapped at her as if

swatting away a fly or a bedbug. Her bleary eyes opened and she stared angrily at Abbie.

'For Christ's sake, Abbie, get off me, let me be,' she screeched as Abbie tried to kiss her again.

Roughly, Ellen freed herself from the two skinny arms that had crept round her neck, and she forcibly pushed Abbie away.

'Can I come in your bed for a quick cuddle, Mammy?' Abbie pleaded. 'It is my birthday, so can I have a cuddle?' she asked again, hopefully.

'Cuddle? At your age! Bugger off and leave me to get some shuteye before I belt you one.'

'It's my birthday, Mammy,' Abbie repeated forlornly. 'You haven't even given me a kiss!'

She stood by the side of the bed, shifting uneasily from one foot to the other, knowing it was dangerous to ask, but she simply had to know. 'Mammy, did you get me a hoop for my birthday?' she asked in a tiny voice that was little more than a whisper.

'Hoop! No, I didn't get you a bloody hoop, I've already told you I haven't money to waste on rubbish.'

'So you got me new shoes, did you? Can I wear them to church?'

'Shoes? I haven't bought you any new shoes, I haven't bought you any bloody thing. Now clear off and leave me in peace.'

Abbie fought to keep back her tears as she called for Sandra so that they could walk to church together as usual. She wished Sandra didn't know it was her birthday, she wished no one in the world knew, then she wouldn't have to explain that her own mammy wasn't giving her any sort of present at all.

Sandra, dressed in a pale blue dress, white socks and black shoes, and with a blue bow in her shining fair hair, was jumping up and down on her doorstep impatiently as Abbie approached. 'Come on, run,' she shouted, 'or we won't have time to look at your present.'

'I haven't got a present,' Abbie muttered, and the tears she had been struggling so hard to hold in check began to slowly trickle from the corner of her eyes and channel their way down her thin cheeks.

'Yes you have,' Sandra giggled, her pretty face wreathed in smiles. She grabbed hold of Abbie's hand and dragged her over the doorstep and into the living room.

It was a light, airy room, where everything was shiny and smelled of lavender furniture-polish. The walls were painted cream and there were flowered curtains and matching cushion covers. There was a vase of artificial roses in the middle of a highly polished table. At each end of the mantelpiece were two white china dogs, and in between them was a big mirror.

'Here,' Sandra grabbed a huge, thin package wrapped up in gaudy paper that was propped up against the wall. 'Happy birthday,' she said as she passed it to Abbie. 'Go on then, open it!' Sandra giggled, her grey eyes sparkling with excitement.

It was such pretty paper that Abbie tried to take it off as carefully as she could, so as not to tear it, but Sandra was impatient for her to see inside the parcel and grabbed one end of the paper and ripped it from top to bottom.

'There!' she exclaimed.

Abbie stared, too choked to speak as she gazed at the wonderful bright-blue hoop. It was exactly what she had set her heart on owning. She couldn't believe her eyes.

'You do like it, don't you?' Sandra asked anxiously. 'Your mam hasn't bought you one as well, has she?'

'It's wonderful,' Abbie breathed, her blue eyes shining, a smile splitting her thin face almost in two. 'It's exactly what I dreamed of having. The best present in the world!'

'Your Sam told me that your mammy was buying you a pair of new shoes,' Sandra commented. 'Why aren't you wearing them?'

The light went out of Abbie's face for a moment. 'Well, she didn't do that either,' she muttered.

'So what did she buy you?'

Abbie didn't answer, simply shook her head.

'You two had better get a move on or you'll be late for church,' Mrs Lewis told them briskly. 'I'll stand your new blue hoop alongside Sandra's red one, Abbie, until you come back.'

Abbie hesitated. Now that she had the hoop in her hands she didn't want to let go of it, in case it was all a dream and it vanished into thin air.

'Come on, Abbie, it will be quite safe with me.'

Reluctantly, Abbie passed it over to Mrs Lewis, but not before she had run her hand all the way round its smooth, shining edge.

Then, on impulse, she flung her arms around

Sandra's mother's neck and kissed her fervently on her soft plump cheek.

'Happy birthday, Abbie!' Mo Lewis returned her hug and kissed her on the brow.

Her birthday was going to be special after all, Abbie thought happily, as she and Sandra set off for St Anthony's.

There was more to come. Sam bought her a bar of milk chocolate which she shared out with him, Sandra and Peter Ryan. Peter's mother gave her a bright blue bag, which had a long strap so that she could wear it like a satchel. Inside it was a white handkerchief trimmed with lace with an 'A' embroidered in blue silk in one corner, and a little mirror, and a blue comb.

By the time she went back to her own home, eager to show off all her birthday presents, her mother and Billy were already back from late Mass.

'Put all that rubbish up into your room and help our Sam lay the table,' her mother told her sharply. 'I stuck a chicken in the oven before I went to Mass, seeing as it's your birthday, and it's probably cooked by now.'

Abbie's heart lifted. Her mammy did love her after all, she thought happily, as she cleared away the dirty crockery, the overflowing ashtray and the empty beer bottles.

From a dismal beginning, her eleventh birthday had become the happiest day of her life, Abbie reflected when she went to bed that night, her new blue hoop leaning against the wall where she could reach out and touch it.

Chapter Two

Abbie and Sandra spent every moment they could after school each night playing outside with their hoops. The long July evenings meant that it was often well after nine o'clock before they went home to bed.

Peter often joined them and they'd try and keep up with him, trundling their hoops as he rode up and down Bostock Street on his bike. Abbie, because she was thinner and taller than Sandra, usually managed to do so. When they reached the corner they would wait until Sandra, puffing and panting, her short plump legs aching with the effort, caught them up.

Mo Lewis came out into the road occasionally to make sure they were all right. Sometimes she brought them a jam butty each, or a piece of her home-made seed cake, which Abbie loved but Sandra wouldn't eat because the caraway seeds stuck in her teeth. Maggie Ryan would often join her for a gossip and she never came empty-handed either. She usually brought them some biscuits or a wedge of Wet Nelly.

Sam, too, would join them after he'd finished making deliveries in the Scotland Road area, riding up and down Bostock Street on his delivery bike and circling around them, wobbling like crazy because the big metal basket fastened to the front of his bike made turning in tight circles difficult.

Life had never seemed so wonderful, even though her mammy was forever scolding her. And when school broke up towards the end of July, Abbie looked forward to spending even more time playing out with Sandra and the others.

She was in tears when her mother told her that now the school holidays had started she would be taking Abbie along to work with her each day.

'Why do I have to come with you?' she asked sulkily.

'Our Sam will be working and he won't be able to keep an eye out for you, that's why.'

'I'll be all right on my own. I'll be playing with Sandra and Peter, and Mrs Lewis or Mrs Ryan will give me a butty if I'm hungry.'

'You can stop scrounging off those two,' Ellen Martin said. 'I've told you before to find someone else to play with. We don't want charity off the likes of them!'

'It's not charity,' Abbie protested. 'And if you think it is then let me bring them back home for a scoff, and that will pay them back.'

'Feed that horde! You must be out of your mind. Takes me every penny I earn to put food on the table for my own lot, without feeding the rest of the street,' Ellen snapped. 'You'll come with me, starting Monday morning. You're big enough to give me a hand so let's not hear any more about it.'

Abbie resented having to accompany her

mother to work. Ellen was employed as a cotton picker, and worked along with a dozen other women in one of the huge sheds on the dockside. Their job was to hack open the great canvas-wrapped bales that had been damaged and tease out the cotton inside them into usable strands again.

The damage that was caused by the salt water, whether because of storms or because the bales had accidentally fallen into the sea, was considerable. The cotton, which had already been packed in as tightly as possible, turned into a solid cake once the salt water impregnated it.

When they'd ripped away the outer canvas they then had to hack out the contents using a sharp, curved knife like a cutlass. One slip and there were cut hands and nicked fingers.

Each wedge they hacked out had then to be torn apart into strands, until it was once more as soft and downy as when it had been first picked from the bushes in southern America.

It was back-breaking work and their hands at the end of the day were raw, their fingertips sore and their nails torn and often bleeding.

Abbie found it was so hot and dusty inside the warehouse sheds that she could hardly breathe. Her mother, like the rest of the women, wore a heavy long black skirt to protect her legs against the roughness of the bales, and an old blouse or shirt. When the weather was cold or wet they each wore a thick black shawl that they could pull up over their heads if necessary. Most of them also wore a man's cap to keep the dust and the flying

17

downy fragments from the teased cotton out of their hair.

Abbie had always considered her mammy to be a big woman, but some of the others who worked there were taller and broader and even stronger than her mammy. One woman, Abbie saw to her amazement, could move the huge bales, which were as big as the kitchen table at home, on her own.

They all made it clear right from the start that they didn't like Abbie being there.

'The sort of things we talk about while we work aren't for a little kid's ears,' one grumbled.

'She's no little kid, Ruby Stacey, she's eleven years old, so you can keep your big gob shut,' Ellen told her.

'Doesn't bloody well look it. Skinny as a rabbit, arms and legs like sticks. Ever tried feeding her?'

'She gets her share!' Ellen scowled.

'Wouldn't like to see the rest of your lot then,' Ruby Stacey retorted. 'No wonder your old man buggered off! Probably went to look for a square meal.'

The other women sniggered and Abbie felt her cheeks burning with shame.

Ellen glowered, but said no more. Ruby Stacey was a florid-faced aggressive woman, much bigger than her, and from the murmurs around her the other women seemed to be siding with Ruby.

Ellen wasn't prepared to let such taunts slide by, though. She waited her time, watching Ruby like a hawk, determined to have her revenge.

At midday, when work stopped, they all sat on

the floor with their backs propped up against the cotton bales, to eat the chip butties or lumps of Wet Nelly they'd brought with them, and it was then Ellen saw her chance.

Ruby Stacey had pulled off her big clumping boots to give her aching feet an airing. Tucked into the top of the thick woollen socks she was wearing was a small wad of something wrapped in newspaper. As she got up to go and relieve herself in the bucket that stood screened off by a piece of canvas in a corner of the shed, the wad dropped to the ground with a dull thud as she walked past Ellen.

Swiftly, Ellen stuck out her leg and flicked her long black skirt so that it covered the package. She waited to see if anyone else had noticed, but no one seemed to have done so. Carefully, she leaned forward as if scratching her leg, and slid the wad into the palm of her hand, and then, still appearing to be scratching herself, hid it away in the front of her blouse.

She saw Abbie was watching her open-mouthed, her blue eyes saucer wide, and gave her a warning frown that she was to say nothing.

Ruby returned, collected up her bits and pieces and went back to work. Ellen did likewise. The moment she got Abbie on her own she turned on her fiercely.

'Now, you keep your mouth shut and say nothing to no one about what you saw, you understand!' she warned.

'Was there money in that newspaper . . .?'

'I've told you! One word and I'll tan your

backside, and that's just for starters. You've seen nothing! Understand? Now get outside and take a breather in the fresh air and think about what I've told you,' Ellen continued, pushing her towards the open doors.

A heat haze shrouded Liverpool. Across the Mersey, which was as smooth as a millpond, Abbie could see, to the left, Cammell Laird's shipyard at Birkenhead, black smoke pouring from its chimneys. Away to her right, though, was the holiday coastline of Seacombe, Egremont, and New Brighton, and she wished she could be there instead of having to go back inside the hot, dusty cotton shed for the rest of the afternoon.

'What you going to do with that money, Mammy?' she asked as they left work and began to make their way home up Water Street and Dale Street towards Scotland Road.

'What money?'

'The money that woman dropped!'

'The heat in that shed has addled your brains. I know nothing about any money.'

'You picked it up. I saw you.'

'You want to watch your tongue, saying things like that!' her mother warned her. 'Keep your trap shut about what goes on in the shed, and about anything you hear, do you understand?'

Abbie nodded, but it worried her. What would Father Patrick say when her mammy confessed to him that she'd picked the money up and kept it. He'd think she was a thief. He couldn't tell the police, of course, because everything you told Father Patrick when you went to confession was strictly between you and him and God. He'd know, though!

It was such a big secret that she had to tell someone. She mustn't tell Sandra in case she told her mother, and her mother told her dad and then they told the police. There was only one person she could tell, and that was Sam.

The minute they'd finished their meal, Ellen shooed Abbie and Sam out to play. 'Billy and me's got a bit of business to see to, so we might not be here when you get back. Put yourselves to bed and no larking about, mind.'

'Where are you going, Mammy?'

'Out!'

Abbie felt uneasy. She was sure it had something to do with the money her mammy had picked up off the warehouse floor earlier that day. She was longing to confide in Sam, but her mother's threats stopped her. She'd had a pasting from her mammy before, and well remembered how her mammy's heavy-handed slaps had left her bruised for days afterwards.

She couldn't put it out of her mind, though, and she came in from playing with Sandra early, complaining she didn't feel well.

'What you got then, a bellyache?' Sam asked.

She shook her head.

'You haven't fallen out with each other at last, have you?' Sam grinned. 'Like a pair of Siamese twins, you two. See one, see the other.'

'It's nothing like that.'

'So what's bothering you?'

'I got things to think about, that's all. I'm going to bed.'

Abbie found it was impossible to sleep. She sat by the window, staring out, watching people come and go until it grew so dark and she became so cold that she was shivering.

She'd undressed and crept under the covers when she heard her mammy and Billy coming down the street, singing drunkenly at the top of their voices. Immediately she knew what sort of business they'd had in mind.

'Have you heard those two?' Sam said, coming into her room. 'It's only the beginning of the week! Where have they found the money to go boozing?'

Abbie bit her lip. Should she tell him? She was bursting to do so. Could she trust him to say nothing. She was sure she could.

'Mammy picked up some money in the warehouse today, that's where they got the beer money from,' she said in a dramatic whisper.

'Picked it up? What do you mean? Some sort of bonus?'

Abbie gave a hysterical giggle. 'No, she stole it, stupid. You mustn't tell anyone you know, or that I told you,' she added quickly. 'She said she'd skelp me if I told on her.'

Sam stared at her, his brown eyes widening in disbelief. 'So whose money was it, and how did she come to steal it?'

In hurried whispers Abbie told him all about the wad of newspaper-wrapped money falling out of Ruby Stacey's sock, and her mother picking it up and saying nothing.

'Silly cow! Everyone down the Docks knows that Ruby Stacey will fight anyone. She beats her old man to a pulp when he steps out of line. She'll make mincemeat out of Mam if she finds out.'

'You won't tell, though, will you?' Abbie pleaded.

Before Sam could answer, the bedroom door burst open and Billy stood there staring at them. He lurched into the room, holding on to the doorpost for support.

'I'm fed up with telling you about coming in here and pandering to that little bitch,' he snarled. Seizing Sam by his mop of thick hair he began shaking him.

'Leave off, you're scalping me,' Sam growled as he tried to struggle free. 'I only came in because the noise you and Mam were making woke Abbie up and she was frightened.'

'Frightened! I'll tan her backside in a minute if she doesn't shut up and get to sleep, and then she'll have something to be frightened about. So will you if I take my belt off to you.'

As she heard them arguing, Abbie cowered down in bed and stuffed a corner of the pillow into her mouth so that Billy wouldn't hear her crying.

When her mother came stumping up the stairs, Abbie hoped she was coming to see if she was all right. She wanted the chance to tell her mammy to keep out of Ruby Stacey's way because she didn't want her to get hurt.

A moment later she heard her mother slam her

bedroom door shut, and she felt completely rejected.

She knew Sam wouldn't be able to come back to her room so she pulled the bedclothes over her head and sobbed herself to sleep.

Chapter Three

Abbie sensed there was going to be trouble from the moment she woke up the next morning. Billy didn't even put in an appearance before Abbie and her Mam left for work, and her mother, still hungover from her binge the night before, said she felt too ill to walk from Scotland Road to the dockside. They took a penny ride on one of the Green Goddesses, but as the tram swayed violently from side to side Ellen had a hard job not to throw up, and they had to get off at the top of Water Street and walk the rest of the way.

Abbie felt ashamed to be seen with her mother as she lurched from one side to the other, belching loudly and bumping into people if they got in her way.

'Do you think you should go back home, Mammy?' she asked worriedly, when Ellen was violently sick as they approached the grim-looking five-storey warehouse.

'Keep your trap shut. When I want your advice I'll ask for it,' Ellen muttered, wiping her mouth with the back of her hand. 'I'll be all right now I've brought that lot up.'

In Abbie's opinion she was far from being all right. She followed her mother into the ground floor of the warehouse. She hated it in there. The air was thick with dust, and the enormous spiders' webs that hung from the ceiling were coated with fibres and hung like grey clouds above her head. As usual she started sneezing. Quick, dry sneezes in such rapid succession that they brought tears to her eyes and left her choking and gasping for breath.

'Pinch your nose between your thumb and finger, chooks,' one of the women told her. 'That'll stop you sneezing, luv.'

She did as she was told, hurrying after her mother who was scuffling along sending up clouds of dust from the cotton-strewn floor as she weaved her way unsteadily between the massive bales.

'What happened to you this morning then, Mrs Martin?' Polly Hicks, the forewoman, demanded as she eyed Ellen up and down. 'Overslept? Or were you too bloody drunk to get up?'

Ellen belched loudly, but didn't answer.

When they reached the bale assigned to her, Ellen slithered to the ground, rested her back against it and closed her eyes.

'I've already docked you an hour for being late,' Polly Hicks rasped. 'If you sit there a moment longer then I'll stop another hour out of your wages.'

Ellen opened her eyes, ran her hand over her face, and struggled to her feet. Picking up the cotton-hook lying on top of the bale, she slashed away savagely at the canvas covering.

'You'd do better if you cut off the steel bands

first, wouldn't you?' Polly Hicks muttered scathingly. She handed Ellen a pair of heavy shears and watched, frowning, as Ellen tried to use them.

'Give them here, you daft cow.'

Snatching the shears back, Polly Hicks deftly cut through the steel bands that held the bale intact.

'Now get on with it!' she snapped as she walked away.

It took Ellen several more minutes to open up the bale enough to reach the tightly packed, water-soaked cotton inside, then she sank down on the floor again, completely exhausted. Leaning against the bale she dropped her head on to her knees.

'You make a start on it,' she muttered, pushing the vicious looking cotton-knife towards Abbie.

Abbie looked at the sharp, curved blade and shook her head. 'I can't, Mammy. I don't know how to use this knife.'

'Take hold of it and hack out as many wads as you can. You know how to tease it out with your fingers until it's like cotton wool. You've seen me do it, now get on with it.'

Abbie tried, but the cotton was rock hard and the sharp knife simply skittered over the surface. She did her best at digging the point in and then twisting it to try and free even a small wedge, but she hadn't the strength in her small hands to do even that.

Abbie made another attempt, tears of frustration trickling down her cheeks. She stabbed wildly at the bale. The knife spun out of her hand and, rebounding from the iron-hard surface, landed point down on her bare knee drawing a thin trickle of blood. Abbie screamed in fright.

'Give it here!' A scrawny woman who had been watching her antics snatched the knife from her hands and slashed out a dozen wedges. 'There you are, luv, pick those up off the floor and start teasing 'em out. That should keep you going for a while. Perhaps your mam'll be feeling more herself by the time you've done that and then she can take over again.'

'Not her! By the looks of things she was on the booze again last night and she's had a skinful!' Ruby Stacey snarled. 'Beginning of the week, too, so I wonder where the drunken bitch got her money from?'

The women paused in what they were doing and an expectant hush fell on the warehouse. One or two of them nudged each other and grinned, as if they knew there was a row brewing and they were looking forward to whatever happened next.

Ruby Stacey looked round at all the expectant faces and smiled grimly, then she strode across the warehouse and stood, arms akimbo, in front of Ellen. 'I suppose yer didn't pick a nice little wad of money up off the floor by any chance, did you, missus? Four nice, bright, shiny florins wrapped up in old newspaper?'

Ellen groaned, but didn't look up.

Ruby's boot went out and made contact with Ellen's chin. 'I'm speaking to you!'

'Lemme be, can't you, I'm not feeling so good,' Ellen moaned.

'I bet you're bloody not! That was my week's

wages. That was to keep me, me old man and me four kids in grub this week! And you stole it, yer thieving bitch.'

Ellen pushed the woman's boot out of her face. 'I didn't steal yer rotten money,' she muttered.

'You bloody well did! Lulu over there saw you. She saw me drop it, and then she spotted you picking it up and sticking it down the front of yer dress. Too frightened of you to open her gob, the silly bitch. Any decent body would have handed it back to me.'

Abbie held her breath, scared of what was going to happen next. She wanted to run and fetch Polly Hicks, the forewoman, who had gone across to the office about something, but her legs felt like lead and she was rooted to the spot.

'So what you goin' to do about it then, missus?' Ruby thrust one of her large hands under Ellen's chin, forcing her head back so that she had to look up. 'Well, do I get my ackers back or not?'

'I haven't got yer money!'

Ruby Stacey gave a mirthless laugh. 'No, you probably haven't got it now, judging by the looks of yer!' Her hand closed threateningly into a fist.

Ellen screamed with pain as it made contact with the side of her face. Abbie rushed to her side and put her thin little arms around her mother's neck protectively. 'You get away from my mammy, you're nothing but a great big bully,' she stormed, her blue eyes flashing with anger as she stared up at Ruby Stacey.

'Nice try, kiddo, but this is between grown-ups,' Ruby said contemptuously. She grabbed hold of

Abbie and, picking her up with one hand, swung her feet off the ground then dumped her on top of the nearest cotton bale. 'Stay there or you might get hurt as well,' she warned. 'Your mam's got no right bringing you here with her. The Gaffer would do his nut if he knew.'

She turned back to Ellen who was nursing her bruised face. 'Well?' she barked, dragging her unceremoniously to her feet. 'What have you got to say for yerself?'

Ellen tried to wriggle free, but Ruby's grasp became even tighter, shaking her as if she was a rag doll. Ellen lashed out with her feet and caught the other woman a resounding blow on her shin with the toe of her boot.

'Want to play rough, do you?' Ruby snarled.

She released her hold on Ellen without warning and Ellen landed in a heap at her feet amidst a cloud of dust.

Ruby regarded her scornfully. 'Now give me my money or get up and fight,' she ordered.

'How can I?' White-faced and shaking, Ellen stared belligerently at her opponent. Normally she knew Ruby wouldn't want to fight her because they were much the same size as each other, but Ruby knew how groggy Ellen was feeling at the moment.

'For the last time, are you going to give me my money back, or am I going to beat it out of you?'

'I told you, I haven't got your money,' Ellen muttered sullenly.

'Better find it, then, hadn't you!'

The other women left their bales and congregated round in a semicircle, watching with avid interest. Ruby had a reputation as a fighter and most of them had felt the power of her fist at some time, and they were keyed up to see what the outcome of the altercation would be.

With a grunt like a Samoan wrestler, Ruby pitched into Ellen. She punched her, butted and kicked her until Ellen was almost senseless.

Crouched on top of one of the bales, Abbie was witness to all that was happening. As Ruby raised one of her big muscular arms to take another swipe, Abbie was sure the woman was going to kill her mother.

Ruby finally stopped, leaving Ellen lying on the floor in a pool of blood and vomit.

Abbie's heart was pounding with fear as she tried to climb down to see if she could help her mother. Ruby heard her move and swung round and barked at her to stay where she was.

In the second that Ruby's attention was diverted, Ellen managed to get up off the floor and snatch up the sharp, curved cotton-knife that Abbie had been using.

As she brandished the knife with the intention of stabbing her opponent, a warning scream from one of the onlookers alerted Ruby. Despite her massive size she twisted away, so that instead of the knife plunging into her chest it was deflected and sliced through her sleeve into her upper arm.

With a scream of rage Ruby jumped on Ellen, tearing her clothes almost off her back. Blood from Ruby's arm pumped out over the pair of them, soaking their clothes and running into a pool on the floor.

The noise and screams could be heard outside the warehouse, alerting the Gaffer who came storming into the shed, shouting at the top of his voice and demanding to know what was happening. Like mice, the onlookers scurried back to their bales and pretended to be working.

'What the hell's going on,' he raged. He gawped at Ruby. 'You're bleeding like a stuck pig, woman! Someone call the scuffers and an ambulance!' he yelled over his shoulder as he turned back to Ruby to apply pressure to her arm, to try and stop the blood that continued to pump out at an alarming rate.

As he spotted Ellen leaning exhaustedly against a bale he called to the forewoman to come and look after Ruby.

'You two bitches been fighting?' He hauled Ellen to her feet. 'You were the one who used the bloody knife on her, weren't you? That'll have to be reported to the scuffers, you know that, don't you?'

'And while you're at it, tell them that she stole my week's money,' Ruby added weakly. 'Lulu's a witness.'

Ellen was trembling and frightened, but she refused to get in the same ambulance as Ruby Stacey.

Since, apart from torn clothes, bruises and a cut lip, she didn't seem to be hurt too badly, the Gaffer shrugged and told her she'd better get off home once the police had finished with her.

'And take your kid with you, and don't ever bring her back here again. Understand! I've warned you before about it. This is no place for youngsters and it will be no place for you if you cause another brawl.'

'It wasn't my bloody fault, the woman's mad,' Ellen defended.

'You'd be mad an' all if someone pinched your money and you knew that you and your kids would have to go hungry all week,' one of the women muttered angrily.

The Gaffer wheeled round angrily. 'I don't want to hear any more about it, so shut your mouth,' he raged. 'Get back to work, or the lot of you will find yourselves with no money for grub at the end of the week. I'll sack the whole bunch of you if there is any more trouble.'

Chapter Four

It was two days before Ellen Martin was out of pain sufficiently to face going to work. Her mood and her temper became worse every time she thought about the money she was losing from her pay packet.

On the Friday morning she dragged herself out of bed, knowing that if she didn't make the effort to go in then she'd get no money at all. As it was there would only be her wages for Monday to come.

'Make sure you don't get into any mischief, Abbie,' she scowled as she stood in the doorway, ready to leave, but still debating whether to go or stay at home.

'I won't have time. I'll be too busy doing all the chores you've told me to do,' Abbie told her sulkily.

'Mind you do the lot, and do them properly or I'll tan your backside when I get home,' her mother snapped peevishly.

'Couldn't I do some of them today and the rest tomorrow?' Abbie pleaded.

'You do them all today, my girl! Now don't forget you're to donkey-stone that front step first, it hasn't been done in months. After that, scrub the kitchen floor and then tidy up the bedrooms. And mind you get the whole lot finished before you go off out to play,' Ellen Martin repeated. 'Go on then, get the apron on and get started. I've left the pumice stone for the step out ready.'

Pulling a face, Abbie tied the piece of canvas sacking that her mother used as an apron around her middle. It was far too big so she had to double it over. The moment the door slammed shut behind her mother she whipped it off, dropped it in a heap on the floor, and shot out of the back door straight round to the Lewis's house to see if Sandra was up.

Mrs Lewis, wearing a flowered pinafore over her dress, answered the door. 'Sandra's still having her breakfast, luv. Did you want to come in and talk to her?'

Abbie nodded hopefully.

'Come on then, ducks. Go and sit at the table with her and I'll make you a jam butty.'

'Me mammy's gone back to work,' she told Sandra as she pulled out a chair. 'She's left me an awful lot of jobs to do, though, probably take me all day before I can get out to play. What are you going to be doing?'

Sandra shrugged. 'I'm not sure. Shall we do something together?'

'Like what?'

'Ssh!' Sandra held a finger to her lips. 'It's a secret!'

'Why?'

'Because I think my mam would stop me if she knew.'

'Go on then, tell me.'

'Wait till she's brought in your butty.'

'There you are, luv!' Mrs Lewis handed Abbie a plate with a doorstep of bread oozing with strawberry jam. 'Get that down you.'

'So what are we going to do, then?' Abbie asked, her mouth full.

'We could go round all the posh shops in town,' Sandra told her.

'Why go into town? There's plenty of shops in Scotland Road we can look at, and even more on Great Homer Street, and they're only at the bottom of our street.'

'The shops there are bigger and better than the scrubby little ones here,' Sandra sniffed.

'So, what difference does that make? We haven't got any money to spend, have we!'

'We can take a look. Could be fun.'

Abbie took another large bite and contemplated the idea while she chewed. 'We'd have to walk there, we've no money for the tram.'

'So? It's a nice day and it's not all that far.'

''Tis when you're coming home.'

'Do you want to come with me or not?' Sandra said, slightly miffed by Abbie's lack of enthusiasm.

'Yes, of course I do, but I have all the jobs me mammy told me to do first.'

'I'll help you with those. We'll finish them this morning and then we'll have all afternoon to go into town. My mam goes to work at one o'clock, and I'll tell her that I want to play with you instead of going with her. I'll ask her to leave us some sarnies.'

Abbie looked doubtful, but the thought of Sandra helping her with all the cleaning jobs that she'd been told to do persuaded her that perhaps it wasn't such a bad idea after all.

'I'll do the front step and you can scrub the kitchen floor,' Sandra said bossily when they got back to Abbie's house, 'then we'll do upstairs together.'

Abbie shook her head. 'That's no good! I'll have to be the one who does the step. If someone sees you doing it they're bound to tell my mammy that you were cleaning our step.'

'So? What does that matter?'

Abbie pursed her lips. 'She told *me* to do it, so she'd probably leather me for letting you come in, as well as for getting you to do it. You know what she's like. She hates me to bring anyone home because it's always in such a mess here.'

Sandra gave an exaggerated shrug. 'Orright! I'll do the kitchen floor and you do the step, then.'

It was nearly midday before they finished.

'I'm whacked,' Sandra exclaimed dramatically, throwing herself down on to Abbie's bed.

'Me, too!' Abbie flopped down beside her. 'Shall we leave walking into town until another day?'

Sandra sat bolt upright, a heavy frown marring her pretty round face, her grey eyes stormy.

'You're a cheat, Abbie Martin. You promised to come with me if I helped you with your cleaning. I don't have to scrub floors or even tidy around at home and my house always looks much better than yours. Your place is a tip, and your brother Billy's room is like a pigsty, with the cigarette ends all over the floor and beer bottles under the bed.'

'It's Sam's bedroom as well,' Abbie reminded her.

'It's not his fault he has to share with your Billy. I know it's not Sam who makes it a mess like that,' Sandra defended. 'His clothes were all hung up on nails, and your Billy's were in a heap on the floor.'

Sandra climbed off the bed. 'Are you coming into town with me or not? If you're not then you can't have any of the sarnies me mam left for us.'

A rumble of hunger in her stomach decided Abbie. ''Course I am, I was only teasing,' she grinned.

'I'm going to put on a clean dress,' Sandra announced the moment they'd finished eating the potted meat sandwiches that Mo Lewis had left on the kitchen table. She regarded Abbie critically. 'You'd better borrow something of mine because there's doormen on the big posh shops and they'll never let us in with you looking like that.'

Sandra was plumper than Abbie, and Abbie was much taller, so Sandra's clothes looked completely different on Abbie than they did on Sandra. She loaned Abbie a blue dress that had a white Peter Pan collar and white trims on the puff sleeves, and she decided to wear a green one with white daisies printed all over it.

'I'm not wearing your shoes, they're all too tight, I wouldn't be able to walk all that way in them,' Abbie told her.

'You can't go in those old plimsolls with your big toe sticking through the top.'

'I haven't got any others.'

Sandra chewed on her lip for a moment, trying to decide what to do. 'I know!' she said at last, 'wear your plimsolls to walk in and take a pair of my shoes to put on when we get there!'

Even though the sun was very hot there was a cooling breeze coming off the Mersey, and, revived by the sandwiches, the journey didn't seem nearly as far as Abbie had thought it would be. They sang the latest songs, 'Yes, We Have No Bananas', and 'Red, Red Robin', at the top of their voices as they walked along.

When they reached Dale Street they cut through Crosshall Street and into Whitechapel, and within minutes they were in Church Street and feasting their eyes on the wonderful window displays.

'We'll go into C&A's in Church Street first,' Sandra said, taking charge. 'You'll have to change your shoes first, though.'

She waited impatiently as Abbie sat down at the entrance to a shop doorway and removed the offending plimsolls and put them into the canvas bag that had held Sandra's sandals.

'They're pinching something chronic,' Abbie moaned as she stood up and took a few tentative steps.

'That'll soon ease off,' Sandra told her. 'They only feel tight because you've had those great, wide boy's plimsolls on,' she added dismissively. 'Hurry up.' Impatiently she led the way into C&A's and Abbie hobbled after her.

Inside, the store was very busy. The two girls roamed from one floor to the next, looking at all the dresses and blouses and coats hanging on the rails.

'This is nothing but clothes,' Sandra said. 'We'll go further up Church Street to Bunney's. They do everything.'

It had been busy in C&A's, but Bunney's was absolutely packed. Men, women and children of all ages surged around the busy department store. Sandra took charge. 'Come on,' she ordered. 'I've been here before with my mother, I know where everything is.'

She headed straight for the toy department and they spent a glorious half an hour looking at all the dolls and wonderful toys that were on display, and wishing they could afford to buy them.

'We don't want to look at any clothes again, we saw all we wanted to in the last shop,' Abbie said, as they left the toy department and made their way down the wide marble staircase.

'Well, not clothes, perhaps, but you'll love the department where they sell scarves and necklaces and ribbons and hair slides,' Sandra told her.

Several times they found themselves separated. The crowd was so dense that Abbie felt a sense of panic in case they couldn't find each other again. Sandra didn't seem to mind a bit. She was in her element, her eyes were shining and she was smiling happily.

'I love going round shops, don't you?' she said gleefully.

'My mammy never has time to do things like this. She says there's no point if you haven't got any money to spend.'

'You're enjoying it today, though, aren't you?' Sandra frowned.

Abbie smiled weakly. 'Yes, but I'm afraid of losing you and not being able to find my way home,' she confessed.

Sandra laughed. 'We'd better hold hands then, hadn't we, at least until we get out of here.'

They were still holding hands when they found the haberdashery section. It was an Aladdin's cave of delights. They tried on hair-bands, held slides up to their hair to see which colour or design looked best, and even tried wrapping scarves round their necks and pirouetting in front of the cheval mirror.

'And what exactly do you two think you are playing at?'

The stern authoritative voice startled them. In his chocolate-brown uniform piped with cream braid the shop-walker was a very forbidding figure.

'We're only looking,' Sandra said boldly.

'You're doing a little bit more than looking,' he boomed. 'I've been watching the two of you, you've been picking things up and putting them down for the last ten minutes. Are you intending to buy anything?' he asked, looking directly at Abbie.

Blood rushed to her face. 'I . . . I haven't any money, sir,' she blurted.

'Just as I thought! Right, then I think the pair of you had better come this way to the Manager's office and he can call a policeman and we'll see what he has to say!'

'Leave off!' Angrily, Sandra shook away the detaining hand he placed on her shoulder. 'We ain't done anything wrong. We're simply looking!'

'Looking? We've already established you were doing more than looking, young lady. We'll leave it for the police to decide, shall we?'

Despite her struggles his grip on Sandra's arm tightened, and with his other hand he took Abbie by the shoulder and began to march the two of them towards the door.

'Abbie . . . Abbie Martin? Is it you? And Sandra Lewis! What in the world is going on?'

The shop-walker stopped as Maggie Ryan approached them, a look of bewilderment on her face.

He paused uncertainly. 'You know these young girls, madam?'

'Yes, I know them both, for goodness' sake. What is it they are supposed to have done, and why are you marching them off like that?'

'I've been watching them for some time. They've been behaving in a highly suspicious manner, picking things up and trying them on.'

Maggie smiled broadly, her blue eyes sparkling. 'Well, don't we all do that when we come into a shop like this? There's so many lovely things on display that most of us would buy up the whole lot if we had the money to do so.'

'That's the point, madam! These two girls haven't any money.'

'So? Don't they call it window shopping?' She gave a warm friendly laugh. 'I know they're doing it inside the store, but it's the same thing really, isn't it? When I need a new pair of shoes I often pop in the week beforehand to see what you have on offer, and I sometimes try on half a dozen pairs before I can decide exactly what I want. I don't buy them right then, I check out how much they are going to cost me and then come back later in the week, or sometimes it's the following week, whenever it is I've got the money together.'

He looked uncomfortable, charmed by her friendly smile and the Irish lilt in her voice. 'Yes, madam, but that is somewhat different.'

'It is?' Maggie looked at him in surprise. 'Now why do you say that?'

'Well, madam, you are a grown-up, and understandably you are budgeting for your next purchase.'

'Quite right! And these young girls are doing the same. Their mams will be proud of them when I tell them. It's a lesson a girl can't learn too soon in life. In a few years' time they'll be married and have to plan their budget and their spending so that their families don't end up in debt.'

'Yes, madam, but . . .'

'I'm sure you're a busy man and we've taken up quite enough of your time with all our chattering,' Maggie Ryan told him with a broad smile. 'If it's all right with you I'll see these two home before their mams start worrying and think they've got lost.'

She divided her bags of shopping between Abbie and Sandra, then possessively took each of them by the arm and smilingly escorted them out of the store before the shop-walker could make any further protest.

Once they were back out in Church Street and well away from Bunney's, Maggie Ryan stopped, reclaimed her shopping from the girls, and drew a deep breath.

'Whew! Do you realise you almost got yourselves done for pilfering?' she asked them.

'It wasn't our fault, Mrs Ryan, honestly,' Abbie told her. 'We were only looking!'

'And trying things on! You never want to do that unless you intend to buy something.'

'It's her fault,' Sandra muttered sulkily. 'When he asked us if we intended buying, she told him she had no money.'

'Well, it was the truth!' Abbie retorted.

'You mean you haven't even got your tram fare home?'

Abbie shook her head. 'We walked.'

'And we'd better start walking home now,' Sandra said. 'My mam comes home around five and she'll wonder where I am. She knows I'm playing with Abbie, but she said I had to be home and have the table laid by the time she got in.'

'Well, you won't manage to do that if you walk,' Maggie Ryan told her. 'It's after half-four now. Here,' she began to pick up the bags she'd rested on the pavement, 'give me a hand with these and I'll pay for your tram fares.'

Chapter Five

'You're not going to say anything to your mam about what happened today, are you?' Sandra asked anxiously, after they had carried Mrs Ryan's bags as far as her door and were hurrying home along Bostock Street.

Abbie shook her head emphatically. 'I might tell Sam, but I won't be telling my mammy. She'd only wallop me if I did. She'd say I shouldn't have been there in the first place and that I was daft to get caught pinching something.'

'We weren't pinching anything,' Sandra said huffily. 'We was only looking.'

'We more or less got accused of pinching, though, didn't we, so we might just as well have been,' Abbie said resentfully. 'That man was a right pig!'

'Yeah, but it all turned out all right in the end, didn't it,' Sandra giggled. 'Good job Mrs Ryan spotted us and saw we were in trouble.'

'She was ever so kind, wasn't she,' Abbie agreed. 'I like her a lot. She's always nice to me.'

'You mean you like Peter Ryan a lot, don't you,' Sandra said craftily.

Abbie's face turned bright red. 'He's nice, too,' she admitted.

'More than nice! Come on, I've seen the way you keep looking for him when we're playing out.'

'So! You're always looking for our Sam!' Abbie retorted crossly.

When she saw that Sandra didn't look at all pleased at being teased, Abbie quickly changed the subject. 'You coming into my place so that I can take your dress and stuff off and give them back to you?'

Sandra shook her head. 'No, my mam will be home by now. Bring them round later on, after tea, but don't let my mam see you with them, though.'

'Why not? She knows I borrow your clothes sometimes.'

'Yes, but if she sees you in my blue and white dress then she's bound to ask why you needed it, because she knows I don't lend you my best dresses just to play out in the street.' She paused, looking thoughtful. 'I don't think you should tell your Sam anything about what happened today.'

'Why don't you want him to know?'

Sandra shrugged. 'No reason, but it's probably best if no one except us knows anything about it.'

'Mrs Ryan does.'

'She won't tell. She wouldn't want to get you into trouble with your mam. She knows the sort of ruction your mam would kick up if she did hear about what happened.'

Abbie looked startled, but said nothing. Sandra was right, she thought, as she made her own way home. Mrs Ryan was especially nice to her. She always made her welcome whenever Abbie called there or she saw her talking to Peter, and it had been kind of her to speak up for them in Bunney's.

She shivered as she thought what might have happened if the shop-walker had taken them to the Manager's office and called the police. It would have been their word against his, and she knew which one the police would listen to.

She was relieved to find that she was the first one home. She changed out of Sandra's dress and put her own shabby clothes back on. She rolled up the dress and the shoes which Sandra had lent her into a bundle, and hid it under her bed. She'd find a way of smuggling them out and taking them back to Sandra when she went out to play later on in the evening.

The fire was almost out, so she raked out the ash from the bottom and then made it up with more coal, and then put the kettle on the gas ring so that it would be boiling when her mammy came in.

She looked in the larder to see what she could find for their meal, but apart from half a loaf, a dish with a lump of margarine in it, and two sausages lying in a pool of yellow fat, there seemed to be nothing. Perhaps her mammy would bring some fish and chips for their tea, she thought hopefully.

Sam arrived home first, whistling cheerfully, a big smile on his face when he saw her.

'Where d'you get the money from for a ride on the Green Goddess this afternoon, then?' he asked. He walked over to the kitchen sink and turned on the cold water tap, and tipped his head underneath it to get a drink, letting it run over his face to cool himself down.

'Seeing things now, are you,' Abbie grinned, as she passed him the threadbare towel that hung from a hook behind the kitchen door so that he could dry himself.

'I saw you and Sandra getting off the tram. So where'd you been, kiddo? Both of you were all dressed up. And why were you both helping Mrs Ryan to carry her shopping home?'

Abbie hesitated, remembering what Sandra had said about not telling anyone, not even Sam, about what had happened, and then decided to tell Sam as much as she felt he needed to know.

He liked Sandra a lot so he wasn't likely to squeal on them if she said Sandra didn't want her mam to know they'd walked into town. It couldn't possibly hurt to tell him that they'd bumped into Mrs Ryan in town and she'd paid for them to come home with her on the tram. There was no need to tell him about what happened in Bunney's, she reasoned.

'You won't say anything, Sam? Not to Mammy or anyone else, promise,' she begged, after she'd explained.

'Your secret's safe with me, kiddo,' he grinned. 'You both must be daft, though, walking all that way just to look into shop windows on a scorching hot day like this.'

'It was a killer, I can tell you,' she smiled. 'I was dead whacked walking all that way, because Mammy had said I had to scrub the kitchen floor and clean the front step and tidy the bedrooms before I could go out. Not fair, really, you boys get away with it, you're never asked to do any housework.'

'I have to go all the way to the cooperage in Bridgewater Street to collect the leftover scraps from the barrels, and I always bring in the coal. I usually have to clean out the grate and re-lay the fire when it goes out,' he reminded her.

'Yeah, but earlier on in the week when Mammy wasn't feeling well I had to do almost everything. She even had me doing the washing, and that made my arms and legs ache, as well as my back, because we haven't even got a dolly tub like other people. It's not fair! Our Billy doesn't help out at all around the house.'

'I don't remember our Billy ever having to do deliveries after school, or work all through his summer holidays, either,' Sam told her.

'Lucky dog!'

'No he wasn't, not really. I'd sooner be delivering things than be penned up in reform school like our Billy was for a couple of years.'

'Didn't do him much good, did it,' Abbie observed. 'He's still a layabout.'

Sam nodded in agreement. 'Work and booze, that's all he's interested in. Anyway, what's for tea? I want to be off out early, got things to do and people to see.'

'Where are you going?'

Before Sam could answer, their mother and Billy arrived home.

'I expected you to have a cuppa brewed and

waiting for me when I got in,' Ellen grumbled irritably, as she flopped down into a chair and looked round the room in a disgruntled manner. Her ribs were still hurting and after a long day at work she wanted to vent her anger on someone.

'The kettle is boiling, Mammy, and I've laid the table,' Abbie told her quickly. 'I didn't know what to start getting ready for tea because there's nothing in the larder.'

Ellen's scowl deepened. 'Sam, run down to the fish shop for a couple of bits of fish and three-penny worth of chips.'

'How many pieces of fish?'

'Better make it three, I suppose. You and Abbie can have a piece between you.'

'Orright.' He began whistling cheerfully, then stopped and held out his hand, 'Where's the money then, Mam?'

Ellen regarded him angrily. 'I haven't got any bleeding money. Been off sick for almost a week. You've got money! It's Friday so you got paid today, didn't you? You buy them.'

'But, Mam . . .' He gave her a pleading look, but, seeing the anger on her face, turned away. It was quite true, he had been paid, but it was only a pittance. If he bought fish and chips for them all then he'd only have about a shilling left, which meant he'd have nothing to spend for the rest of the week.

Billy had been paid as well, he thought resentfully. Billy might only be a casual labourer down at the docks, but he earned a man's wage, not a couple of shillings like he did as a delivery boy, so why couldn't Billy be the one to pay out?

He was about to explain this to his mam, but as he turned round to do so, he saw Billy watching him. There was a calculating look in his brother's small dark eyes, and a cynical sneer on his mouth. Sam decided to keep quiet. If he said anything and it started an argument, it wouldn't only be his mother he'd have to deal with, but Billy as well.

As Billy exhaled a cloud of acrid smoke, Sam felt the familiar sickening drop in his belly as he avoided Billy's eyes. He decided that the best thing he could do was to leave things as they were, and get out of the house before Billy asked him to bring back some fags as well as fish and chips. If that happened then all his money would be gone, and if he refused then Billy would probably hammer him and take his money from him.

By the time he got back, Abbie had plates ready, bread cut and the tea already made and brewing.

The thought that it was his money that had bought the fish and chips, which Billy was wolfing down, spoiled the meal for Sam. As soon as he'd finished eating his own share he pushed back his chair to go out.

Abbie followed him out of the back door and into the back jowler.

'Where you going to, then, in such a hurry?'

Sam tapped the side of his nose with his forefinger, 'That's for me to know and for you never to find out.'

'I will find out, I'll ask Sandra,' Abbie told him

determinedly. 'I know you tell her all your secrets,' she teased.

'You leave Sandra out of this,' Sam scowled.

'OK. I'll keep your secret if you keep mine!'

'That's a deal. Now I'm off, and you'd better start washing up those dishes or Mam will give you a belt round the ear like this,' he told her, playfully cuffing her ear.

As she washed up the pile of greasy plates and put them away, Abbie daydreamed about what life could be like if she lived in a house like the Ryans'. Everything there was so clean and shining, there never seemed to be any shouting or squabbling, and Peter always had shoes and socks to come to school in and usually looked cleaner and tidier than anyone else.

Abbie liked him a lot; he was always so nice to her. He wouldn't let anyone bully her. He even took her side whenever Billy came out into the street shouting at her for something she was supposed to have done wrong. She sometimes thought he was as nice, or even a tiny bit nicer, than Sam was, and yet she loved Sam more than anyone else in the world. She'd never been afraid of him like she was of Billy.

Sam and Billy were still out when she went to bed that night. Her mother had gone upstairs earlier, complaining that sitting in a chair only made her ribs ache worse. Abbie had made her a cuppa and taken it up to her in bed, but Ellen complained that it didn't taste right.

'Billy'll be bringing me back a bottle of stout so

I'll wait and have that,' she'd muttered, pushing the tea aside.

Abbie intended to stay awake until Sam came in, so that she could get him to tell her where he'd been. She wondered if he'd gone out with Sandra on their own and that was why he wouldn't say where he was going.

She didn't want him getting too friendly with Sandra because then he'd have less time for her. It was all right for Sandra; her mammy kissed and cuddled her and worried about her, and even took her out when she wasn't working. She wished her own mammy was like that, instead of always being tired and grumpy.

Despite her determination to stay awake, Abbie drifted into sleep, still thinking about the good times she and Sam had when they went out with Peter and Sandra as a foursome.

Chapter Six

Abbie was quite relieved when the summer holidays were over and it was time for school to restart, since anything would be better than the sheer drudgery of having to tackle mounds of housework every day and getting the family's meals ready. It wouldn't be so bad, she thought, if her mammy was pleased with what she did, but usually she did nothing but grumble.

When she'd cleaned the windows, even though she'd rolled up old newspapers and used them to shine the cracked, scratched glass, like Mrs Ryan had told her to do, her mammy had complained that they looked streaky.

It wasn't her fault that after she'd lugged all the dirty sheets, towels and vests all the way to Frederick Street wash house, and boiled them all for almost an hour, that she found there was a red handkerchief mixed in with them and everything was streaked red.

She still couldn't see what all the fuss was about, since it was the first time that any of their clothes had been boiled for months and months. Her mother usually put dirty clothes to soak in the same water as they'd used when they'd had their weekly bath. She would leave them there in the tin bath to soak overnight, but sometimes she forgot about them for days. When she eventually rinsed them out they were such a dismal grey that she was ashamed to hang them out on the clothesline stretched across the jigger. Instead, she'd drape them on the guard around the fire after they went to bed, and leave them there to dry. Often they were still there days later.

Abbie wished they had an airer in their kitchen, the same as the Ryans and the Lewises had. They lowered it down to put the wet clothes on and then pulled it back up to the ceiling when the clothes were on it, and left them there until they were dry.

Even when she'd made some briquettes from the coal dust and wet newspapers, her mam had grumbled that they were too small to be any good.

At playtime on the first day of the new term back at St Anthony's, Abbie and Sandra looked for Sam, but he kept well out of their way.

'He said not to expect him to talk to us any more,' Abbie told Sandra as they walked round the playground, hand in hand.

'Why not?'

'He said that the other boys would tease him if they saw him talking to us.'

'That's daft! He's your brother and we've always talked to him at playtime.'

'I know that, but it's different now he's older and in the top class.'

'I'm beginning to hate school,' Sandra sighed. 'I don't even like the teacher we've got this year. Sister Mary is so strict!'

'I bet we're going to find the work's a lot harder, too,' Abbie agreed.

'The minute I'm old enough I shall leave and get a job,' Sandra vowed.

'I bet your mam won't let you. She'll want you to go to a commercial college, and learn to type and do shorthand and things like that.'

Sandra pulled a face, but before she could express her opinion on the matter the bell went, and they had to go back to their classroom and Sister Mary, and no more talking was allowed.

The two girls settled in far quicker than they had anticipated. The lessons were more difficult, but they had both expected that, and the routine seemed to be as dull as ever.

It was better than being at home, though, and if she worked really hard, Abbie thought, then maybe she'd be able to get a good job, like Mrs Lewis was always talking about, when she left school.

One Tuesday, a few weeks later, there was an unexpected excitement. At the beginning of afternoon playtime, two policemen arrived. They looked so imposing, in their navy serge uniforms with bright silvery buttons and their big dome-shaped helmets, that everyone stopped what they were doing and watched as they walked across the school yard.

They were met by one of the Sisters and taken inside. Almost immediately the bell went, but instead of going back into their classrooms they were all told to line up outside.

'What's going on?' Sandra whispered, as she and Abbie were jostled into line by the rest of their class.

There was an immediate call for silence. Then Mr Tomlinson, the headmaster, appeared, alongside the two policemen. 'The police have come here to inform me that a bicycle was stolen yesterday evening from Monks's Cycle Shop in Great Homer Street, and that one of the pupils from this school is responsible. Now, I want that boy or girl to step forward and own up.'

He stopped speaking and waited expectantly. There were whisperings and nudges and the sounds of suppressed laughter, but no one moved or spoke up.

'Silence!' His voice brought immediate quiet.

'For the last time, I am giving the culprit the chance to come forward.'

Still no one spoke or moved, so he turned to the policemen. 'You have a name?'

They nodded, and one of them took his notebook from his top pocket and read out, 'Peter Ryan! Is there a Peter Ryan here?'

Abbie and Sandra squeezed hands and stared at each other in shock. There must be some mistake. It couldn't be Peter, he never got into any trouble.

They watched in disbelief as Peter stepped forward. In his grey shorts, navy blue V-necked ribbed jumper and white shirt, he looked to be one of the most respectable boys in the school. He even had on proper black shoes and knee-length grey socks.

'Is your name Peter Ryan?'

They watched as Peter nodded. He tried to speak, but his voice seemed to have dried up and though his lips moved, no sound came out.

'Did you steal a bicycle from a shop in Great Homer Street last night?' the policeman demanded.

Peter shook his head. 'No,' he croaked. 'Why would I want to do something like that, I've got a bike already.'

Some of the older children started laughing, but they were quickly silenced as Mr Tomlinson glared in their direction.

'Can you tell us where you were last night?'

'At home, of course!' Peter mumbled. 'Where else would I be?'

'Right. We don't need lip from you!' He looked Peter up and down carefully and then referred back to his notebook. 'You answer the description we were given of the boy who was in the bicycle shop around the time the bike went missing,' he said ominously. 'You'd better tell us exactly what you did when you left school yesterday afternoon.'

Peter bit his lip. 'The usual. Walked home with my friends and then went out on my bike with Sam Martin for a bit, and then I went home for tea.'

'So you admit you were riding a bicycle?'

'Yes, but it was my own bike.' He stopped and stared boldly at the policeman. 'It was my own bike, I've had it for almost a year. My dad bought it for me the last time he was home from sea.'

'And did you go out again after you'd had your tea?'

Peter looked uncomfortable. 'Only for a few minutes. I'd chipped some of the paint on the back mudguard so I nipped out to get some touch-up paint.'

'Did you get it from Monks's in Great Homer Street?'

Peter nodded.

'So who was your accomplice?'

Peter looked puzzled. 'I went there on my own.'

'And while Mr Monks went through to his storeroom at the back of the shop to fetch a tin of black enamel, you stole a bike from the front of the shop. Right?'

Peter shook his head. 'Of course not,' he said indignantly. 'I wouldn't do a thing like that. I've already told you I have a bike, so what would I want with another one?'

'Stop lying, son. You stole a bike, admit it. You wheeled outside one of the bikes that were on display in the front of the shop, propped it against the kerb, went back in, paid for your tin of enamel, and then came out of the shop and rode the bike away, as bold as brass.'

'No, I didn't. Someone else was in the shop at the same time, he'll tell you I didn't do anything like that.'

The policemen exchanged knowing looks. 'Are you going to tell us what you did with the bike?'

'How can I when I didn't take it?' Peter protested, his voice quavering.

One of the policemen placed a hand firmly on Peter's shoulder. 'Come on, we're taking you back to the police station with us for further questioning.'

He turned and thanked the headmaster for his cooperation. 'The rest of you remember, if you steal or do anything else wrong, then we will get to hear about it and come after you,' he warned.

With Peter walking between them, the two policemen started to move towards the school gate.

'Stop, stop, you can't do this, he's not done anything wrong, he never does anything wrong!'

Her dark hair flying, her blue eyes blazing, Abbie pushed her way through the lines of other pupils and chased after the trio. She clutched at Peter's jumper, trying to pull him away from the policemen.

'And who are you?' One of the policemen grabbed her firmly by the arm, halting her in her tracks.

'I'm his best friend.'

'I see!' The policeman regarded her sternly. 'And can you tell me where Peter Ryan went yesterday evening after he visited the cycle shop in Great Homer Street?'

Abbie hesitated, wondering if she should lie, but afraid they would only find out if she did and take her along to the police station as well. 'No!' she said miserably. 'He's already told you, though, that he was at home with his mam most of the evening, and that's where he usually is.'

The policeman frowned. 'I think you are wasting our time,' he said gruffly. 'We've had information from someone who was in Mr Monks's shop at the same time. Come on,' he took Peter firmly by the arm and began to walk off.

Abbie grabbed at the policeman's stiff blue jacket to try and stop him. 'He's not done anything wrong,' she insisted, pummelling with her fists on the policeman's back, 'he's already told you that!'

He tried to shake her away but she grabbed him more tightly, latching on to one of the silver buttons on his jacket. As he pulled back, the button tore away from the blue serge.

Angrily, he prised it from her fingers. 'Get back with the rest of your bunch before I run you in as well,' he barked.

Tears streaming down her face, Abbie turned away and followed the other children back into the school. She was shaking with anger that Peter should be taken away. It wasn't fair. She was sure that he wouldn't dream of pinching a bike. He didn't even nick other kids' balls or tops or anything. And, as he'd told the scuffers, he already had a bike, so why would he want another?

The incident was the talk of the school. Abbie found herself publicly reprimanded by the headmaster, and ridiculed and teased by all the other kids for sticking up for Peter. Even Sandra ignored her and pulled her hand away when Abbie went to take it as they crowded back into the classroom.

That night she didn't wait for Sandra, but ran home as fast as her legs would take her. She didn't go straight to her own house, but went to Mrs Ryan's, banging on the door as if the devil himself was on her heels.

She breathed a sigh of relief when Maggie Ryan answered the door because she had been afraid Mrs Ryan might have been called down to the police station and still be there.

'Is Peter here?' she asked anxiously.

Maggie Ryan shook her head. Her eyes were red-rimmed and puffy from crying and for once she wasn't smiling. 'They've kept him at the police station,' she said. 'Do you want to come in? Your mam won't be home from work for a while yet, will she?'

'No, and our Sam's out doing his deliveries.'

'Come on in, then, and I'll find you a biscuit or a piece of cake.'

'He didn't do it, Mrs Ryan. I know Peter wouldn't do something like that,' Abbie told her as she followed Maggie Ryan through to the living room.

'Peter told me how you stuck up for him,' Maggie said with a gentle smile.

'It didn't do any good, though, did it,' Abbie muttered stubbornly. 'They still took him away. Wouldn't they believe you, either?'

Maggie shook her head. 'They said they had proof, but they wouldn't say what it was. Peter has to stay there until they've finished their enquiries and then he will have to appear before a magistrate. His dad will be out of his mind with worry when I write and tell him.'

'Perhaps you shouldn't tell him,' Abbie said sagely.

Maggie smiled. 'We'll see, luv. The trouble is his boat docks in a couple of months' time.'

'That's ages away! By the time he comes home it will all be forgotten and someone else's name will be mud,' Abbie said hopefully.

Abbie was wrong. Since there was only his mother's word that he had been at home that night, the police insisted that he had been the one who stole the bike, and they thought he probably had an accomplice who had actually taken the bike while Mr Monks was serving Peter. Since they couldn't locate the bike, and Peter wouldn't admit to an accomplice, they adjudged he was guilty.

Later, when Peter appeared before the magistrate, even though the police still couldn't trace the bike, he was found guilty and sent to a reform school for three years.

Abbie and Sam were both convinced he was innocent. Sandra wasn't sure and said that if he did do it then he was a fool to get caught.

Remembering how close they had come to being wrongly accused of pinching things in Bunney's store, and probably would have been if Mrs Ryan hadn't spoken up for them, Abbie thought that Sandra was being very unfair and told her so.

She was so annoyed with Sandra that she refused to play with her that night and went home early. She liked Peter a lot, and next to Sam she thought he was the nicest person in the world.

Abbie was so upset that she couldn't get to

sleep that night for thinking about Peter and what might be happening to him. Sam felt the same, and without her having to ask him he came into her room and they curled up together for comfort, until they heard Billy and their mam coming down the road, roaring drunk.

'Where have they found the money this time, to go boozing this early in the week?' Sam murmured.

Abbie stared at him, wide-eyed. 'I wonder if it was Billy who stole that bike?' she whispered. 'He was having a good laugh when I was telling you about Peter being kept in custody and having to go before the magistrate, and he was in Monks's shop around the same time.'

Sam shook his head. 'He wouldn't let Peter take the blame, that would be low even for Billy,' he muttered.

'Well, they've had a skinful, and I don't know where else they'd get the money from,' Abbie persisted, as the noise from downstairs became louder and more raucous.

'You mean you think Billy pinched the bike then sold it to someone?'

She nodded. 'That could be why the police say that they can't find it.'

Sam looked doubtful.

Abbie struggled to her feet. 'I'm going downstairs to ask him.'

'Abbie! Don't be so stupid! He's drunk, he might hit you, you know what he's like.'

'I don't care! Peter is in a reform school being

punished and Billy's out enjoying himself, swilling beer,' she declared angrily.

Before Sam could stop her she was running down the stairs. Reluctantly, he followed her, fearful of what might happen.

'What the hell're you doing down here?' Ellen muttered as she turned and saw Abbie in the doorway.

'I want to ask Billy where you got the money from to go to the boozer tonight.'

'You cheeky little brat!' Ellen's massive hand swung out, but Abbie ducked and it went over her head.

'Well?' She faced Billy. 'Where did you get the money?'

'Abbie!' Sam shouted a warning but he was too late.

'You were the one that stole that bike, weren't you, Billy? And you've sold it, and that's where you got the money from for you and me mammy to go boozing.'

Billy's sallow face turned a dark red colour, his small dark eyes glittered menacingly and he let out a low growl as he lunged towards her.

Abbie stepped back out of reach and Sam grabbed her by the arm and pulled her towards the back door. Seconds later they were out in the back jigger, running barefoot down the alleyway towards Great Homer Street with Billy in hot pursuit.

Sam pushed Abbie behind some sheets of rusty corrugated iron that were propped against one of the walls and shushed her to silence.

They crouched there, shivering with fright as they heard Billy pounding to the end of the jigger and then back again. As soon as Sam felt they were in the clear, he took her hand and ran with her to the other end of the alleyway and then round the corner into Scotland Road and finally back into their own street.

'We can't go back indoors tonight, he'll murder us,' Sam told her.

'I'm sorry, it's all my fault,' Abbie whimpered. She felt cold and frightened and her bare feet were sore and hurting. 'What are we going to do?'

Sam's face was grim. 'There's only one thing we can do, he told her. 'We'll go to Mrs Ryan's, and see if she will take us in.'

Chapter Seven

Abbie missed Peter far more than she would admit to either Sandra or Sam. Because Sam had begun to spend a lot of time with Sandra, her friendship with Peter had grown closer. Now, with him gone, she was more lonely than ever.

All three of them talked about Peter a lot, wondering how he was getting on. They asked Mrs Ryan to take messages when she went once a month to visit him. They sent along comics and sometimes a Fry's chocolate bar as well, which Sam paid for out of his Saturday earnings.

Abbie spent more and more time with Mrs Ryan, because when they came out of school in the afternoon Sandra now went straight to the corner shop where her mother worked. 'I have to, because me mam says she wants to keep an eye on me so's I don't get into trouble like Peter Ryan,' Sandra confided to Abbie.

'Peter didn't do it, he didn't steal that bike,' Abbie told her emphatically.

'Well, if he didn't then who did? And if you think you know who did steal it, Abbie Martin, then you ought to go and tell the police.'

'No good doing that if I haven't got any proof, is it,' Abbie said miserably.

'Well, you seem to think you know who it might be?' Sandra persisted.

Abbie shook her head. 'I'm not saying.'

Sandra looked at her shrewdly, her grey eyes wary. 'It wasn't Sam, was it?'

'Of course not!' Abbie's face coloured up with indignation. 'You know quite well that Sam wouldn't do a thing like that!'

She had to bite her tongue not to confide in Sandra that she and Sam both thought it might be Billy. Sam had warned her not to breathe a word to anyone. They were both quite sure that he was involved, though.

That was a night neither Abbie nor Sam would forget in a hurry. They'd still been talking things over when Billy and their mother had arrived home so drunk that they could hardly stand up. They'd fallen through the door into the passage-way and cursed each other for a good ten minutes as they'd tried to pick themselves up.

Then they'd started pushing and shoving each other so hard that in the end it had come to blows, and Sam had had to step in and stop them. He'd got a kicking from Billy, as well as a black eye, the result of his mother's elbow jabbing him in the face.

Ever since then Billy had been surly and aggressive, cuffing Sam round the ears whenever he got the chance. Abbie felt his small mean eyes follow-ing her whenever she was in the same room as him, and she knew she only had to do or say something that annoyed him and she'd feel the force of his hand around her own ears.

As it was, he vented his spleen on her by making her clean his shoes, and iron the white cotton shirt that he wore at the weekends when he went out drinking. No matter how well she did these jobs he was never satisfied. If his boots didn't gleam enough he made her polish them again, and if there was a crease down the sleeve of his white shirt he threw it back in her face and told her to iron it properly.

Abbie couldn't see that it mattered if there was a crease since he always had his jacket on anyway. Ironing was not something she was very good at. She found heating up the flat iron over the coal fire, and then making sure it was perfectly clean before she began using it, was tricky. More often than not she burned herself, either lifting it off the trivet or when she was cleaning the bottom of it and around the edges with a piece of old towel.

Sometimes she forgot to spit on it, to test it and make sure it wasn't too hot, and then there would be a brown singe mark on whatever she was ironing. Yet, if she didn't have the flat iron hot enough then it was a waste of time using it because it wouldn't remove the creases.

Although her mother usually left a pile of washing or ironing for her to do when she got in from school, and also expected the table to be laid and the kettle boiling, Abbie still managed to fit in a visit to Maggie Ryan's most evenings.

To do this she worked out a clever plan. She dashed home from school and filled the big iron kettle and put it on the trivet over the fire. If it wasn't quite boiling when she got back from Mrs

Ryan's then she poured the water from it into the tin kettle they used on the gas ring. She always made sure that she was back home in time to be in the middle of whatever other chore it was she was supposed to be doing when her mother and Billy came in from work.

'You'll have to buck your ideas up, young lady, when you come to leave school,' Ellen would grumble, when she found her doing the ironing on a corner of the table or leaning over the sink up to her elbows in dirty sudsy water. 'If you go to work in a factory where you're on piece work you'll starve to death, the time it takes you to get anything done.'

Abbie would concentrate on what she was doing and say nothing. Sometimes Ellen would let it pass, at other times she'd yell at her, 'Answer me when I speak to you, you insolent little brat!'

As winter approached and it was dark earlier and earlier in the evenings, Mrs Lewis insisted on Sandra staying indoors after tea.

'Is your mam trying to stop us seeing each other or something?' Abbie asked. 'Sam was saying he hasn't seen you for ages, either.'

Sandra went bright pink and avoided Abbie's eyes. 'I told you, she's worried about me getting into trouble.'

'We don't get into trouble, though, do we!'

'Only because we don't get caught! Look what happened when we went into town together. And then there was that time when we tied Mrs Kelly's door knocker on to Mr Parsons's door handle so that when he came out and shut his door her knocker banged.'

'That was ages ago,' Abbie said indignantly, 'when we were in infants' school, and it wasn't us, it was Peter and Sam who did that.'

'We were out playing with them! My mam says that Mrs Kelly is always going on about it whenever she comes into the shop.'

Abbie shrugged. 'It didn't work properly, anyway. If Mrs Kelly had any sense she would have known that it wasn't really anyone knocking on her door.'

'She told my mam she was frightened out of her life because she thought it was the scuffers coming after her Liam.'

Abbie laughed. 'Serve her right, he's always in trouble. He does cruel things like tying a tin can on to a cat's tail and picking up dog turds and putting them through people's letterboxes.'

Deprived of her playmate, and anxious to get out of her own house after she'd washed up the dishes and put them away after their evening meal, before she was landed with more chores or in trouble of some kind, Abbie would sneak down the back jigger to the Ryans' house.

Maggie was always pleased to see her and when Michael wasn't there she would sit and listen to her, show her photographs of Peter and Michael when they were small, and talk to her about everything under the sun.

One evening Abbie had even confided in her that she couldn't understand why her own mammy was always so cross with her and didn't seem to want to spend any time with her.

'I think that perhaps my sister Audrey dying so young upset her a great deal,' Abbie sighed.

Maggie Ryan looked startled, but said nothing.

'I don't know anything about what happened, because nobody ever wants to talk about it,' Abbie went on. 'It was around the same time as I was born, wasn't it?'

'More or less,' Maggie Ryan agreed evasively.

Skilfully, Maggie changed the subject. 'Now, didn't I say we'd make some of those fairy cakes you like so much? We'd better get started or they won't be cooked before you have to go home.'

Whenever she was baking, or preparing a meal for herself and Michael, Maggie would let Abbie help and would teach her how to cook and make cakes.

Usually, too, there was a sample to be enjoyed at the end of their task. If Abbie couldn't wait until the cakes or pies were cooked and ready to eat, then Maggie Ryan always saved her a taster until the next time she popped in.

The only thing that spoiled this wonderful friendship for Abbie was Michael Ryan. He was an older version of Peter. He was good-looking, tall and lean with black hair and eyebrows and deep blue eyes. He said very little, even to his mother, and seldom spoke to her except to mutter 'Hello' or 'Goodbye'. He made Abbie feel uncomfortable because he seemed to watch her closely all the time she was in their house.

When she first started going there every evening

she tried to get him to talk to her by asking him about his work.

'Do you like being a porter at Lime Street station?' she asked shyly.

He shrugged, and took a packet of Lucky Strike cigarettes out of his pocket and lit one.

'Do you want to be a guard or an engine driver and travel on the trains someday?' she asked.

He took a deep drag on his cigarette. 'Not really,' he said, and blew out a cloud of blue smoke.

'You could see lots of other places, if you did,' she gabbled on.

Michael shrugged. 'Only different stations.'

'Is it hard work being a porter?'

'It's just a job.'

'Do you meet lots of interesting people?'

He shrugged again. 'They're only on the platform for a few minutes so I wouldn't know if they're interesting or not.'

She waited hopefully for him to go on, but he didn't. He concentrated on lighting a fresh cigarette from the stub of the one he'd just finished.

After that she confined herself to saying 'Hello' or 'Goodbye', the same as he did.

She remarked on it once to Maggie Ryan, and Maggie had merely smiled.

'Perhaps he doesn't like me coming here,' Abbie said worriedly.

'No, of course he doesn't mind,' Maggie Ryan assured her.

'He's not friendly like Peter,' Abbie persisted. 'I miss Peter a lot!' she added wistfully.

'Take no notice of Michael. He's a man of few words and a bit on the shy side,' Maggie said reassuringly.

'Is that why he hasn't got a girlfriend?'

Maggie Ryan looked taken aback. 'I don't know whether he has or not,' she said slowly. 'He certainly hasn't brought one home yet.'

After that, Abbie decided not to visit when Michael was there, if she could help it. His presence definitely seemed to mar the atmosphere between her and Mrs Ryan, and that was so special she didn't want it spoiled in any way at all.

Instead, she counted the days left until Peter came home. Mrs Ryan helped her to make a chart and every time she visited they marked off the days.

'It's going to be a big chart,' Mrs Ryan sighed. 'Peter won't be home until 1929, just before his sixteenth birthday in September.'

'Shall we plan a very special birthday for him?' Abbie suggested.

'We can, but it's an awful long time away.'

'We could have a party. Some of the friends he had at school could come, and, of course, Sandra and Sam. I could help you to get everything ready and do some extra baking.'

'That's a great idea! You make a list of the people we should invite and a bit nearer the time I'll buy extra food for the store cupboard each week. We'll have a special baking session a few days before he's due home so that there's plenty of cakes and little pies . . .'

'And could we have jelly and custard?' Abbie

interrupted wistfully. 'Sandra's mam used to make it as a special treat on my birthday when I was little, but she doesn't do it any more. I can still remember what it tasted like, though.'

'We'll go even better,' Maggie Ryan promised. 'We'll make a trifle with sponge cake and tinned fruit in it, and decorate the top with real cream. How about that? And we'll make a big birthday cake and you can help me decorate it, and we'll put Peter's name on it in coloured icing.'

Chapter Eight

Maggie and Abbie planned the party for when Peter would be released in September 1929 over and over again. They constantly changed the menu and even the names of the people they would invite. It was a bit like playing a game, and one they both thoroughly enjoyed.

Since it was such a long time away, Maggie suggested they should keep it a secret until nearer the date of Peter's release, so whenever Michael was around they talked about something else.

When that happened, Abbie hugged the secret to herself and elaborated on their plans when she was at home and in bed. It was like living in another world; one of her own making where everything was exactly as she wanted it to be. In her dream world she was wearing a lovely blue dress that matched her eyes and she had on shiny new shoes, and Peter told her how pretty she looked.

Abbie was now on such friendly terms with Maggie Ryan that she no longer knocked on the door when she visited. Instead, she simply called out 'Hello' as she opened the back door and went in, so it was quite a shock when she walked in a few nights before Christmas to find Paddy Ryan in the kitchen.

He was away at sea for such long stretches that for a minute she didn't recognise him. She had forgotten that he didn't look a bit like Michael and Peter. He had thick copper-coloured hair and a dark red beard, and the most massive shoulders and muscled arms she had ever seen. His face, what she could see of it, was weather-beaten, and his dark grey eyes were sharp and penetrating.

'And hello to you, young lady,' he grinned, 'how can I help you?'

'I ... I've come to see Mrs Ryan,' Abbie told him, her face going red.

'Visitor for you, Maggie,' he bellowed.

Maggie came rushing into the kitchen looking very flustered, a worried frown on her face. 'Hello, Abbie,' she hesitated, looking anxiously at her husband and then back at Abbie. 'I was just coming round to tell you ...'

'Abbie? Abbie who? It's not Abbie Martin, is it?' Paddy Ryan challenged. His welcoming smile changed to a heavy scowl.

'It's all right, Paddy, Abbie's only popped in for a second with a message for me.'

'A message? What sort of a message? What the hell is she doing walking into my house without even knocking? Come to that, what is she doing under my roof at all?' The affable look had gone from his face; his eyes were no longer friendly, but steely grey as they darted from Abbie to Maggie and back again.

'It's all right, Paddy,' Maggie Ryan murmured soothingly, 'I can explain.'

'Bloody well get on with it then, and it had

better be good,' he growled, his hands clenching into fists as if he was having difficulty containing his temper.

Abbie reached behind her for the handle of the kitchen door. 'I'll come back some other time,' she said hastily as she backed away. Paddy Ryan looked so fierce and angry that she felt herself trembling all over. For a minute she'd been afraid he was going to attack her.

She was used to her mammy screaming at her, and Billy shouting and swearing at her, but there was something so intense about Paddy Ryan and the way he was looking at her that she felt sure he meant to do her some harm.

She couldn't think why. As far as Abbie knew she'd never spoken to him before, so she had no idea how she could have upset him.

'You'd better go, Abbie,' Maggie Ryan whispered. Her face was white, her lips trembling, and she avoided Abbie's eyes.

Abbie didn't stop to question why Mr Ryan was so angry. She felt so scared she couldn't get out of the Ryans' house fast enough.

Paddy Ryan was probably so upset about what had happened to Peter that he didn't want to see any of Peter's friends, so that was the reason he didn't want her there, she reasoned as she ran back home, her heart still pounding.

Christmas 1926 was on a Saturday, and it was the most miserable one Abbie had ever known. Paddy Ryan was still at home, which meant she couldn't go round to the Ryans' house and she had been looking forward to doing so. She knew there wouldn't be much celebration in her own home, apart from her mammy and Billy getting drunk, and she couldn't stop thinking about all the treats Maggie had promised her.

She had helped Maggie to make a Christmas pudding and a Christmas cake and she'd been looking forward to tasting them. They had been planning that on Christmas Eve they would make a batch of mince pies, and Maggie had said that Sam could come round, as well as on Christmas Day.

'It will have to be fairly late on in the day, because in the afternoon I'm going to visit Peter,' Maggie explained. 'I'll leave everything prepared ready, and when I get back I'll be able to tell you how Peter is getting on.'

Now, with Paddy Ryan at home, that was going to be impossible, Abbie thought sadly. He had seemed to be such a nice man when she'd walked into the kitchen. A beaming smile, a hearty greeting and then, the moment he had heard her name, he'd become a bad-tempered ogre. She kept asking herself why? She hadn't said or done anything to upset him. Maggie had looked so flustered that she hadn't dared ask. She couldn't put it out of her mind, though, and once Paddy Ryan went back to sea she would certainly ask Maggie what had gotten into him causing him to have acted the way that he did.

She knew that Sandra had invited Sam to her place on Christmas Day, but so far she didn't know if he had accepted or not. If he went, then it meant she was going to be on her own. Except, of course, for her mammy and Billy, and with Christmas Eve being on a Saturday they'd both have a hangover until the middle of the morning and then they'd probably be in a drunken stupor for the rest of Christmas.

Unless Sandra asked her to come round as well, and somehow she didn't think that would happen. Lately, Mrs Lewis seemed to think that it was better for the two of them to be kept apart in case they got into any trouble. Why Sandra would get into trouble going out and about with her, and yet it was all right for her to go out with Sam, Abbie couldn't work out.

As predicted, Abbie found herself staying at home with her mammy and Billy on Christmas Day. Both of them were bad-tempered, having had far too much to drink the previous night. Her mammy had bought a chicken, but made no attempt to cook it.

'If you want it then you'd better stick it in the oven before you go to Mass,' she told Abbie. 'And stick some spuds in alongside it as well.'

'And mind there's some stuffing and some good thick gravy,' Billy told her.

'I'm not sure how to make stuffing,' Abbie replied.

'Then bloody well find out. Go and ask Maggie Ryan, you're as thick as thieves with her most of the time.'

'I can't go down there, Paddy Ryan is home from sea.'

Billy gave a nasty laugh. 'Doesn't want you around the place, eh, kiddo! Hear that, Mam?' He turned to Ellen, a smirk on his face. 'Paddy Ryan doesn't like the look of Abbie's face.'

'Huh! That's not surprising. Told you to sling yer hook, did he?'

Abbie shook her head. 'Not really. He didn't seem very pleased to see me, though.'

Billy and his mother exchanged knowing glances.

'Then you'd best stay home where you belong and do a bit more for your own folks, hadn't you, instead of gallivanting out all the time,' Ellen told her. 'Now get on and see to that chicken or else there'll be nothing for any of us to eat.'

Abbie didn't see or hear anything from the Ryans all over Christmas and the New Year. The weather was cold and miserable and she felt desperately lonely.

She saw hardly anything of Sam because he spent more and more time with Sandra. They had plenty to be excited about because on Monday, January 2nd, he would be starting work full time at Nelson's Jam Factory.

The whole thing had come as a surprise. One of the travellers who called at the shop where Mo Lewis worked had said there would be a vacancy at the factory after Christmas. He'd said if she knew of a likely lad then he'd put in a good word for him.

It was a chance in a lifetime. A job being handed out on a plate, when half the boys who left school couldn't find work, and more and more men were being laid off because of the rising unemployment.

Sandra had been in the shop and overheard

their conversation, and said she knew someone who was working as a delivery boy and was looking for better employment. The upshot had been that Sam had got the job.

It meant that, in future, instead of Sam being at home in the early evening to take her part when her mother and Billy arrived home, she would have to face them on her own.

Sam would come in soon afterwards, but he would probably be tired out from his long day and in no mood to listen to her trivial problems. Like his mother and older brother he'd be ravenous and expect to find his meal on the table. Later in the evening, when normally they would have had time to talk to each other, Sam would be going round to see Sandra.

Now that he was about to start work, Sandra went round telling everyone that Sam was her boyfriend. Abbie thought she was being stupid since she was only eleven, and they wouldn't be old enough to marry for years and years. When she said this to Sam, Sandra accused her of being jealous.

'You'll see things differently when Peter comes home,' she retorted smugly.

At school, Sandra began to avoid Abbie and go around with a bunch of other girls, arms linked, all singing and sniggering together. Sometimes the song was 'I can't give you anything but love', or else, 'Let's do it, let's fall in love'.

Abbie tried to pretend she didn't care what they were doing or what they were saying. Deep down, though, she felt lonely and unhappy and longed for Peter to come home from reform school, but it seemed to be a lifetime away. She missed him so much, and she wanted to be reassured that he was still her best friend, the same as before he was sent there.

If the day ever came when he told her that he loved her then that would be the happiest day of her life. When that happened she would sing 'Let's fall in love' at the top of her voice, even though she knew she'd be out of tune and sound more like a frog croaking than a nightingale warbling.

Chapter Nine

Christmas had been dismal, but the start of 1927 was even worse for Abbie. Her mother and Billy had celebrated New Year's Eve, which had fallen on a Saturday, with a drinking binge that had started on the Friday night.

Sam had been late coming home because he and Sandra had gone into town to see the New Year in, so there had been no one she could turn to when Billy and her mammy had arrived home, roaring drunk, very early on Sunday morning.

Their New Year resolution seemed to be to see how much booze they could get down them in one night, Abbie thought miserably. She cowered under the bedclothes with her hands over her ears as they shouted and yelled at each other and sang rowdy songs that ended in bursts of raucous laughter.

When she finally heard them stumbling up the stairs she prayed that neither of them would come into her bedroom.

When she came downstairs on New Year's Day she had to pick her way over discarded coats and boots, pools of vomit, and a broken chair. The living room was in such a state of disorder that it looked as though they'd been robbed.

Except that they had nothing worth taking,

Abbie thought bitterly, as she set about clearing out the ashes and stirring the fire to life with bits of rolled-up newspaper and firewood. Resignedly, she set about clearing up the mess before she went off to Mass.

If her mammy used one quarter of what she spent on drink and cigarettes on making their home comfortable, it could be every bit as nice as the Ryans' or Lewis's, she thought wistfully. They could have a rug on the floor to take away the chill that went through your feet and legs first thing in the morning. They could have pretty matching cups and saucers, instead of a collection of chipped mugs and battered cups that didn't match up with any of the saucers. They could have proper sheets and woollen blankets on the beds instead of having to use old coats for extra warmth.

The list was endless. She could go on and on, but what was the point. Practically every penny Billy and her mam earned, and some of Sam's wages, went on beer and cigarettes, and she couldn't see that changing. She supposed she should be grateful that her mammy paid the rent regularly. At least she kept a roof over their heads, even if half the time their bellies were empty.

She wondered if things would be any better, now that Sam had a better job and would be bringing more money home each week. He'd be expected to hand it over, of course, and she wondered if it would be set aside for housekeeping or used as extra beer money.

She was pretty sure she knew the answer, but

Sam might have something to say on the matter and if he did then she'd certainly back him up.

In some ways she wished Sam hadn't got the job at the Nelson's Jam Factory. She knew he had been lucky getting taken on since there were dozens of boys in Liverpool who would have jumped at the chance. It meant, though, that he would have to travel to Aintree each day, so he would be going out of the house even earlier than her mammy and Billy. That meant she'd be expected to clear up and tidy the house all on her own before she went to school.

1927, Abbie decided, was going to be anything but a happy new year. She wished she was old enough to leave school but it would be another year and a half before that was possible.

Perhaps if she could make the house nicer, Abbie thought, as she continued to clean out the ashes, then Sam wouldn't want to go out with Sandra every night. Her mammy might even begin to take an interest in making the place more comfortable once Sam started bringing more money home.

It would be Sam's fourteenth birthday in ten days' time, so perhaps she'd try and put on a special tea for him and ask Sandra to come round. She'd keep it a secret and ask Sandra not to breathe a word about it to Sam.

She planned all the details in her head as she cleaned the place up. Then she made a cup of tea and took it upstairs to her mammy so that she could tell her all about her wonderful idea.

Ellen looked terrible. Her face was yellow, there

were bags under her eyes, and her hair was so tangled and matted that it looked as though it hadn't seen a comb in weeks.

'Happy New Year, Mammy, I've brought you up a cuppa,' Abbie told her. She felt so full of hope for the future that she leaned over and kissed her mother's cheek.

Ellen pushed her away. 'Gerroff with you! What you after, smooching around me like wet echo. If it's money then you can forget it, I'm bloody skint!'

Abbie pulled back as if stung. 'I don't want money!' she muttered, her happy mood shattered. 'I wanted to tell you what I thought we could do for Sam's birthday.'

Ellen heaved herself up in bed, took the cup of tea and slurped a mouthful. 'What do you mean, do for his birthday? He's got his present and a damn good one it is and all.'

'Oh!' Abbie looked taken aback. 'I didn't know you'd bought him anything.'

'Buy him anything?' Scowling, Ellen pushed her hair back out of her eyes. 'He don't need me buying him anything. He's got his birthday present, the lucky little bugger, he's got a decent job at long last and it's been handed to him on a plate.'

'That's not a present, well, not a present from us, is it!'

'It's all he's going to get so he'd better make the best of it!'

'I thought that perhaps we could put on a nice tea for him and ask Sandra to come round and . . .'

'Have Sandra Lewis in here scoffing my grub! You must be out of your mind, girl. If she wants to have her tea with Sam then she'd better be the one to invite him to her house. Her mam's got a sight more food in her pantry than I've got in mine. Gets it all cut price from that corner shop where she works!'

'I don't know anything about that . . .'

'No, you don't know anything about most things. Now bugger off and clean up downstairs and let me get some bleedin' shuteye. My head's thumping like a steam hammer without listening to your stupid twaddle.'

Nothing more was said by either of them about it, and Sam's birthday would have passed by unnoticed had it not been for Sandra inviting him to her house for a meal.

'She said you can come as well if you like,' Sam told Abbie.

Abbie hesitated, wondering if it meant that she and Sandra could once more be good friends.

'If she wants me to be there then why couldn't she ask me herself?'

Sam shrugged. 'I don't know. Ask her yourself!'

'Won't I be in the way if it's special for the two of you?' she asked tentatively.

'Sandra's mam will be there as well, so of course you won't be in the way.'

Abbie's face lit up with a wide smile. 'Then I'd love to come. Do you want me to tell Sandra or will you?'

'She's taking it for granted that you'll come.'

Abbie boiled up a kettle of water and washed

her hair in the sink, rinsing it three times to make sure there was no soap left in it. Then she rinsed out Sam's best shirt and a blouse for herself and dried and ironed them.

She felt really excited. She hadn't been out anywhere all over Christmas. The winds blowing in from the Mersey had been icy, making it too cold to walk around the streets, so she'd stayed indoors, and now she was fed up with her own company and was really looking forward to going to Sandra's place.

Abbie felt a sharp stab of jealousy when she found that Sandra had bought Sam a present. She would have loved to have been able to give him one but she had no money.

Sandra's present wasn't very big, but it was wrapped up in glittering gold paper and tied with an elaborate ribbon bow.

When Sam opened it Abbie heard him catch his breath in surprise as he pulled out the shiny new mouth organ.

'This is great!' he exclaimed, his brown eyes shining. Eagerly, he put it to his lips and began to play. The tone was beautiful, soft yet powerful.

Sam stopped and examined it carefully. 'This is a double reed *Echo*,' he said in awe. 'Gosh! Thanks, Sandra. It's the very best you can get!'

'Well, I didn't think you'd want one of those cheap *Bandmaster* mouth organs like the rest of the boys have,' she sniffed. 'Go on, play us something.'

'He can't play,' Abbie told her.

'Yes I can! Well, a bit. I ought to practise first, though!'

'Rubbish. I'd sooner hear you play that thing badly than listen to you whistling,' Sandra joked. 'When you were on your delivery bike I always knew it was you coming along the road by the way you whistled,' she told him archly.

'All delivery boys whistle. It's to make sure people get out of our way, especially when we're riding on the pavement,' he grinned.

'Yeah, but none of them whistle as badly as you used to! I'm glad you won't be doing that any more.'

The tea was terrific. Abbie's eyes widened when she saw the loaded table. Mo Lewis had brought home all sorts of tasty things to eat from the corner shop where she worked. Little chocolate cakes, a swiss roll that had jam and cream in it, chocolate biscuits, and some little tiny biscuits with coloured icing stars on the top.

To start off their meal, Mo Lewis cooked a pan of sizzling pork sausages and served a mountain of chips to go with them.

As they sat happily round the table, laughing and joking and tucking into the plentiful spread, Abbie felt she had never enjoyed herself so much and wished things could be like this in her own home, even if it was only on special occasions.

Her bubble of happiness burst when Sandra began pointing out how different she was from Sam. Abbie felt as if a black cloud had suddenly descended, and all she wanted to do was get out of the house.

It was so silly really, she told herself, Sandra didn't mean to make her feel like that. It had been a light-hearted remark but it ruined the occasion for Abbie.

'You and Sam don't look a bit alike,' Sandra said in a puzzled voice. 'Sam's hair is brown and so are his eyes. Yours aren't! You've got black hair and blue eyes.'

'Sam takes after Mammy,' Abbie told her. 'She's got brown hair and brown eyes.'

'And so has our Billy,' Sam pointed out.

'You're as tall as Sam, even though he's two years older than you,' Sandra persisted.

'Mammy's short. And so is Billy,' Abbie reminded her.

'Was your dad tall, then? And did he have black hair and blue eyes?'

'I don't know!' Abbie grinned. 'I never met him, did I!'

'Why? Did he die when you were very little?'

'That will do, Sandra,' Mo Lewis interrupted. She shook her blonde head slightly and there was a warning in her grey eyes as they locked with Sandra's.

'Sorry! I just wondered. No one ever talks about him, and I've never seen him, and now Abbie says she hasn't either,' Sandra said with an innocent smile.

'That's because he cleared off when Abbie was a couple of weeks old and we've not heard from him since,' Sam said sharply.

'Oh!' Sandra clapped her hand over her mouth. 'I didn't know that or I wouldn't have brought it up. I suppose you must take after him in looks, Abbie, that's why you have such black hair. Was he a gypsy?'

Abbie felt too choked to answer. Sam reached out and squeezed her hand, and his brown eyes were full of concern when he saw how upset she was.

'Stop teasing her, Sandra,' he warned. 'Dad went into the Army and he was listed as "missing" when the war ended.'

'That certainly wasn't a very nice thing to say,' Mo Lewis agreed. 'Now, if we've all had our fill, what about you helping me to clear the table and wash the dishes, Sandra?'

'I'm going home, Sam,' Abbie told him the moment they were left on their own. 'I wish I hadn't come. Fancy Sandra asking if Dad was a gyppo!'

'Don't be daft. She was only pulling your leg.'

'Well, I didn't like it. It was a horrible thing to say. You stay here if you want to, but I don't want to be here a minute longer.'

'Sandra's got all sorts of games for us to play and she has a new record for her wind-up gramophone of "Bye Bye Blackbird" for us to listen to. And she'll put on the other one you like singing along to, "When the Red Red Robin comes Bob Bob Bobbin' Along".'

Abbie shook her head. 'I don't want to listen to any of them.'

'Not even if I play an accompaniment on my new mouth organ?' he grinned.

'No, not even if you do that,' she said tearfully. 'I'm going home and I'm going right now.'

Chapter Ten

Abbie had never seen Sam so happy. He seemed to find his new job perfect in every respect.

The Nelson preserving company had only been established for about eight years at its site in Long Lane, Aintree, but already it had become a household name for quality, and was famous worldwide for its jams.

Sam was so intrigued by what they produced that he didn't seem to be able to stop talking about it. Each night when he came home he had something new to impart to Abbie as he washed his face and hands at the kitchen sink and waited for her to put his meal on the table.

'They use countless different types of fruit and it comes from all over England, and they also ship in strawberries and raspberries from eastern European countries. You should see all the other fancy fruits, like apricots, that they import, too. They bring in huge crates of bitter oranges to make marmalade,' he went on, his round face glowing with excitement. 'The colours and the smells when they open up the crates of different fruits makes your head swim!'

'So what do they do with them all?'

'The fruit goes into enormous copper pans and they are boiled up in those, along with the finest crystal sugar, to a special recipe for each type of fruit . . .'

Abbie clapped her hands over her ears. 'You sound as though you are reading it from one of their labels,' she exclaimed.

'I've read them so many times I know it off by heart,' he grinned.

'So what happens to the fruit when it's taken out of the pans?' she asked.

'The pans have special spouts, so that when the fruit is properly cooked and about ready to set then it's poured out of the pans and into seven-pound tins or one- or two-pound jars.'

'Isn't that dangerous?'

'Of course it is! The jam is boiling hot, so the pans have to be tilted very carefully to make sure there's no splashing and that the jam doesn't spill over from the tins or jars. The people doing that are properly trained and very skilled.'

'What happens next?'

'When it's been poured into the big tins or small glass jars, you mean?'

Abbie nodded.

'The tins and jars are stacked in wire cages until they've cooled off. After that, all the containers are sealed and then they pass along an assembly line where girls label each one according to what sort of jam is inside it. Then they pass them along to the packers who crate them up. Then they stick on a label showing the shop or destination they're going to on the outside of the package.'

'So what's your part in all this?'

Sam grinned. 'I shovel the fruit out of the casks,

where it's been stored from the moment it arrives at the factory, into the copper pans. Girls and women do all the packing and labelling stuff. The men do all the heavy work like lifting the crates and loading the lorries when the crates are ready for delivery.'

'So how many women and girls work there?' Abbie asked.

Sam puffed out his cheeks and looked thoughtful. 'Hundreds! They all wear white overalls and white turban things over their hair. They stand in long lines, putting the lids on and making sure the seals are tight before they pass them along to the girls who put the labels on.'

Abbie listened with interest, but inwardly she resolved that when she left school she'd make sure she didn't go to work in a factory.

The only good thing she could see about Sam's job was that, unlike Billy, he was always in the dry and working in a nice clean place. That, and the regular pay packet he received every Friday. Ten shillings a week, every week, less the money for his insurance stamp, seemed to be an awful lot of money to Abbie.

At the end of the first week Ellen demanded that he should hand his pay packet over unopened, but Sam refused to do so.

'No, Mam! You tell me how much you want me to pay for my keep and I'll give you that and keep the rest,' he told her.

'I want the lot!' she told him brusquely. 'You hand it over to me and I'll give you some pocket money back.'

Sam shook his head. 'That's no good. I have to pay out for tram fares every day and I need something to eat and drink at midday.'

'Take some bleedin' sarnies and a bottle of cold tea, like other lads do.'

Sam pulled a face.

'That's what the rest will be doing!' Ellen insisted.

'Maybe, but they probably have a mam who makes up their sarnies and has them all ready by the time they leave home in the morning.'

'If you're too bloody idle to make your own then get your sister to make them for you, she doesn't do much else,' Ellen told him.

Sam still wouldn't agree to hand over his pay packet.

'If you don't I'll chuck you out, and then you can see if Mo Lewis will take you in as a lodger,' Ellen threatened.

Sam remained tight-lipped. 'You tell me how much you want from me and I'll hand it over,' he told her stubbornly.

'Right, if that's the way you want it then let's have eight shillings.'

Sam shook his head and his mouth tightened. 'That doesn't leave me enough for my tram fares, let alone spending money.'

'Money to waste on that Sandra Lewis, you mean,' Billy sneered. He had been listening to their argument with a cynical smile on his face.

'No! Money for ciggies and beer.'

Billy's lips curled. 'You're too young to drink!'

'You used to go out drinking with mam when you were fourteen,' Sam reminded him.

The row went on for almost a week. When she realised Sam was refusing to give in to her browbeating, Ellen finally agreed he should turn over seven shillings a week.

'You pay for your own grub at midday, though,' she told him.

'I only need a cob of bread, I can have all the jam I want to put on it,' he grinned. 'Tell you what, you give me the bread and I'll bring you home some jam every week. There's always dented tins or cracked jars going for free.'

Sam was as good as his word. From then on they never went short of jam or marmalade. Abbie knew that he also brought some home for Mo Lewis. In fact, he spent so much time round at Sandra's house, and had so many meals there, that Abbie thought it should be Mo Lewis who received his seven shillings a week.

It was the second week in February 1927 before Paddy Ryan went back to sea, and until then Abbie felt she dare not go and knock on Mrs Ryan's door.

She'd not even bumped into Mrs Ryan all over Christmas and the New Year, and she was desperate to know how Peter was. She'd asked Sandra a few times if either her or her mother had heard, but they hadn't seen anything of Mrs Ryan either.

'My mam said that the whole lot of them had gone over to Ireland to see Paddy Ryan's old folk,' Sandra said.

'If that's true,' Abbie said worriedly, 'then it means that Peter hasn't had any visitors since Christmas. I wish I'd known and then I would have gone along to see if they would let me visit him.'

'Of course they wouldn't. You're not a relation!' Sandra told her. 'They're awfully strict about such things.'

'It might have been worth a try.'

'I think you're mad to go on holding a torch for him. He won't be home for another couple of years, and by then he'll probably have forgotten you.'

'Of course he won't. I send messages with his mam every time she goes to visit him, and he sends me messages back.'

'He'll have changed, though! Locked up in there all that time with ruffians of every description, he won't be the same Peter Ryan that we used to know.'

Abbie's blue eyes misted. She didn't want to believe Sandra. She carried a picture of Peter engraved on her brain. Even at this minute she could see his face, his very dark hair that he wore brushed back but which always fell forward over his forehead, his straight dark brows framing his intensely blue eyes, his wide smile and firm chin. He was much better looking than Sam, as well as being head and shoulders taller than him.

She wondered if he had grown any more, if so he would be nearly six foot by now. She was glad about that because she was tall, much taller than Sandra and taller, even, than Sam was.

She was pretty sure he would never let himself be influenced by the type of boys he had to associate with, even if they were rough and uncouth.

'He'll be nearly sixteen by the time they let him out,' Sandra commented. 'He'll have a job finding work. His reputation will be against him for one thing.'

'He doesn't have to tell them he's been in reform school!'

'Don't be daft! It will be on his records. Anyway, they'll want to know what he's been doing with himself since he left school.'

'Out of work and looking for a job like most of the other school-leavers.'

Sandra looked smug. 'Yes, Sam's been dead lucky, thanks to me and me mam getting him the job at Nelson's.'

'Well, he must be good at it or they wouldn't be keeping him on there, would they,' Abbie retorted sharply.

'I've been thinking I might go there to work when I leave school,' Sandra went on. 'I'd be able to keep an eye on Sam and see he behaves himself with all those girls he has to work alongside.'

'Good luck to you! I wouldn't work in a factory if you paid me!'

'Oh my, Miss Hoity-Toity, and where do you think you'll go to work, then?'

'Frisby Dyke's, or somewhere like that.'

'Bit behind the times, aren't you, luv,' Sandra said loftily. 'They're in real trouble and about to go bankrupt!'

'Well, there's other big stores, Lewis's or Bon Marché, I'm not too fussy.'

'You mightn't be, but I bet they are and they may not want someone whose boyfriend has been in reform school.'

Abbie's cheeks went scarlet. 'You do talk rubbish, Sandra Lewis,' she said hotly.

'It's been a long time since you were last here – I've missed you,' Maggie Ryan commented when, eventually, Abbie went round to see her.

'I wanted to come before, to find out how Peter was the last time you saw him.'

Maggie shook her head despondently. 'I'm worried about him,' she admitted.

'Why? He's not ill, is he?'

'No, but he's changed such a lot, Abbie. You'd hardly know him!'

Abbie's heart thumped anxiously. 'In what way?' she asked tentatively, and gritted her teeth as she waited to hear the answer.

'All the fun has gone out of him,' Maggie said sadly. 'He's so serious, as though he has the cares of the world on his shoulders.'

'He probably hates being in there, that's why!'

Maggie pushed her dark hair back from her face, and her eyes were puzzled. 'No, I don't think it's simply that, luv. He seems to be so sombre. Keeps telling me about all the studying he's doing. In fact, he never even mentions how long it will be before he's released. He's working away all the time at some exam or other. I can't make head nor tail of it, but he seems to think it is very important.'

'I didn't know they studied and did exams while they were in reform school.'

'Oh yes. Education is considered to be very important. If you work hard you get points or something, and that all goes to help when your case comes up for review.'

'So, if he's working so hard, does that mean he will be released earlier?'

Maggie looked taken aback. 'I never thought about that, Abbie. I'm glad you've mentioned it. I'll ask him, next time I go in to see him.'

'Apart from that, Mrs Ryan, how has Peter changed? Does he look different?' Abbie asked anxiously.

Maggie Ryan sighed. 'Well, he's grown quite a bit; he's a lot taller than his dad now. And he's broadened out as well. He's quite a handsome-looking lad, in fact,' she added proudly.

Abbie's heart beat faster. 'He always was, but it sounds as though he's improved even more,' she smiled.

Chapter Eleven

The next few years flew by, and all Abbie could think about was how much she was missing Peter. She still counted the days to his release, but at the very start of 1929, she also began to mark off the days until she left school. Because her birthday was not until July she was expected to stay until the summer holidays. Sandra's birthday was in May, but her mam thought it would be a good idea if she stayed on until the end of July as well.

'The sooner you leave school and start earning some money, the better off we'll all be,' Ellen told Abbie. 'It's a pity you can't find yourself a Saturday job, like our Sam did. Lazy lump, lying around the house all the time.'

'Will you be better off?' Abbie questioned. 'When I start work I won't have time to do all the cleaning and washing and ironing,' she pointed out.

'Less of your bleedin' cheek,' Ellen flared. 'Who the hell do you think you're talking to? I put the food on the table and buy all your clothes so the least you can do is pull your weight around the place.'

'I do more than pull my weight, as you put it, I practically run this house,' Abbie reminded her.

'Most of my clothes and shoes come from Paddy's Market and are someone else's cast-offs!'

Over the last couple of years, Abbie had come to realise that no matter how hard she tried she would never be able to win her mother's love and approval, and now she no longer tried to do so. She was taller than her mother and her two brothers, and she no longer felt intimidated when her mother and Billy began shouting and swearing, whether it was at her or each other. Generally, she simply ignored their outbursts and filled her head with other thoughts.

Most of the time she thought about Peter, who was due for release in September, and about the difference between her home and the Ryans'. She had long since stopped comparing her mam with Peter's mam because there was such a vast difference between the two women.

Ellen was a tough sort of person; cold, aggressive, untidy and raucous. She wasn't interested in cooking, or making their home comfortable. Maggie was the exact opposite. She was warm-hearted, her shoulder-length curly black hair was always clean and shining, her blue eyes continually sparkling, and she had a warm, ready smile. She was a good homemaker, and an excellent cook.

Maggie Ryan had shown her more love and affection since Abbie had been visiting her regularly, while Peter had been in reform school, than her own mother had shown her all her life, Abbie thought sadly.

She still couldn't understand why Paddy Ryan had taken such a dislike to her. Maggie didn't seem to want to discuss it, but she was sensible enough not to take offence. Without being asked, she steered clear of the Ryan house whenever Paddy was at home.

As summer heightened, Abbie started thinking more and more about where she was going to go to work. She turned a deaf ear when her mother kept hinting to Sam that he should ask if they were taking on school-leavers at Nelson's. Although Sam still seemed to like his job there, and he had been promoted to helping on the vans, she still didn't intend to go and work in a factory if she could help it.

Maggie Ryan said that with her lovely dark looks and tall figure she would easily get a job in one of the Lyon's Corner Houses, but she didn't really fancy being a Nippy, either.

Sandra said she wouldn't be going to work in a factory after all. Her mam was going to ask Mrs Pringle, the woman who owned the hairdressing salon in Great Homer Street, if she could start there as an apprentice. Mo Lewis went every fortnight for a marcel wave, and sometimes to have her fair hair bleached with peroxide.

Abbie looked at Sandra enviously. A hairdresser! She had never thought of trying to do something like that, but it certainly sounded better than working in a factory.

'If she wants more than one girl to start there, perhaps she'd take you on as well,' Sandra suggested. 'Shall I get my mam to ask her?'

'That would be wonderful,' Abbie agreed, her eyes shining enthusiastically.

Suddenly, life seemed to be full of promise. Since Sam had been working, and had had some money in his pocket, she'd seen hardly anything of Sandra because Sandra had been out with Sam all the time. If she and Sandra were working together, though, it might put things back on the old footing. She hoped so, they'd been such close friends when they'd been younger that she missed seeing her every evening and sharing secrets.

When Sandra said that her mam was going to ask Mrs Pringle the next time she went to have her hair done, Abbie could hardly wait to find out what the answer was.

She could tell by the look on Sandra's smiling round face that the news was good, the moment she saw her.

'So, when do we start, do we have to go and see her for an interview first?'

'No! Normally we would have to, but my mam is such a special customer, and Mrs Pringle has known her for such a long time, that she took my mam's word that you would be suitable. She didn't need any sort of reference for me, of course. She's cut my hair ever since I was about six years old, so she's known me for as long as she's known my mam.'

Abbie looked enviously at Sandra's shining fair hair, which was cut in a sleek bob. 'That's probably why it always looks so nice,' she told her.

Sandra studied Abbie's 'pudding basin' cut critically. 'Perhaps you ought to try and do something to your hair before you start work. It badly needs cutting. Would you like me to do it for you?'

'Could you!' Abbie's face lit up. This was like old times, doing things for each other, sharing things and taking an interest in each other.

'Come round this evening after tea. Tell your Sam I won't be going out tonight.'

'Shall I tell him why?'

Sandra shrugged her plump shoulders. 'No, keep him guessing, do him good.'

'He might be worried?'

'So? You shouldn't let boys know everything, or take you for granted, Abbie. You've got to have a life of your own, you know.'

Abbie bit her lip and said nothing. If Peter was interested enough to ask, she would certainly tell him where she would be and what she would be doing.

'Haven't seen you here for quite a while,' Mo Lewis greeted Abbie when she turned up about half past seven.

'Sandra is going to cut my hair,' Abbie told her. 'Thank you very much, Mrs Lewis, for speaking to Mrs Pringle. I'm really looking forward to starting work there.'

'That's all right, Abbie.' Mo Lewis gave her a fleeting smile. 'I hope you will behave yourself and work hard, and not let me down,' she added.

'Of course I won't. I'm very grateful.'

'Come on, we don't want to take all night doing your hair,' Sandra said impatiently. 'Come into the kitchen.'

Sitting on a hard kitchen chair with a towel tied

round her neck, Abbie felt apprehensive as she heard the scissors snipping away. Sandra tilted her head first one way and then the other. She wished there was a mirror so that she could see exactly what Sandra was doing.

When Sandra finally finished and handed her a small hand-mirror, Abbie gasped. She looked so different. Her face-framing bob and central parting were gone. Most of her hair was swept back behind her ears in a ragged, uneven style, and there was a badly chopped-off fringe covering her forehead.

'Well? Do you like it? It makes you look more grown-up.'

Abbie turned her head this way and that. 'It's so different I don't know what to say,' she murmured.

Mo Lewis was taken aback. 'You don't sound very grateful! I think our Sandra has done a good job. It shows she's cut out to be a hairdresser.'

Abbie wasn't so sure. Her hair didn't feel right, and she couldn't wait to get home and take a good long look at herself in the mirror.

When she did she was aghast. She couldn't possibly go to work in a hairdresser's looking like that! She didn't even fancy going to school in the morning with her hair in such a state.

Biting back her tears she slipped out of the house again. It was late, but she was sure Mrs Ryan wouldn't mind the intrusion, and there was no one else she could think of who would be able to help her.

Maggie Ryan gasped and then started laughing when she saw Abbie.

'Oh my goodness, what have you been doing?'

She listened sympathetically as Abbie explained about the forthcoming job and Sandra's attempt to cut her hair so that she would look better.

'If I was Mrs Pringle I would send you packing before you started work,' Maggie told her. 'With hair like that you'd frighten off all her customers!'

'Can you do anything to put it right?' Abbie begged.

'I'll try! Come on into the kitchen.'

Once again, sitting on a hard chair with a towel round her neck, Abbie listened to the snip of scissors and wondered what on earth she was going to look like this time.

'There you are!' Maggie held out a hand-mirror for her. 'Does that look any better?'

Abbie studied the results with relief. The style remained the same, but this time her hair was cut smoothly into the nape of her neck. It was all the same length and hung neatly behind her ears. The heavy ragged fringe had been transformed into a neat wispy one that curved over her right eye.

'It's wonderful, thank you so much! I could never have gone out looking like I did.'

'Well, it's not all that much different,' Maggie said modestly. 'I've tidied it up, that's all.'

They looked at each other and grinned conspiratorially. 'Our secret?' Maggie said.

'You mean let Sandra think that this is how she actually cut it!'

'I don't think she will say anything, do you?'

'I don't know what I would do without you,' Abbie told her. Impulsively she flung her arms round Maggie Ryan's neck and hugged her.

If Sandra noticed the improvement she said nothing. Even though she knew she looked better than she had ever done in her life, Abbie still felt nervous when, a week later, she and Sandra started work.

Maggie had bought her an Amami shampoo, and shown her how to comb her hair after washing it so that it hung sleek and smooth. She had also helped her to make a new dress from a length of lovely blue material Abbie had bought in the market with money Sam had given her for her birthday.

In the window of the salon there were two models' heads. One had a smooth blonde wig that showed the perfection of a marcel wave that cost one and sixpence, while on the other one there was a dark brown curly wig advertising the advantage of a steam perm at nine shillings and sixpence. On shelves down one side there was a display of hairnets; coloured ones to sleep in at night, and very fine ones to protect the hair during the day. On shelves on the other side of the window, combs and brushes were displayed, and Amami shampoos at fourpence each, in different coloured sachets for blondes, brunettes or red-heads.

The salon itself was a long narrow room that was spotlessly clean. There was a reception desk immediately inside the door. At the far end of the room there were two wide white bowls side by side, where the apprentices washed the customers' hair. The rest of the room was divided up into eight curtained-off individual cubicles, ensuring that whatever treatment the customers had done was carried out in complete privacy.

Alice Pringle was a forbidding-looking lady in her late forties. She was immaculately dressed in a smart white blouse and a plain black skirt. Her brown hair had a rigid marcel wave, and her frosty smile was turned on and off like a light, depending on who it was she was dealing with. Her manner with her staff was stern and cold; with customers, smooth and ingratiating.

'Well, Sandra,' Mrs Pringle looked down at the gold watch on her wrist, 'I'm pleased to see you have arrived on time. Bad timekeeping is something I will not tolerate.' She looked Abbie up and down. 'And this is your friend. Hmm! You are rather tall to be a hairdresser, young lady. I hope you won't be complaining of backache every whipstitch.'

Without waiting for an answer she signalled to a red-headed girl in her late twenties. 'Beryl, come and take charge of these two new girls. Find them some overalls and show them what to do.'

'Yes, Mrs Pringle.' Beryl hurried across the salon.

'They can start by washing the dirty towels from yesterday.' She turned to Sandra and Abbie. 'I'm sure you both know how to use a dolly-tub so get on with it.'

It was mid-morning by the time they had finished and hung the towels out to dry on a line stretched between two posts in the yard at the back of the shop.

'While those are drying you can sweep up the floor, and wash out the basins after each customer,' Beryl told them. 'At lunchtime, you make tea for the rest of the staff and then you can stop for fifteen minutes to eat your own snack.'

It didn't sound too bad, but they found there were countless other tasks which Beryl didn't bother to mention. They were constantly being asked to run errands for other members of the staff, or even for some of the customers. They were expected to keep the floors in each cubicle clean by continually brushing up hair. Half the time they didn't know which cubicle they were needed in, and if they went into the wrong one the assistant working there told them off.

In the afternoon they had to bring in all the towels they had washed in the morning and hung out to dry, fold them up neatly and stack them away on a shelf. At the same time they had to collect up all the towels that had been used during the day, wash them, and hang them to dry in readiness for the next day.

By the time the salon closed at seven o'clock that night, both Sandra and Abbie felt dog-tired as they made their way home.

'It's a lot harder than I thought it would be,' Sandra grumbled.

'Perhaps working in a factory might be easier after all,' Abbie giggled.

Sandra sniffed. 'You go and do that sort of work if you want to, but my mam says I am worth something better than that, and after her getting us the jobs I'm sticking it out. It's bound to get better.'

Chapter Twelve

Although there was another young apprentice and four qualified hairdressers working at Mrs Pringle's salon, Abbie and Sandra seemed to be the ones who were sent to wash out the towels and make the tea. After the first few days, however, most of the others who worked there became a little more friendly towards the two newcomers.

Mrs Pringle spoke to them only very occasionally, and then it was usually because there was an errand she wanted one of them to run, but they sensed she was watching them closely.

On the Thursday morning she instructed the senior stylist, Marcia, to let Beryl, the other junior, attend to the towels.

'I want you to instruct Abbie and Sandra on how to shampoo,' she told her.

'Do you want them to practise on each other?'

'No, Mrs Harding will be arriving in five minutes' time and she has agreed that they can try out their skills on her. Let one of them apply the shampoo and let the other one rinse, and report back to me on how they get on,' she ordered.

Although it looked fairly simple, Marcia turned it into a complicated art-form.

'Before you start to shampoo you must make sure that the client is well protected,' she instructed. 'Use two towels. A small thin one, which you tuck inside their collar, and a large thicker one over that. You must make sure that the thick towel completely covers their shoulders and protects the front of their clothes. Do you understand that?'

Both girls told her they did.

'There is a right and wrong way to apply shampoo,' she continued. 'First you must carefully measure it out into the palm of your hand, and then it must be massaged into the scalp using firm yet gentle movements. Every strand of hair must be perfectly covered to make sure it is clean. Rinsing off is equally important. Every particle of shampoo must be removed. Remember that the hair must be squeaky clean. You then wrap a clean towel around the client's head and move them into one of the cubicles ready for the stylist.'

Again, both girls murmured that they understood what she was telling them and assured her that they had no questions.

'Right. Well, we will see how you get on with Mrs Harding. I'll stand behind you so that I can be sure you are doing it properly, and if anything goes wrong I can deal with it.'

Sandra placed the towels round Mrs Harding's neck as they'd been told to do and then reached out for the shampoo.

'Wait,' Marcia held her arm. She studied Sandra's plump little hand and then turned to Abbie. 'Hold your hands out,' she ordered.

Marcia nodded her head as if reaching an

important decision. 'You have much longer fingers,' she told Abbie, 'so I think you will be much better at massaging the shampoo into the scalp. Anyway, you do it this time and we'll see how you get on.'

Abbie felt nervous as she tipped shampoo into her hand. She knew Sandra was scowling, annoyed because she had wanted to be the first one to do it.

As she gently but firmly worked up a lather, and made sure it covered every part of Mrs Harding's scalp, the woman murmured her appreciation.

'There, I thought you would be best for that job,' Marcia exclaimed, pleased by her decision. 'Now, Sandra, let's see how well you can rinse it all off. Squeaky clean, mind!'

Sandra picked up the rubber attachment that was fixed to the tap, digging Abbie hard in the ribs to make her move out of the way. As she did so, a jet of hot water shot out of the spray nozzle at the end, missing Mrs Harding but soaking Marcia, who screamed as the hot water hit her full in the face.

Abbie grabbed at the hose to try and deflect the spray away from Marcia, but Sandra pushed her out of the way causing the water to shoot straight at Mrs Harding, soaking the front of her clothing.

Mrs Pringle, hearing all the screams and commotion, came hurrying out of her office to see what was going on. She arrived on the scene at the precise moment that Abbie grabbed the spray.

After that it was bedlam. All the staff seemed to

be milling around Marcia and Mrs Harding, everyone trying to help. Countless dry towels were passed from one to the other. Marcia was calmed within a few minutes, but Mrs Harding remained very irate.

'Look at the state I'm in,' she ranted. 'My blouse and skirt are completely ruined, and I'm soaking wet right through to my knickers!'

Even though it was a blazing hot August day, she claimed she would probably catch her death of cold from being soaked to the skin like that.

Mrs Pringle did her best to calm her down. Brenda was dispatched to make Mrs Harding a cup of tea to counteract the shock she had suffered. More towels were handed to Mrs Harding to wrap round her shoulders to keep her warm. Mrs Pringle assured her that a taxicab had been called to take her home and that she would pay for it.

Then Mrs Pringle turned on Abbie, blaming her for the whole incident.

'I didn't do anything wrong,' Abbie protested, her voice trembling and tears streaking down her cheeks. 'I grabbed hold of the spray to try and prevent Mrs Harding from getting wet. If you ask Marcia I am sure she will tell you the same thing.'

Mrs Pringle refused to listen.

'Ask Sandra, then,' Abbie told her. 'I'm sure she will tell you it was all a dreadful accident.'

'I'm not interested in what Marcia may have to say, or what she may think. I have already spoken to Sandra. The poor child is distraught and from what she has told me it is obvious that you were to blame. She says you deliberately pushed her.'

Abbie felt angry about the injustice of the accusation. After so many years of being brow-beaten by her mother and Billy, Mrs Pringle's raised voice and angry stance had less effect on her than it would have had on most young girls.

Automatically, she straightened her shoulders, standing so tall that her eyes were on a level with those of Mrs Pringle. 'That is not true,' she said firmly, her dark head held proudly. 'All I did was to try and turn the spray away so that the water went into the washbasin and not over anyone.'

'So why did Mrs Harding and Marcia get soaked to the skin, then?' demanded Mrs Pringle.

Abbie met her accusing gaze with a contemptu-ous look. 'It happened because Sandra tried to twist the hose out of my hand,' she explained angrily.

'That's quite right, that is what happened,' Marcia piped up.

Mrs Pringle looked flummoxed. She waved a hand imperiously to quieten Marcia. Realising that she was probably in the wrong, but having no intention of admitting this, Mrs Pringle glared at Abbie and said frostily, 'Report to my office, Abbie Martin, we'll finish this discussion in pri-vate where there will be no further interruptions!'

Once they were in her office, and Mrs Pringle was seated behind her desk, she wasted no time in venting her spleen by dismissing Abbie and telling her to leave the premises immediately.

'And don't expect any wages or a reference,'

Mrs Pringle told her. 'In fact, I ought to make you pay for a new blouse and skirt for Mrs Harding, as she is one of our most valued customers and I doubt if she will ever put a foot over our door again.'

'She probably won't when she hears how unfairly you've treated me,' Abbie told her quietly as she turned on her heel and walked out.

Once she was standing on the pavement outside the hairdresser's, Abbie's bravado evaporated. She'd been working there less than a week and already she'd been sacked!

She wished there was someone she could talk to. Someone who would understand her predicament and advise her on what she ought to do. Mrs Pringle was in the wrong. It had been Sandra's fault. Yet Sandra had blamed her and played the innocent.

As she walked down Great Homer Street, turning her back on Pringle's Hairdressing Salon for good, Abbie had to admit that it would probably have been even worse for Sandra than for her if Sandra had been the one who'd got the sack. Sandra really would have been in deep trouble, because her mother knew Mrs Pringle well and had asked her to give them the job.

She would be in hot water herself when her own mother got to hear about what had happened. She'd never wanted her to go there in the first place, but Abbie had always vowed that she would never work in a factory. Now, she thought miserably, it looked as if she'd have to go back on her promise to herself.

Too upset to go home, she decided to walk into the centre of Liverpool and look at the shops.

She gazed into the windows of the big department stores, wondering if the day would ever come when she would be able to afford to buy some of the wonderful clothes on display. As she stopped to look in the windows of Frisby Dyke's, she remembered telling Sam and Sandra that one day she intended to work there.

And why not, she asked herself. She'd never wanted to be a hairdresser. Why didn't she go in and ask if there were any jobs going. She had nothing to lose.

She stared at her reflection in the glass window, then, smoothing down her dark hair and straightening her dress, she marched boldly into the store.

Once inside she had no idea what to do next. Taking a deep breath she marched up to one of the shop-walkers. 'Do you have any jobs going?' she asked quickly, before her nerve deserted her.

He looked at her, startled. 'You'd have to ask in the office. Top floor. Take that lift over there and it will take you all the way up there.'

Once she was inside the lift she felt so scared that if it had stopped at any of the intermediate floors she would have got out of it and run. As it was, when it bumped to a stop and the doors opened she found herself right outside the General Office.

Knees knocking, she pushed open the heavy wood and glass door, and found herself in front of a polished mahogany counter. The girl perched on a high stool behind it gave her an encouraging smile.

'I . . . I wondered if there were any jobs going?' Abbie stuttered.

'You mean here, in the office?'

'No. Down in the shop, serving behind the counter,' Abbie said quickly.

'All those jobs have already been filled by this year's school-leavers,' the girl told her.

'Thanks!' Shoulders dropping, Abbie turned away. She should have stuck to her guns and come after a job here the day she left school, and not bothered with the hairdresser's, which was not what she had wanted anyway, she thought despondently.

'Wait a moment,' the girl called out as Abbie reached the door. 'I've just remembered, one of the new girls didn't turn up. She met with some kind of accident. I don't think anyone else has been taken on in her place. Hang on a minute and I'll ask.'

She was back in seconds. 'Miss Breck says she'll see you. Will you follow me,' she said, and opened a door that led into a corridor. When they stopped outside another door, the girl tapped lightly and then opened it and indicated to Abbie that she should go in.

The woman sitting behind the desk was in her thirties. Abbie had never seen anyone who looked so neat. Her brown hair was drawn back into a bun from her oval face, which was as smooth as ivory. She was wearing a dark grey costume the same colour as her eyes, and a white blouse which was buttoned right up to the neck.

'You are looking for work?'

Abbie nodded.

Miss Breck drew a notepad towards her and picked up a pen. 'And what is your name?'

'Abbie Martin.'

'Where have you been working until now?'

'I . . . I've only just left school.'

'I see! When were you fourteen?'

'On the eighteenth of July.'

'And you want to be a counter hand?'

Abbie relaxed. 'Yes, I've always wanted to work here, ever since I was quite small,' she replied, smiling.

Miss Breck studied her more closely and Abbie pulled back her shoulders, glad she was wearing the new dress Maggie had made for her, and that she had washed her hair only the night before when she'd gone to the public baths so she knew it was clean and shiny.

Miss Breck smiled kindly and indicated to Abbie that she should sit down. 'Well, we finished taking on new junior staff in July but we do still have one vacancy. It's in one of the fashion departments so we need someone who looks attractive and has a nice manner.' She studied Abbie carefully. 'Where do you live?'

'Bostock Street.'

'I'm not sure where that is?' Miss Breck remarked.

'It's one of the roads between Great Homer Street and Scotland Road.'

The smile vanished, and a frown marred the smoothness of Miss Breck's ivory face.

'I see!' She twiddled the pen between her thumb and forefinger thoughtfully. Then she looked up and scrutinised Abbie once more. 'Well, you certainly look quite respectable, and you appear to have a nice personality, so I think we can give you a trial. You will be on probation, you do understand that? If, after the first month, we decide you are not satisfactory, then you will have to go.'

Abbie nodded vigorously. 'I understand.'

'You will be paid five shillings a week during your first month. After that, if your work is satisfactory, we will increase your wages to seven shillings. Deductions will be made each week for your Insurance Stamp. Your hours are from eight o' clock in the morning until seven at night, Monday to Friday, and until nine o'clock on Saturdays. You will have a half-hour break in the middle of the day; this will be on a rota system with the other members of your department. There is a rest room where you can eat your sandwiches or you can use the staff canteen. Is there anything else you wish to know?'

'It all sounds perfect,' Abbie said enthusiastically. Her relief at getting a job overshadowed everything else.

'Right. You can start next Monday morning, then. Report to Miss Webster in the Coats department. Do you know where it is?'

'No, but I am sure I can find it. I'll go and have a look now, while I'm here, to make sure I know where to go on Monday.'

'Yes, well I think it might be even better if I took you there myself and told Miss Webster who you are. It might save a lot of time and misunderstanding on Monday morning.'

Chapter Thirteen

Abbie walked home on air. Her head was spinning, her heart was singing, and she couldn't wait to relate all her day's adventures to Maggie Ryan.

Her only worry was how she was going to explain to her mam at the end of the week when she had no money to hand over. Perhaps, though, when she heard that she would be earning five shillings a week, and not three and sixpence, she wouldn't take it too badly.

Since she never goes to a hairdresser's herself, it probably won't worry her too much when she hears that I've been sacked from Pringle's, even before I've been there a week, she told herself.

Frisby Dyke's! The name repeated itself over and over in Abbie's head. It was where she'd always dreamed of working, though she'd never even thought about which department. To be starting in Coats was even better than she could have hoped for.

Maggie Ryan was as pleased as Abbie when she heard the news.

'That's wonderful, luv. Far better than working at a hairdresser's. You've more chance of getting on and being promoted. Better money as well! I'd say it was a lucky break for you, and I wouldn't let what happened at Pringle's bother you any more.'

'When I was a small kid I always said I wanted to go and work at Frisby Dyke's,' Abbie smiled.

'Well, there you are, then, it was meant to be.'

'Will you tell Peter when you go in to see him next time?'

'Of course I will, luv. He'll be as pleased as punch for you. Now that you've left school they may let you visit him. Would you like me to ask, next time I go there?'

'Would you!' Abbie's eyes shone with excitement. 'I'd like that more than anything. It would have to be on a Sunday, of course, because I'll be working every day for the rest of the week.'

'We'll try and fix something up,' Maggie promised. 'Anyway, he'll be home soon. All you have to do now is tell your mam about what has happened.'

Abbie's eyes clouded. 'That's not going to be easy.'

'Rubbish! She'll be delighted when you tell her about your new job.'

'I'm not so sure. Mrs Pringle hasn't paid me, so mam'll have plenty to say about that!'

Maggie looked thoughtful. 'Need you tell her that bit?'

'I shall have to, because she's already told me I've got to hand over two shillings and sixpence a week.'

'Oh, I see!' Her face brightened. 'I know what we can do; I can lend you the money you should have earned. How about that?'

Abbie stared at her, open-mouthed. 'You'd do that for me?'

'Of course!'

'I promise I'll pay you back,' Abbie assured her.

'I know you will. Shall we say at a shilling a week, then if you give your mam the two and sixpence she's expecting you'll still have some spending money left over.'

'Thank you, Mrs Ryan, thank you so much!' Abbie hugged her. 'You really are my guardian angel,' she said gratefully.

'I'll get you the money right now,' Maggie smiled as Abbie released her. 'You can hang on to it until "handover" day, but at least you know you'll have it ready,' she smiled.

Ellen and Billy were already there when Abbie reached home. As soon as she walked through the door Ellen launched into a diatribe about the fire being out and Billy was cursing loudly because there was nothing ready to eat.

'Well, I'll be here tomorrow when you get in and your meal will be ready and waiting for you, and on Saturday as well,' Abbie told them.

Ellen stopped what she was doing and stood there with her hands on her hips, glaring at Abbie. 'Why's that?' she demanded.

Abbie told them. She recounted her story in detail. The only thing she omitted was the fact that Mrs Pringle had refused to pay her.

Instead of her mother being riled, as she had expected, Ellen rocked with laughter. And so did Billy. It wasn't the raucous laughter that she was used to hearing from them when they came home late at night in a drunken stupor. It was real laughter, as though they were both amused and pleased about what had happened.

'Oh my God!' Ellen wiped the tears from her eyes. 'You're a right caution! I wish I'd been there to see it all happening.'

'So what are you going to do now?' Billy asked. 'You going to stay home and look after this place and cook our food?'

'She certainly bloody well isn't,' Ellen rasped. 'Our Sam can ask around and see if he can get her taken on at Nelson's, or at one of the other factories out at Long Lane.'

'There's no need for him to do that,' Abbie told her quickly. 'I've already got another job. I'm starting on Monday at Frisby Dyke's.'

'You're doing what?' Ellen's mouth gaped in surprise. 'How the hell did you manage that?'

Abbie shrugged. 'I went in there and asked for a job.'

'And you got it just like that?'

'I was lucky. One of the new apprentices hadn't turned up because she'd had an accident, and I've got the job instead of her.'

'They're dead posh in there,' Billy muttered. 'I've never fancied the place, not with that dolled-up fella in the doorway, bowing and scraping, the silly old sod.'

'Yeah, it's posh all right!' Abbie said. 'Ever so. I suppose you mean the doorman, the man who is all dressed up in a frock coat.'

'Isn't that the place where, when you leaves the shop, they gives you a special handle with their name on it to hook your parcels on to carry them home?' Ellen asked.

'Yeah!' Abbie smiled and nodded.

'Wonder they bloody well let you in!' Ellen exclaimed. 'Probably only because you was dressed up, like.'

'The lady who interviewed me was ever so nice,' Abbie told them.

'Did you have to tell her where you live?'

'Of course. I don't think she really knew where it was, though!'

'I bet she didn't. Uppity they are, those who work in there. And most of the customers are toffs, or come from Wallasey and think they are! You'll be expected to do a lot of bowing and scraping, you know! I bet you won't like that.'

'Have to put up with it, I suppose,' Abbie grinned. 'I start on Monday in the Coats department.'

'Wait till I tell the other shawlies down at the cotton shed that you're going to work at Frisby Dyke's!' Ellen guffawed. 'That'll give them something to think about. Going up in the world, that, and no mistake!'

'Something to go out and celebrate,' Billy grinned. 'You going to treat us, kiddo?'

'No I am not!'

'Hoity-toity already, are we,' he leered. 'I suppose you'll make out you don't recognise me if I walk into the store!'

Abbie felt hot waves of embarrassment sweeping over her as she regarded the scruffy, unshaven figure in front of her. With his greasy trousers tied under the knee with old shoelaces, his grubby shirt frayed at the collar, and a button hanging by a thread from the cuff of his filthy jacket, he looked more like a down-and-out than a working man. Her mother, in her long coarse black skirt, stained blouse and black shawl, didn't look much better.

Not for the first time, Abbie longed to be able to get right away from her slummy home and surroundings. Their place was probably the most run-down house in the whole of Bostock Street, she thought, as she looked round the shabby living room.

Mo Lewis and Maggie Ryan both kept nice tidy homes. It wasn't simply that their front steps were cleaned with pumice stone twice a week, or that their washing was sparkling white, and not a dull, dirty grey collection of rags, when they hung it out on the lines stretched across the back jowler between their street and Kew Street.

There was more to it than that. When you went in the door of the Ryans' or the Lewis's you were met with a smell of furniture polish and good cooking, not a damp rancid smell like there always was in the Martins' house.

The entire atmosphere was different, too. There was a feeling of friendliness and warmth that made you feel cosy and welcome, even if you were only staying for a few minutes.

Even the rent man wrinkled up his nose, signed their book to show they'd paid, and didn't hang around in their place any longer than he had to do.

Sam never brought Sandra home with him, and

Abbie wondered whether it was because he was ashamed of the dump they lived in, or whether it was because Sandra wouldn't come there. Their home being so shabby could be one of the reasons why Billy never brought a girl home, either. Most chaps of his age, except Michael Ryan, were married or going steady.

To do that, of course, you had to be in love, but love was something that Billy and her mam didn't seem to know the meaning of, as far as she could tell. She couldn't remember the last time her mam had hugged her or kissed her. Even when she was quite small, her mam had never tucked her up in bed and kissed her goodnight.

Maggie Ryan had shown Abbie more affection than any of her own family had ever done, apart from Sam. Sam would still hug her now and again, when he could see that she was particularly down in the dumps, but even with Sam there was less of that these days, now that he was going out with Sandra.

She longed for Peter to come home. He'd be almost sixteen when he was released, and, even though she hadn't seen him for three years, and his messages had become few and far between, she hoped he hadn't changed all that much.

In the past he'd always been telling her how much he cared about her, but Maggie had said several times how much he'd altered, so Abbie couldn't help wondering if he would still feel the same way about her. It wasn't something that she felt she could ask Peter's mother to find out.

After her last visit Maggie had said, 'Do you

know, Abbie, Peter's become so serious that I sometimes wonder if I still know him!'

It seemed to worry her. Yet, she also seemed to be very proud of the fact that he was doing a lot of studying.

'I'm sure he's working far harder at his books in there than he would have done if he'd been at home. I suppose it's because there's not much else for him to do.'

'Better for him to be studying and reading than getting in with a bad lot and learning all their tricks,' Abbie had reminded her.

'Yes, there's that to be thankful for,' Maggie Ryan agreed. 'The only trouble is, I wonder what it means for the future. Several times he's talked of going to sea like his father does when he gets out, and that's something I don't want him to do. With two of my menfolk away at sea my life would be pretty bleak.'

Her own life would be bleak as well, if Peter went to sea, Abbie thought. Like Maggie, she hoped it wouldn't happen, especially now, when she had landed herself such a good job and there was such a bright future for them to look forward to.

Chapter Fourteen

Peter Ryan lay with his eyes wide open, staring into the darkness and listening to the ragged breathing of the other twenty boys in his dormitory. It was almost midnight on his very last night of incarceration.

At eight o'clock tomorrow morning, Friday 13th September 1929, he would be free, released into the outside world once again. In three days' time it would be his sixteenth birthday.

Never again would he have to wear the prickly khaki-green shorts and harsh yellow top that had become his uniform ever since he had entered the reform school two years earlier.

His first pair of long trousers, grey worsted ones that his mother had brought in for him, were in a brown paper parcel underneath his bed, together with a white shirt and a blue pullover.

As the door to the dormitory opened and a glimmer of light appeared, followed by the slow, measured tread of approaching footsteps, he closed his eyes quickly. All his other senses were alert, waiting and listening.

Slowly, Tobias Prescott's feet came closer. There was an accompanying sound of the thin cane he always carried being thwacked lightly but rhythmically against his trouser leg.

He would pause every now and then by one of the beds, and there would be a rustle as the coarse bedcovers were thrown aside. Then came the padding of a pair of bare feet as their owner scurried along the scrubbed wooden floor in the direction of the door.

Peter sensed Tobias Prescott's presence as he reached the foot of his own bed and paused. The man was grossly overweight and his breathing was heavy and laboured.

Ignore him; take no notice. Keep your eyes shut. Breathe slowly and steadily; pretend he's not there, Peter warned himself silently as he heard the cane whipping against the man's leg like a beating heart.

It seemed to be an interminable time before Tobias Prescott moved on. When he eventually did so, Peter felt his tense muscles relax. Opening his eyes a mere fraction, he looked on as Prescott stopped twice more. He watched with rising anger as he saw bedclothes being thrown back and frightened young boys, clad only in striped flannel nightshirts, scramble out of bed and run for the door, trying to escape the thwack of the cane on their bare legs.

Peter shuddered. That was mild compared to what they would endure before they crept back to their beds again, weeping, distressed and ashamed.

He remembered the first time it had happened to him. The selected boys were told to line up in the masters' common room, to lift their nightshirts up over their shoulders and to bend forward, hands on their knees, their bare backsides exposed.

They'd been left standing like that for about half an hour, heads hanging so that the blood rushed to their faces making their eyes bulge.

Then Tobias Prescott had walked down the line, wielding his cane. Each boy received five stinging strokes. He'd had so much practice that he was an expert in making every stroke felt. The cane was so thin that it was like a whip. It seared the flesh, stinging like a wasp and drawing blood.

Anyone who cried out, or moved, received an extra lash. As the air reached the cuts, the pain became excruciating, but there would be another slash of the cane for any boy who dared to jerk away or straighten up.

Five minutes, ten minutes, or even longer, they were left standing there, bending forward, their hands on their knees. The ungainly stance ensured that every scrap of self-esteem and dignity was eroded. And then came the final punishment, and that was even more degrading.

Peter had been so utterly shocked that he had almost fainted.

He had told his mother about a great many of the indignities he had suffered, but never about that. He knew she would find it so terribly repulsive that he couldn't find the words to do so.

Instead, each time it took place he refused to acknowledge what was happening. He tried to pretend it wasn't him or his body that was being treated so vilely, and he refused to dwell on it afterwards. He confined each incident to the darkest corner of his mind and kept them there, locked away even from his own thoughts.

His attitude separated him from the others. They talked about what had been done to them. For some it cleansed the incident from their mind. Others revelled in what had happened and covertly indulged in a replay with each other, of what had taken place.

Peter wanted no truck with what they were doing. He regarded their behaviour as an endorsement of the abomination that they were being subjected to by Prescott, the master in charge of their dormitory.

Isolated and scorned, he spent long, lonely hours on his own. He used much of the time to mentally rebel against the injustice of what had happened that had brought him into such a place.

Someone had lied and told the police that they had seen him taking the bicycle he'd been accused of stealing. His mother had said that both Sam and Abbie were convinced that it had been Billy. They were sure that he'd been the one who had stolen the bike, but they had no proof.

Peter thought a lot about Abbie and wished she was allowed to visit him. His mother brought messages from her every time she came in, and continually told him that she had grown into a lovely girl.

Peter listened avidly to news about her. She was the only girl he'd ever really known well, certainly the only one he'd ever cared about. He wondered how she felt about him. If she was as pretty as his mother claimed, then she must have plenty of boyfriends, he reasoned. He'd not seen or spoken to a girl since the day in the Magistrate's Court when he'd been found guilty.

Knowing what he did now, he worried that Abbie might be suffering unspeakable abuse from her brother Billy and be afraid to tell anyone. If she did, he wasn't sure if Sam would be a match for Billy. Sam wasn't very tall or very muscular, and Billy was such a mean, nasty character. When he was under the influence of drink he seemed to lose all self-control, and was aggressive even towards his mother.

Peter's memory of Abbie was so different from his mother's description of what she was like now. He remembered her as a skinny kid who always looked so frightened and wistful, because she was always being shouted at by her mother and bullied by her older brother. He remembered how he used to put his arm around her shoulders and promise to protect her from the world for the rest of their lives.

He smiled to himself at the memory. He'd been pretty puny himself in those days. Now, he was over six-foot tall, broad-shouldered and muscular. It was his physique as much as anything that had kept him safe from bullying and abuse. He was bigger and taller than most of the other boys, and many of the masters. His fearless attitude of looking them straight in the eye, even though he might be quaking inwardly, had stood him in good stead, except where Prescott was concerned. And even Prescott had not singled him out for special attention for the last six months.

He wondered how Abbie would see him when he was released. His mother never mentioned that she had any other boyfriends. She always said how much Abbie was looking forward to him coming home. He wasn't sure, though, if that was true, or whether she told him that to keep his spirits up.

He had given quite a lot of thought to his own future. Not all the masters were depraved like Tobias Prescott. The master who was in charge of their education, Mr Walters, was elderly, grey-haired, and concerned for their mental welfare rather more than their physical well-being.

'You've got a good brain, young Ryan, why don't you make use of it,' he said quietly after the first lesson Peter had attended.

So Peter had. He'd worked at his studies, not only in class but in his spare time as well. Mr Walters had encouraged him. Yesterday, at his final lesson, aware that it was the eve of his discharge, Mr Walters had wished him well in the future and given him a folded piece of paper. On it was a name: Frank Lewis.

'That's the name of a man at the Royal Liver Friendly Society. Go and see him as soon as you get out of here and he will give you a job as a clerk.'

Peter had been grateful, but doubtful of his chances. Three years in a reform school was hardly a good recommendation.

'Thank you, but won't I need a reference?'

Mr Walters shook his head. 'Don't worry about

that, my boy. I've already spoken to Frank Lewis about you. Good luck.'

Peter still couldn't believe it would be possible to walk straight into a job, not these days when there were hundreds of men and boys unemployed in Liverpool, the same as in the rest of the country.

To work at one of the most prestigious new buildings in Liverpool, to be able to live at home with his mam and to see Abbie regularly, all seemed too good to be true.

On the one occasion when his father had been on shore leave and visited him, he had expressed such disgust that one of his sons should be in such a place that Peter wondered if he would ever manage to rid himself of such a stigma.

'You'll have to go to sea when you get out of here. No one in Liverpool will take you on,' Paddy Ryan had warned. 'Go to sea, sign on for a long trip so that everyone here forgets all about you. When you come home again in a couple of years' time, then, with any luck, they'll have forgotten all about your past.'

Peter knew that going to sea was the very last thing he wanted to do. Months spent aboard ship in a confined space with only men for company would be like another sentence. The only thing that had kept him sane while he'd been in the reform school was the thought of being back at home again once his punishment was complete.

Each day, as he downed the thin watery porridge at breakfast-time; the grey-looking stew made mostly of vegetables with a few lumps of meat that was little more than gristle and fat at midday; or the slice of dry bread and margarine served as an evening meal, he yearned for his mother's home cooking.

The memory of the bowls of rich tasty scouse, the steamed puddings, the fruit cakes and scones that he'd taken for granted when he'd been at home, not only made his mouth water, but gave him something to look forward to in the future.

He'd made a calendar, a list of all the days he had to endure before he would be free again, before he would enjoy the blissful comfort of his home and be able to talk and laugh with Abbie. Each night he marked off one more day. Tonight he'd marked off the very last one.

With a contented sigh he turned on to his side, ready to sleep, knowing that when he woke it would be to a new life and freedom.

Chapter Fifteen

Working at the Frisby Dyke emporium was like entering another world for Abbie. The people she found she would be working with were all so prim and proper. They spoke in quiet, refined voices and wore such smart clothes that Abbie realised from the outset that she was going to have to tread warily. Even though she was wearing the blue dress that Maggie had made for her, she knew she didn't quite measure up to the others.

Her very brief experience at Pringle's Hairdressing Salon had taught her how important it was to be careful not to do anything to upset those in authority.

She had no idea at all what her duties would be when she reported to Miss Webster, but she was quite unprepared for the look of horror on Miss Webster's face as she hurried her off the shop floor and into the stockroom.

'My goodness! Thank heaven there are no customers to see you dressed like that,' she exclaimed. 'Now, remember to stay in here out of sight until you are fitted with a uniform. There's plenty for you to do. You can start by unpacking those boxes,' she went on, indicating a stack of very large cardboard boxes. 'It's the new stock of winter coats. Put each one on to a hanger and then on to one of the mobile rails, ready to be taken out into the showroom once any creases have dropped out of them.'

The woman handed Abbie a box of shaped wooden hangers, each one printed with the company's name, and bustled away leaving her to tackle the mountain of boxes.

The pile reached almost to the ceiling and Abbie was trying to reach the top one to start unpacking when another consignment was wheeled in.

'You're new!' the young man pushing the forked trolley commented, as he deposited his load on to the floor at the far end of the stockroom. 'Need some help?'

He was wearing a uniform of brown trousers and a brown jacket with 'F.D.' embroidered in gold thread on the top pocket. He had red hair and freckles and he didn't look to be very much older than Abbie was, but he was so tall that he had no difficulty in picking the top four boxes off the pile and putting them on the ground by her feet.

'Is that enough or shall I get another pile down?' he asked.

'I think I can manage to reach the others, thank you very much.'

'They're quite heavy, perhaps I'd better lift a few more down for you,' he insisted. 'I'm Jamie Greenslade, by the way,' he told her with a friendly smile. 'I work in the warehouse so we'll probably be seeing quite a bit of each other as I'm always bringing new stock up here.'

Abbie smiled shyly. 'Thank you for your help, Jamie.'

'I was hoping you were going to tell me your name?' he grinned.

'It's Abbie. Abbie Martin.'

'And this is your first day! It must be,' he smiled, 'because you're wearing your own dress, and it suits you. That blue is the same colour as your eyes!'

Abbie felt her cheeks burning. 'I think I had better get on with the work I've been told to do,' she said quickly, and began to fiddle with the thin string around the top package.

'Here, let me show you the easy way to do that,' he told her. Expertly, he slid the string to one corner of the box and slipped it off the edge so that it fell in a tangled heap on the floor and the lid could be lifted off without any difficulty. 'Break your nails trying to undo the string on each parcel,' he warned. 'You straighten the string out afterwards and then it is saved and sent down to the packing room so that it can be reused.'

'Thank you, I'll try and remember.' Abbie smiled nervously. 'I really should get on now and do the work I've been told to do.'

'I'll see you again, then.'

Without waiting for her to say anything he wheeled his trolley away. Left on her own, Abbie began unpacking a coat from each of the boxes as she had been instructed to do.

They were all so beautiful that they took her breath away. Jewel colours, wonderfully soft, warm fabric and, in some instances, trimmed with fur collars and cuffs.

They must cost the earth, she thought, smoothing them on to the hangers and then arranging them on the rail.

She stacked the boxes one on top of the other against one of the walls, smoothed out the tissue paper into neat sheets, and laid out the lengths of string beside them.

She was on the last box in the pile she'd been told to unpack when Miss Webster returned.

'My goodness! You are a tidy worker,' Miss Webster smiled. 'Are you as good at wrapping up parcels as you are at unwrapping them?'

'I . . . I don't know. I've never tried.'

'Well, never mind about that at the moment. Run along to Gowns. Miss Miller is waiting there to fit you with a uniform. Do you know where it is?'

Abbie shook her head. 'No, but I am sure I'll be able to find it.'

'It's on the floor below this one. Don't take all morning about it as there's lots here to be done.'

Miss Miller was a thin, angular woman in her late fifties. Her grey hair was drawn back in a severe bun and her dark eyes were sharp and cold. She was wearing the regulation high-necked black dress and looked extremely forbidding.

'Abbie Martin? This way.' She turned on her heel before Abbie could reply and stalked off into the staff room at the rear of the department. Abbie hurried after her.

The minute the door closed behind Abbie, Miss

Miller produced a tape measure and expertly measured Abbie's bust, waist and hips. With equal speed she selected a black blouse and skirt from a rail. 'Try that on, it should fit!'

'You mean now?'

'Of course I mean now! We can't have you wandering around the store without a uniform. That dress barely covers your knees!' she added in shocked tones.

Shaking with nerves, Abbie pulled her own dress over her head and took the garments that Miss Miller held out to her. As she stood there in her cami-knickers and lisle stockings, which were held up by pieces of elastic as garters, she was conscious of the look of disapproval on Miss Miller's face.

'You are quite well developed, so you really should be wearing a liberty bodice or one of these new-fangled brassieres,' Miss Miller stated in an extremely critical voice.

Abbie kept her head lowered, biting her lower lip to avoid her embarrassment. No one had ever seen her undressed before, except Maggie Ryan when she had been trying on the blue dress Maggie had made her for her birthday. Then she had been wearing a liberty bodice and navy cotton knickers. Maggie had given her the cami-knickers, saying that she had bought them for herself, but that they were too small. Abbie knew they were a little on the large side for her, but she hadn't minded that. The feel of the soft silky material against her skin, after the stiff prickly knickers she had been wearing, was wonderful.

'You'll need to wear a slip under your uniform,' Miss Miller went on, 'otherwise you'll find it clings to your legs in a most unpleasant way. Have you got one?'

Abbie shook her head.

Miss Miller tut-tutted in disapproval. 'What do you young girls spend your money on,' she admonished. 'What you are wearing underneath is as important as what you are wearing on top. Now remember that in future.'

Abbie nodded.

'Right, well into those clothes and let's see how they look on you.'

She drummed impatiently on the back of a chair as Abbie put on the straight black skirt, which hung several inches below her knees, and then the black top, which buttoned up to a high banded neck and had long sleeves that fastened with buttoned cuffs.

'Tuck the top inside the skirt,' Miss Miller ordered. 'There, that looks better!' she commented, once Abbie had done so. 'Now you look like one of our girls.'

Abbie smoothed the waistband and then undid the top button of the blouse because she felt as if it was choking her.

'No! That stays done up,' Miss Miller told her sharply. 'Turn round so that I can check if the skirt is hanging right at the back.' She gave it one or two small sharp tugs, then stood back, a satisfied look on her angular face.

'Now, look in the mirror and take note. I expect to always see you looking as trim as you do now.'

Abbie stared at her reflection in disbelief. She could hardly recognise the tall, slim figure, dressed almost to the ankles in black, that was staring back at her. She had never worn black before, and it made her skin look so white and her eyes such a bright blue that it seemed to transform her features. She looked solemn, but she also looked elegant, and it rather took her breath away.

'When you've quite finished admiring yourself you'd better get back to your work,' Miss Miller told her caustically.

'Here,' she handed Abbie a package. 'That's another top. You needn't unwrap it as it's exactly the same as the one you have on. You are only issued with one skirt, but you get two tops. They must be changed regularly, at least once a week, and they should be washed very carefully and properly ironed. Is that understood?' She gave her a crumpled piece of brown paper. 'You'd better wrap your own dress up in that, and don't forget to take it home with you tonight, otherwise it will go out with the rubbish.'

As she made her way back to the Coats department, Abbie felt that every eye was on her, even though she knew that, now she was dressed exactly the same as all the other counter assistants, she simply blended into the general background.

'Ah! That looks better,' Miss Webster greeted her. 'We won't have to hide you away in the stockroom any more.'

The rest of the day passed in a whirl of activity. Abbie made tea, swept the floor, dusted counters and fitments. In between, she held pins for the alteration hand, who was called in to make an adjustment to a coat that didn't quite fit one of the customers, and then she had to clear up the pins and lengths of cotton that were still on the floor afterwards.

She also discovered that after the store closed there was still work to be done. All the coats that were out on display had to be covered over with dustsheets, and every counter cleared. Whatever was on display had to be put away safely in drawers or glass cabinets.

Everyone had a part to play and, even though it was only her first day there, she found she had to help tidy up the stockroom so that everything was put away and the room was as neat and tidy as if it had never been used.

Then and only then could she leave.

'Is that your dress and second top in those parcels?' Miss Webster asked her, as she was about to walk out.

'Yes!' Abbie said in some surprise.

'You had better open them up so that I can check the contents.'

Abbie's face flamed. 'Why? Do you think I am pinching something?' she asked indignantly.

Miss Webster sighed. 'No, of course not, Abbie, but it is one of the rules. Before you take anything out of the department I have to check and issue you with a receipt, which you must then show to the doorman as you leave the building.'

When she finally made her exit from the Frisby Dyke building, Abbie had another surprise. Jamie, the boy from the warehouse, was waiting for her.

'Hello,' he grinned. 'I didn't like the idea of a pretty girl like you having to walk home on her own after her very first day at work. Shall I carry your parcels for you?'

'No thank you!' Abbie clutched the two parcels tightly to her chest. 'I can manage quite well.'

'You said that this morning, but in the end you let me lift down some more boxes for you.'

'Well, they were heavy and these aren't,' she told him primly.

'You look different in your uniform, you know,' he told her. 'Very prim and proper,' he added with a cheeky sideways look of appraisal. 'Are you in a hurry to go home?' he asked when she made no reply. 'If not, we could go and have a coffee at the Kardomah.'

Abbie stopped, and turned and faced him. 'Look, Jamie, I was grateful for your help this morning but I've already got a boyfriend.'

For a moment he looked taken aback. Then he laughed. 'I was asking you to go for a coffee, not to marry me,' he called back over his shoulder, as he stalked off in the opposite direction.

Chapter Sixteen

Did she have a boyfriend? Were things still going to be the same between her and Peter when he came home? It was something that bothered Abbie all the way back to Bostock Street.

She quite liked Jamie and she wondered if she had acted rather rashly in turning down his offer of friendship. As a new girl, who knew no one else of her own age working at Frisby Dyke's, perhaps she had been rather too hasty in spurning his attentions.

Still, Peter would be home in a few weeks and then she would know exactly where she stood. Three years was a long time, he had probably changed a great deal. For that matter, so had she. She'd been a skinny unattractive schoolgirl when he'd gone away and now she was almost grown-up.

She caught a glimpse of her reflection in the shop windows as she walked along Lord Street. In her long black skirt she certainly looked different, and she wasn't at all sure she liked what she saw. She hoped she wouldn't meet Sandra on her way home. She'd been quite envious about the dress Maggie had made for Abbie and she'd be bound to have something disparaging to say about her new black look, Abbie thought self-consciously.

Thinking of Sandra reminded her of the fracas there had been at Mrs Pringle's. She wondered if she ought to go and see Mo Lewis and tell her she was sorry about what had happened, since she'd been the one who'd helped her to get the job there.

What had happened had been Sandra's fault, she reminded herself, so perhaps it would be best to say nothing. She still didn't know what Sandra had told her mother and she didn't want to say something that might get her into any trouble. As things were, she felt she probably had the better job now, and that was probably why Sandra was avoiding her.

Even though Sandra was no longer very friendly towards her, Abbie knew she was still as thick as ever with Sam. The two of them seemed to be so full of each other that they had no time for anyone else. Abbie couldn't help feeling a little bit miffed about this because she and Sam had always been so close when they were younger.

At one time they had shared all their secrets and comforted one another when things were bad at home. Now, she hardly ever saw him, and when she did he was usually getting ready to go out with Sandra and wasn't very interested in what was happening in Abbie's life.

Even when she had told him about her new job he had merely raised his eyebrows in surprise. 'Frisby Dyke's, eh! Going up in the world, aren't you. You'll have to learn to talk posh if you want to get anywhere there.'

She wondered if he was jealous. Sam wasn't a rough, tough type of character. She was surprised that he had settled down to working in a factory as well as he had done. Perhaps it had something to do with the fact that most of the other workers were women. The wages were better, too, than what he would get working in a shop, and, if Sandra was to be believed, Sam was saving up so that as soon as she was seventeen they could get married.

A half smile played on Abbie's lips as she recalled the plans she and Sam had harboured for so many years. When Billy and their mam had been so drunk they couldn't stand up and were shouting and bawling at each other, the two of them had clung together and said that as soon as they were old enough to go out to work they would set up home together and move right away from Bostock Street. And Peter had always said he would come with them. In his case it hadn't been because he was unhappy at home, but because he had wanted to be with her.

Abbie wondered if he still wanted to be with her, and whether he had thought about her while he was in the reform school, as much as she had about him.

He hadn't written to her. Maggie said it was because all their letters had to be read by the teachers and headmaster before they were posted, and Peter didn't want them to know about his feelings or private life.

'He doesn't write to me much, either, luv,' she'd said when Abbie's eyes had filled with tears.

'He could give you a note to give me,' Abbie

had pointed out. 'You get to see him every month.'

'No, luv, it would be difficult. There's a master on duty all the time I'm there. He walks up and down between the tables and we're not allowed to pass anything at all between us.'

'You take cake and sweets and stuff for him.'

'I have to hand them over when I go into the building and they are given to him later after they've been inspected,' Maggie told her.

'You never said!'

Maggie sighed. 'No, luv, there's a lot that's gone on in there that I've never said anything about, to you or anyone else. No point in making you more unhappy than you already are.'

There was so much to learn, so many new faces to remember, that the next few weeks at Frisby Dyke's flew by. Any day now Peter would be home and he'd be able to tell her what it had been like in reform school. Even more important, she would be able to find out if he still felt the same way about her. Maggie kept saying he'd changed. That he was so much more serious than he had been. From the little she had gleaned from Maggie about what it was like in there, then it was no wonder all the laughter had gone out of him.

She hoped, though, that he wasn't too serious. She and Maggie were still planning a welcome home party for him, because it would be his sixteenth birthday on the Sunday after he came home.

'He'll be released on the Friday so it won't give him very much time to come to terms with being back at home,' Abbie said thoughtfully. It would also give her a few evenings to get to know him again, she thought. One more week of waiting, that was all.

Like Maggie, she was on tenterhooks. During the day, her mind was fully occupied in learning about her new job and memorising the names of all the new people she was meeting.

She'd been relieved to find that Jamie hadn't taken offence by her refusal to have a coffee with him. The next day he greeted her with a wide smile and was as chatty and helpful as he had been on her first day.

In the days that followed, Jamie introduced her to several other members of staff who were about the same age as them, and this had helped a great deal in putting her at ease.

Miss Webster and most of the other senior staff frowned upon too much fraternising. There were occasions, though, when she was sent to another department with a message or goods, and it was reassuring to see a face she knew when she got there. It also helped when she passed people in the corridor or on the stairs, because she often recognised them and knew which department they worked in.

When a crowd of them met up in the staff restroom, Abbie tended to listen and say as little as possible. Some of those with posh accents, she discovered, came over on the ferryboat from Wallasey each day. Others lived in the better parts of Liverpool, like Aintree, Edge Hill, or Aigburth. She envied them as they talked about their semis and big detached houses, but she was careful never to mention where she lived. She was afraid someone might know that Bostock Street was a row of terraced houses off Scotty Road, and everyone knew that was the most notorious part of Liverpool.

Jamie had told her he lived in Wallasey, in Palmerston Road. From what he said about his home life she was sure that, like most of the others she had met at Frisby Dyke's, he would have been slightly shocked if he heard she came from Bostock Street, one of the slummiest areas of Liverpool.

Peter was released the following Friday. She would have liked to have been there when he arrived home, or better still to be at the gates when he was released, to be the one to greet him first. Knowing that was impossible, she went off to work with a heavy heart and found it difficult to keep her mind on what she was doing.

When she eventually left work that night she didn't stop to join one of the long queues of people waiting for a tram, but ran most of the way home. It was a warm September evening, but a fine mist was falling, and by the time she reached Bostock Street her uniform was clinging to her and her hair was hanging in rats' tails.

She knew she ought to go home first and change, before knocking on Maggie's door. In her dreams about her reunion with Peter she had envisaged that she would be wearing the lovely blue dress Maggie had made for her, and that her hair would be sleek and shining as it framed her face.

That would take precious minutes and her need to see Peter mattered more than anything else did in the world. Yet she felt nervous and shy, and although she usually walked in the back door she couldn't bring herself to do so.

Her heart was beating so hard that it sounded as loud as the knocker did as she rapped on the Ryans' door. She had her fingers crossed, praying it would be Peter not Maggie who opened it.

In her dreams, his face lit up with happiness the moment he saw her and he pulled her into his arms as if he couldn't wait a moment longer to hold her close. Then his lips covered hers as she melted into his embrace and he whispered how much he loved her. With his arm around her shoulders he led her into the living room and they could hardly answer each other's questions for the need to kiss and kiss again.

Peter did answer the door. For a moment he stood there, a tall, lean figure with broad shoulders, looking down at her enquiringly, waiting to know what she wanted. His pale face was sombre, his mouth a thin line. If it hadn't been for his thick dark hair and vivid blue eyes she would have thought it was a stranger.

'Welcome home, Peter!'

'Abbie? I didn't recognise you! You look so . . . so different.'

'So do you!'

They stared at each other in bewildered silence.

'You'd better come in, you look half drowned. Mam's in the kitchen,' he added awkwardly.

Maggie, hearing Abbie's voice, came out into the passageway. 'Heavens above, girl, you're soaked to the skin. You'd better run home and change, hadn't you. Why don't you come back after tea and then you can have a good long talk with Peter.'

Too choked to answer her, Abbie nodded.

'See you later, then, Abbie. You and Peter can have a good chat and catch up,' Maggie said again as she left.

She didn't answer. Her mouth was so dry that she couldn't even swallow. The ground seemed to be spinning before her tear-smeared eyes. This wasn't how it was supposed to be!

All her dreams evaporated into the mist. To think she'd turned down the chance to go for a coffee with Jamie Greenslade because she had wanted to stay true to Peter. She'd told Jamie she had a boyfriend. Now she wasn't sure if Peter was even a friend! He'd been so cool towards her, cold almost. He hadn't even recognised her, well, not at first. He didn't even seem pleased to see her. They might as well have been complete strangers.

When she reached home she ran straight upstairs to her bedroom. She leaned her arms on the rickety chest of drawers that served as a dressing table and stared into the flyblown mirror hanging above it.

Her reflection sent a shudder of hopelessness through her. What on earth had she expected? She sat there, staring deep into her own despairing blue eyes, wondering who she was and what she could ever hope to have from life. Her hair hung in rats' tails around her face, her uniform clung to her body like a black shroud, and she had a haunted look that was almost frightening.

No wonder Peter hadn't recognised her, or, if he had, that he had hidden his feelings from her. Seeing her standing there on the doorstep so bedraggled must have been a terrible shock for him. It had probably shattered all his dreams, that is if he had ever harboured any, she thought bitterly.

Feelings of self-hatred flooded over her. Perhaps this was why her mam had no time for her, why Billy treated her as if she was something revolting he had trodden in.

The only person in the world that she could think of who really cared about her was Maggie . . . and she had more or less told her to go home and come back when she had tidied herself up.

Chapter Seventeen

Peter had changed so much she'd hardly recognised him, Abbie thought ruefully, as she changed out of her wet clothes into the pretty blue dress and went back round to his house.

This time, however, he certainly seemed more pleased to see her, and gradually, as they talked and exchanged memories, and Abbie related her experiences at the hairdresser's and told him about her new job at Frisby Dyke's, some of their former rapport returned.

She still wanted him to tell her what his feelings for her were, but she realised that he wasn't likely to do that with Maggie sitting there. Instead, she listened to what he was prepared to tell them about his stay in the reform school, and plied him with questions about what he was planning to do now that he was home.

'First thing Monday morning, I'm going for a job,' he told them.

'You should have a word with Sam and see if there are any jobs going at Nelson's Jam Factory,' Abbie suggested. 'There's an awful lot of chaps on the dole, you know. Things have got worse since you've been inside, haven't they, Maggie?'

'Yes, unemployment figures are up,' Maggie

agreed. 'It mightn't be as easy as you think to get fixed up, Peter.'

'Oh, we'll see,' he said quietly.

'I hope you don't find that you have to go to sea like your dad suggested,' his mother said worriedly.

'I don't think I'll be doing that!'

'Well, don't be too sure,' she warned. 'I don't want to sound depressing, but as Abbie has said there's an awful lot of men and boys out of work. Lads coming up to twenty who've never managed to find work since they left school.'

Peter adroitly changed the subject. He asked Abbie how Sam and Sandra were, and about some of the people he had known while at school. His mother told him about the proposed party she was planning for the coming Sunday but he shook his head. 'No, Mam, I don't want to do anything like that. I simply want to slip back into my place here as if nothing has happened.'

'But Peter, we've planned it all. We were only waiting for you to come home so that we could invite everyone.'

He frowned anxiously. 'You haven't done so yet, though, have you?'

'No! We left that until the last minute in case you didn't get out on the day you were supposed to. Abbie is going to contact everyone; Sam and Sandra will help her . . .'

'No! There isn't going to be a party, or a fuss of any kind. Is that clear?'

He rose, and walked up and down the small

room agitatedly. 'I'm sorry if it's spoiling your plans, but that's the way I want things to be.'

Maggie looked very taken aback. 'Well, if that's what you want, luv, then of course I won't organise anything. I thought you would enjoy having all your old friends round, having a nice meal and catching up with all that's been happening.'

'No!' This time his voice was so hard and authoritative that Abbie and Maggie exchanged surprised looks.

'Would you like me to ask Sam and Sandra and Abbie round for tea on Sunday, then, seeing that it's your birthday?' Maggie persisted.

Peter crossed the room and took her by the shoulders. 'Can't I make you understand, Mam, I don't want any special tea or party. I don't want to celebrate my birthday, I want to slide into the background without anyone noticing. I want it to be as though I've been on a holiday, or away on a trip like Dad, and come home again. I don't want a barrage of questions about what it was like in there. I don't want people staring at me and questioning me as if I've come from another world. Answering all the questions you two have fired at me has been bad enough. I want to be left alone to get on with my life. Is that understood?'

Abbie stood up. 'I think I'll be going,' she said, her voice unsteady. This was the second time tonight that all her hopes and plans had been trampled in the mud, and she didn't think she could take any more.

She felt sorry for Maggie because, like her, she

had been looking forward to putting on a party for Peter, to spoiling him and making a fuss of him, and now he had made it quite clear that he didn't want any of it. He resented their interference in his life and in the plans he had obviously already made.

As she walked the few yards back to her own house, Abbie wondered where she came in his scheme of things. He certainly wasn't aching to take her in his arms, or to tell her he loved her as she had been dreaming he would do. She was burning up with her need for him to do so, but there was such a coldness about his manner that she was too intimidated to even kiss him on the cheek in case he rejected her.

On Saturday, Abbie had to work until nine o'clock, and she felt so tired when she left the store that she went home and straight to bed. She'd have plenty of time to see Peter the next day, Sunday, she told herself.

When she did call at his home in the middle of the morning, hoping he would walk to church with her, Maggie said he'd been to early Mass and now he'd gone for a walk.

Abbie hoped he'd call and see her later, but although she waited in all day he didn't show up. Pride wouldn't let her go to the Ryans' house again that day.

For all Peter's aloofness, however, Abbie couldn't keep away from the Ryans' house. She called round on Monday evening when she had finished work, but Maggie said he wasn't in. He'd gone out early in the afternoon and hadn't come back yet. Even as they were speaking, Peter came in. He looked confident and pleased with himself as he told them his news, that he was starting work on the following Monday.

'You've got a job already? How have you managed that? Where is it?'

He held up his hand, warding off the questions fired at him by his mother and Abbie as if they were blows.

'I've got a job with the Royal Liver Friendly Society,' he told them.

'You mean the insurance company in that big building down at the Pier Head? The one with the Liver birds on the top of it?' Abbie exclaimed in astonishment. 'What're you going to be doing there, then?'

'Working as a clerk.'

'They're ever so posh! I thought you had to pass your School Certificate before they'd even look at you,' she said in surprise.

'I *have* passed it.'

Abbie stared at him in disbelief. 'When did you do that? You weren't even in the top class at school . . .'

'I passed while I was in the reform school' he told her. 'I did a lot of studying and reading while I was in there, far more than I would have done otherwise. The master who taught us was very supportive and he recommended me for this job.'

'And yet you never said a word when we were saying about all the unemployment and how difficult it was for lads to get work!' Maggie said.

Peter shrugged. 'I've told you often enough that I've been doing a lot of studying.'

'You never mentioned anything about a job!'

'I've learned never to take anything for granted. If I'd told you that I was going after this job then you would have been all keyed up. As it is, I hope it has come as a nice surprise for you.'

'For me an' all,' Abbie breathed, as Maggie went off into the kitchen to put the kettle on. 'I never dreamed you'd be able to get a job like that, Peter. I thought you'd end up in a factory like our Sam, or working as a docker like our Billy.'

His mouth tightened and his blue eyes were icy as he stared back at her. 'You mean because I was sent to a reform school?'

She bit her lip, remembering how sensitive the old Peter had been. She didn't want to hurt his feelings, but he was quite right, that was what she had been thinking.

'No!' she defended. 'It's just that, what with the General Strike and the Depression and everything, and so many people out of work, I thought you'd be lucky to get a job at all.'

'Look, Abbie, I never took that bike. I was innocent, as you well know. I have been punished for something I didn't do, but I don't intend to let it make me bitter for the rest of my life,' he stated. 'Getting this job isn't pure luck, I've worked hard for it. Now I intend to make a new life for myself.'

'Does that new life include me, Peter?'

He shrugged. 'That remains to be seen. You're not the scrawny little schoolgirl I left behind. You have changed so much. You've grown up, you're beautiful and you've got your own life.'

'Not completely,' she said softly. 'I've dreamed of you coming home, Peter, of us picking up the threads. I've always loved you and I thought you cared for me in the same way.'

'You're talking about when we were kids.'

'We used to be so close, we shared all our secrets. Remember the times whenever my mam and Billy were legless after one of their drinking binges, and we came running to your mam for protection? Sam and me used to say that once we were old enough to work and earn money we'd run away from here and find a home of our own, and you always said you wanted to come with us.'

He smiled cynically. 'Kids' talk!'

'There was more to it than that!'

'Perhaps! Now you've got your own life, Abbie, your own friends.'

'Friends, yes. That's all they are, though. I've never gone out on a date because I've always thought of you as my boyfriend and I've stayed true.'

Peter laughed, a dry humourless sound. 'Love is a feeling I dispensed with a long time ago. Being shut up, a prisoner for all that time, not allowed visitors apart from a visit from my mother once a month, and from my father when he was home from sea, killed off any feelings I had for other people, Abbie,' he said bitterly.

'Oh, I thought about you from time to time,' he added, as if trying to quell the hurt he saw in her eyes, 'but that was all. Memories of how we played together, sometimes on our own, sometimes with Sam and Sandra, but it was as though it was someone else's life. Not mine! I knew that things between the four of us could never be the same again, so what was the point of hankering after them?'

'Now that you're home, do you feel the same? About us, I mean?' Abbie persisted.

Peter sighed expressively. 'It's nice to see you again, but quite frankly, Abbie, I'm a little scared of you. You are so worldly, so grown up and so very pretty, that I can't imagine why you would be interested in someone like me. You must meet plenty of young men who are keen to take you out and have a good time. I don't know how to enjoy myself any more.'

'Perhaps I can teach you!'

He shrugged. 'For the moment it's going to take all my concentration to cope with my new working life.'

'Well, perhaps I can help you over that.' She blushed furiously. 'If we saw each other in the evenings then we could talk about it, discuss any problems you're having. That might help you to settle in better, don't you think?'

His mouth tightened. 'You are trying to be kind, Abbie, but I've learned to fight my own battles and deal with my own problems. I prefer to do things that way.'

'Does that mean you don't want to see me any more?' she asked desperately.

'I'm sure I'll see quite a lot of you. You seem to

be good friends with my mother and I'm sure you'll be popping in to see her.'

His remarks made Abbie's hackles rise. 'Look, Peter Ryan, I've been carrying a torch for you throughout the time you've been away. I've never dated anyone else, because I thought it wasn't fair to do so with you shut away. I've had plenty of offers. Boys at work have asked me out, but I've always turned them down. I may not have visited you, but that was because the authorities refused to let me do so while I was at school. I've sent you messages and things whenever your mam has been visiting you, and I always came round to ask her how you were the minute she got home again.'

'Abbie! I'm sorry. I didn't mean to hurt you, I just don't want you building your hopes up about us, or our future together,' he told her.

'Oh, don't worry, you've made it quite clear that we have no future!'

He passed a hand over his thick dark hair. 'I don't know what to say. I'm so mixed up inside, Abbie. So much happened to me while I was in that place. You had to be hard in order to survive. There are things that happened to me that neither you nor my mam know about, and which I don't ever want to talk about.'

'You're not in that place now, though, are you,' she said quickly.

He stared at her, his handsome face haggard with indecision.

'Please, Peter,' she begged. 'You are the person I love most in the world! I've looked forward so much to you coming home. I really thought you would still love me, but even if you don't I'd like us to be able to go out together and have some fun. Won't you give it a try? It might help you to forget some of the bad things that happened to you.'

Chapter Eighteen

Abbie found that it took Peter several months to settle back into normal life, and even then their relationship was still on a formal basis. She wondered if they would ever regain the fun and the feelings of closeness they had known in the past, but she refused to give up hoping.

She still loved him with all her heart, and she was never happier than when they were together, whether it was at his home or when they went out with Sam and Sandra.

She hoped that seeing Sam and Sandra kissing and cuddling when the four of them went to the pictures, or on the rare occasion to a dance, would stir some passion in Peter. Apart from a cool kiss when they met or said goodnight, though, he seemed determined to keep his feelings tightly reined.

Abbie felt frustrated. She yearned for a display of deeper feelings of love from Peter. She wondered if there was something wrong with her, that no one seemed to show her affection the way she wanted them to do. Her mam had never loved her, never had any interest in what she did or what she thought about things. Billy either teased her or sneered at her. Sam, who had at one time been so close and protective, was now utterly besotted by Sandra, who was so possessive and jealous that she couldn't bear to see them exchanging confidences or laughing and joking together.

Abbie had hoped that she would be able to forget or ignore how unhappy she felt about losing Sam when Peter came home. She had envisaged that there would be the same kind of relationship between herself and Peter as there was between Sam and Sandra. She had planned and dreamed of their life together, once Peter was home again. She'd thought they would be inseparable, that he would never tire of telling her how much he loved her and how deep his feelings were for her.

Instead, even though she had been patient all these many months, he was so wrapped up in his job at the Royal Liver Friendly Society that he didn't seem to notice if she was around or not. Persuading him to go out with her was such hard work that she sometimes wondered why she bothered, especially when she often had other offers that she turned down.

As Christmas approached, she received so many invitations to parties from her friends at Frisby Dyke's that she decided to accept some of them, despite the fact that Peter said he didn't want to go with her.

Perhaps if she went on her own to some of the parties it would make Peter realise that she wasn't content to wait forever for him to pay her the sort of attention she desired. Instead of feeling so frustrated by Peter's behaviour, she'd make this new attitude her New Year resolution, she resolved.

Abbie kept to her New Year resolution, and from the very start of 1930 she concentrated on enjoying every moment, both when she was working and when she wasn't.

She concentrated heart and soul on partying and having a good time. She teased, cajoled, begged, or threw a tantrum when Peter wouldn't go with her, and then went on her own. Her mother became tired of her mood changes and threatened to kick her out if she didn't change her ways.

'I'll not stand for it any longer, you little slut,' she bellowed at her. 'You'll be fifteen on your next birthday, my girl, and unless you mend your ways then out of this door you go, bag and baggage. I'm not putting up with you coming home all hours of the night and morning, like you're doing these days, it gives the place a bad name.'

'It might do if you hadn't already done that,' Abbie told her derisively. 'At least I come home sober, not staggering all over the place and shouting the odds at the top of my voice for all the neighbours to hear, like you and Billy.'

Although Billy frequently raised his fist to her, and would quite happily have given her a hiding, his mother restrained him. 'Wait until her next birthday. Do it now and the scuffers'll claim she's only a kid and have you in the nick for hitting her. After July she won't be a kid any longer and then you can belt all hell out of her, for all I care.'

Abbie laughed off her mother's threats, but deep inside she felt hurt and resentful. She retaliated by doing less and less around the house. She kept her own room tidy, but that was all. She ate most of her meals out, either snacks in one of the milk bars near where she worked, or fish and chips that she bought on the way home. Towards the end of the week, when she had very little money left, she made do with a twopenny Mars bar. She looked forward to Sundays, when she was usually invited to a meal with Maggie and Peter.

At work, when she was finally allowed behind the counter to serve customers, she felt as if her life was changing for the better at long last.

She would never forget the thrill she felt the first time she actually made a sale. Bursting with importance, she loaded the customer's bill and money into the little round wooden container, screwing the lid back on and then putting it into the little metal cage above her head. Then she pulled the wooden handle that sent it winging its way along the wires suspended under the ceiling to the office. A few moments later it came winging back with a sharp pinging sound, and as she unscrewed the wooden ball, took out the receipt and change and handed them over to the customer, she felt as proud as any mountaineer who had scaled the highest peak.

When she had been given her promised pay rise after her trial period, her mother had made her hand it over for her keep. Since then, she had said nothing to her mother about the other rises she'd received. Instead, she used the extra money to buy herself pretty clothes and make-up.

She had become very friendly with two girls of her own age; Molly, who worked in the dress department, and Pearl, who was on the cosmetics counter. They kept her informed about all the wonderful bargains that were available when prices were reduced on shop-soiled items or end of season lines.

For her fifteenth birthday on Friday the 18th July 1930, she bought herself a brilliant red, Spanish-style, tiered skirt, and a low-necked black top trimmed with lace to wear with it. She combed her sleek black hair back behind her ears and pinned it in place with two red combs. Jamie gave her a single red rose and she pinned this high on one shoulder of her top.

'You look like a real Spanish dancer,' one of the girls told her as they all met up with Peter, Sam and Sandra after work at the Kardomah café.

'That's what she is,' Jamie laughed. 'Why do you think I brought my guitar along?'

'You can't play it in here,' Peter warned him, looking round the packed café.

'I know that!' Jamie laughed. 'I'm going to play it afterwards, though, and Abbie is going to dance for us, isn't that right?' He gave Abbie a wink that made her giggle.

'For goodness' sake you two, behave your-selves,' Peter told them in a disapproving voice. 'People are looking, you're showing us all up!'

'OK. Drink up and we'll move on,' one of the other boys told them. 'It's Abbie's fifteenth so we ought to celebrate with a proper drink.' He looked at Peter, 'Are you coming?'

'Of course he is,' Abbie giggled, clutching hold of Peter's arm. 'He's my guardian angel,' she tittered. 'Peter makes sure I don't get into any trouble.'

'Oh, is that all,' laughed Pearl, 'I thought he was your father he's so staid!'

Still laughing and joking they made their way out of the Kardomah and into the nearest pub.

Knowing the devastating effect that having too much to drink could cause, Abbie had always sworn she would never get drunk. She found the very smell of beer and stout obnoxious, but it was her birthday and all her friends wanted to enjoy themselves.

When Jamie gave her a small glass containing a deep red liquid she took a tentative sip and found she liked it. This wasn't beer, it was smooth and as sweet-tasting as nectar. This was delightfully different! It wasn't drinking, not in the sense she recognised. She took another sip; it slid down effortlessly. She felt so happy and relaxed that she blithely accepted another and then another.

'You do know that's port you're drinking,' Sandra hissed. 'It can make you very tipsy indeed,' she warned. 'You'd better watch yourself, or you'll end up smashed out of your mind and rolling down the street like your mam and your Billy do most weekends.'

Peter took hold of Abbie's arm. 'Come on, I'll walk you home before you make a spectacle of yourself,' he told her firmly. 'You shouldn't be

174

drinking at all, you're not old enough! You're only fifteen, remember.'

'Oh no you don't!' Her dark hair flying and her eyes sparkling dangerously, she pulled away from him. 'You go home if you want to, misery guts! This is my birthday and I'm going to enjoy it. Jamie's going to play his guitar and I'm going to dance. Isn't that right, Jamie?'

'Whatever you say, my Spanish beauty,' he chuckled, giving a low sweeping bow as he lifted the strap of his guitar over one shoulder and began strumming.

'Not in here you don't, mate,' the barman told him. Putting down the glass he was holding under one of the pumps, he dashed round to their side of the counter and began hustling them out through the door. 'Bloody load of rabble, that's all you are,' he stormed as he pushed them outside. 'Any more trouble and I'll call the scuffers, so don't try and come back in.' He looked at Peter, 'I'm surprised that you're associated with this lot, you look like a decent bloke,' he exclaimed, as he slammed the door behind them.

They crowded together on the pavement, laughing and giggling as they emerged into the warm July evening. It was not even properly dark and they all agreed it was much too early to go home. Arms linked, they surged like a tidal wave along the streets. Peter tried to pull Abbie to one side and reason with her, but it was pointless. She was in high spirits and determined to dance as she had said she would.

On the steps of St George's Hall they gathered

round in a group as Jamie once more began to strum on his guitar. He played 'Dancing on the Ceiling' followed by 'Puttin' on the Ritz' and then 'You Made Me Love You'. They screamed for more, they yelled for Abbie to dance for them, so she pirouetted and stamped her heels as Jamie strummed wild chords of music. With her full red skirt billowing in the evening breeze she twirled madly to the frenzied beat of his music.

Crowds streaming home from the pictures and pubs stopped to take in the spectacle, whistling and cheering her on.

Oblivious to them and to everything else that was going on around her, Abbie was taken by surprise when a hand grabbed at her arm, pulling her to a standstill.

'Gerroff,' she screamed, and tried to go on dancing. Then, suddenly aware that Jamie had stopped playing, she looked around in surprise and tried to steady herself. Her head was spinning and she found it difficult to stand upright and still at the same time.

'I think you've been celebrating rather too well, haven't you, miss,' the policeman holding her arm stated. 'Come on, let your friends take you on home before you do anything daft.'

Abbie grinned up at the tall, broad-shouldered figure in a blue uniform and high-domed hat. 'Thank you, officer, but it's my fifteenth birthday and I don't want to go home, not yet. I haven't finished celebrating. Look,' she waved her arm, 'all these people are my friends . . .' She stopped and looked round her, puzzled. Everyone except

Peter had disappeared. It was as if the night had swallowed them up. A short distance away, Sam and Sandra were watching her antics uneasily. Only Peter remained, standing at her side.

'Abbie, come on,' Peter muttered worriedly as he took her arm.

'Yes, miss, do as your boyfriend asks,' the policeman insisted.

'Don't you want to know my name so that you can write it down in your notebook?' Abbie grinned. 'It's Abbie. Abbie Martin.'

'Right then, Abbie Martin, let's see you on your way home.'

'Aren't you going to arrest me?' she stuttered, looking up into his handsome, clean-shaven face provocatively.

His brown eyes twinkled. 'Not this time, but if I ever catch you dancing on the steps of St George's Hall again, or causing any more disturbances, then I will have to,' he told her severely.

He turned to Peter. 'I'll walk along with you to make sure there isn't any further bother. Do you have far to go?'

Peter looked embarrassed. 'Bostock Street, off Scotland Road,' he told him.

The policeman nodded. As they turned into Whitechapel he said, 'You should be able to manage to get her home safely from here.'

'Hold on!' Abbie grabbed at the policeman's arm as he was about to walk away. 'I told you my name but you haven't told me yours!' She squinted at the number on the shoulder of his blue uniform, 'I can't even read that in this light,' she announced.

'The name's Fisher. PC Fisher,' he told her politely.

'Aren't you going to wish me a happy birthday, then, PC Fisher?' Abbie challenged.

'Most certainly not!' he said firmly. 'You are not legally old enough to be out drinking, and if you cause any more disturbance then I will have to take you into custody,' he added gravely.

Abbie pouted. 'It is my birthday,' she persisted.

'I know!' He smiled. 'I'll wish you a happy birthday the next time we meet, providing you're sober! Now, let your friends take you home before you get into any more trouble.'

Chapter Nineteen

Sandra was furious. She could hardly wait until the policeman was out of earshot before she caught up with Abbie and began lambasting her.

'You idiot, Abbie Martin,' she railed. 'You could have got us all locked up with your daft carry-on. Behaving like that on the steps outside St George's Hall is enough to get us all in trouble.'

'Nothing daft about it at all,' Abbie defended. 'I'm only having a bit of fun and celebrating my birthday. I'm wearing a Spanish skirt so what's wrong with dancing a fandango.'

'Fandango! You're drunk!'

'Sandra's right. It's lucky for you that that policeman was in a good mood and not much older than us. If it had been one of the older bobbies we'd have found ourselves chucked into a cell for the night and up before the beak in the morning,' Sam agreed.

'Don't talk so stupid,' Abbie flared. 'We weren't doing any harm, only having a lark around and a good time. We hadn't robbed a bank or broken any windows or anything.'

'No, but Jamie was strumming his guitar like some demented banshee and you were cavorting as if you had lost your senses.'

'Sandra is quite right,' Peter said grimly. 'We

were causing a disturbance and that officer had every right to charge us. It's pure good fortune for all of us that he didn't.'

'Pure good fortune,' Abbie mimicked Peter's voice. 'Rubbish, and you know it. He was a good sport and he would probably have liked to have joined in. He would have done an' all, if he hadn't been in uniform,' she added with a grin.

'If, instead of being so lenient, he'd arrested us, think of what the results might have been,' Sandra went on, ignoring Abbie's light-hearted comments.

'Oh stop being such a misery guts,' Abbie scowled. 'You're ruining my night out.'

'If we'd been arrested then I would probably have lost my job and Sam might have, too,' Sandra pointed out. 'Peter most certainly would have been in serious trouble because of his previous record. You wouldn't be laughing, either, Abbie Martin, when we all ended up in court.'

'I would have told the magistrate that I didn't know any of you and that you were trying to restrain me, and then he would have had to let you all off,' Abbie giggled.

'You are impossible!' Sandra snapped. 'We should have cleared off like the rest of your so-called friends and left you to get on with it on your own.'

'Sandra's right,' Sam agreed. 'I thought you had more sense than to behave like that. I thought you'd seen enough of our mam and Billy getting drunk to never let yourself end up legless like them.'

'I wasn't legless! I was dancing a fandango! How could I have been doing that if I was legless?' Abbie argued petulantly, her lip quivering at the injustice of Sam's accusation.

'Oh leave her alone, Sam, she's still pissed out of her mind,' Sandra exclaimed witheringly. 'Are you going to see me home or do I have to go on my own?'

'Of course I'm going to walk you home, luv,' Sam told her quickly. 'I can't help being concerned about my sister, though, can I?'

'Leave her to Peter,' Sandra said scornfully, 'I don't want to have anything more to do with her.' Her voice broke and she began to sniffle. 'I don't know what my mam would say if she knew I'd been stopped by the police!'

'There's no need to say anything to her about it. It wasn't you that was doing anything wrong, it was our Abbie,' Sam protested. 'Don't get upset about it, luv.' He pulled out his handkerchief and dabbed away her tears. 'It's all over now, they don't even know our names.'

'Yes they do! Your Abbie was stupid enough to tell that copper her name.'

'Well, he didn't write it down so you can bet your boots he'll have forgotten it by now. Come on,' he took her arm, 'I'll take you home. You'll see Abbie back safely, won't you, Peter?'

'That's right, Sandra, turn on the waterworks, make sure you get every bit of sympathy you can squeeze out of our Sam,' Abbie said sarcastically. 'I suppose you think you're really clever because you've won him over to your side, and it's you he's worrying about and not me. I've watched the way you make up to him. You think you've got him exactly where you want him, you weepy little wimp!'

'At least I have a boyfriend who wants to marry me and I can keep a job, which is more than you can do, Abbie Martin.'

'Keep a job!' Abbie's tone was scathing. 'Washing old women's hair all day! You call that a job? I call it skivvying. What I do is a job. Counter Assistant in the poshest store in Liverpool.'

'If it's the poshest store then why is it always in trouble. Everyone knows that Frisby Dyke's is going bankrupt and that they will be closed down soon. Then you'll be out of work again,' Sandra added spitefully, 'and being toffee-nosed won't be of much help to you then, especially if you have a prison record!'

'Prison record? I haven't got a prison record,' Abbie retaliated.

'You nearly had one tonight. I would never have forgiven you if you'd landed us all in court. If you think you can drag Sam down into the gutter with you and the rest of your drunken family then you've got another think coming.'

'Oh yes!' Abbie laughed derisively. 'You've got our Sam under your thumb, haven't you!'

'We're not having anything more to do with you. We're not going out with you ever again,' Sandra told her. 'Peter can do what he likes, but if he has any sense he'll drop you as well.'

'That's what you'd like to happen, isn't it, Sandra Lewis?' Abbie said contemptuously.

'You'll never get my brother to stop talking to me or going out with me, will she, Sam?' She looked imploringly at him, but he wasn't listening, he had already turned away from her and was trying to persuade Sandra to stop quarrelling.

'Come on, Sandra, let's go,' he muttered, taking her arm. 'We don't want that scuffer coming back and finding you two scrapping like alley cats or he might change his mind about letting us all off.'

'Letting us ALL off,' she screeched. 'You needn't drag me into this. It's your stupid sister that's caused all the trouble tonight. I'm never going to speak to her ever again, so you can like it or lump it.'

Flinging his arm away from her she started to stalk off. Sam ran after her, pulling on her arm, then slipping his arm round her waist and holding her tightly against his body as he matched his stride to hers so that they were walking in unison.

Tears flooded Abbie's eyes as she watched them. Sandra was right. Sam does care more for her than he does for me these days, she thought bitterly.

Sam had always been there for her; ready to protect her from the time she could crawl. In the past he would never have dreamed of walking off and leaving her like this.

Sandra, with her pale round face and big soft grey eyes, had stolen his affection. Her sweet, pretty, toadying manner had got under his skin. She'd seduced him!

Abbie felt she couldn't bear it. What had meant to be a night of celebration was turning out to be a parting of the ways. She would never feel quite the same about Sam. How could she, when he had let her down like this? As for Sandra, she would never speak to her again for as long as she lived.

'Do you want me to walk you home?'

Peter's subdued voice brought Abbie back to the present. Of course she expected him to see her home, but she wanted far more than that. She didn't want him to do it because he felt it was his duty, she wanted him to do it because of his feelings for her. There was a time when she had been so certain of his unwavering affection and had been sure he loved her deeply. She had considered herself to be his girlfriend and was confident that he would do anything in the world to please her.

Now she was no longer sure about that. Ever since he had come home from the reform school he had seemed cold and distant. Not really interested in her or her life. He was so serious, so unresponsive to her chatter. His mind seemed to be occupied by other things; his work, the night school he was attending, and his hopes of promotion.

He didn't talk to her about these things himself, she learned them from his mother. He didn't share his hopes and dreams for the future with her any more. She had no idea whether she featured in them or not.

She had always been sure of his love, and of Sam's, but now she seemed to have neither.

Maggie had changed, too. While Peter had been away she had been so welcoming, eager to share her thoughts and for them to do things together. Now, Maggie was so wrapped up in Peter, and everything she did was for his benefit.

At that moment, Abbie felt that if she disappeared off the face of the earth it wouldn't affect Maggie's or Peter's life one iota. Or Sam's, either!

She shrugged. 'Please yourself! Scarper like all the others if you want to,' she muttered belligerently.

'You know I wouldn't do that, Abbie. It's not safe for you to walk down Scotland Road on your own. Come on,' he took her arm. 'It's starting to rain, let's hurry or you'll get soaked and your new dress will be ruined.'

Peter's sombre mood sobered her. Without a word she fell into step alongside him. She was anxious to make amends for all that had happened that evening, for all that had gone wrong, but she couldn't find the right words.

She knew she had gone too far, but it had only been for fun, that and high spirits. Sandra's accusation that she'd been legless like her mam and Billy had rankled. She would never let herself be like them; she despised their behaviour and lack of self-control.

Sam taking Sandra's side had hurt. She had always depended on his support, but now, or so it seemed, she had turned him against her.

The fine drizzle became heavier, covering the wet pavement and reflecting the streetlights in a shiny black film. The rain clung to her face, to her painted eyelashes, so that she had to blink to see where she was going. She felt cold and miserable.

What had started out as a warm July night full of promise was now dank and depressing. She wished she had stayed at home.

When they reached Bostock Street, Peter made no attempt to walk all the way to her door with her. He paused by his own doorstep but didn't kiss her goodnight or ask her in.

'Night then, Abbie. See you later in the week, perhaps,' he said non-committally, shrugging his collar higher around his ears. 'I'll wait here until you reach your own door.'

'Oh don't bother,' she said dismissively. 'You might ruin your suit if you do.'

Hot tears were blinding her eyes as she stumbled the few extra yards to her own door. She went inside without even a backward glance.

Chapter Twenty

The display of affection between Sam and Sandra was in such stark contrast to the cool reserve that Peter showed towards her, that Abbie felt bitterly jealous.

Peter was so polite and formal that sometimes she wanted to scream. She tried to make him jealous by talking about Jamie and some of the other boys who had been celebrating with them on her birthday, but it had no effect whatsoever.

'Don't you lark around and have a bit of fun with any of the girls in your office?' she asked.

He shook his head. 'Certainly not! Mr Norris, the Senior Clerk, wouldn't approve of any nonsense of that sort,' he said coldly. 'Anyway, there are no girls in our department, only men.'

'There must be secretaries and telephonists working at the Royal Liver,' Abbie persisted.

'Of course there are, but I don't know any of them and have no occasions to speak to them.'

'So I'm still your only girlfriend, then?'

He frowned. 'Of course you are. Whatever makes you ask?'

Abbie shrugged. 'Nothing!'

'I'm not very good company these days, am I,' he said ruefully. 'I'm sorry, Abbie. I find it hard to let go and lark about like Jamie and the rest of the crowd you work with, because I think there's so much more to life than just having a good time. I want to get on in my job, to be promoted, to earn a good wage so that I have a secure future.'

Her blue eyes widened. It was the first time he had opened up and said that this was how he felt, or told her what was on his mind. He looked so serious in his dark suit, crisp white shirt, and sober blue-and-grey tie, that she often found it hard to believe that he was the same age as Sam. Now, listening to him making such solemn statements, he sounded like a man of thirty.

She couldn't wait to get away from Bostock Street and have a home of her own, but she wanted some fun first. She didn't want to be tied down to being a wife and mother for years and years.

'Perhaps you need to get out and have fun. We used to have some great times when we made up a foursome with Sam and Sandra.'

'I don't think that's possible, Abbie. I think they want to be on their own,' he told her, his handsome face serious. 'I think Sandra made it quite plain on your birthday that she doesn't like you coming between them.'

'Sam's my brother, and whether Sandra likes it or not she's not going to stop me seeing him,' Abbie said huffily. 'Anyway,' she went on, 'that spat between us was nothing. Sandra's like that. We're always falling out, but it soon blows over. She flares up over nothing and Sam feels he has to agree with her to keep the peace.'

Peter pushed back the lock of dark hair that had

fallen over his forehead. 'I don't understand such behaviour, Abbie,' he said wearily. 'I think we should all try and get along together.'

'That's what I'm trying to say. Let's go out as a foursome more often, and have fun.'

Peter shook his head. 'I have a lot of studying to do,' he prevaricated.

'So you don't want to go out and have a good time?' she persisted doggedly. 'Is that what you're trying to say? You'd sooner stay at home poring over dry as dust books than come out with me.'

'Of course I'm not saying that, Abbie. I do want to go out with you, but not every night of the week.'

'I see! So you want to come out with me when you are bored with your books. Great! And what am I supposed to do on the nights you want to stay in?'

He frowned. 'What did you do in the evenings while I was away?'

'Came round to your place to see your mam.'

'Well, there you are, then!' His face brightened. 'You can come round and see her while I'm studying. What could be better?'

'What could be better!' she mimicked, a scowl distorting her pretty face, her eyes glacial. 'I've already told you, Peter Ryan, what could be better. It would be better if you took me out more often, if we went to the flicks, or dancing, or even a walk and then dropped into the Kardomah or a milk bar.'

His face hardened. 'I've already explained to you, Abbie, that I have to study. I want to study,' he added, emphasising the word 'want'. 'It's for the future . . . our future.'

Abbie bit her lip. It had been well over a year now since Peter had begun working at the Royal Liver and he was still spending most of his evenings studying. She had no idea how to deal with such dedication. She had thought that once he was settled she would be able to tempt him to reconsider his plans or at least modify them in some way so that they could see more of each other.

She shook her head, letting her dark hair fall over one eye provocatively. 'Please, Peter. After working all day I want some fun in the evenings. Can't we compromise? Can't you give up a couple of evenings a week to take me out?'

He shook his head firmly. 'No, Abbie. I'll take you out at the weekends, but during the week I want to study. Now that I'm going to night school two evenings a week I need the other evenings to do the homework they set. Surely you can understand that?'

She pouted prettily. 'I'm so lonely and fed up when I can't see you. I like your mam but I don't want to spend every evening with her!'

Visiting Maggie every evening while Peter had been away had been fine, because it was a way of keeping close to him. Now he was at home, although she still enjoyed Maggie's company, she wanted to be with him. She was jealous of Sandra and her hold over Sam. She wanted Peter to behave like a boyfriend should, and to give her the same sort of attention as Sam showed Sandra.

'Then go to night school, the same as I'm doing. I'm sure there's a course of some sort you could do that would help you to get promotion.'

Her winsome look changed to one of scorn. 'You must think I'm mad if you think I'm going to spend my evenings studying!'

'Then find something else to do that will make you happy,' he snapped.

'OK, I will.' She turned away from him, slamming the door as she left, not even calling out goodbye to Maggie.

She'd find something else to do with her evenings, she vowed, as she walked back down Bostock Street to her own house. And it wouldn't be cleaning up the hovel she lived in, either, she thought disdainfully as she looked round the squalid living room with its piles of dirty cups and plates scattered everywhere.

She'd show Peter Ryan that he wasn't the only pebble on the beach. She thought of all the invitations she'd had from Jamie and several of the other lads working at Frisby Dyke's. She'd always turned them down. In the beginning it was because she didn't think it was fair to Peter for her to go out with them when he was shut away in reform school.

He wasn't shut away now, but he might just as well be, she thought rebelliously. Well, she'd show him. She wasn't going to mope around every evening any more. She was going to do what she should have done a long, long time ago. Put herself first and have a good time.

You're only young once, she reminded herself.

From now on she'd accept every invite that came her way. She'd have a rip-roaring time.

Abbie tried to be patient. For the next twelve months she left Peter to study while she pursued her own social life. By the time Christmas 1931 came, Abbie was known to the entire younger element at Frisby Dyke's as a good-time girl. She'd go to anyone's party and she'd accept a date from anybody, except at the weekends. What she did from Friday to Monday morning, no one knew, but she was never free, no matter how alluring the invitation might be.

Because Christmas Day fell on a Friday it meant a really long weekend. They would close on Thursday night and not open up again until the following Monday morning.

There were so many parties planned for the Thursday and Saturday nights that Abbie was swamped with invitations. Everyone seemed to be staying at home on Friday, though, and celebrating with their families.

Her own Christmas Day was a complete blank, apart from going to Mass.

Sam had said he was going to Sandra's for his Christmas dinner, so Abbie waited hopefully for an invitation from Peter or Maggie to go to their house, and was bitterly disappointed when she didn't get one.

It meant spending Christmas Day with her mam and Billy. Her mam had bought a chicken for their dinner, and as usual was expecting her to cook it along with all the trimmings, but she felt it would be a complete waste of time. They would both be out cold from drinking themselves into a stupor the night before, and they'd push it around their plate because they had no appetite.

They'd be ready for a glass of port afterwards, though. Probably finish the bottle and she'd be left to clear away all the mess.

Life wasn't fair, she decided. She didn't blame Sam for wanting to get out, even if it did mean marrying Sandra and moving in with Mo Lewis. He'd be better fed and looked after there than he had ever been at home, she thought cynically.

Perhaps that was what she ought to do; get married!

The idea grew in her mind. She began dropping hints to her mother and Billy that she and Peter were thinking about getting married.

'I thought you'd have seen sense by now and stopped going around with that po-faced straight-jacket,' Ellen commented. 'I know you and him played together when you were kids, but I thought that now you were old enough to take your pick you'd take up with someone else.'

'Then you thought wrong,' Abbie told her defiantly. 'There's never been anyone else for me except Peter.'

'Oh no! Then what's the gossip I've heard down the cotton sheds about you being seen out with a different bloke every night?'

'A load of rubbish,' Abbie said defiantly, her face reddening. 'Whoever told you that?'

'Oh, word gets round, especially when you're making a spectacle of yourself. Make sure you behave yourself on New Year's Eve. We don't want to start off 1932 with your name splattered all over the *Echo*!'

'I've never had my name in the paper,' Abbie protested.

'Not yet, you haven't, but you got pretty near it with that bit of showing-off when you were celebrating your birthday outside St George's Hall a year or so back,' Ellen told her.

'How do you know about that? You've never mentioned it before.'

'Keeps me mouth shut when it's none of my business,' Ellen smirked. 'Anyway, I'm glad you've found yourself some new boyfriends and are playing the field before you settle down. It means you're not seeing so much of that Peter Ryan.'

'So why're you bringing it up now, then?'

'Just warning you to behave yourself on New Year's Eve,' Ellen told her. 'The scuffers have got their eyes peeled for anyone causing a disturbance.'

'It's you and Billy that need a warning,' Abbie retorted. 'I'm sick to death of being woken up in the middle of the night when you two arrive home legless and singing your lungs out. You're just as bad as our Billy. No wonder he can't find anyone to marry him.'

'What the hell would he want to get married for, when he has all the home comforts here and none of the responsibilities,' Ellen cackled. 'Billy's all right, so you leave him alone. He helps to keep a roof over our bleedin' head. We all know he likes his pint, so what? So do I!'

'We all know that as well,' Abbie agreed contemptuously. 'Everyone who lives in Bostock Street knows it. You make quite sure they do when you're pissed out of your head.'

'That'll do. You seem happy enough to stay here and yet you do damn all to help keep the place going. It's like a pigsty most of the time. All you use it for is a dosshouse these days,' she added angrily.

'Well, there you are. I don't like it here and you don't like me being here, so if I make a New Year resolution that I'm going to marry Peter Ryan and move out then we'll all be happy, won't we!'

'Anyone but him!' Ellen told her firmly. 'I told you before, forget that po-faced prig, you can do better than that for yourself!'

'You wouldn't be satisfied if I told you I was going to marry the Prince of Wales! I bet you think Sandra Lewis isn't good enough for our Sam, either.'

'Humph!' Ellen snorted. 'She's not given our Sam much choice, has she, the lying little bitch!'

Abbie's curiosity was roused. 'What do you mean by that?'

Ellen cackled and tapped the side of her nose with her forefinger. 'That's got you worried, hasn't it!'

'Not really, because I don't know what you're on about.'

'Why do you think Sam's in such a hurry to get

married? It's because he doesn't like the way Peter Ryan's always around at the Lewis's place.'

'Peter? Around at Sandra's?'

'He says he's looking for you. They know you're out with other fellas, but they don't split on you because Sam says Sandra feels sorry for him. Sam's in a hurry to get wed because he thinks Peter will take Sandra off him.'

'That's ridiculous!'

Ellen Martin grinned. 'Is it? Mo Lewis encourages her and Peter. She thinks he's much more respectable than our Sam and that he could provide Sandra with a better future. Our Sam's only a factory worker. Peter Ryan goes to work in his best suit and wears a smart trilby not a greasy old cap!'

Chapter Twenty-One

Abbie didn't want to believe her mother's insinuations. On New Year's Eve when she went to a dance at the Tower Ballroom in New Brighton with Peter, Sandra and Sam, she was aware of how well Peter and Sandra were getting on, and she wondered if, after all, there was some foundation for her mother's remarks.

She watched Peter and Sandra dancing together. Sandra barely reached up to his shoulder and Abbie noticed that he seemed to be looking down at Sandra in a way he had never looked at her.

That's because I'm on eye-level with him, she told herself, but she knew there was more to it than that. As she and Sam danced close to them she saw the warm smile on Peter's face and the concentration in his gaze, as if there was no one else in the world but the two of them.

She also noticed the flirtatious glances Sandra was darting up at Peter. There was a half smile on her lips and the hand that should have been resting on his shoulder was around his neck, as if she was going to pull his head down towards her at any moment and kiss him.

Sam seemed edgy and uncommunicative, which was unlike him, and Abbie suspected that he had noticed the closeness between Peter and Sandra, the same as she had, and was just as worried about it.

At the time, it didn't seem tactful to mention it; not on New Year's Eve. At midnight it would be 1932, the start of what she hoped was going to be a wonderful year. Peter would be taking some important exams after Easter, and if the amount of time he had spent studying had anything to do with it then he would pass with flying colours.

After that he was bound to get promotion. Once that happened, and he was earning a man's wage, then the possibilities for changes in her future as well as his were bright.

She'd enjoyed having a good time with the friends she'd made at work, but the endless hops at third-rate dance halls, visits to the flicks, or hanging out in a milk bar, were beginning to get a bit boring.

She'd be seventeen in July, time to start thinking of getting engaged and planning a home of her own.

Either that or looking for promotion at work. There were not all that many openings. She was too young to be considered for a Head of Department job, she hated sewing so she didn't want to become an alteration hand, and she didn't stand a chance of getting the one job she really coveted, being a mannequin.

There were only two of them in the whole store. Zara, who was the model for dresses, was in her twenties. She had a very good figure and was very pretty with long blonde hair and big grey eyes. Abbie knew that the chances of ever getting her job were nil. She was walking out with one of the Accountants and it was rumoured that he was about to be made a Director, and that was how she had got the job in the first place.

Minette, who modelled the coats and outerwear for their department, was almost forty, and all Abbie's friends said she would be far better. She was tall enough, slim enough and she had the looks. The only trouble was that she was too young to even be considered for the job.

Weighing everything up, Abbie decided, the best thing she could do was settle down with Peter. It wouldn't be a very exciting future, but it would be a secure one. He'd be a hard worker, and he'd always be reasonably well paid at the Royal Liver Friendly Society, so they should be able to afford to move away from the slummy Scotland Road area, perhaps over to Wallasey.

She could never understand why Maggie hadn't moved out of Bostock Street years ago. Abbie was sure she could have afforded to do so.

After all, Michael was still living at home and he had a good steady job as a railway porter at Lime Street station. Maggie herself had now started working part-time as a cook, and Paddy Ryan must be pretty well paid because he was a Chief Petty Officer. Maggie didn't smoke and only took a drink on special occasions.

On Christmas Day, when she and Peter had taken Maggie with them to Sandra's place in the evening for a drink, Maggie had had one small glass of port and then said she felt tipsy after it!

She'd seen her own mam down half a bottle of the stuff and it hadn't had any effect on her at all!

Maggie had said that she felt so strange that Abbie had offered to take her home and see her into bed. Peter had stayed at the Lewis's, she remembered, which was unusual because Peter was usually very protective towards his mother.

She'd stayed with Maggie for almost an hour because Maggie kept feeling sick. When she left, Peter still wasn't back, so she was surprised when she went home and found Sam already there.

'Is the party over?' she asked. 'I just popped in to pick up my cardigan because I was feeling cold, and then I was going to come back to the Lewis's.'

Sam shrugged. 'I'd had enough!' he muttered.

'Peter's still there, though, isn't he? He hadn't arrived home when I left Maggie.'

'Yeah! He's still there, but I'm off to bed. I shouldn't bother going back if I were you. Sandra and her mam will think you're still with Maggie Ryan,' he added.

She hadn't known what to make of this, or what to do, so she'd gone to bed herself. Christmas Day had always been something of a let down, ever since she could remember, and as she still wasn't getting on too well with Sandra she wasn't keen to go back to her house.

Now, as she sat there on her own watching the way Peter was holding Sandra, and the look on her face as she gazed up into his eyes as they circled the ballroom to the strains of 'Dancing in the Dark', Abbie wondered whether her decision on Christmas night had been wise. Her mother had been right. It would seem that Sandra had obviously got to know Peter extremely well while she'd been entertaining him on her own.

Not a good start for 1932, Abbie thought angrily. She may not find Peter terribly exciting but she regarded him as hers. She always had, and she certainly wasn't going to let Sandra steal him away.

She had no intention, either, of letting Sam be hurt. He adored Sandra; he'd never been out with any other girl. He'd saved hard ever since he first started work and he'd confided in Abbie that he was about to buy Sandra an engagement ring.

She wondered if he'd already done so. If so, was he planning to propose to her tonight, on New Year's Eve.

She felt uneasy; she didn't want him to see Peter and Sandra dancing together so intimately, and she felt it was up to her to do something about it.

The band was still playing 'Dancing in the Dark'. Pushing her way across the crowded dance floor she tapped Peter on the shoulder. 'This is our favourite tune, shouldn't you be dancing with me?'

Sandra glared at her and clung more tightly to Peter. Abbie was afraid she was going to cause a scene, or refuse to let him go, but when Peter smiled down at her she seemed to melt. With a little giggle she released her hold on him and walked away. Peter looked so uncomfortable that, against her will, Abbie found herself saying, 'Do you think we should make sure she is all right?'

They found Sandra and Sam sitting together, so

instead of dancing they stayed with them, having a drink until it was time to herald in the New Year. As the four of them linked hands for 'Auld Lang Syne' the atmosphere was uneasy. It was as if they were all slightly on edge and not happy about being in each other's company, Abbie thought uncomfortably.

Two months later, on St Valentine's Day, when once again the four of them were at the Tower Ballroom, Abbie discovered the reason for Sam's moodiness.

She thought at first that he was irritated because Peter was dancing with Sandra, but as she sat having a drink with him she was shocked when he revealed the real reason for his concern.

'Sandra's preggers.'

Abbie spluttered into her shandy. 'Am I hearing right?' she asked, her blue eyes wide with amazement.

Sam ran his hands through his short brown hair. 'Yeah! Bloody lovely, innit!'

'What're you going to do about it? Get hitched?'

'Have to in the end, I suppose,' he said gloomily. 'Trouble is she wants a roof over her head, first.'

'Nothing wrong with that! You could live at Mo Lewis's place for the time being if you have to, though. I'm sure she wouldn't mind,' she added quickly as she saw a heavy frown darken Sam's features.

'Sandra wants a place of her own, a corpy house and all the trimmings; you know what she's like.

What's more, she says she doesn't want kids, not for a while, anyway.'

Abbie laughed. 'She hasn't got much choice if she's already in The Club, has she!'

'She wants rid of it, so can you help?' he asked abruptly.

Abbie stared at him, open-mouthed. 'What makes you think I know how to go about doing something like that?'

He shrugged. 'You've been knocking around with Peter for years and you've never fallen for a kid so you must know something.'

'Yeah! Like keeping me legs crossed for one thing,' she told him tartly. 'I haven't slept with Peter Ryan or with any other bloke.'

Sam looked at her through hooded eyes. 'So who do I ask, then?'

Abbie played with a strand of her hair. 'You could ask Mam, she's bound to know someone.'

'I don't think Sandra would go for a backstreet job! Anyway,' he rubbed a hand over his face, 'I don't fancy some old shawlie messing her about. Too bloody dangerous!'

'Get something from the chemist, then.'

'Like what?'

'I don't know!'

'I can hardly go in and say "me Judy's in the Puddin' Club, so what can you dish out to get rid of it, whacker?" now, can I.'

'Then she'll have to go to the doctor and ask him to help her.'

'They're not allowed to do abortions, so it

would have to be a backstreet quack, though, wouldn't it?'

Abbie shrugged helplessly. 'Unless you have some sort of grounds why she can't have kids.'

'Like what?'

'I don't know! Heart trouble, liver trouble, insanity? You tell me. Mind,' she nodded in the direction of where Sandra and Peter were dancing, 'she looks too fit and healthy to be able to convince them about any of those things . . . except perhaps of sanity!'

'Bitch!' Sam scowled at his sister and took a long drag on his cigarette. 'Come on, our Abbie, you must know someone or something. How about all those smartarses you mix with at work? Surely one of them must have some answers.'

'I'll ask around,' Abbie promised, 'but I can't promise anything. The best thing you can do is get hitched. At least you're covered, then, if she can't find a way to get rid of it. Has she told her mam yet?'

'Christ, no! Mo Lewis will do her nut. You know what she's like, and she's got Sandra's dad under her thumb so he'd raise the roof as well. He's such a wet echo he'll side with her. I don't want to be around when they find out!'

'When is it due?'

'Sandra says around the end of August or the beginning of September. She's not too sure.'

'She'll have to do something pretty quick, then, or it'll be too late,' Abbie warned. 'I'll ask the girls at work but don't get your hopes up.'

'What about Maggie Ryan. Do you think she might know someone?'

'She's the last person you want to ask, she's too strict a Catholic for anything like that!'

'Yeah! You're probably right,' Sam said sheepishly. 'The trouble is, Abbie, I can't think straight, not since Sandra told me the news. I don't know what to do for the best.'

'Nip off and get spliced on the quiet, that's the best advice I can give you,' Abbie stated firmly. 'If you and Sandra are married then she might feel differently about having the baby.'

'I don't think so,' Sam said gloomily. 'She wants to have a big white wedding and everything.'

'Even if it means her kid's a little bastard?' Abbie asked cynically.

'I don't think she sees it like that. She just doesn't want to have kids until she can have everything nice for them. You know, the big pram to push 'em out in, the cradle and shawls and all the rest of the fancy gear.'

'Then she should have kept her legs crossed and you should have had more sense. It's her own fault! She's a tease. Look at the way she's flirting right this moment!' Abbie said angrily, looking across the dance floor to where Sandra and Peter were dancing cheek to cheek.

Chapter Twenty-Two

Sandra's outspoken fury, when she returned to where Sam and Abbie were sitting and discovered that Sam had taken Abbie into his confidence about her being pregnant, made Abbie cringe.

Sam was taken aback and Peter was shocked, but Abbie felt a sudden hatred towards the girl who had been her friend since childhood. To blame Sam for what had happened was so unfair.

It was as much Sandra's fault as his, and while she could understand Sandra might be a bit put out by the news being made known, Abbie still didn't think it warranted tearing Sam apart in public. After all, she reasoned, Sam had only told her in the hope that she might be able to help. Now, she decided, she wouldn't lift a finger to help Sandra. If she did and it went wrong, then Sandra might publicly berate her like she had done Sam, and Abbie wasn't standing for that.

She had to admit to herself that she felt secretly rather pleased that Peter was seeing for himself how churlish Sandra could be, without any need for her to say a word.

He had gone as white as a sheet when he heard Sandra admit that she was pregnant, and he'd looked absolutely thunderstruck when she had let fly at Sam because he had mentioned it.

Even so, Abbie felt sorry for her. She knew how worried she would be if she ever found herself in that sort of predicament. She told herself she was being mean not to try and help Sandra in some way, since they had, after all, been friends since schooldays.

'I've been telling Sam that the best thing you two can do is get married,' Abbie said quietly when Sandra finally stopped ranting at Sam.

'Oh, you did, did you! So we have your permission, do we!' Sandra sneered. 'And what business is it of yours? Your Sam getting me in the family way can hardly bring disgrace on the Martin name, can it, not with a drunken mother and layabout brother like you two have.'

Tears streamed down Sandra's face and she sobbed noisily like a small child. When Sam tried to take her into his arms to comfort her she fought him off like a wild cat and turned to Peter, clinging to his arm and burying her tear-stained face in his shoulder.

Abbie felt her anger rising. There was a limit to her sympathy. As she saw Peter patting Sandra's shoulder and mopping at her face with his handkerchief, while Sam slumped dejectedly, elbows on his knees and his head in his hands, she felt she had had enough.

'I'm off home,' she stated. 'Are you coming, Peter?'

He looked unsure. She knew he was embarrassed by what had happened, but she was also aware that it was Sam, not him, who should be comforting Sandra.

She put a hand on Sam's shoulder. 'See you at home later,' she said quietly.

He looked up, grabbing hold of her arm to stop her going. 'You will ask around, see what you can find out? You promised,' he added as he saw the look of hesitation on her face.

'You needn't bother!' Sandra flung at her. 'I don't need your help. And don't go opening your big gob and spreading rumours about me, neither.'

Abbie shrugged. 'All right, if that's the way you want it!'

Sandra's small round face twisted grotesquely. 'Don't come the holier-than-thou act with me, either, because I know different. I've heard of the way you carry on with the lads at Frisby Dyke's!'

Abbie felt outraged. Sandra, not content with messing up her own life, was doing her best to spoil things between Peter and me, she thought bitterly.

She'd never tried to hide the fact that she'd gone out with Jamie and his friends. They'd gone to the flicks, dancing, and to milk bars, but it had always been in a group and she'd never let any of them lay a finger on her.

None of them had ever seen her home or even kissed her goodnight because she had always made it plain that Peter was her steady boyfriend. Judging by the look on his face she was going to have quite a job convincing him of that, she thought angrily.

'I'm going.' She stood up and walked towards the door, her eyes sparkling with tears. She didn't wait to see if Peter was following her. She didn't care. Not about Peter, or Sandra, or even Sam at that moment.

She'd never speak to Sandra again as long as she lived, she resolved, as she left the Tower Ballroom and ran along the promenade and on to the pier to catch the boat back to Liverpool.

The strong wind coming off the Mersey was icy, and Abbie couldn't stop shivering. She found herself a corner seat inside one of the covered saloons and hunched there worrying about Sam and Sandra until she felt the boat grate against the Liverpool landing stage.

In the days that followed, Sam badgered her persistently to find out what Sandra could do to get rid of the baby, but Abbie remained resolute.

'If she wants my help then she can come and ask for it herself,' she snapped. 'And she can apologise to me in front of Peter, and take back all she said about me.'

'She didn't say anything about you except that you went out and had fun with the boys at work.'

'Boys and girls! Remember that. We went out as a group. There was no pawing. No pairing off, no sneaking off into dark corners, no pinching each other's partners.'

'If you're still sore about Sandra making up to your Peter then forget it,' Sam scowled. 'I've already told her that she wasn't playing fair and she's said she's sorry and promised not to do it again.'

'Only because she knows she hasn't much

chance with him now that she's got a bellyful. Another couple of months and she'll be the size of a house, and no chap will give her a second look!' Abbie said spitefully.

'Another couple of months and it will be too late for you or me to do anything to help her,' Sam muttered. 'Come on, Abbie, we've always looked out for each other, don't let me down over this one.'

By the time Abbie agreed to help it was far too late. She did find out the name of a woman living in one of the nearby streets, but when Sandra went along the woman took one look at her and shook her head. 'You're too far gone for me to touch you, luv,' she said firmly. 'What are you, five months?'

'No, not even four,' Sandra lied glibly. 'Can't you even give me something to take?' Sandra begged. 'Some medicine or pills, like. You wouldn't be involved, then, if anything went wrong,' she added hopefully.

'Need bloody elephant pills to shift what you've got in there!' the woman told her coarsely. 'You'd better find some poor bugger daft enough to marry you and give it a name before it's too late! That's the best advice I can give you.'

A month later, Sam and Sandra were married in a registry office. There was no fuss and no invitations.

Sam wore his one and only suit. It was navy blue and too short in the sleeves and in the legs because although he hadn't put on any weight he had grown taller since Billy had handed it down to him.

Sandra wore a loose-fitting, button-through, green cotton dress that concealed her bump, and a beige swagger coat over it. She didn't have a bouquet; there were no flowers of any sort, and no confetti afterwards.

Neither Mo nor her husband Dan were exactly pleased about Sandra marrying Sam Martin. Although she'd been going around with him ever since she was at school, Mo had always looked on her friendship with him, Abbie, and Peter Ryan as kids growing up together.

She knew she'd been naïve. Dan had warned her often enough in the past that she was building up trouble, but she had always laughed and reminded him that there was safety in numbers. She had never seriously thought that Sandra would ever marry Sam, and she knew Dan had never thought Sam was good enough for their Sandra.

In fact, as she had seen the interest Sandra had been showing in Peter Ryan lately, she'd thought that Sandra was growing up at last and had seen for herself that she could do better than Sam Martin. Peter had been in trouble, of course, but he was well over that.

Every time she saw him she thought how smartly dressed and well-spoken he was. He appeared to be such a serious young man, and seemed to have very good prospects for his future.

She and Dan weren't thrilled at the idea of having a grandchild, either. They'd had heated words over Sandra and Sam moving in to live with them. Dan didn't approve, but as Mo said, where else could they go. She certainly didn't want Sandra living at the Martins' place.

'It's better for them to move in with us than into that dump,' Mo told him. 'I've never understood how Abbie has turned out as nice a girl as she has, with a mother like Ellen Martin.'

'Never mind about that, is Sandra going to stay home and look after this baby?' Dan asked worriedly.

'That goes without saying!' she told him emphatically.

'It's only temporary, mind,' Mo warned Sandra and Sam when she agreed they could move in. 'I want a promise from you both that you'll try and get a place of your own as soon as possible.'

'Of course we will! The minute we're married and can go on the list, we'll put our name down for a nice little corpy house as far away from Scotty Road as we can get,' Sandra told her.

'Well, mind you do,' Mo insisted. 'Me and your dad are too old to start having screaming kids around the place. I never have liked small babies. They're nice enough when they get a bit older, but not when they keep you awake half the night, squalling their heads off and needing to be fed and have their nappies changed every five minutes.'

Sam wanted Peter to be one of the witnesses but Abbie was dead set against it. 'Let's keep out of it,' she told him. 'Sandra has tried to come between us as it is, and I don't want to have anything more to do with her.'

'You still talk to Sam!'

'He's my brother, I'll always be there for him,' Abbie told Peter.

'Even when he's married to Sandra?'

Abbie shrugged. 'He's got to do his duty for the baby's sake. Doesn't mean I have to be her friend, though, does it.'

Peter had kept his own counsel about the newlyweds after that, and Abbie never ventured any further information. Neither of them went to the wedding.

Ellen Martin was furious when she found out that Sam was not only getting married but that they were moving in with Sandra's mam and dad.

'That's his pay packet gone! That only leaves our Abbie and she barely tips up enough to cover her food,' she fumed as she told Billy the news.

'Then make her pay up a bit more. She must have had increases in her wages during the time she's been working at Frisby Dyke's,' Billy muttered.

'Yeah! You're right! Look at all the clobber she's bought herself and the way she's always out gadding about. You don't do that on peanuts.'

'Probably gets the boys to pay for her, if I know our Abbie, like all the rest of the young bints these days. That's all most of them want a bloke for is to pay for them when they go out,' Billy remarked sourly.

'She's smart, she knows what she's doing. Got her head screwed on, I'll say that for her. You don't see her getting caught out. Still looking for Mr Right is our Abbie.'

'Well, she won't find him while she's knocking

around with that bloody Peter Ryan. I thought you would have put a stop to that before now. Great pansy! Have you seen the way he goes to work these days, all dolled up in his pinstripe suit, stiff white collar and a bowler hat?'

'I see him down by the Liver Buildings now and again.'

'A proper day's work on the dockside would kill him,' Billy said scornfully.

'He's clever from what our Sam says.'

'Yeah? All this studying at night school, though, what's he think he's going to do, end up as General Manager of the Royal Liver Friendly Society?'

'According to what Maggie Ryan tells everyone, when he passes his next exam he'll be promoted to Manager of a department,' Ellen said, as she helped herself to a cigarette from Billy's packet that was lying on the table.

'Forget about him, he's nothing to us,' Billy said with a surly laugh. 'What's important is that our Sam's gone, so that means Abbie'll have to dib up more ackers. Get what you can off her now, before she moves out.'

'She can't get spliced until she's eighteen, not without my say-so,' Ellen said smugly.

'That won't be so very long, though, will it!'

'At least another year. Abbie won't be seventeen until July.'

'So that leaves plenty of bloody time for her to get knocked up like that Sandra Lewis,' Billy prophesised.

'She'd better not! I hope she's got more sense than to let that happen!'

Chapter Twenty-Three

As a treat for her seventeenth birthday in July, Peter took Abbie to the new Grafton Ballroom.

They both dressed up for the occasion. She wore a floor-length dress, a stunning creation in shimmering pale turquoise with a fitted top and very full skirt, which she'd bought at a special staff-discount price.

It was cut daringly low at the back, almost to her waist, so, although it was sweltering hot, Peter persuaded her to keep on the lacy white stole that Maggie had tactfully offered her in case later on in the evening it turned cool.

Peter wore a black suit, and a white shirt that was frilled down the front, and he had smart silver cuff-links and a silver pin in his grey silk tie.

He looked so handsome that Abbie's heart beat faster. Tonight was going to be a very special occasion, she was sure of that, and she could barely wait for him to find the right moment to propose.

She was seventeen at last, so now Peter could ask her to marry him with a clear conscience.

She smiled to herself; he was such a stickler about such things. As soon as they were officially engaged she was sure he would show her more affection. Once she'd promised to marry him he would feel free to be more demonstrative. They'd be able to behave more like Sandra and Sam towards each other.

Thinking of them brought her up with a start. She wouldn't let things go quite as far as Sandra had! At the moment, eight months pregnant, she looked like a hippo, with her bulging stomach and rolling walk. Her round face was so bloated that all her pretty looks had gone.

For a second, Abbie felt guilty that she hadn't done more to help Sandra earlier in the year. It wasn't her conscience that had stopped her from helping Sandra to get rid of the baby, it had been jealousy. She hadn't liked the way Sandra had flirted with Peter whenever they'd gone out together over Christmas and the New Year.

For a horrible moment she'd actually thought that perhaps Peter was going to drop her and take up with Sandra, and she knew that would have had a devastating effect on Sam as well as her. He'd adored Sandra, ever since they were small kids, in fact, the same length of time as she and Peter had been close.

That was all in the past now, she thought, as she looked across the table at Peter. She was the lucky one, not Sandra. Peter was tall, good-looking, smartly dressed, and now that he had been promoted to Head of a department he was earning good money. She was pretty sure he wouldn't want them to get married until she was eighteen, so that meant they had a whole year to save up and plan their future together.

A whole year to wait, but at least at long last

he'd be free to show his feelings. There would be no more chaste kisses on the cheek, or a gentle hug, but real snogging sessions. She'd be able to tell him how much she loved him and, best of all, he'd do the same in return.

She really longed to hear him express his feelings for her, to feel wanted and loved. To know that her thoughts and her every action mattered to him. Sam had been the only one who ever came anywhere near to doing that. She could never remember her mam ever hugging or cuddling her, not even when she had been very small and had fallen over and hurt herself, or when she wasn't feeling well.

Maggie had been more affectionate towards her, and more interested in her than her own mam had ever been. That was until Peter came home. Now he was the centre of Maggie's life and she couldn't do enough for him.

Sitting at one of the little round tables at the side of the dance floor, sipping the glass of sweet white wine that Peter had ordered, Abbie waited expectantly for him to lean across the table, take her hand in his, and pop the question. She had seen him slip a small box into his pocket before they left the house so she knew he had the ring. She wondered if he was nervous, but from the confident way he had studied the wine list before ordering she was pretty sure that Peter could handle any occasion quite calmly.

That was the difference between them, Abbie thought reflectively. Peter was so cool and concise, he always thought things through, never rushed into any situation until he was quite sure he was doing it right. Sometimes she wished he would throw caution to the wind and be a little more reckless.

She took another sip of her wine and, as she put her glass down, a thought came unwillingly into her mind. Perhaps it was as well that Peter was so cautious. If he had been the reckless type then he might have dropped her and dashed off with Sandra, and she wouldn't be sitting here now, on the verge of becoming engaged to the handsomest man in the room.

Her nerves were on edge as she waited for Peter to say the words she was longing to hear.

She tried to catch his eye, but he was staring at the whirling couples on the dance floor and she wondered if he was waiting for a more intimate moment. Was he waiting until he was holding her in his arms so that he could whisper the magic words seductively into her ear?

'Shall we dance?' she suggested.

His sweeping dark brows drew together in a frown. 'Wouldn't you prefer to finish your drink first?'

Abbie shrugged, letting the lacy shawl slip so that her bare shoulders gleamed in the artificial light.

'I thought you might like to,' she murmured. She lifted her wineglass and held it out towards him. 'To us!' she grinned, then raised it to her lips and drained it.

The wine waiter appeared at her side by magic and began refilling her glass, but Peter reached out and held his hand over the top of it. 'I think you should go easy on the wine, you're already looking a little flushed, Abbie,' he cautioned.

Deftly she moved the glass from under his hand and held it out towards the waiter. 'To the brim, please! It's my birthday!'

He bowed and filled her glass. 'Happy birthday!' he smiled as he returned the bottle to the ice bucket at the side of their table.

'Thank you!' She raised the glass to her lips and took a long slow drink, her blue eyes sparkling. Then putting the glass down on the table she stood up, and, grabbing hold of Peter's hand, pulled him towards the dance floor.

Peter tried to resist. When she pouted and threw back her dark head, letting her lacy shawl slip from her shoulders, he gave in and followed her, discreetly putting the shawl back into place.

The band was playing 'Night and Day' so he was able to guide her sedately around the dance floor. When they changed the tempo to the more stirring rhythm of 'Dancing on the Ceiling', Abbie began to give vent to her high spirits. She danced with abandon, pulling off the white lace shawl and throwing it carelessly over Peter's shoulder, lifting up her long skirt and making such a show of herself that people were gasping.

Peter tried to calm her, to lead her back to their table, but it made no difference at all. Stubbornly, she clung to him, keeping him in the centre of the room as she twirled like a dervish, her head thrown back and only Peter's arm preventing her from skidding full length on to the floor.

Other people moved aside to make room for them, or retired to the safety of one of the tables dotted around the edge of the dance floor. The manager appeared and ordered the band to stop playing. Then he walked over to them and laid a restraining hand on Peter's shoulder.

'If you don't mind, sir . . .' He didn't bother to finish his sentence, his look said it all. Firmly, he escorted them both off the dance floor, not back to their table but towards the exit where the liveried doorman was standing with one hand already on the door handle, waiting to open it for them.

'Hold on!' Peter murmured. 'We haven't finished our drinks!'

'I'm sorry, sir. This is The Grafton and you are causing a disturbance that is unacceptable to our clientele. If you have left anything behind on your table then I will send a waiter to collect it for you.'

Peter's face was white with embarrassment and his mouth tightened into a grim line. 'Thank you, there is no need,' he said curtly.

'Thank you, sir. Goodnight, sir, goodnight, madam.' He gave a stiff little bow and signalled to the doorman to see them off the premises.

Outside on the pavement, Peter was shaking with anger. 'What the devil did you have to behave like that for, and have us thrown out,' he railed.

The cool night air cleared Abbie's woozy head like a douche of cold water. 'I was only trying to show you how well I could dance,' Abbie pouted.

'Dance! That wasn't dancing! Throwing yourself

around like a madwoman, taking your shawl off and flaunting your naked body.'

Abbie raised her eyebrows. 'You can be a right prude at times, Peter,' she said scathingly. 'Naked body! My shoulders were bare, that is all.'

'And what about when you hitched up your skirt and waved your legs in the air?'

'They weren't naked! I was wearing silk stockings.'

'You were making a spectacle of yourself. Come on, we're going home.'

'Peter! It's my seventeenth birthday. We're supposed to be celebrating!' She took his arm and looked up into his face. 'I thought you had something special you were going to say to me tonight.'

'The only thing I have to say to you tonight is come on home before you make a bigger show of yourself!'

The scorn in his eyes cut through her like a knife.

'And what if I don't want to go home?' she protested. What was wrong with him. He was acting like he had on her fifteenth birthday, trying to ruin her fun.

'Then I'll say goodnight to you here, right now,' he told her stiffly, and turned on his heel and began to walk away.

'Peter! Peter, come back! You can't leave me here to walk home all on my own,' she pleaded, running after him, her heels tapping frantically on the pavement.

He paused and turned. 'Come on, then, I'll see you home.'

'I want another drink first,' she pleaded. 'You haven't wished me a happy birthday yet, or given me my present.'

His jaw jutted. 'Are you coming?'

'No!' She tossed back the mane of black hair that framed her face, her eyes challenging. 'You'll have to come back here and make me.'

He didn't rise to her bait. Shrugging his shoulders he strode off, deaf to her shouts and protests.

She stood where he'd left her for a few minutes, then made her way across the road to the King's Tavern. She'd never been into a pub on her own before, and it took her a moment to summon up the courage to do so.

I'm no better than my mam; it must run in the blood, she thought bitterly as she elbowed her way through the smoke-filled room to the bar counter.

She groped in her purse for some money and then stood there for several minutes trying to catch the barmaid's eye so that she could buy herself a drink.

'Excuse me, you aren't Audrey Hepburn by any chance, are you?' a voice whispered in her ear.

Abbie turned quickly. A flashily dressed man, with receding slick dark hair, a Charlie Chaplin moustache and sharp green eyes, was standing beside her, looking at her appraisingly.

'I'm Edmund Styles,' he announced, holding out his hand, and Abbie caught the gleam of a diamond signet ring as she rested her hand in his.

He tipped his Brylcreemed head to one side and studied her. 'No, you are too pretty for Audrey Hepburn. It was the style of your dark hair and those big innocent eyes that fooled me. If you were on the stage alongside her, then, believe me, she'd be a past number! Can you sing?'

Abbie shook her head. 'Not really. Croak like a frog, though.'

He gave her a foxy grin. 'So what are you good at?'

'I work in a shop . . . a very posh shop.'

'Ah! That accounts for the lovely dress you are wearing. Very glamorous! Can you dance?'

Abbie giggled. 'I've just been chucked out of the Grafton Ballroom because they didn't like the way I was dancing!'

Edmund Styles's dark eyebrows lifted. 'I think we should have a little drink together and talk about this,' he said, fingering his moustache thoughtfully. 'You may be just the girl I'm looking for.'

When he'd bought their drinks and found a table where they could sit down, he again broached the subject of her dancing.

'Perhaps dancing is what you should be doing for a living,' he said pointedly. He selected a fat cheroot from a gold case and lit it. 'Serving in a shop, even if it is a posh one, is hardly the sort of job a lovely-looking girl like you should be doing.'

Abbie felt flattered. 'And where would I find a job where all I had to do was dance?'

'I can offer you one!' He drew deeply on his cheroot and then let out a long stream of blue smoke. 'That's after I've seen you dance, of course.' He held up a hand as she was about to speak. 'If you've been turned out of The Grafton because of the way you dance then I'm pretty convinced you are exactly the sort of girl I'm looking for to perform at the Floral Pavilion over in New Brighton.'

'As a dancer?'

'That's right!' He took a sip of his whisky. 'If you can deliver, then the job is yours,' he told her as he replaced his glass on the table. His fingers moved up her arm and crept tenaciously round her breast. 'Perhaps we should go somewhere quiet so that you can show me what you can do?'

Abbie knew she had drunk too much and that her brain was in a spin, but she was sufficiently in control of her senses to realise that she couldn't trust Edmund Styles.

'Lemme go! Gerroff! Keep your hands to yourself,' she said angrily, pushing him away from her.

Edmund Styles's elbow caught his tumbler as he pulled back, spilling the whisky in it. He let out an oath as he thrust his chair backwards to try and avoid the residue that was running off the table and down the trouser leg of his flash suit. His chair crashed against the ankle of the man sitting behind him who let out a roar of pain and threw a punch that landed squarely on Edmund Styles's chin.

Immediately, the entire pub was in turmoil. There was uproar as fighting broke out. Chairs were pushed back, men threw indiscriminate punches and women screamed with fright.

Abbie tried to make a run for it, but the doors were already shut fast and the police whistles were sounding.

She felt a strong hand grab at her arm and spin her round, and she found herself looking into a pair of stern brown eyes, and a handsome face that she recognised immediately.

'Well, well? I seem to have had this pleasure once before,' the police constable said in a slightly amused voice. 'What have you been up to this time, Abbie Martin?'

He took her by the arm and led her to the far corner of the room, leaving his colleagues to quell the mêlée that was still going on.

Chapter Twenty-Four

'So, what are you doing here? How have you managed to break the law this time?' Bradley Fisher asked. 'Not wild dancing again, I hope?'

Abbie avoided his keen brown eyes. 'It started with dancing,' she admitted.

'What here, in this pub?'

'No, in the Grafton Ballroom. They didn't like my style of dancing so we were thrown out.'

'We?' Bradley Fisher frowned. 'Who were you with and where are they now?'

Abbie bit down on her lower lip. 'I was with my friend, Peter Ryan. He was upset because we got chucked out, we had a few words and then he stalked off and I came in here.'

'On your own!'

She nodded. 'I know, stupid, wasn't it,' she admitted, giving him a tremulous smile.

'Extremely!'

'Then this chap started chatting me up.'

'A stranger?'

'Yes!' She giggled nervously. 'He said he thought I was Audrey Hepburn and he offered me a job as a dancer over at the Floral Pavilion in New Brighton.'

Bradley's frown deepened. 'That wouldn't have been a man called Edmund Styles, would it?'

Abbie's eyes opened wide in surprise. 'Do you know everyone?' she asked.

'Only those with a dubious reputation.'

She bit her lip. 'Does that include him?'

'I'm afraid it does. Especially where pretty young girls are concerned. I hope you turned him down.'

'I was going to accept his offer, but then he started getting a bit fresh. When I tried to stop him pawing me he knocked his drink over. That was what started all the hullabaloo.'

Bradley Fisher shook his head despairingly. 'You really are trouble; you shouldn't be allowed out! Come on,' he took her firmly by the elbow.

'You're not going to arrest me, are you?' she protested. 'I wasn't involved in the fight. I was about to go home, but the landlord shut the doors the minute you arrived.'

'That's to make sure that criminals like you get their just deserts and don't go anywhere else and disturb the peace,' he told her severely.

Abbie tried to pull her arm free. 'You're not going to arrest me, surely!'

'Not this time, but I am going to make sure that you go straight home and that you arrive there safely. Once these doors are open again there will be a mad stampede. I want you to wait over by the bar until I've finished dealing with this lot and then I'll walk you home.'

'There's no need,' Abbie told him quickly. 'I promise I'll go straight home.'

'Please yourself. Either do as I say and let me

see you home or I shall have to arrest you. I can't take the risk of abandoning you.'

Abbie wasn't sure whether he was joking or not, but it was a nice feeling to have someone so concerned about her. It made her feel warm inside, protected and safe.

'Very well,' she said meekly, 'I'll wait by the bar counter for you.'

Afterwards, as they walked towards Scotland Road, she gave him a censured version about what had happened during the earlier part of the evening.

'Celebrating your birthday again? So how old are you now?'

'Seventeen!'

'Old enough to be taken out on a date, then.'

'If the right sort of person asked me,' she teased.

He gave her a penetrating look. 'Do you think I might fit the bill?' he asked.

'I could think about it!'

He grinned. 'You do that, and if the answer is yes then be at Lime Street station next Tuesday night at seven.'

'Not on your life!' Abbie laughed. 'Hang around outside Lime Street station? You must be kidding! What do you think I am, a Mary Ellen?'

He grinned back at her. 'Not so daft after all, are you!'

'Don't think that just because you're a copper you can take the mickey out of me like that,' she snapped.

'Sorry!' He held up his hands. 'I was only having you on.'

Abbie's spirits sank. For one moment she'd thought he really was asking her for a date and she'd had every intention of accepting, if only to prove to Peter Ryan that he wasn't the only man in her life.

'I did mean it about taking you out, though,' Bradley Fisher went on in a more serious tone. 'Will you come out with me one evening, Abbie? We could go over to New Brighton for a walk along the prom, or do anything else you fancied.'

'Yes, I'd like that,' she said eagerly. 'I haven't been to New Brighton since St Valentine's night and it wasn't the right time of year to be walking along the prom.'

'OK,' he agreed. 'That's on, then. We'll catch the seven o'clock ferryboat from the Pier Head, go for a walk and then have a meal or go to one of the shows over there.'

'You know how to spoil a girl!'

He looked at her sharply. 'You will turn up?'

'Of course I will. Even if it's raining cats and dogs,' she promised.

'Good. I'll be waiting.'

As they reached the junction of Scotland Road and Cazneau Street, Abbie stopped and held out her hand. 'I'll say goodnight, I know my way from here,' she grinned.

'No, I'll see you to your door.'

'What, and have the neighbours think I'm in some sort of trouble being brought home by a scuffer! Me mam'd kill me!' she joked.

'All right. If that's the way you want it. I'll be in

my own clothes when we meet on Tuesday; do you think you'll be able to recognise me?'

'Probably not. Perhaps you'd better be carrying a copy of the *Echo* or something because if I'm accosted by a stranger I might scream for a policeman!'

'Right, I'll remember that. And you remember it's the seven o'clock boat we're going on and don't be late.'

Abbie found herself looking forward to her date with Bradley Fisher, especially when she didn't hear a word from Peter.

She'd felt quite flattered that Bradley had remembered her name from the incident on the steps of St George's Hall. And she'd been even more impressed when he'd told her that he hadn't been able to put her out of his mind ever since then.

She'd thought about him once or twice. He was good-looking with his brown eyes, short dark hair and fresh face, and he looked very impressive in his navy blue police uniform. He had a nice friendly manner and was so easy to talk to. He didn't seem threatening or a bully like so many policemen were.

What she liked most of all was that even though he barely knew her, he seemed genuinely interested in her and what she had to say. When she told Peter things although he listened to her he either lectured her on what she should have done or ought to do, or else he dismissed what she'd told him as being of no consequence.

Bradley Fisher wasn't like that. He asked questions or made comments that made her feel important and interesting.

She hadn't intended to say anything to her mam or Billy about what had happened, but when Sam called round he let slip that he'd heard that Peter had arrived home on his own from The Grafton, and that he'd been in a very bad mood.

'Said you'd showed him up doing some fancy dance or the other,' he grinned. 'You should have known better, you know Peter's become a bit of a stuffed shirt now he's got his promotion.'

Abbie shrugged. 'There's plenty more fish in the sea,' she said, flicking her hair back behind her ears.

'I've been telling you that for ages,' her mother cackled. 'I never could fathom out why you stuck to him like glue, or why you even bothered going around with him at all. Look at you! Sandra's getting wed and having a kid and she's no older than you, and now you've fallen out with Peter Ryan you've got no fella at all!'

'That's where you're wrong,' Abbie told her. 'I'm going out on a date on Tuesday night.'

'Who with?' Ellen asked nosily. 'That Jamie from work, or one of that crowd you work with that you're always on about?'

'No. With someone else. He's quite special. Tall, dark and handsome,' she grinned and then added quickly, 'you don't know him.'

'What's his name? Anyone I know?' Sam asked.

'Bradley Fisher.'

Billy pricked up his ears. 'I've heard that

232

moniker somewhere,' he said suspiciously. 'What's this geezer do for a living? Does he work down the docks?'

Abbie tapped her nose. 'None of your business,' she told him. 'He's my date, not yours!'

She left the room quickly, before Billy could remember where he'd heard Bradley's name from and started asking her any more questions about him. She knew Billy would be livid if he discovered that she was going out on a date with a policeman.

Billy had had so many run-ins with the law that the sight of a policeman walking down Scotland Road was enough to make him quake in his shoes for all his bluster.

Her mam felt much the same way, so the less they knew about her friendship with Bradley Fisher, the better it would be.

The less he knew about her family for the moment, the better it would be as well, which was why she hadn't let him walk her all the way home.

He knew she lived somewhere off Scotland Road and that was bad enough. If he found out that she lived in the slummiest house in Bostock Street he might drop her like a hot brick.

Time enough for him to know those sort of details if they started becoming serious about each other and then she'd have to tell him about her family.

For the moment it was simply a matter of having a night out in New Brighton and a chance for them to get to know each other a bit better.

Chapter Twenty-Five

The sky hung like a thunderous black curtain over the Mersey. Ships' klaxons and foghorns sounded continuously. It was raining so hard that it was blowing in through the open doors of the cotton sheds, where that morning dozens of damaged bales had been unloaded and swung inside the shed from the ship docked alongside.

The noise of the rain drumming down outside almost drowned the voices of the women working in there.

'If they don't turn the bloody tap off before knockin' off time we'll be like drowned rats by the time we get to the top of the floating roadway,' one of them commented loudly.

'Sooner get bleedin' soaked than hang on here any longer. Getting back to me own fireside is all I give a damn about. What's a drop of rain, anyway, only cold water,' another piped up.

'It's only a summer storm; there's another hour to go yet, so with any luck it'll have eased off by then. At least we're working inside so we're out of it. Think of the poor buggers working out on the dockside, they must be like drowned rats!' Ellen Martin shouted back, pulling her black shawl more firmly round her shoulders.

'See for yourself, here's your Billy. Look at the state he's in!'

Ellen looked up as Billy, soaked to the skin, water skidding off the peak of his greasy cap, walked across to the corner of the warehouse where she was working.

She put down her sharp, curved knife and held out her hand. 'Orright' then?'

He nodded, shoving a tin box into her outstretched hand, pulling a face and turning his jacket collar up around his ears all at the same time.

'See you at home later, then.'

Billy grunted and turned away.

'Why the hell does he have to bring his snack tin over here, Ellen, for you to carry home for him?' Ruby Stacey asked. 'Lazy bugger!'

'Have to wait on him 'and and foot at home as well, do yer?' another laughed.

Ellen didn't answer. She put the tin Billy had brought underneath her own, and taking off her black shawl wrapped them firmly together in a bundle. Then picking up her curved knife she returned to hacking out a wad of the iron-hard, salt-damaged cotton, ready for teasing.

Her fingers itched to look inside Billy's tin, but she knew better than to even show a flicker of interest about what was in it. There were too many curious eyes, too many loose tongues, and too many women who would be more than ready to land her in trouble if she gave them the slightest chance.

The women who worked in the cotton sheds

were the roughest of the rough. Most of them lived in the dingy courts that were built around the Scotland Road area. Very few of them could read or write, but they were streetwise and hard, and they had an inborn craftiness that got them through life.

Many of them were married to men who were casual labourers on the docks, or men who were on the bottom rung when it came to jobs. Burly men who were rough and ready, and quick with their fists at work as well as at home.

Even though most of the women she worked alongside were well able to stand up to their menfolk, they regularly appeared with black eyes, cut lips and bruises. She knew only too well that they would have no compunction about throwing a punch her way if they knew the contents of Billy's snack tin.

Ellen grinned to herself. They thought themselves smart, but they were no match for her and Billy. When the pair of them worked as a team the rewards were always well worth the risks they took.

It was still raining when the hooter sounded, but Ellen barely noticed. All she wanted to do was get home and see what was in Billy's tin.

As the other women dithered about going out in the rain, she made to leave.

'You can't go out in that lot, you'll be half-drowned long before you can reach the tram stop,' Ruby Stacey yelled.

'Gerroff! I won't melt! A drop of rain never did anyone any harm,' Ellen argued. Angrily she shook Ruby's hand away from her arm and elbowed her way past the others.

'Well, at least put your shawl up over your head, you silly bitch,' one of the women at the front advised. She made a grab for the black shawl that Ellen had tucked underneath her arm. There was a scuffle and a tussle and the shawl was dragged free, spilling its contents. The lid on the tin Billy had entrusted to her flew open.

'Flippin' 'eck! Wha's all that, then?' one of the women exclaimed, as a man's silver watch and a handful of mixed silver lay scattered on the warehouse floor.

They pushed and shoved to pick the pieces up and then slowly handed them back to Ellen.

She took them without a word of thanks and thrust them as fast as she could into the deep pocket of her black skirt.

'Hang on a minute. Let's have a gander at that watch,' one of the women demanded.

Ellen pushed her aside. 'Sling your 'ook and mind your own bleedin' business, Florrie Smith.'

The woman was taller than Ellen, with a pock-marked face and brawny arms. She stood with them akimbo, as she glared suspiciously at Ellen.

'I think it is my bloody business, Ellen Martin,' she said menacingly. 'That's my old man's watch you got there.'

'Don't talk so bleedin' wet,' Ellen blustered. 'How the hell would I have your old man's watch?'

'That's something I'd like to know,' Florrie Smith told her. 'It was in that tin your Billy brought over and we all know what a right tea-leaf he is! It doesn't take a barrack-room lawyer to work out what's going on!'

Ellen tried to push Florrie to one side. 'Out of me way, I haven't got time to stand here argy-bargying with you. I got a home to go to, even if you haven't!'

'Oh no you don't!' Florrie grabbed her by the hair and spun her round. 'You ain't tear-arsing off nowhere, not wi' my old man's watch in your pocket, so hand it over.'

'And who's going to make me?'

'Me and me mates are!' Florrie Smith told her aggressively.

Ellen looked round at the rest of the women, trying to gauge who was on her side and who would be likely to support Florrie.

'What makes you think it's your old man's, anyway?' Ellen parried.

'Turn yer pocket out and let's take a dekko. If it's my Jack's watch it's solid silver and as sound as Big Ben, and it's got J. S. engraved on the back of it.'

'Give over, you barmy sod! It's only a bit of tat,' Ellen told her. 'Probably given away with a pound of tea or else it came out of a Chrissy cracker or from Paddy's Market,' she added derisively.

Florrie's face reddened. 'I think it's time to stop jangling and take a dekko,' she demanded nastily.

There was a murmur of agreement from the other women, and before Ellen could avoid it she was surrounded and her black skirt almost torn off as hands dived for the pocket where she had secreted the watch and money.

Polly Hicks, the forewoman, screamed for help. The warehouseman came running to see what all the commotion was about. He took one look at the milling mound of women, all clawing and fighting, and then yelled at the top of his voice for someone to call the scuffers.

Within seconds, police whistles were sounding the alarm and there was the dull thud of pounding feet as three policemen who had been on the dockside invaded the shed, batons at the ready.

It took the three of them ten minutes to separate all the women and find out what the fuss was about. They confiscated all of Ellen's loot. One of the policemen took out his notebook and asked her for her name and address, but she refused to give it.

'Helen. Mury Helen!' one of the other women cackled. 'Can't you see she's a scruffy Mury Helen from her shawl and black skirt?'

'That'll be enough,' the sergeant in charge snapped. Along with another officer he marched her away to the police station, leaving the younger policeman to pacify the rest of the women.

'So when're you going to let my old man have his watch back?' Florrie demanded.

The young police officer shrugged. 'You'd better ask down at the station. They may need to hang on to it as evidence. Depends if they charge her or not.'

'Wouldn't mind bettin' that if my old man's realised it's gone then him and his mates are looking everywhere down on the docks for it,' Florrie babbled.

'You'd better tell him to report his loss, then, and we'll see if he can prove it's his.'

'Yer wants to track down her son, Billy. He's the real villain, not her. He's the one what stole the watch. He brought it over here and gave it her to carry home for him,' Florrie went on.

'Right, I'll do that. What's his full name and where does he live?'

'Bostock Street, off Scotland Road.'

'The number?'

'Gawd, how should I know that. You wanting me to do your job for you!' she sneered in mocking tones. 'Look for the scruffiest house in the road, dirty doorstep and dirty ragged curtains at the window, that'll be it.'

He nodded.

'What's yer name, so that I can tell me old man who it was said he was to come to the station and ask for his watch?'

'Constable Fisher.'

'Well, you damn well make sure you nab that Billy, Constable Fisher,' Florrie called after him as he walked away.

It wasn't until he reached Scotland Road and was looking out for Bostock Street, that Bradley Fisher realised he hadn't made a note of the accused woman's surname before his colleagues had marched her off, so he didn't know Billy's name, either.

He debated whether to go to the station first and find out, or whether, since he was virtually on the doorstep, he should follow Florrie Smith's directions and look for the scruffiest house in the road.

It stood out like a sore thumb! Even in a road of slummy houses, this house had the edge. The front step looked as though it hadn't seen a pumice stone in years. There was a cracked pane of glass in the front window and the grimy curtains were in tatters. As he hammered with his fist on the front door he noticed it was chipped and scarred, as though it had been kicked in a few times.

There was no reply. He knocked again, then put his shoulder to it and gave it a firm push. A dank, sour smell came from inside as he stepped into the dark passage.

'Anyone at home?'

His voice echoed. In the living room, ashes spewed from the grate into the hearth. Mugs and dirty plates with leftover food on them cluttered the rickety table and sideboard. He went to the bottom of the stairs and shouted out again, but there was still no answer. He made his way up to the landing and looked into the bedrooms. Two of them were in a state of complete disorder, the beds unmade, clothes dropped on the floor. The smaller of the bedrooms, however, was neat and tidy, but the thing that caught his attention was the full-length turquoise frock hanging from a nail on one wall.

He walked across the room and fingered it, momentarily unable to believe it was the same dress, hoping he was mistaken.

'What do you think you are doing!'

He had been so engrossed in the dress that he hadn't heard anyone come in, and he turned around startled to face Abbie.

'Bradley, what are you doing in my bedroom?' she gasped in astonishment.

'Your bedroom? This is where you live? Billy is your brother? Your mother's name is Ellen?'

She nodded, the colour draining from her face. 'Why all the questions? Is something wrong?' she asked anxiously.

He shook his head, unable to believe Ellen was Abbie's mother, wondering how to tell her what had happened.

'Has there been an accident? Are they hurt?' she persisted, her voice quivering.

Again, he shook his head. 'No, there's not been an accident,' he said hesitantly.

'What, then?'

'There was an incident at the cotton sheds and your mother has been arrested for possessing stolen goods.'

Abbie stared at him, chewing on her lower lip.

'She's been taken to Atholl Street police station,' Bradley added, almost apologetically.

'You arrested my mam!'

He squared his broad shoulders. 'Yes, I arrested her, but I didn't know she was your mother,' he said stubbornly.

'So why are you here, turning the place upside down?'

'I'm looking for your brother, Billy. According to information received, he is the real culprit and your mother was his accomplice,' he told her stiffly.

Chapter Twenty-Six

After Bradley Fisher left the house, Abbie lay on her bed, dry-eyed, staring up unseeingly at the cracked, dirty ceiling. She felt as if the bottom had dropped out of her world. She couldn't believe that Fate had dealt her such a cruel blow. For Bradley to find out where she lived was bad enough, but for him to have taken part in arresting her mam, and to be looking for Billy so that he could arrest him as well, was the final straw.

The look on his face when she had walked into the house and found him fingering her evening dress had sent goose-bumps chasing along her spine. When he had turned around he'd looked as if he was seeing a ghost, and she had been just as shocked as him.

The thought that what her mother had done might ruin their friendship made her realise how much she liked him.

Over the last few weeks, since she'd been going out with Bradley, she'd thought that at last she had found someone who was not only interested in everything she said or did, but really did like her a great deal.

For her entire life her mam and Billy had treated her as if she was of no importance. Neither of them had ever shown her any affection or love.

Her childhood closeness to Sam and Peter had now been eroded. Sam had transferred his love to Sandra; Peter seemed to have channelled all his energies into his work. Even Maggie Ryan seemed to have lost interest in her.

Meeting Bradley, and discovering someone who was not only interested in her, but who seemed to love her, had been such a wonderful experience; like starting a new life. Each kiss they'd exchanged had filled her with wonder. It had been like renewing a pledge of their love, and a promise of all the happiness that was still to come; and now those hopes were all turning to dust.

She dare not let herself dwell on what he must think of her. She wished fervently that right from the beginning she'd told him everything about herself. She should have told him where she lived, explained about her family background. She'd meant to, once they got to know each other. Then, because she was so much in love with him, she'd been afraid to do so in case it changed his feelings for her.

Looking back, she knew it would have been far better for this run-in between her mam and Bradley to have happened earlier on in their relationship, before he had come to mean so much in her life. She might have felt unhappy at losing him, but she wouldn't have been as broken-hearted as she was now. She wouldn't have known this terrible emptiness, as if someone had ripped out her heart.

When Billy arrived home and discovered his mother wasn't there he flew into a rage.

'Where the hell is she?' he demanded, barging into Abbie's bedroom and angrily kicking at the legs of her bed.

'At Atholl Street police station.'

'What! What did you say?'

'Mam's been taken to Atholl Street police station. She's been done for causing some sort of affray down at the cotton sheds.'

'How do you know?'

'The police were here when I got in from work. They're looking for you.'

'What the hell for? What's it got to do with me?'

Abbie shrugged listlessly. 'I don't know. I think Bradley said it was something to do with stealing a watch.'

'Bradley! That fella you're knocking around with? What's it got to do with him?'

'He was the one here looking for you. His lot arrested Mam.'

Billy looked at her in growing fury. 'Bradley . . . Bradley Fisher. I thought I knew that name. He's a bloody scuffer, isn't he!'

Abbie nodded.

'You've been knocking around with a bloody scuffer, opening your great gob and telling him all he wants to know about our goings-on,' Billy railed.

He caught hold of Abbie's arm and pulled her off the bed, hauling her to her feet and shaking her like a rag doll until her teeth were chattering.

'You'd better get yourself down the cop shop and find out what's going on!' he snarled, pushing her towards the door.

'Go yourself!' she muttered, pulling back from him and sitting back down on the bed.

'How the hell can I! You said that your Bradley Fisher was here looking for me! He wasn't doing that so that he could invite me to a bleedin' party.'

'So what have you been up to?'

'The less you know, the less you can mouth off to your boyfriend,' Billy snarled.

'I don't suppose there's much chance of that,' Abbie said bitterly. Her eyes filled with tears. 'Now that Bradley has found out about my family I don't suppose I'll ever see him again.'

'Lucky for you, you stupid bint. If I see you talking to him again I'll bloody well thrash you within an inch of your life!'

Abbie looked at him disdainfully. 'You'll have a job. Any minute now one of those scuffers will be back here looking for you, and when they hear what you've been up to you'll be behind bars in Walton Jail!'

Billy frowned, a desperate shifty look on his face. 'Mam won't spill the beans; she'll keep her trap shut,' he said confidently. 'All I've got to do is bugger off where that dozy-arsed copper can't find me.'

'Go on then, scarper!' Abbie said derisively. 'Be just like you, Billy, to leave our mam to fend for herself when she's charged for something you've done. What'll you care if she ends up inside?'

'They won't send an old biddy like her to the Dogs' Home,' he blustered.

Abbie shrugged. 'If they find her carrying whatever it is you've nicked, they're bound to do just that. Bradley said something about a watch,' she added, eyeing him closely.

Billy hesitated, as if trying to make his mind up about what he ought to do.

'Can you lend us some money, kiddo? I'm skint,' he said at last.

'Lend you money so that you can make a getaway and let mam take the can back for you! You must think I'm stupid.'

'Stop whingeing! Open your purse up and hand over some ackers,' Billy snarled. 'The sooner I'm away, before that bloody scuffer of yours comes back, the better. Me mam knows how to deal with the scuffers. She'll tell them that some fella she didn't know asked her to look after the ticker for 'im.'

'And you think they'll believe her?' Abby asked caustically.

'Don't see why not.' His thin lips twisted into an ugly grin. 'It's as near the truth as she can get!'

'Maybe, but the police know exactly who that mystery fella is,' Abbie pointed out. 'The women in the cotton sheds saw you hand it over to her and they've already told the police, and that's why they came here looking for you.'

Billy ran a hand over his scant brown hair. 'So what the hell am I supposed to do?'

'Own up?' Abbie said scathingly.

'If I do that they'll want the low-down on about a dozen other offences!'

'You have been busy! And has Mam been involved with those as well?'

Billy scowled. 'Some!'

'What about the bike you nicked that Peter Ryan got put away over?' Abbie said softly.

'Shut your trap! What the hell's the point of bringing up something like that after all this time. They've wiped that one off their slate years ago.'

'Only because he took the rap for it. It was you that pinched it, wasn't it, Billy,' Abbie persisted.

'Give over nagging! They'd never prove anything. Let's have some ackers and I'll be out of here, and you won't see nor hear from me ever again.'

'I'd like nothing better, but I've already told you I haven't got any money, not until I'm paid tomorrow.'

Billy's eyes narrowed. 'You get paid tomorrow. And then you'll give me enough to skedaddle?'

Abbie shook her head. 'I never said that!'

Billy grabbed hold of her. 'Say it now, then!' he ordered, twisting her arm behind her back until she was white with pain.

'What about Mam?'

'I've told you, she can take care of herself,' Billy snarled. 'Anyway, what're you so worried about her for; the pair of you hate each other's guts!'

'That's got nothing to do with it. It's not fair that someone who's innocent should be taking the rap.'

'Innocent be beggared. She's as much involved in what went on as I am. I told you before, don't worry your head about her, she knows the score and she knows how to take care of herself. She's been doing it long enough! The last thing she'll want me to do is put me own head on the block. It won't save her skin any, only give the scuffers a bloody good laugh.'

Abbie bit her lip. Billy was in an ugly mood and she was afraid of what he might do next. She didn't know what to say or do for the best. She was so frightened that she couldn't think straight. She knew she ought to turn Billy in, and she hated him, but he was her brother.

She wondered if the police would come back to the house looking for him, or if Bradley would throw them off the scent for her sake?

Even if he did manage to do that, it would only be a temporary measure. They already had her mam in custody and they knew that Billy was her accomplice and that, sooner or later, he would return home.

The sound of the front door opening startled them both. Billy let out an oath and looked round wildly for some place to hide.

'Get rid of the buggers!' he hissed as he scrabbled underneath Abbie's bed and pulled the coverlet down to hide him.

Shaking like a leaf, Abbie went out on to the landing. 'Who is it? Who is it down there?' she called out nervously.

'Who the bleedin' hell do you think it is? I lives here, don't I! Get the soddin' kettle on and let's have a decent cuppa, the muck they give you down at the cop shop is like gnats' piss.'

'Mam! Is that really you?' Abbie called as she tore down the stairs.

'It's me, so get the bloody kettle on, then!' Ellen ordered.

Rubbing away her tears with the back of her hand, Abbie did as she was asked.

'Is our Billy here?'

'Yes. He's hiding underneath my bed.'

Ellen gave a belly laugh as she flung her shawl over the back of a chair and sat down and eased her feet out of her boots.

'Crafty sod! Go on, then, call him down, tell him I'm home.'

Billy had already heard his mother's voice and was halfway down the stairs when Abbie went out into the passage.

'Is she all right?'

'Ask her yourself.'

'They let you home then, Mam!' he grinned as he sidled into the room.

'No thanks to you!'

'What's happened?' Abbie demanded. 'Are they still looking for Billy, and are they going to charge you both?'

'Charge us with what?' Ellen asked, her mouth open in surprise.

'For pinching the watch, of course,' Abbie said.

'Watch? I never pinched no watch.'

'Well, Billy did, didn't he?'

They exchanged warning glances.

'Got the wrong end of the bleedin' stick, haven't you?' Ellen snapped.

'What did they take you in for, then?' Abbie asked bewildered.

'For causing an affray. Once they got me down the station and asked some questions they realised the rumpus was nothing to do with me, and so they let me go!'

Abbie looked at Billy in surprise. 'The watch. Bradley said you'd stolen it and then passed it over to Mam...'

'Bradley? That the name of the young scuffer who nicked me?'

'One of them.'

'Didn't take you long to find out his name, did it! Fancy him, do you?'

'She's going out with the bugger,' Billy said glumly.

'*Was* going out with him,' Abbie corrected him. 'After what has happened, and now he knows where I live and that you're my family, I doubt if I'll ever see him again,' Abbie added miserably. 'Anyway, Mam, you've still not told me the whole story about what happened.'

'There's nothing more to tell,' Ellen muttered.

'Yes there is,' Abbie persisted. 'What about the watch that Billy stole, where is it now?'

Ellen shook her head and scratched herself. 'There was a watch. It was on the floor and it was smashed to smithereens. Some woman tried to say it was her old man's, and that Billy had nicked it from him. The scuffers reckon she'd pinched it, though, and was going to flog it off.'

Abbie shook her head. 'I don't believe you,' she said flatly.

'Orright, then, here's the truth, if it will make you feel any better,' Ellen sneered. 'Billy did nick the watch, and he brought it over to the cotton sheds in his snack tin and handed it to me to bring

252

home. The tin fell on to the floor but I managed to stuff the watch into my pocket.'

'And the police found it there?'

''Course they bloody well didn't. I made sure it was on the floor when the fight started. That's how it got smashed up. There was no evidence at all against me, except that woman's word, and, as I've just told you, the police reckoned she was the one who'd taken it from her old man and that she was going to flog it.'

Chapter Twenty-Seven

'Abbie Martin, Miss Breck wants to see you in her office right away,' Miss Webster told her officiously.

Abbie looked taken aback. 'Do you know what it's about?'

'No, but it seems to be very urgent.'

As she hurried along to the Staff Manager's office, Abbie's mind was in a whirl. Why on earth was she being summoned? As far as she knew there was no reason for Miss Breck to want to see her.

Her heart pounded. Could it be something to do with her mam or Billy, she wondered. Surely they hadn't got themselves into any more trouble and been arrested again.

'Abbie.' Miss Breck looked rather puzzled. 'There is a young man downstairs who is asking if you can go home immediately.' She hesitated. 'It is bad news, I'm afraid. Your brother's wife is seriously ill and is asking for you.'

'Sandra? She's expecting a baby any time now!' Abbie said in an anxious voice.

'I understand that is part of the problem,' Miss Breck murmured. 'Apparently there are complications. I think you had better collect your coat and run along. I will explain to Miss Webster that you have been unavoidably called away.'

'Yes, Miss Breck. Thank you.'

Feeling slightly dazed, Abbie walked to the door. As she opened it, Miss Breck said, 'We shall expect you back at work in the morning, Abbie. If it is not possible for you to come in then you must be sure to let me know.'

'Thank you, Miss Breck, I'll do that.'

Abbie's mind was still whirling as she hurried towards the entrance. Although she and Sandra had had very little to do with each other since their fall out earlier in the year, they had been friends since they were quite little and she couldn't help but feel concerned about her.

When she reached the ground floor she looked round for Sam, then drew in a sharp breath of surprise when she saw that it was Peter Ryan who was waiting for her. He looked very smart in his dark business suit and her heart missed a beat. She hadn't seen him for weeks, not since she had started going out regularly with Bradley Fisher.

The feelings she'd had for him since she was a small girl were long gone. His reserved indifference had made sure of that. He had changed so much. He was so prim, so cold, so unable to express his feelings. She occasionally wondered why she had spent so much time trying to win back the affection Peter had shown towards her when they were growing up, when he obviously no longer had any feelings for her.

Bradley was not much older than Peter, but he had been so utterly different. He'd been warm and loving, and so ready to tell her how much he cared for her that being with him had transformed her life.

Seeing Peter standing there was like turning back the calendar and reviving all the heartbreaking events of the past year that she'd been so determined to put out of her mind.

'Peter, what are you doing here? I thought it was Sam who had come to fetch me?'

He shook his head. 'That was why I didn't give a name, I thought you mightn't come down and it is very urgent, Abbie,' he said grimly. 'Come on,' he took her arm and hurried her towards the door. 'I've got a taxicab waiting.'

'Where is Sandra?' she asked over her shoulder as he followed her into the cab.

'At the Liverpool Infirmary. They rushed her in at ten o'clock this morning.'

'I didn't think the baby was due until the end of August or early September?'

'It's premature. She had it about an hour ago. The baby is fine; it's Sandra who is giving cause for concern. They don't hold out much hope for her, I'm afraid, Abbie. She was asking for you, that's why I came to fetch you.'

Abbie felt choked, but before she could ask for any more details the taxicab pulled up in front of the hospital.

After he'd paid it off, Peter hustled her inside, up two flights of stairs and along a corridor that had frosted-glass windows. He pushed open the glass-panelled door at the end of the corridor. 'Wait a moment,' he said when they were inside the ward, 'I must let the Sister know that we are here.'

The smell of disinfectant caught in Abbie's throat as they were taken to the far end of the ward, to a bed screened off with blue- and pink-striped curtains.

Sandra was so white and motionless, and there were so many tubes and drips attached to her body, that for a moment Abbie thought she had come too late. Then, as they approached the bed, Sandra turned her head and the moment she saw Abbie she seemed to rally.

Giving a weak smile she reached out and clutched at Abbie's hand, almost as if she was afraid she might walk away.

'Hello, Sandra,' Abbie said awkwardly. She felt at a loss for words yet desperate to comfort her in any way she could.

'Have you seen the baby?' Sandra's voice was a hoarse whisper.

'No!' Abbie shook her head. 'I've only just this minute got here and Peter brought me straight to see you.'

Sandra closed her eyes, fighting for breath. Then summoning up all her strength she opened her eyes again and clutched even tighter at Abbie's hand. 'It's a little boy. You will look after him, Abbie? Promise me you'll look after him,' she begged.

Stunned, Abbie stared down at Sandra, wondering if she knew what she was saying.

Sandra's ashen face contorted as she sensed Abbie's reluctance to answer.

'Please, Abbie, promise me you will,' she begged, her grey eyes pleading.

Abbie still hesitated. How could she make a promise like that? She was out at work all day. Surely Sandra's mother was the right person to be looking after the baby until Sandra was well enough to do so herself.

'Of course Abbie will look after him, Sandra,' Peter affirmed, signalling at Abbie with his eyes for her to confirm what he had said.

'Yes, don't worry, Sandra. Of course I'll do all I can,' Abbie told her. She looked round, 'Where's Sam? He should be here with you.'

Sandra turned her head restlessly from side to side and muttered something, but her voice was so faint that Abbie couldn't catch her words. She bent lower. 'I didn't hear what you said, Sandra.'

Sandra gave an enormous gulp, tears flooded from her eyes and rolled down her cheeks, her chest heaved, and then there was stillness.

'Sandra!' Abbie felt a wave of panic wash over her as the hand she was holding seemed to lose its grip on hers. 'Sandra!' she said again, her voice high and almost hysterical.

Peter whipped back the curtain and called for someone to come and help. A nurse was there in seconds, followed by the Sister.

Abbie and Peter were told to wait outside the ward as the nurses began to try and resuscitate Sandra.

Abbie stood by one of the windows, staring at the fuzzy impressions made by the frosted glass. She felt drained and frightened. She was sure

Sandra was dead, and there were so many unanswered questions in her mind that she felt utterly bewildered.

When the Sister came out into the corridor to speak to them, Abbie was aware that Peter's hand was gripping her shoulder and she braced herself, knowing her worst fears were going to be confirmed.

It was all over. They hadn't been able to save Sandra.

Abbie felt numb and in something of a daze as Peter led her away and went to find a chair so that she could sit down. She still couldn't believe what had happened.

'Would you like to see the baby?' he asked uncomfortably.

Abbie's blue eyes were pools of horror as she stared up at him. 'The baby has taken Sandra's life!' she said in a strained voice.

'You must try not to think about it like that,' he said uneasily.

She shook her head as if trying to clear her thoughts. 'Where's our Sam, why isn't he here? He should have been at Sandra's side, holding her hand, comforting her, not us!'

Peter chewed on his lower lip. 'There's something you ought to know, Abbie.'

'About Sam?' She frowned. 'He's not in any trouble, is he?'

'No, of course not.'

'Then why isn't he here?'

She stood up and began pacing backwards and forwards. She felt as if the whole world was spinning round her, as if she was going mad. Things were happening all wrong. Where was Sam, where was Mo Lewis, or even her own mam; they should all be here at a time like this.

'Abbie, listen to me and try to understand what I am telling you,' Peter said stiffly. 'Sam isn't here because he found out that the baby Sandra was carrying wasn't his.'

Abbie stared at him, bewildered. 'Not Sam's? But that was the reason why they got married, because Sandra was expecting his baby.'

'Yes, I know.' Peter ran his forefinger between his neck and his stiff white collar as if he was struggling for breath. 'I'll try and explain things if you'll give me a chance!'

Abbie shook her dark head, perplexed. She didn't want to hear what Peter had to say, she was still wrapped up in her own thoughts, in the events of the last few minutes.

'I promised Sandra that I would look after her baby! Is that why she asked me, because she knew Sam wouldn't?'

'Possibly,' Peter agreed uneasily.

Anger welled up in Abbie. 'How could she, how could Sandra make me promise such an undertaking when she knew all the time that the baby wasn't our Sam's and that she was dying.'

Peter looked uncomfortable. 'She . . . she probably wanted what she thought was best for the baby,' he said helplessly.

'Why can't her mother look after it? I know nothing at all about caring for babies. Anyway, I don't want to look after it if it isn't Sam's. If it had been Sam's then perhaps I would be feeling differently.'

Abbie held her head in her hands and rocked backwards and forwards. 'What have I done,' she moaned, 'making a promise like that to a dying woman. How can I possibly keep that promise when I hate this baby even before I see it? How could she have done something like this to Sam!'

Peter took her by the arms and tried to calm her. 'Listen to me, Abbie, you'll feel better once you have had time to get used to the idea. Why don't you come and have a look at the baby, you may feel differently towards it once you've seen it.'

She shook her head. 'I don't think so.'

'Please!' he implored. 'Come and see it.'

'They may not let me! If it isn't Sam's child then I'm not even a relation, am I,' she protested stubbornly.

Peter didn't answer. He walked back into the ward on his own and she heard the mumble of voices as he talked to the Sister, but she had no idea what they were saying to each other.

They came out of the ward together, and the Sister took them to a small annex further along the corridor and left them. Peter urged her inside and guided her across to a crib. As she looked down into it her heart almost stopped. The baby lying there appeared to be perfect in every way and completely healthy, but very tiny. Its head was covered in a thick down of fair hair, the colour Sandra's had been.

Abbie felt her heart turn over as she looked down on the baby, and when it opened its eyes and stared up at her she gasped in surprise. The baby's eyes were as blue as her own were!

There was something so familiar about the baby that she had a premonition of what Peter was about to say, even before he began speaking.

'There is something you have to know, Abbie,' he said awkwardly, 'and it may make you realise why Sandra asked for your help.'

She stared at him unflinchingly. 'Go on!'

'I was trying to tell you earlier . . .' His mouth tightened and he took a deep breath.

Abbie felt as if an ice-cold hand was grabbing her heart as he added, 'Sandra's baby isn't Sam's, it's mine!'

Chapter Twenty-Eight

They left the baby at the Liverpool infirmary until after Sandra's funeral, which had been arranged for Thursday 25th August.

Although the baby was perfectly healthy it was underweight, and there were minor feeding problems to be dealt with because it was slightly premature, before the hospital would let them take it home.

No one in authority had even asked where the baby would be going when it left hospital.

Both Maggie Ryan and Mo Lewis were too upset by what had happened to discuss the issue either with the authorities or with each other.

The baby's fate hung in the air; a spectre at Sandra's funeral, a problem for which no one had a solution.

Several times during the week Abbie had made a point of going up Brownlow Hill in order to walk past the old, smoke-grimed Workhouse building, trying to convince herself that, whatever happened, Sandra's baby mustn't end up in there.

Even the bedraggled, barefoot existence of the children who were brought up in the sun-starved courts and back streets around Scotland Road was better than being shut away inside that grim building, she told herself.

Her promise to Sandra lay heavily on her mind. Why had Sandra picked her, of all people, she kept asking herself? Perhaps she had been delirious and not really meant it like that.

Abbie wanted to talk about it, explain to Mrs Lewis that she and her husband were in a much better position to bring the baby up than she was, but Mo Lewis was so overcome with grief at losing Sandra that it was impossible to do so.

Maggie Ryan didn't seem to want to talk about it, either. She avoided her completely, and Abbie wondered how much she really knew about the situation.

Gradually, she persuaded Sam to tell her the truth about what had happened and how Peter Ryan came to be the father of Sandra's baby. When he finally broke his silence he was bitter and resentful, and he blamed Abbie!

'If you'd helped Sandra to get an abortion when we asked you to do so, then this wouldn't have happened,' he said accusingly.

She bit back her own angry retort. Sam looked so ill that, even though she smarted under the accusation, she didn't feel it was the right time to row with him. He looked so drawn and haggard and talked in such a despairing way that she was afraid he might do something foolish in an attempt to get out of the mess he found himself in.

One thing which Sam made quite clear was that he wasn't prepared to bring up the baby. The shock of finding out that Sandra had been unfaithful had broken his heart. He couldn't bear to hear her name mentioned and he didn't even want to look at the baby. As for its future, he didn't care who looked after it or brought it up, or even what happened to it.

He was bitterly angry with Abbie when he heard that she had promised Sandra she would take care of the baby.

'How could you do such a thing!' he exploded angrily.

'I didn't know she was going to die. I didn't know it wasn't your baby, either,' she snapped. 'I thought I was helping you! We've always stuck together and looked out for each other, ever since we were kids, that's why I made that promise.'

Realising she would be getting no help from Sam, Abbie tackled Peter. She had hesitated about approaching him, knowing how deep her feelings had always been for him in the past.

She felt icy cold, her emotions suspended, as he told her his side of the story.

'It happened at Christmas,' Peter said morosely. 'After my mam had had too much to drink and you had taken her home. Sam went home after that, but I stayed on at Sandra's and we ended up in bed together.'

'As simple as that?' Abbie asked sarcastically. 'I suppose you'd both had too much to drink as well and so you couldn't control yourselves?' she added caustically.

Peter bristled, his face flaming. He opened his mouth to refute what she was implying, then thought better of it. Tight-lipped, he said stiffly, 'We possibly had. I'm not used to drink, as you very well know.'

He chewed his lower lip. 'I bitterly regretted what happened. It haunted me afterwards.'

'Really?' Abbie looked at him contemptuously. 'So that was why you flirted with Sandra on St Valentine's night when we went to the Tower Ballroom at New Brighton?'

Peter ran a hand through his thick dark hair. 'I regretted that, too! After that I did everything I could to put things right.'

'You mean you showed some interest in me until the night you took me to the Grafton on my birthday, and then you knew that I didn't measure up to Sandra's sweet and lovely ways!'

He shook his head. 'You did disgrace us both, Abbie. I have never been thrown out of anywhere before in my life. It was most upsetting, because I do have my reputation to consider now that I am a Manager at the Royal Liver Friendly Society.'

'So how do you think they are going to react when they hear about the baby,' she asked, her blue eyes locking with his.

Peter shuddered. 'I'm afraid to even think about it,' he admitted. 'Somehow it's got to be kept from them.'

'So how will you do that? Stick the baby in the Workhouse or in an orphanage?'

Peter looked shocked. The colour drained from his lean face. 'I was hoping that Sandra's mother would bring the child up.'

Abbie gave a dry laugh. 'Mo Lewis is a control freak. She hates you to even walk into her poxy house unless you take your shoes off first. She's hardly likely to take on a young baby with its messy feeding habits and sticky fingers everywhere.'

'Not even when it's her own grandchild!' Peter said in amazement.

Abbie shrugged. 'Try asking her yourself!'

'Well,' he asked desolately, 'who else is there who can look after it?' He looked at her speculatively. 'Except you. Remember, you did promise Sandra you would look after it, so will you take it on, Abbie?'

'Me, take on a young baby! How can I afford to do that? I'm out at work all day.'

'You needn't be. I have a decently paid job now, so you could stay home.'

'Are you suggesting I should be a kept woman?' she asked scornfully.

'Not exactly!' His face brightened. 'We could get married. We'd have a home of our own.'

'And our own ready-made family? How very cosy!'

'You used to love me, Abbie.'

'I thought I did when we were growing up because you always followed me round like a faithful dog. When Sam and I tried to plan what we were going to do when we were old enough to earn money and get away from Bostock Street, you always begged to come with us. Remember?'

'So why not marry me now? We could move over the Mersey to Seacombe or New Brighton and you'd be well away from Bostock Street. A home of your own, Abbie,' he persisted.

'And a baby that is not my own! A child whose mother stole my brother's affection away from me and then treated him so shabbily that he is now almost insane. Do you think *that* is a good start for a happy family life, Peter?'

He shrugged. 'As I see it, for us to set up home together is the perfect solution.'

'Perfect solution for you, maybe. No one you work with need ever know the truth. That's what you mean, isn't it, Peter?'

'Partly. Above all, I want you back, Abbie. Since we've stopped seeing each other I realise how much I care about you.' He reached out and took her hands. 'I really do mean that, Abbie. I do love you! Being separated from you makes me feel as if I've lost part of myself. We have always been so close.'

Abbie pulled her hands away and shook her head. 'That's not true. We've grown further and further apart since you've come home.'

'Only because I found it so difficult to readjust. I was shut off from you and everything I knew for almost three years, Abbie. At that age it's a lifetime. You changed so much. I resented the fact that you never once visited me . . .'

'Only because I wasn't allowed to do so because I was still at school,' she interrupted sharply. 'I wanted to come and see you. I sent messages. Sam and I sent you comics and sweets that we bought with the money Sam earned doing deliveries.'

'I know, and I appreciated them, but what I really wanted was to see you. Then, when I did get out, you had a life of your own. You were working and you'd made new friends and you seemed to find me dull and uninteresting.'

'Only because you always had your nose in a book, studying!'

'I was doing that for you. I wanted to get on, make something of myself. To prove myself in your eyes. To get a promotion so that we could get married,' he said glibly.

'No, you wanted to get on, to justify yourself in your own eyes,' she told him. 'All that night school and studying was to make you feel good and it had nothing to do with me, or how I felt. You didn't like my new friends, you thought them shallow. I wanted some fun but you didn't. That's why we drifted apart, Peter.'

'Are you saying that you still love me?' he asked hopefully. 'That Jamie, and Bradley Fisher, and all the rest of them mean nothing to you?'

A shadow flickered over Abbie's face as he mentioned Bradley Fisher's name. That was still an unhealed sore and something she didn't want to even think about. Her feelings for him had been deep and genuine. She believed that what she had felt for him was true love, and she'd been sure that he had felt the same way about her.

She blamed the fecklessness of her mother and Billy for what had happened. Once Bradley knew the sort of family she came from, how could she expect him to go on seeing her when it might be putting his career in jeopardy.

'Please, Abbie. Say you'll marry me and make a home with me and the baby,' Peter pleaded. 'You'll never regret it. I can afford to provide you with a good home, right away from here. We can start afresh, the sort of future you promised yourself when you were growing up. I'll devote every moment of my life to you, and I know you will be a wonderful mother. If the baby grows up believing you to be its mother then it will love you as much as I do.'

Abbie shook her head doubtfully. She was very tempted. The thought of being first and foremost in someone's life was a tremendous incentive. She wanted so much to love and be loved. She still cared for Peter, she told herself, even if those feelings were nothing like as deep and as strong as the ones she had for Bradley.

Was that enough to ensure their future happiness? As for the baby, poor little mite, could she ever love him, knowing that he was Sandra's child? Her feelings were in such turmoil that she couldn't find an answer.

'Please, Abbie, I'm begging you,' Peter pleaded. 'If you don't want to get married right away then just move in with me and see how things go.' He took both her hands again, raising them to his lips.

'I need time to think about it,' she prevaricated, pulling herself free.

'Promise me you'll consider the idea,' he begged.

She nodded, too choked to speak.

'When will you give me your answer? The hospital aren't prepared to keep the baby any longer now that Sandra's funeral is over.'

Abbie took a deep, shuddering breath. He was rushing her and she was so afraid of doing the wrong thing. She needed time to talk to Sam, to talk to Mo Lewis, to her own mother, even, and eventually to Maggie Ryan. Her decision affected all of them in one way or another. The decision couldn't be hers alone.

'Soon, Peter. I'll give you my answer as quickly as possible,' she promised. 'I must talk to Sam, first. Sam and others,' she added vaguely.

Sam was still too upset about what had happened between Sandra and Peter to be able to talk reasonably about it.

'I feel cheated,' he said bitterly, running his hand through his thick brown hair. 'Sandra never told me until she went into labour. I couldn't even think straight after that. I loved her so much, Abbie, and yet I wasn't even there when she died. My life is such a mess that I can't hang around here any longer. I've found a ship and I've already signed up. I'm sailing in two days' time.'

Abbie looked shocked. 'Sam, you can't do this. The baby. What about the baby?'

He shrugged. 'It's not mine, is it,' he said flatly.

'Peter has asked me to move in with him and for us to bring the baby up. How do you feel about that, Sam?'

He stared at her, shaking his head as though he couldn't believe what he was hearing.

'It's up to you,' he said at last. 'I think you're mad to get involved. He cheated on you, remember, the same as Sandra did on me, but you do whatever you like.'

'Does Mam know you're going to sea?'

'I've told her, but she doesn't seem to care one way or the other. The only one who will miss me is you, Abbie, and it looks as if your life is going to be pretty full.'

'You mean if I go ahead and do what Peter is suggesting,' she murmured dubiously.

'Don't do it unless you are sure it's what you want,' he warned.

Her mind in a whirl of indecision, Abbie went to see Mo Lewis. Despite what she had said to Peter earlier, she half hoped that once Sandra's mother heard what Peter was planning she would step in and demand the right to bring up the baby herself. She was, after all, the child's grandmother.

'No,' she told Abbie coldly, 'me and Dan have talked it over and we've decided it would be too heavy a responsibility for us to take on. Dan will be retiring in about ten years, just when the child would be at that noisy, demanding stage, wanting bikes and football and such like. You know what boys are like, and it would be more than Dan could stand,' she added dismissively.

'It is your grandson we are talking about,' Abbie reminded her.

Mo Lewis sighed. 'If it had been a little girl then I might have thought differently. It would have been like having Sandra back and she was so sweet at that age. Her daddy always called her his little princess. I always kept her looking so pretty,' she said sadly. 'And for such a thing as this to happen. I blame your Sam. He was never good enough for her.'

'She was quick enough to marry him when she found out that she was pregnant, though, wasn't she!' Abbie pointed out angrily.

Mo Lewis sighed again. 'It's such a pity she didn't tell all of us the truth about what had happened and then she could have married Peter. He is such a refined young man, he would have offered her so much more than your Sam ever did.'

'You didn't think Peter Ryan was such a nice, refined young man when he was sent off to reform school,' Abbie reminded her sharply.

Mo Lewis shrugged. 'It wasn't his fault, though, was it. He didn't steal that bike. Everyone round here knew that it was your Billy.'

Abbie bit her lip. There was no point in discussing that matter any further since it was all in the past.

'Anyway,' Mo sniffed, 'it's Peter Ryan's baby and he has a good job so it's up to him to provide for it.' She dabbed at her eyes, 'If it hadn't been for him our Sandra would still be alive today.'

Abbie wondered if she should even bother to tell Mrs Lewis about Peter's plans, then she decided that it was better that she should hear about it from her than from anyone else.

Mo looked taken aback when Abbie told her it was Peter's idea that they should move in together and bring up the baby.

'Looking for a good home for yourself, are you. I can't see Peter Ryan taking up with you again for any other reason than finding someone to look after the baby. I suppose I can't blame you!' she said scathingly. 'You Martins will cash in on anything, won't you.'

Abbie clenched her hands into fists to keep her

temper in check. 'And what is that supposed to mean?' she asked icily.

Mo Lewis shrugged her shoulders again. 'I don't want to talk about it. It won't bring my Sandra back. You do whatever you like.'

There was only one person who still needed to be told what was happening, Abbie thought wearily, and that was Maggie Ryan. She seemed to have kept very quiet about the whole affair, but, by now, the way tongues had been wagging, surely she must know that Peter was the father of Sandra's baby.

Chapter Twenty-Nine

Abbie was relieved to find that Michael and Maggie were both at home when she went round to the Ryans' house that evening.

She'd still not told her mother or Billy that she was thinking about marrying Peter and bringing up Sandra's baby. It was time enough to do that when she finally made her commitment, she decided. It wasn't as though either of them would care or even be all that interested.

The only thing that might concern her mam was the fact that if Sam was going to sea, and she was leaving home to marry Peter, then there would be less money coming in.

Maggie Ryan answered the door, but there was no warmth at all in her greeting. It touched Abbie's heart to see how much Maggie seemed to have aged over the past couple of weeks. She hoped that Maggie would feel relieved when she heard her decision and that the news would lift some of the burden from her shoulders.

Peter looked at her questioningly as she entered the room, and she felt very nervous as her eyes met his and she gave a small nod to signal her agreement to the arrangement they had discussed earlier in the day.

The look of relief on his lean, handsome face

restored her belief that she was doing the right thing. She waited nervously for him to break the news to his mother.

When he did, the reaction, not from Maggie, but from Peter's brother Michael, left her open-mouthed with astonishment.

'No!' Angrily he rose to his feet and stared round at the three of them as though trapped. 'It's completely out of the question!'

'Michael! That will do!' Agitatedly, Maggie tried to push him out of the door.

'Give over. I'm not leaving until the matter has been cleared up. I'm not letting that happen!'

'It has nothing to do with you, Michael!' his mother shouted, tears streaming down her face.

'Of course it has!' he exclaimed hopelessly. 'It's history repeating itself!'

'What are you on about?' Peter looked from his mother to his brother in bewilderment. 'Mam's right, this has nothing to do with you, Michael. Abbie and me have made our minds up that it's the best thing to do. We're going to get married and bring up the baby as our own.'

'No you are not!' Michael rubbed a hand over his face. 'It wouldn't be right,' he said dully.

'It's my baby, don't you understand that,' Peter said looking agitated. 'He's my responsibility and if Abbie is prepared to play her part then what business is it of yours or of anyone else?'

'Abbie can't do it. Nor can you.' Michael's darkly handsome face contorted with suppressed emotion. 'You two can't marry each other!'

They stared at him, waiting for an explanation, but he seemed too upset to go on.

'I'm afraid Michael's right,' Maggie Ryan said emphatically. 'The two of you mustn't marry.'

Abbie felt a frisson of unease. 'Why ever not?' she demanded. 'Surely that is for me and Peter to decide.'

Maggie shook her head. 'Are you going to tell them, Michael, or shall I?'

'You two are not getting married because I forbid it!' Michael Ryan repeated stubbornly.

'Too bad, but it's none of your business,' Peter fumed.

'Oh yes it is. I'm Abbie's father!'

'You're what?' Abbie stared at him, open-mouthed, disbelief in her eyes. 'You're my father?' She looked from him to Peter, hoping for an explanation, but Peter was as thunderstruck as she was.

'What Michael says is true,' Maggie told them ruefully.

'I don't believe it, not one word of it!' Abbie exclaimed hysterically. 'You are only saying this to stop us getting married. It's rubbish! I don't know why either of you are making such a preposterous claim!'

Michael seized her by the shoulders and turned her round to face the overmantel. 'Look in that mirror,' he ordered. 'Look at the colour of your hair and the colour of your eyes. Recognise where you have seen them before? Now look at my eyes, my hair, and then look at Peter's. Satisfied? Now do you believe me?'

Abbie pulled away from him, covering her face with her hands. 'Maggie, tell me it's not true,' she whispered tearfully.

'I only wish I could,' Maggie said in a low voice. 'It's the truth, Abbie. Michael is your father,' she added, her voice breaking.

Abbie uncovered her eyes and stared hopelessly at Peter. 'Did you know about this?' she asked bitterly.

He shook his head. 'I swear to you this is the first I've ever heard of it,' he assured her.

With a strangled cry, Abbie turned and made for the door, rushing out into the street in a blind panic.

She didn't believe them. She was sure they weren't telling the truth, though she couldn't understand why. There was only one person who could confirm if it was true.

'Mam! Mam!'

Her voice was a moan, an agonised cry coming from deep inside her as she burst into their house. 'Mam,' she clutched at Ellen as if she was grabbing hold of a lifebelt, 'tell me it's not true!'

Ellen shook her clinging hands away. 'What the bleedin' hell is the matter with you? What you carrying on about now?'

'Lost another of your boyfriends, have you?' Billy jibed.

'Michael Ryan . . . Michael Ryan . . .' She kept saying his name over and over again, unable to repeat what he had told her.

Ellen's face hardened. 'What about him?'

Finally, in a voice heavy with despair, she stuttered, 'He ... he ... says he's my dad!'

'So the bugger's owned up at long last. Better go and live with him, then, hadn't you,' Billy guffawed.

Ellen rounded on Billy, slamming her open hand hard against the side of his face. 'Shut your great trap, you stupid oaf!'

'Mam, are you saying it's true?' Abbie gasped, her cheeks hot with humiliation.

'Oh, it's true all right!'

The colour drained from Abbie's face as despair and disbelief surged through her. She stared at Ellen as if seeing her for the first time in her life.

'You mean that you're not my mam,' she whispered incredulously.

Ellen's face hardened. 'Of course I'm bloody well not!'

Abbie stared at her in disbelief. Realisation swept over her like a wave. The lack of affection from Ellen, all the times she had pushed Abbie away, slowly began to make sense. She had thought Ellen was her mam, and had never been able to understand why she didn't kiss her, make a fuss of her, love her, worry about her, even. Now she knew! Ellen wasn't her mam, that was why she had never loved her or cared for her.

So, if this bleary, scruffy woman in her long black skirt, coarse blouse and thick black shawl, whom she had always thought was her mam, wasn't really her mother, then who was?

'Are you going to tell me about it?' she pleaded in a strained voice.

Ellen scratched under her armpit and pulled her black shawl tighter. 'Hasn't Michael Ryan already done so?'

Abbie shook her head. 'All he said was that he was my dad.'

'Why did the silly bugger tell you that, then?'

'Because of Sandra's baby.'

'What the bloody hell has that got to do with this?'

Abbie looked from Ellen to Billy and back again, like a trapped animal. 'It's not our Sam's baby,' she said in a strangled whisper. 'It ... It's Peter Ryan's.'

Ellen stared at her blankly as if unable to take in the meaning of what she was saying.

'Same as before! Them bloody Ryans, there's no stoppin' the buggers,' Billy chortled loudly.

Ellen rounded on him, her face ravaged. 'Shut your gob!' she ordered.

He held up his hands as if in surrender.

'Are you going to tell me who my mother is, then?' Abbie asked.

Ellen sighed. 'Yes, I suppose it's time you knew the truth,' she said dully.

'So? Who was she?'

Ellen's haggard face softened and her eyes had a faraway look in them. 'Your real mam was Audrey! My little Audrey who died when she was thirteen.'

Abbie felt a tingling shiver run through her. 'You mean you're my grandmother!'

Ellen looked vague and didn't answer for a moment. Then she nodded.

'What happened?' Abbie persisted uneasily.

'Like I said, my little Audrey was your mam. She was only thirteen and still at school. She was a lovely girl, as pretty as a picture with curly fair hair, big brown eyes, and a smile that would melt your heart!'

She sighed heavily. 'She and Billy and Michael Ryan knocked around together all the time. The three of them were inseparable, except when they were at school.'

'Go on!'

'I'd just started working down at the cotton sheds when it happened. Left on their own all day they got into all sorts of mischief. I'd expected our Billy to keep an eye on young Audrey, but he was too busy looking after number one to see what they was up to . . .'

'Come off it, Mam,' Billy interrupted indignantly. 'I was nearly fifteen and I'd just got my first job, that's why I wasn't around to see what those two little buggers were doing. It would have happened anyway, Michael Ryan was crazy about our Aud.'

'By the time I found out that she was in the club it was too late to do anything about it. Poor little bitch, she didn't know what had happened to her, she was only a young kid herself.'

Ellen Martin paused and rubbed the back of her hand across her eyes.

'The Ryans wouldn't admit that their Michael had had anything to do with it,' she said bitterly. 'Not even after you were born and our Audrey had died. They kept well out of the soddin' picture; they always have.'

'Yeah, they left you holding the baby, eh, Mam?' Billy guffawed.

'It was up to me to take you, or for you to go into the Workhouse or some sort of home,' Ellen went on. 'They said at the hospital that all young babies had blue eyes and just fuzz on their heads, and that the colour of both would change later. I was so upset at the time about losing my own little girl that I believed them.'

'So you decided to bring me up as your daughter?'

Ellen nodded. 'I thought if you grew up looking like my Audrey then you would take her place.'

She paused and dabbed again at her eyes, this time with the corner of her shawl. 'Bloody fool, wasn't I? You were nothing like my little girl! Every day you looked more and more like the Ryans. You'd got their dark hair, as well as their blue eyes.'

'Surely the Ryans were aware of this?' Abbie said stiffly.

'They didn't want to see it, did they! That Michael was sent back to Ireland for a couple of years, out of the bloody way, and never a word was said against him. Maggie Ryan kept herself to herself and no one twigged what had happened. Instead, everybody blamed my little Audrey,' Ellen said bitterly.

'They accused her of being fast and feckless,' she went on. 'Blamed me because of the way she'd been brought up.

'Her father couldn't take all the evil gossip, so what with that, and a baby that cried night and day, and his despair at losing his precious little angel, he buggered off.'

'So he didn't go into the Army?'

Ellen shrugged. 'How the hell should I know. He left me to face all the wagging tongues in Bostock Street and bring the lot of you up single-handed. Billy was working and earning a few bob a week, but it wasn't enough to keep body and soul together. Sam was only a toddler, only a year or so older than you were.'

Ellen sighed. 'Many's the times I walked up Brownlow Hill, past the Workhouse, carrying you in my arms, and wondered about dumping you on their doorstep. It was only the fact that you were my little Audrey's kid that stopped me from doing so.'

Ellen wrapped her arms around her body and rocked to and fro. 'I didn't love you then and I've never loved you since. God knows, I've tried, for Audrey's sake, but all I can think about every time I look at you is that you killed my lovely little girl. That, and the fact that you look just like the Ryans!'

Chapter Thirty

'How can I possibly marry you, Peter,' Abbie exclaimed exasperatedly. 'If Michael is my father then you're my uncle!'

'We could live together, even if we don't get married,' Peter argued. 'If we move over to Seacombe or Liscard no one there need ever know.'

She shook her head. 'I couldn't bring myself to do that.'

'There's the baby to think about, Abbie,' Peter Ryan protested sulkily.

Abbie looked at his dark, brooding face, the selfish gleam in his blue eyes and the petulant twist of his mouth, and wondered how she could have ever thought herself to be in love with him.

'The baby is your problem, Peter, not mine,' she told him defensively. 'Ask your mother to help! Even though she didn't take any responsibility for your brother's child she might help you with yours,' she added scathingly.

She turned away, tears streaming down her cheeks as she remembered how many times as a small child she had run to Maggie for comfort when Ellen and Billy were rip-roaring drunk and fighting like cat and dog. The Ryans' home had been an oasis of safety when Ellen and Billy were smashing up the furniture or threatening her and Sam with a good thrashing.

All her life she had thought Maggie was so kind and wonderful, even longed to be one of her family. And all the time she was. She was Maggie's grandchild as much as she was Ellen Martin's.

The constant rows and drunken brawls she'd witnessed as she'd been growing up began to make some sort of sense to her.

Instead of talking matters over with the Ryans and reaching some sort of agreement with them to share the responsibility, Ellen had shouldered the extra burden. Ellen had been bitter over losing her own daughter and resentful about having to bring up a child that had been fathered by Michael Ryan, and that was why she'd turned to drink and vented her pent-up feelings by fighting with Billy.

She wondered why Billy had stood for it all these years, why he hadn't left home and made an independent life for himself. The only reason she could find was that he knew his mother blamed him for not protecting Audrey. In addition, she depended on his wages to help support herself and Sam. And to support Abbie!

I have been a burden round her neck all these years, Abbie thought guiltily. No wonder she dislikes me so much and can't bear to touch me. How she must have hated it when I tried to hug her and kiss her. No wonder she always pushed me away.

The thought that she might feel the same sort of

terrible rejection for Sandra's little boy helped her to harden her heart to Peter's pleadings.

They could never marry, and if they should set up home together what sort of life would that be for the child, she asked herself. In time, she was bound to resent the situation she found herself in, and then, heaven forbid, she might start taking her resentment out on the child like Ellen had done on her.

It wasn't as if there was no one else to bring him up. Maggie wasn't all that old, she could still cope with a baby, and it was up to Peter to help her. Perhaps someday in the future he would marry, and then he could make a proper home for his son.

Abbie kept telling herself that to go and live with him merely for the sake of the child would only be building up more unhappiness. As it was, because of Peter's action, she'd lost her best friend, Sandra. She was also about to lose Sam, the brother she'd been so close to for most of her life, if he went to sea as he claimed he was going to do.

She pulled herself up short. Sam wasn't her brother! Sam was her uncle, the same as Peter was!

The realisation shook the very foundations of Abbie's world. She didn't know who she was any more. Had she ever known who she was, she wondered bitterly?

The only place where she felt confident and sure of her identity was at Frisby Dyke's. There, surrounded by people she had come to know and like and respect, she felt reassured. No one there knew her secret. To them she was Abbie Martin, the same person as they had always known.

Those in the department where she worked knew she had lost her sister-in-law in childbirth and they had offered their condolences, but they were ignorant of the details.

She had never talked about her family, not since the first day she'd been there. She'd been quick to notice Miss Breck's hesitation when she had mentioned that Bostock Street was off Scotland Road, and knew instinctively that her background was different from most of the others who worked there, but she hadn't let it depress her.

Instead, she'd made sure that no one ever found out where she lived or that her mam was a shawlie who worked in the cotton sheds.

There had been one or two close shaves when she'd first become friendly with Jamie, and after a night in town he had wanted to see her home. Fortunately, because he lived in Wallasey, he was always worried about what would happen if he missed the last ferryboat, so she always had a wonderful excuse about why he shouldn't see her home.

When they all went out as a crowd, the problem never seemed to arise. They were all too intent on having a good time to worry about how the evening was going to end. When it was time to go home there was always a mad dash to catch a late Green Goddess, or, in some cases, a boat, and in the ensuing mêlée she'd always managed to slip away more or less unnoticed.

Her early background might have been rough

and ready but she had been quick to learn. She aped the manners of those around her and mimicked their accents, so that within a few weeks it had been hard to tell her apart from the others.

Billy had scoffed at her lah-di-dah ways, but that hadn't worried her. Knowing what she did now she felt that everything she'd done had been justified.

Deep inside her, she'd known she was different to him, better than him, even. He might have been her real mam's brother, but he was a slummy born and bred. He'd never tried to better himself. The guilt he carried about what had happened to his sister Audrey seemed to have tainted his outlook on life, which was why his mother could dominate him like she did.

At least she had the satisfaction, now, of knowing that he wasn't her brother, Abbie thought smugly. He might be her uncle, but that was nowhere near the same thing. The blood ties were so much looser that she felt she could dismiss him completely from her life. And she would, she told herself firmly. She intended to walk away from all of them as soon as it was possible to do so.

The only thing that was holding her back was the fact that she didn't earn enough money to live independently.

She could move in with Peter, she reminded herself. He had made the offer. He would always hold down a good job and earn reasonable money, so financially she would never have any worries.

Was that enough to satisfy her need to be loved and wanted, she asked herself? The baby would love her, probably think of her as his mother. He would be dependent on her, so surely she would have all the affection she wanted.

She refused to think about it during the day while she was working, but the moment she went to bed all the problems churned over and over in her head. Even when she slept, the voices of Ellen and Billy and Maggie and Michael, all arguing for and against her and Peter setting up home together, dominated her dreams.

Mo Lewis kept her own counsel. She avoided Abbie as much as possible and refused to even look at the baby.

To friends and neighbours she declared, 'I'm too heartbroken over losing my Sandra to do anything to help with the child. I've never been any good with little boys. If it had been a baby girl, to replace my Sandra, then I might have taken it on. As things stand it's the Ryans' responsibility.'

She was the first to exclaim in shocked tones, 'History repeating itself!' when news leaked out that Michael Ryan was Abbie's real father.

'They've broken up the Martin family and come between Ellen and Abbie, but they're not coming between me and my Dan,' she declared stoutly.

When pressed for her opinion about Abbie moving in with Peter and the pair of them bringing up the baby, she merely shrugged her plump shoulders.

'If that's what Abbie wants to do then good luck to her, it's nothing to do with me,' she said primly.

Abbie eventually decided it wasn't something she could bring herself to do. Any feelings she'd had for Peter were long gone. He was nothing more to her, now, than any other neighbour in Bostock Street. Even the closeness she'd had with Maggie had been eroded when she'd discovered that Maggie was her grandmother, and realised that never once had she spoken out or given any indication of how closely they were related.

Looking back, Abbie felt that the kisses and cuddles and other displays of affection Maggie had shown her when she'd been small had been to fulfil Maggie's needs. Or to allay her own conscience because she felt guilty about the way Ellen and Billy treated me, Abbie told herself sadly.

Michael's rejection rankled, however. She had always been aware of the way he watched her whenever she was in their house, and of the fact that he rarely spoke to her. Now that she knew the true reason she felt resentful. If he had shouldered some of his obligations she could have had a much happier childhood.

Peter was devastated when she told him she had decided that she wasn't prepared to move in with him and take care of the baby.

'I was relying on you, Abbie. I thought you cared for me?'

She shook her head. 'I used to, Peter. I treasured every word you said, followed you about, thought of you as my hero. I dreamed of the day when you would ask me to marry you.'

'So what's happened to change that?'

'We've both grown up! You were so changed when you came home from reform school that you had no time for me. I ached for you to notice me, to show me some affection.'

'No, you were the one who had changed, Abbie,' he told her angrily. 'You had your job and all your new friends. You didn't want to be with me, you wanted to be with Jamie and his crowd.'

'I wanted you to come along as well whenever we went out!'

'They weren't the sort of friends I wanted.'

'You didn't have any others,' she pointed out. 'Except Sam and Sandra,' she added bitterly, 'and look what happened there!'

'It wouldn't have done, if you hadn't behaved the way you did. You showed me up whenever we went out, that was when the rot set in. Sandra tried to make amends, to comfort me when she saw how upset I was.'

'Oh, she did that all right!' Abbie said sarcastically, 'and look where it left our Sam.'

'Sam was only concerned about you . . .'

'Oh, stop repeating yourself, Peter! You've said all this before. It was my fault, Sam's fault, but never your fault. You think you've been hard done by, but think about what your brother Michael did. That's the trouble with you Ryans,' she said angrily, 'you think you can do as you like, sin as much as you want to, and then go to confession and wipe the slate clean again. Well, it doesn't work like that. You've fathered a child, the same as your brother did, but the only difference is that this time you are going to have to face the music and be responsible for bringing it up.'

'I can't do that, Abbie. Not without someone to help me.'

'Then ask your mother to help you. It will give her a chance to atone for her sins of omission as my grandmother!'

'You can't leave things like this, Abbie,' Peter blustered. 'I want you – I need you! Not only because of the baby, but because I love you, I always have!'

'You may have done so at one time, but not since you came home,' she said wistfully. 'Be honest; I embarrass you.'

'Only when you behave outrageously; like a tart.'

'How dare you!' Her face flaming, Abbie turned on her heel to leave.

Peter grabbed her by the arm, spinning her round and savagely pushing her up against the wall, his mouth trying to find hers.

Abbie fought to free herself from his embrace, but he was far too strong for her. Overpowering her, he pinioned her arms behind her and began tearing at her clothes. Twisting her face away from his she gulped in a lungful of air and then screamed again and again and again.

Pushing her down on the floor he straddled her, pushing her skirt up to her waist, trying to force her legs apart.

Fear and outrage lent power to her lungs. Her screams were blood-curdling, alarming passers-by in the street outside.

Maggie came rushing out of the kitchen and

then stopped in the doorway, aghast at what she was witnessing.

Someone had called the police. There was a hammering on the front door, a loud crash as a shoulder was applied to it, then the thud of heavy boots and warning shouts before a hand caught hold of Peter's collar, dragging him away from Abbie and throwing him to one side.

As she was gently pulled to her feet by strong arms she gave a deep shudder, even though she knew she was safe. She heard the policeman who was holding her call out to his fellow officer, 'Can you manage on your own?' and an answering response.

Then the one holding her exclaimed, 'My God! Abbie!'

She had already recognised his voice, but she had been afraid it was simply a delusion because she was so upset.

'Abbie!' The voice was soothing, the hands that held her were strong yet gentle. 'You're safe now.'

She waited for him to speak again, unsure whether she was hallucinating or if it really was Bradley Fisher who was holding her in his arms.

Tears of self-pity began rolling down her cheeks, even though she kept her eyes tight shut. She mustn't attach any importance to him being here, she told herself. He was only doing his duty. The minute he saw she was recovered he would walk out of the door and she would never see him again.

'Abbie! Open your eyes. Please! Speak! Tell me you aren't hurt.'

The concern in Bradley Fisher's voice sent shivers of longing surging through her. Could it mean that he still cared! After all that had happened, and despite what he knew about her family and her background? Was it possible that he still had feelings for her?

Tentatively, she blinked and found herself looking straight into his warm brown eyes, and there was no mistaking the love and concern in their depths.

The pressure of his arms around her body increased. The nightmare encounter with Peter was wiped from her mind. All she could think about was that she was in Bradley's arms and he still loved her.

'Can you tell me what happened?' he asked solicitously.

Abbie shook her head. 'I don't want to talk about it,' she whispered. 'I'd like to go home.'

'This will have to be reported.'

'No!' She shook her head firmly. 'It's a family matter. It's all over now. There's nothing more to be said or done.'

'You're not going to press charges against your attacker?'

Abbie shuddered as she looked across the room to where Peter was sitting on a chair, a policeman at his side. Peter was resting his elbows on his knees, supporting his head between his hands. Maggie was standing near him, ill at ease, her face stark with concern. 'No!' she said tightly, 'I don't want it to go any further. I'm not hurt . . . only frightened.'

Bradley Fisher exchanged an understanding glance with the other policeman who slowly put his notebook away.

'Come on, then,' Bradley took her arm. 'I'll see you safely home.'

As they walked along Bostock Street to her own home, Abbie felt tongue-tied. Now that he knew she was all right, would he simply walk away and she'd never see him again, she wondered?

'I'd better leave you here,' he said as they reached her front door. 'I don't think either your mother or your brother would welcome my presence.'

She nodded. 'I'm sorry about what happened before, it wasn't your fault. You didn't know who my mother was.'

'So why have you avoided me ever since? I've missed you a great deal, Abbie.'

She stared at him, a startled look in her blue eyes. 'I thought that would be what you wanted. I didn't think you would wish to see me again when you knew the sort of reputation my family had.'

'I'm interested in you, not them,' he stated. 'My feelings for you, Abbie, are as strong as they ever were, so when am I going to see you again?'

Her heart thundered crazily. She grinned weakly. 'Whenever you like.'

'I'm talking about a proper date, not rescuing you from some trouble you've managed to get yourself into,' he told her with mock severity.

'So am I,' she agreed.

'Would tonight be too soon?'

'No,' she smiled happily. 'That would be wonderful.'

He looked at his watch. 'Can you meet me in an hour? I'll take you to the State Restaurant in Dale Street for a meal, and we can talk about our future.'

Chapter Thirty-One

Bradley Fisher felt in an optimistic mood as he walked away from Bostock Street. Everything was finally coming together and at last there was a real purpose to his life.

He had felt most uncomfortable about arresting Ellen Martin, as he had had no idea that she was Abbie's mother. They were so utterly different that he wouldn't ever have guessed, even if Ellen had told him her surname.

As events turned out, arresting Ellen Martin had given his career the boost he had needed. Within a few days he had been told he was to be promoted to Sergeant.

His mother had been delighted. 'You'll end up as the youngest Inspector in your division, the same as your father did,' she beamed proudly.

Even that had not lifted his spirits, because he knew that he had upset Abbie; indeed, more than that he had antagonised her so much that he might never see her again.

Yet it seemed that their paths were fated to cross, he told himself as he hurried back to the station to file his report and sign off duty. They had met again, and once more he had the opportunity to put things right between them.

This time he'd make sure that he did. He'd

never felt like this about any other girl. He hoped that Abbie felt the same way about him, as he did about her, because tonight, given the opportunity, he intended to ask her if she would marry him.

He felt a little nervous about what his mother's reaction would be, but surely, he told himself, she didn't expect him to stay at home for the rest of his life!

His father had died when he was fourteen, and ever since then his mother had expected him to be the man of the house.

When he'd been younger he'd been flattered that she consulted him over most things and had taken an intense pride in the fact that he was 'in charge'. Lately, though, when he'd suspected she was using her dependence on him as a ploy to stop him from leaving home, he had grown to resent it.

When he had said he wanted to move out and have a life of his own she'd been quick to offer an alternative arrangement.

'Marry a nice girl and I'll convert this place into two separate flats,' she told him. 'It's really far too big for me, now that your father is gone, and I don't entertain on anywhere near the same scale.'

'Why don't you find somewhere smaller, then, if it's too much for you to cope with?'

'It's our home, Bradley, yours and mine! I'm being sentimental, I suppose, but we've had so many happy years here that I couldn't bear to move. It would make two delightful flats. There are four bedrooms, and with three reception rooms downstairs as well as the kitchen we would be able to have it converted properly. We'll call in an architect and see if he thinks it's possible to even have separate entrances so that we would be completely independent, if that means so much to you.'

He'd looked round the room they were sitting in and his heart had sunk as he compared the middle-class luxury he took for granted with the room he had seen at Abbie's home.

In this room there were polished wood-block floors, a magnificent Persian carpet, a huge three-piece suite upholstered in dark red velvet, and matching wing-backed armchairs. There were occasional tables, a glass cabinet, and a bookcase that spanned most of one wall and reached almost to the ceiling.

The dining room across the hallway was fitted wall to wall with celadon green Wilton, and there was an impressive, highly polished mahogany table that could seat ten people. There was also a matching sideboard and a side table for serving, and a huge bow-fronted cabinet filled with cream Spode china and elegant glassware.

All the windows at the front of the house were screened with identical Nottingham-lace curtains in addition to the heavy velvet drapes with their matching pelmets.

His mother's bedroom was enormous, with a fitted walk-in wardrobe and a canopied bed. Even his own bedroom was probably larger than the whole of the ground floor at Abbie's place.

He knew, though, that the difference in their

living accommodation wouldn't be the only reason that his mother wouldn't approve of Abbie as her future daughter-in-law. Once she found out about Abbie's family background she would be mortified.

Leonora Fisher was in her mid-fifties. She was smartly dressed and very house-proud. Her husband, Robert, Bradley's father, had been much older than her. He had been an Inspector in the Wallasey police force so they had been able to afford to live in Seabank Road, which was within walking distance of Manor Road Police Headquarters and was one of the most respectable areas in Wallasey.

Leonora was a stickler for routine. Always on a Friday morning, while a woman came in to clean the house, she had a regular appointment with her hairdresser where she had her mousy-blonde hair shampooed and was given a henna tint and a marcel wave.

Ever since her husband had died, Leonora had received a pension that was adequate for her to go on living in the same house and in the same style.

Robert had always told Bradley that he wanted him to go to University, but after he died Leonora was quick to point out that this was no longer possible unless she made stringent economies.

'Your father,' she told Bradley proudly, 'was the youngest Inspector in the Wallasey police force at the time of his promotion. He managed that without going to University, and I am sure you can be as successful as he was if you put your mind to it.'

Young, and easily flattered, he had believed her and set that as his goal in life. The moment he was old enough to do so he had applied to enter the force. His mother had been unable to understand why he had joined the Liverpool police and not the Wallasey force.

'Everyone at Manor Road knew your father and would be only too willing to help you in your career,' she pointed out. 'The Chief Constable there was a special friend of your father's, they played golf together and they were both in the Masons.'

'It's for those very reasons that I've joined a different force,' Bradley told her. 'I want to succeed because of my own achievements, not because everyone knew my father.'

His mother was very put out at the time, but later, once he began to succeed by his own efforts, she became inordinately proud of his achievements.

When he had been told he was to be made Sergeant, she threw a party to celebrate. She invited half a dozen girls of his own age who were the daughters of her closest friends.

They were all nice girls in their twenties, wearing the very latest style of silk party dresses and high-heeled shoes. All of them were eager to be married and have a home of their own and they'd been primed in advance by their own mothers about how suitable a catch Bradley would be.

They could see for themselves that he was very

tall, with broad shoulders and slim hips. He was clean-shaven and extremely handsome.

Those who flirted with him found he had a pleasing personality. He looked boyishly attractive in his blue uniform, and most of them thought he would look positively terrific when he was finally wearing his Inspector's uniform.

For his mother's sake he played the part she'd allocated to him. He charmed them all, but he didn't lose his head or his heart over any of them.

He'd already lost his heart to black-haired, blue-eyed Abbie, even though he knew his mother would consider her to be totally unsuitable.

Abbie's only redeeming asset was that she worked in Frisby Dyke's. On the face of it that might make her acceptable, but the moment his mother heard a whisper about her background then she'd have an attack of the vapours and have him running for her smelling salts.

This particular frailty was her favourite ploy when he upset her in any way. When he had been much younger it used to leave him cowering under the bedclothes, scared that she might die. As the years passed and her attacks not only never proved fatal, but usually only lasted for about an hour, he stopped taking them seriously.

This time, however, it was a more sombre matter. He wanted his mother and Abbie to meet. Above all, he wanted them to like each other, since, if Abbie accepted his proposal and agreed to marry him, then they would be the two most important people in his life.

*

Abbie found it hard to believe that she had met Bradley Fisher again, and that he had asked her out.

She'd dreamed about it happening countless times, but she'd never really thought it would come true.

What was more, there had been something excitingly significant in the tone of his voice and in his dark brown eyes, as well as the way he had cradled her so tenderly in his arms.

She was confident that his concern about what had happened to her had been far greater than he normally showed to people who had been attacked.

She smiled to herself, her heart singing because he'd asked her out to dinner so that they could talk things over.

She wondered if he had missed her as much as she had missed him. Her spirits soared as she remembered the anxiety in his voice. There had been so much more than mere concern for her safety. He had been so tender, so anxious about her, and she was sure that what she had seen in his dark brown eyes was love.

What had happened before hadn't been entirely his fault or his mistake, she told herself. After all, he had only been doing his job, and since Ellen hadn't given him her full name how was he to know who she really was?

Would it have made any difference if he'd known that, she asked herself? Probably not! He had been doing his job. They were the ones who had been in the wrong.

Yet, knowing this, fully aware that they were villains, he still wanted to see her. Or was she building up false hopes? Was he going to try to explain why he couldn't see her again?

Her thoughts went back to the moment when he and another policeman had burst into the house and found Peter attacking her. Once again she recalled the timbre of his voice and the look in his eyes, and she was overcome by a crazy gladness because she knew she loved him, and instinctively, from deep in her heart, she was sure that he loved her.

Chapter Thirty-Two

It was the first time Abbie had ever been to the State Restaurant in Dale Street and she felt extremely nervous. She wasn't used to eating out in such places. Even though she was wearing a new dress, a pretty floral voile one that she'd bought in the summer sales, and knew she was looking very attractive, she still felt on edge.

When she arrived and found that Bradley wasn't outside waiting for her, all sorts of doubts began crowding her head. Had he changed his mind? Was she too early? Had something prevented him from being there? Had she made a mistake about the time he had said to meet him?

She paced up and down the pavement for another few minutes, looking hopefully at every tram that trundled past, hoping that Bradley might be on it. She checked the time with the great clock-face on the Liver Buildings, and then decided she was either quarter of an hour early or over a quarter of an hour late.

It had started to rain. What started as a fine sea mist quickly turned to a steady drizzle, turning the cobbled road into shiny black glass. Not only was her hair getting wet, but if she stayed out in it any longer, even though she was wearing a coat, her dress would be ruined, so she took shelter in a shop doorway.

The minutes ticked by and she started wondering if Bradley had already arrived and was waiting for her inside the restaurant. She tried to remember what his exact words had been, but she'd been so excited at seeing him again and finding he wanted to take her out that her mind had been in a whirl.

It was ridiculous hanging about outside in the rain, she told herself, so taking a deep breath she ventured into the restaurant.

The moment she entered the doors she felt overcome by fright, as a tall pompous man wearing black evening dress and a stiff-fronted white shirt bustled forward with a clipboard in his hand and asked if she had reserved a table.

Unable to speak, her mouth so dry that her tongue was sticking to her teeth, she could only gulp and shake her head as she turned to leave.

Then she heard her name called, and Bradley appeared as if from nowhere, his coat collar turned up, his brown hair almost black with rain. 'Abbie! I'd given you up!'

'I'd given you up!'

'I've been sheltering in one of the doorways!' They spoke in unison, then stood there holding hands and grinning at each other like two school kids.

Suddenly aware that the head waiter was still waiting patiently to know if they had reserved a table, Bradley let go of Abbie's hands and gave him the necessary information.

'Do you want to go to the Ladies' room,' he asked, as they were shown to their table and he took her coat and handed it over to a waiter who was hovering solicitously.

Abbie shook her head. She didn't want to let Bradley out of her sight for one minute in case she lost track of him again.

The waiter pulled out her chair and she sat stiffly on the edge of it, waiting nervously until Bradley had taken his place opposite her before she could relax.

Waves of noise ebbed and flowed all around as people laughed and chattered; the sound swelled like some strange music, making her feel dizzy.

She looked at the beautifully laid table, the crisp white damask cloth and napkins, the single flower in an elegant cut-glass vase in the centre of the table, and at the gleaming array of silverware and glasses, and wondered if she was going to be able to cope with it all.

Until now, her eating out had consisted of visits to Lyons Corner House, the Kardomah, or a milk bar. The nearest she had got to this sort of setting was when Peter had taken her to the Grafton Ballroom and they had sat with their drinks at one of the little tables that circled the dance floor.

She'd drunk rather too much wine that night and had made a complete fool of herself, she remembered ruefully. She must be very careful not to repeat that mistake tonight, she reminded herself.

A new feeling of panic surged through her as the waiter handed them both a large, leather-bound menu. She tried to read what was on it, but her eyes became blurred with embarrassment when she realised that she didn't understand half of what was written there. Some of the words describing the dishes were in French, and even those dishes that were in English had names which she didn't recognise.

'Would you like me to order for you?' Bradley asked quietly.

She nodded.

She watched his dark brows knit together in a frown as he perused the list in front of him. Then, in a firm, crisp voice, he placed their order. Before she could sit back with a sigh of relief that the ordeal was over, the wine waiter appeared at his side and once more his attention was diverted.

'Right! Now that's all done we can talk,' he grinned.

He put her at ease, admiring her new dress and talking of trivial everyday matters until she was completely relaxed, and laughing with him over something he described to her.

She was grateful that he hadn't mentioned her family or any of the other events that had caused so much friction and trauma between them. She knew these had to be talked about, but she was thankful that he was leaving that part of their reunion for the moment. Coping with the meal was going to be nerve-wracking enough for her.

The food was delicious. Skilfully, Bradley guided her through the minefield of cutlery and glasses. He didn't press her when she refused a second glass of wine although he refilled his own glass to the brim.

At the end of their meal, as they sat drinking rich, dark coffee from delicate little cups and nibbling tiny, minted chocolate-covered biscuits, she felt she had never experienced an evening like it in her entire life.

There was more to her enjoyment than the appetising food and the wonderful wine, delicious though those had been. It was being with Bradley, knowing how much he cared, how serious he was about their friendship and the fact that he was so anxious to go on seeing her in the future.

By the time they left the State Restaurant the rain had cleared. The warmth of a balmy, late September evening lay over Liverpool. In the velvety dark sky above there was a sprinkling of stars, and a crescent of moon hung like a bright yellow pennant over the Liver Building.

Bradley walked as far as the junction of Scotland Road and Bostock Street with Abbie. She felt uneasy, knowing that the right thing to do was to take him back to her home, but if Billy and his mam were there she wasn't sure what sort of a reception they would give him.

As if reading her thoughts, Bradley stopped and pulled her into his arms. 'I'm going to say goodnight to you here, Abbie,' he said softly.

Gently, he kissed her on the lips, and then, as she clung to him, his kisses became more intense. With tremendous willpower he pulled back.

'Can I see you at the weekend?' he asked. 'If

you are free on Sunday I'd like to take you to Wallasey to meet my mother.'

Abbie caught her breath in alarm. 'Your mother?' Her eyes were wide with shock. The idea scared her stiff.

'Why not? You're the two most important people in my life and you've got to meet sometime. The sooner the better, surely?'

'She mightn't like me!'

'Like you? She'll love you, the same as I do,' he told her confidently. 'We'll catch the two o'clock ferry over to Wallasey on Sunday afternoon and go and have tea with her.'

'I'm not sure. Perhaps we should leave it for a while.'

Bradley shook his head. 'I'm off duty this Sunday and I won't have another weekend free for almost two months.'

Abbie looked relieved. 'Let's leave it until then, shall we?'

Bradley shook his head. 'No,' he said firmly. 'This Sunday. Now do you want me to come to your house and collect you or would you rather meet me at the Pier Head?'

'I'll meet you at the Pier Head,' she told him quickly.

She didn't want him coming to Bostock Street. That could well spoil things between them, even though he had already been there and knew what it was like. On Sunday, both Ellen and Billy would have been out drinking until the early hours of the morning so they would have hangovers and one or the other of them would probably have been sick. The house would smell vile, and there would be dirty clothes strewn everywhere and unwashed dishes piled up on the table and in the sink.

The only place in the entire house that was ever tidy was her own room. Even if she cleaned the house up before Bradley arrived the unpleasant smells would still be there.

She wasn't sure where he lived, except that it was in Wallasey, but she had no doubt that it was far better than her home. He had mentioned his mother several times in conversation during their meal and he had told her that his father had died while he was still at school. Apart from that, though, he had said very little about his family background.

She tried to tell herself that she was being silly to make such a fuss about meeting his mother. He was only a policeman, after all, not a doctor or anyone of any great importance. Well, she smiled to herself, he had been promoted to Sergeant, she mustn't forget that fact. He seemed very proud of his new rank and she felt sure his mother was equally delighted by his achievement.

'Right, I'll meet you on Sunday at the Pier Head in time for us to catch the two o'clock boat,' she promised.

'Don't be late,' he warned. 'The ferry to Seacombe only operates hourly on a Sunday.'

She hesitated, still wishing she could persuade him to postpone the visit to meet his mother. Being back together was still so new. So much had happened in her life since she'd last seen him that she still hadn't told him about.

She should have told him about Sam and Sandra and the baby, and explained why Peter had attacked her.

What was even more important was that she wanted to share with him all the information she now had concerning who her mother and father really were, because she was sure it would make a difference in his eyes.

She felt it was terribly important that she explained all these things, especially the fact that she was not as closely related to Ellen and Billy as he thought she was.

She would have preferred to do this and clear the air properly, so that there were no secrets and no misunderstandings between them, before she became involved with his family.

Chapter Thirty-Three

Abbie was up early on Sunday morning and off across town to the public baths in Cordwallis Street, anxious to be there before a queue formed.

Usually she had a bath on a Saturday night when she knew that Billy was at the pub and wouldn't be back until after midnight. She dragged in the tin bath that hung on the wall outside their back door and boiled up as much hot water as she could, but this was a special occasion.

Lying back in the deep soapy water, after first shampooing and rinsing her hair, Abbie let her mind go over all her preparations for the coming visit to meet Bradley's mother.

She still felt terribly nervous, but at least she'd know she was clean from top to toe, she thought wryly, as she wriggled down deeper so that only her nose was above the water line.

She wished Bradley had been willing to wait a little longer before putting her through such an ordeal. She would have liked to enjoy whatever time they could spend together, just the two of them, getting to know each other better.

There was so much about her and her family that he still didn't know, and she wanted to be able to tell him every detail before he heard it from someone else.

Bradley being in the police force didn't help matters, not when Ellen and Billy were such well-known scoundrels. She supposed it proved how strong his feelings were for her, she reflected, that he still wanted to see her even though he believed a disreputable old shawlie like Ellen was her mother.

Abbie's name wasn't really Martin, though, she'd been given her mother's family name, not her father's. If Michael Ryan was her father then she should be called Abbie Ryan, not Abbie Martin. She wondered how Bradley would feel about this. Would it make her seem any more respectable? Unlike the Martin family, as far as she knew the Ryans had never been in any real trouble with the police. Apart from Peter being wrongly acccused of stealing the bike and being sent to reform school.

It was funny, she reflected, looking back and remembering how all the time she had been growing up she had craved Ellen's love and had always been rejected. She had done everything in her power to win approval from her, yet Ellen would never throw a kind word, let alone praise, her way. Even when she'd been only a toddler she had sensed that there was love for Sam but not for her and she had resented always being pushed away!

Now, to some degree, she could understand the reason for this. Ellen had lost Audrey, the daughter she had adored, when Audrey had been little more than a child herself; and she blamed me for that, Abbie thought sadly. It wasn't my fault, though, so she shouldn't have punished me as she did.

Yet, she asked herself, had Maggie Ryan behaved any better? Maggie had kissed and cuddled her and shown her kindness, but she had never taken her into her home and brought her up as she could have done. After all, if Michael Ryan was her father then surely Maggie, who was also her grandmother, was as responsible as Ellen Martin was for looking after Abbie.

She was better placed to do so as well. Paddy Ryan had a good job and sent money home regularly. Maggie also had a job. In fact, Abbie was at a loss to understand why the Ryans had gone on living in Bostock Street when they could have afforded to move to a much better place.

Was it because of me, she wondered? Was there a guilt factor that kept Maggie there so that she could keep an eye on me and see I was all right?

If that was the case, then why didn't she bring me up? Unless, Abbie reasoned, Ellen Martin refused to allow her to do so. Or had Paddy Ryan been against it, she wondered, remembering his reaction on the day she'd walked into the Ryans' house unaware that he was home from sea.

Perhaps that was the reason, she mused, as she remembered the rows whenever Ellen discovered that she and Sam had taken refuge at the Ryans' house when Ellen and Billy had been fighting. She never created like that if she knew they had been at Sandra's house. Yet she never stopped them from going to the Ryans'.

There were so many questions to which she

would probably never know the answers. Even so, she would have liked to have had the chance to talk them over with Bradley before she met any of his family.

A loud banging on the cubicle door and a raucous voice declaring, 'You've had more than your time, missy, there's a load of others waiting to get in there,' brought Abbie out of her reverie.

The water is cold anyway, she told herself, as, scowling at being so abruptly disturbed, she drained the bath, dried herself, and put her old clothes back on.

Someday, if she was lucky enough to marry Bradley Fisher, she might have a bathroom of her own. Then she would not only be able to take a bath whenever she felt like it, but she would be able to lie in it, soaking away her problems and indulging in her daydreams for as long as she liked.

Ellen was still in bed when she reached home, and Billy, snoring loudly, was sprawled in an armchair where he had been all night.

She was dying for a drink and debated whether or not to make a cup of tea. She was afraid that it might disturb Billy if she started clattering cups, and it was more peaceful to leave him sleeping, so she crept past him and went up to her room.

There was plenty she wanted to do before either of them woke up and started ordering her round and demanding something to eat.

Before she left the house she had hung the dress she intended to wear on a nail on the back of her bedroom door, and she'd also laid out her clean underwear on the bed.

She studied it all carefully, not sure if she had made the right choice or not. She wished she knew a little bit more about Bradley's mother. She didn't want to turn up looking dowdy, but neither did she want to turn up looking overdressed and give Mrs Fisher the wrong impression.

She had thought about asking Bradley what she should wear, but she knew this would be a waste of time because his answer would be, 'You look lovely no matter what you are wearing.'

That was the trouble with men, they didn't seem to realise that knowing you were dressed right helped you to feel confident, she thought worriedly.

She wondered if he had warned his mother that he was bringing her over for tea, and if his mother was fretting about their forthcoming meeting the same as she was doing.

The idea of someone of Mrs Fisher's standing worrying about what she should wear to meet her son's girlfriend brought a smile to Abbie's lips. She probably regards it as something of a nuisance, having her routine upset by having me to tea. She'd probably much sooner have Bradley all to herself, Abbie mused.

From what little she had gleaned from Bradley's conversation, his mother regarded him as the man of the house and relied on him for advice and companionship. Perhaps this was why he didn't appear to have ever had a steady girlfriend.

A frown clouded Abbie's face. If his mother was

so anxious to keep him all to herself then did she discourage him from having girlfriends? If this was the case then how was she going to react when they met, she wondered apprehensively.

'Stop looking for trouble!' she told herself out loud. Mrs Fisher was probably a very nice woman. Bradley is a good son who's happy to shoulder his responsibilities and help her as much as he can since his father is dead, and that is all there is to it.

Plenty of middle-aged women of her type came shopping at Frisby Dyke's. They were usually well fed, contented, stylishly dressed and able to afford to indulge themselves. Their idea of having a good time was going to the pictures, taking tea in town with their friends or visiting each other in their homes.

For all I know I may be just one of a long string of girls that Bradley has taken home to meet her, she told herself sternly. Probably after they've left she points out how unsuitable they are and that is the end of that. He is probably far too comfortable and too well looked after by his mother to ever seriously think about leaving home.

Nevertheless, it still didn't stop Abbie from wanting to look her very best. She spent the next hour and a half drying and styling her hair and trying on everything she had in her wardrobe in case it looked more suitable than the pale green dress with a pleated skirt that she had already chosen.

By then, Ellen was awake and calling out that she wanted something to take away the pain in her head, and Billy was complaining that he had a mouth like the bottom of a birdcage. Slipping her old clothes back on again, Abbie went down to make them a pot of tea and see if they wanted anything to eat.

'Not yet, I've only just come to my senses,' Ellen scowled, holding her head in her hands. 'You can cook us something later on. I'm off back to my bed for an hour or two.'

'I'm going out before two,' Abbie told her.

'Out? Where are you going? Not round to that Maggie Ryan's place to help with that baby, I hope!'

'No, I'm going with a friend to New Brighton,' she said vaguely.

'Sod that! We need you to get us a meal.'

'Then I'll get it ready for you now and leave it in the oven to keep warm.'

'Bloody well do it later, like our Mam said,' Billy muttered. 'I don't want scoff that's all dried up!'

'No, I can't! I've already told you I'm going out.'

'Answer me back an' you'll bloody well be going out with a black eye,' Billy snarled.

As Abbie turned on her heel to go back upstairs, Billy reached out and grabbed her by the arm, jerking her towards him so violently that she screamed out in pain.

'You bloody deaf or something? We want a proper meal, but we want it cooked later on. Mam and me have both got bad heads and we don't want you clattering bloody dishes right now. Understand?'

'Let go of me!' Abbie shook herself free. 'If you

must know, I'm going back upstairs to finish doing my hair, if that is all right with you?' she added sarcastically.

'Less of your bleedin' lip! I heard you sneaking out earlier on. Gone for a couple of hours or more. So where were you, then? Round at the Ryans'? Helping with that soddin' baby?'

'I haven't seen the baby since last week sometime, not that it's any concern of yours.'

Billy belched loudly and sprawled deeper into his chair and closed his eyes.

Abbie waited until he started snoring again and then she made her way upstairs. It was really too early to leave yet, but it was obvious that Ellen and Billy had both had a skinful the night before and were now feeling the ill-effects, so it would be better if she was out of the house before either of them turned nasty.

The sun was shining so she would walk down to the Pier Head. She could always sit on a bench there until Bradley showed up.

Quickly she changed into her dress and combed her hair so that it framed her face. As she was carefully outlining her mouth with lipstick she heard Billy moving about downstairs. Her heart thumped rapidly as she heard his footsteps on the stairs.

Swiftly she moved behind her bedroom door and stood there, holding her breath, praying he wouldn't come in and see that she was all ready to leave.

She heard him pause outside the door and hoped he couldn't see her and that he hadn't noticed her coat and bag lying across the foot of her bed. As his steps moved away and she heard him go into his own room she snatched up her coat and handbag and cautiously tiptoed out of the room and down the stairs.

Ellen was still sitting at the table, her head in her hands, her eyes closed. Biting her lip as she concentrated on not making a sound, Abbie made her way to the backdoor, opened it, and was out into the back jowler before Ellen could look up.

Abbie waited until she reached Scotland Road before she stopped to put on her coat. By then she was so breathless from running that she had a stitch in her side and was gasping for air.

Chapter Thirty-Four

Abbie and Bradley caught the Royal Iris ferryboat, which sailed promptly at two o'clock. Although it was September the weather was mild and the Mersey was like a millpond with gulls dipping and skimming over the surface. Abbie enjoyed every moment of the journey across to Seacombe.

They went up on to the top deck and leaned over the rail, admiring the two giant liners berthed at the dockside, and trying to identify some of the many cargo boats also moored there. They passed the Isle of Man boat coming into the landing stage and the ferryboat Royal Daffodil travelling in the opposite direction to them, heading for Liverpool Pier Head.

It wasn't until they were on one of the bright yellow double-decker Wallasey buses, and already on their way up King Street towards Seabank Road, that Abbie allowed herself to think about the real purpose of their trip. Immediately some of the sunshine went out of the day for her.

Before she could voice her fears to Bradley he was standing up and taking her by the arm. 'Come on, the next stop is ours.'

Abbie looked around her with increasing trepidation as they alighted from the bus. Seabank Road looked so imposing that it took her breath away. The road seemed to go on forever. On the left-hand side there were very large, detached red-brick houses with well-kept front gardens. On the right, row after row of big terraced houses running in parallel lines right down to Egremont promenade.

The whole area spoke of well-off middle-class living and contrasted so sharply with her own background in Bostock Street that Abbie wanted to turn tail and run.

'Here we are!' Bradley pushed open a low wrought-iron gate that led on to a paved pathway, bordered by a wall on one side and a large round flowerbed on the other.

As he slipped his key into the door, Abbie was sure that the lace curtain in the huge bay window stirred just a fraction, and she had the feeling that they were being watched.

Leonora Fisher came into the hallway to greet them. She was smartly dressed, in a dark blue silk dress with a lace-edged modesty vest at the 'V' neckline. Her hennaed hair had been given a marcel wave and she looked much younger than Abbie had expected.

Mentally, Abbie compared her with Ellen. They must be about the same age, she reasoned, yet Ellen, with her raddled face, bleary eyes and stringy unwashed hair, looked twenty years older. She tried to imagine what Ellen would look like if she was dressed as elegantly as Bradley's mother, instead of in her coarse black skirt, flannel blouse and black shawl.

If she had clothes like Leonora Fisher the first

thing she would do would be to take them down to Old Solly's and pawn them, and spend the money in the nearest boozer, Abbie thought bitterly.

'As it's such a lovely day I thought we'd take tea in the conservatory,' Mrs Fisher announced. 'Do take your little friend through, Bradley, and I'll bring in the tea things, I have everything ready.'

Bradley guided Abbie down the length of the dining room to the far end, where French doors opened into a sun-filled room that had glass on all three sides. The floor was a mosaic of blue, green, yellow, white and black tiles. The room itself was furnished with cane chairs and settees upholstered in flowered chintz. In the centre of the room was a round, glass-topped cane table. The double door at the far end of the conservatory was fastened back so that the long garden outside seemed to be an extension of the room.

To Abbie it was so breathtakingly beautiful that she couldn't speak. She perched uneasily on one of the settees next to Bradley, wondering how she was going to cope with the ordeal of drinking tea in such an atmosphere.

As Mrs Fisher appeared in the doorway, pushing a loaded tea trolley, Bradley jumped to his feet to assist her. Abbie watched in dismay as she saw the array of dainty, crustless sandwiches, the elaborate chocolate cake and the cream sponge cake. They all looked delicious, but how on earth would she be able to eat any of them and balance a teacup at the same time!

Before he sat down again, Bradley moved the

glass top table so that it was immediately in front of the settee and laid out plates and serviettes and tiny pastry forks.

'Do you take milk, Abbie?' Mrs Fisher asked as she poured out the tea from an elaborate china teapot into matching cups.

'Of course she does!' Bradley smiled. 'And sugar!'

'Put the sugar bowl on the table, then, Bradley, so that she can help herself,' his mother instructed.

Conversation was stilted. Abbie took a mouthful of her tea and almost choked it was so hot. Blinking back her tears she accepted one of the cucumber sandwiches, grateful for the cool filling. Gaining confidence, she also accepted a slice of chocolate cake and then wished she hadn't because she found that the icing was so sticky that it clung to her fork.

The ordeal of tea over, Abbie wondered if she was expected to help clear away. When Mrs Fisher wheeled the trolley out of the room she asked Bradley in a whisper whether she should offer to help to wash up.

'No! Don't worry about that. Mother will leave everything on the trolley and the woman who comes in to do the cleaning will see to them.'

Abbie felt shocked. No wonder the house looked so perfect, almost as though no one ever used it, she thought. A woman to come in to clean when there was only two of them living there. It seemed to her to be an outrageous extravagance.

To Abbie's relief, when their meal was over, Bradley suggested that the two of them should take a walk as far as New Brighton. 'We can walk along Seabank Road to Rowson Street, then down Victoria Road to the prom. We can catch the ferry back to Liverpool from there or take a bus to Seacombe and get a boat there.'

'Oh dear, I didn't think you'd be planning on leaving so soon!' Mrs Fisher sighed. 'This is a flying visit, isn't it! I've seen hardly anything of you this weekend, Bradley.'

Her voice was so reproachful that it made Abbie feel guilty. She wondered if she was expected to suggest that Bradley should stay with his mother and that she would make her own way home.

Bradley's chuckle as he took Abbie's arm was reassuring. 'I'll be home later this evening if you want to sit up and wait for me,' he told his mother.

'There, that wasn't such an ordeal, now, was it?' Bradley grinned as he took her arm while they walked along Seabank Road.

Abbie frowned worriedly. 'It was all right, but I'm wondering what sort of impression I have made on your mother.'

'She thinks you're lovely, and so do I!' he reassured her, giving her arm a squeeze to emphasise his words.

Abbie bit her lip. She wasn't sure if he was right or not. She had a feeling that when Bradley got home again that night, no matter how late he was, he would find his mother sitting up waiting for him in order to talk about her.

There was nothing she could do about that so she pushed it firmly to the back of her mind, determined to enjoy the rest of her day with Bradley.

Even though it was Sunday, Victoria Road was packed with day-trippers making the most of the late summer weather. Because they were all in holiday mood, they were all smiling and happy, and Abbie found the atmosphere quite exciting.

She'd had no idea there were so many things to see and do in New Brighton. They considered the idea of going to the Floral Pavilion to see a show, but there were no seats left.

'We could go to the Trocadero Cinema,' Bradley suggested. 'Shall we see what's showing?'

Abbie looked doubtful. 'It's such a lovely day that I'd rather stroll along the prom or go for a walk on the pier,' she told him.

They did both, and by then it was getting towards dusk so they decided to catch the next boat back to Liverpool.

Abbie felt it had been the most perfect day of her whole life as she sat next to Bradley on the open deck, his arm around her waist, and watched the receding lights of New Brighton and the myriad of approaching lights from Liverpool.

She wished they could go on drifting forever, locked in each other's arms, just the two of them with no one else to worry about.

'Do you want to stay on this boat for the return journey?' Abbie asked, as they bumped into position alongside the floating roadway and there was a grating sound as the vessel was secured.

'I'm seeing you home first!' he told her. 'You

don't think I'd let you make your own way home at this time of night, do you?'

It was quite dark as they reached Scotland Road. Dark and drab and sour smelling, Abbie thought, wrinkling her nose in disgust. What must Bradley think, bringing her back to this squalor after showing her the lovely area where he lived?

'I can find my own way from here,' she said abruptly, stopping on the corner of Scotland Road and Bostock Street.

'I'm seeing you right to your door,' he told her firmly. 'Don't worry, I'm not expecting you to ask me in, but I do want to make sure you reach home safely.'

As they left the bright lights of Scotland Road and turned into Bostock Street, an ambulance turned the corner at the same time, its headlights splitting the gloom like a searchlight.

'That's not going to your house I hope!' Bradley murmured.

'No, but it has stopped outside the Ryans' house,' Abbie said worriedly. 'I wonder what's happened?'

Bradley frowned. 'That's where Peter Ryan, the chap who attacked you, lives.'

Abbie nodded. 'I wonder what's wrong?' She let go of Bradley's arm and started to run towards the house where several people were already gathered.

Bradley grabbed her arm, pulling her to a standstill. 'Keep away,' he warned, 'I don't want you getting into any more trouble!'

She wriggled free. 'You don't understand, it

might be Maggie who is in trouble,' she called back over her shoulder.

As she reached the Ryans' door, Maggie came out of the house, following one of the ambulance men who was carrying the baby wrapped in a shawl.

'What's going on, Maggie? What's happened?' Abbie called out.

Maggie Ryan shook her head as if dazed. 'I don't know, Abbie. I'm not sure what happened. I asked Peter to keep an eye on the baby while I went to church. When I got back I found him asleep in the chair so I went to check the baby was all right, and he wasn't breathing.'

'We've already told you, missus, that it looks as though the child has been smothered,' one of the ambulance men muttered.

'I've been trying to tell them it must have been some sort of an accident,' Maggie said agitatedly, 'but they won't believe me.'

'Come on, missus, we're wasting precious minutes hanging around here. Get in the ambulance if you are going to and let's get the kid to the hospital and see if they can do anything for him there.'

'Maggie, do you want me to come with you?' Abbie offered, as Maggie clambered up into the back of the ambulance.

'No, luv, no don't do that. Stay here and make sure that Peter's all right. He's still in the house and he's in a terrible state because someone has sent for the police and he thinks they are coming to arrest him!'

Chapter Thirty-Five

Bradley laid a restraining hand on Abbie's arm. 'Come on, let's go. We can go to the hospital, if you wish.'

She shook her head. 'Maggie asked me to see that Peter was all right. I must stay with him.'

'You're not to go in that house. Peter Ryan attacked you, remember,' Bradley said, his voice edged with anger.

'I know that, but I promised Maggie,' Abbie said helplessly.

Bradley's jaw tightened. 'No!'

She was startled by the resentment in his voice. For a brief second she hesitated, then, as she saw the two uniformed figures approaching, she pushed her way through the crowd towards the house and took up a defiant stance on the Ryans' doorstep.

'There's no need for you to get involved, miss,' one of the policemen told her curtly, elbowing her aside.

'Hold it! What's going on?' Bradley demanded.

'Who's asking?' one of the policeman snapped, then as he recognised Bradley he gaped in surprise.

'Well?' Bradley's tone was so authoritative that the policeman responded automatically.

'We're here to take a suspect in for questioning, Sarge. A young baby left in his care appears to have died in suspicious circumstances.'

'Died! I thought they were taking it to the hospital and that it would be all right!' Abbie gasped. 'And what do you mean "in suspicious circumstances"?' she gabbled. 'He wouldn't hurt it, he was its father!'

'Sorry, miss. We have our orders. If you'd just stand aside, please.'

'At least let me go in first and warn him,' she begged.

Before they could stop her she had slipped past them and into the house, calling out Peter's name as she went.

Bradley strode after her. 'Wait, Abbie! Don't be foolish. He's attacked you before . . .'

A sudden piercing scream from Abbie drowned out the rest of his warning. Bradley and the two policemen rushed inside.

Abbie was at the foot of the stairs, screaming and sobbing, and pointing at the dark shape dangling from the stairwell in front of their eyes.

'Christ! He's topped himself,' one of the policemen exclaimed in horror. 'Here,' he addressed his colleague, 'grab his legs and try and take his weight while I cut him down, we may still manage to save him.'

Bradley pulled Abbie into his arms, holding her close, shielding her from the gruesome sight, whispering words of comfort as he tried to calm her.

Her screaming startled the people who were

gathered on the pavement outside the front door and had now been joined by others who had seen the police arrive. All of them were speculating about what had happened.

Once again the ambulance was called to the Ryans' house, although it was quite obvious that Peter was dead and nothing could be done to save him.

After Peter's body had been taken away, Abbie couldn't rid herself of guilt. She felt what had happened was as much her fault as anyone else's. Maggie had asked her if she would look after the baby on Sunday evening while she went to church. Her mind had been so full of her invitation from Bradley, and the thought that she was going to meet his mother for the very first time, that she had forgotten all about it.

When she tried to explain all this to Bradley he merely shrugged.

'Really! Well, it isn't your fault. You're no relation, only a friend, so it was up to Mrs Ryan to make other arrangements when you didn't get back to her. Anyway, even if you had, she couldn't expect you to alter plans you'd already made.'

'It isn't quite as simple as that,' Abbie said hesitantly. 'I meant to tell you long before this, but there is something else that you don't know.'

Bradley's face hardened. 'You're not going to tell me that it was your baby – yours and Peter Ryan's!'

'How dare you! If that's what you think of me

then let's end it here and now!' Abbie flared angrily, her face flaming, her blue eyes icy.

'I'm sorry!' He caught hold of her arm, turning her round to face him, pulling her into his arms and burying his face in her smooth black hair.

She struggled free, placing both her hands on his shoulders and pushing him away from her.

'I think it might be best if you listened to what I have to tell you,' she said forcefully.

Bradley was conscious that the groups of people who had come out of their homes to see what was going on were listening with avid interest to their exchange.

'All right,' he agreed. 'Let's find somewhere quiet.' He tucked her arm into the crook of his elbow and walked back towards Scotland Road. 'There might be a milk bar still open, if not we'll go into one of the pubs and find a quiet corner. By the look of you a drink wouldn't go amiss. I really do understand that you've had a terrible shock, Abbie.'

She waited until they had found a quiet spot in the Newsham Arms and the two brandies that Bradley had ordered were on the table in front of them.

She took a sip from her glass and shuddered as its potency hit the back of her throat. Then she sat up straight and stared at him, almost as if he was a stranger.

'To start with, my name is not really Abbie Martin, but Abbie Ryan.'

Bradley frowned. 'Ryan?' He looked bemused. 'So why all the fuss when I arrested Ellen Martin?'

'At that time I thought she was my mother,' Abbie explained. 'In actual fact, she is my grandmother. My mother was her daughter, Audrey, and she died when I was born. She was only thirteen.'

Bradley let out a low whistle. 'My God, Abbie, what are you saying? Do you mean that Peter Ryan ... ' he stopped and frowned. 'He can't be your father, he's too young, he's only about your age.'

'No, Peter is my uncle. My father, it seems, is his elder brother, Michael Ryan.'

'So Mrs Ryan is your grandmother as well as Ellen Martin?'

'That's right.'

Bradley looked confused. 'And the baby, the one that's just been found dead. In what way is that related to you?'

Abbie shrugged. 'Well, I suppose it's my cousin or something.' She shook her head as if mystified. 'It's very complicated. Sandra, the baby's mother, was married to my brother, Sam.'

She stopped and shook her head. 'Well, that's not quite right, either. I know now that Sam is not really my brother, but my uncle.'

'Sam is the baby's father?'

Abbie shook her head. 'Sandra had been going out with Sam ever since we were at school and they'd not long been married. It seems she had a fling with Peter Ryan last Christmas. No one knew about it and we all assumed that the baby she was expecting was Sam's.'

'And it's not?'

Abbie shook her head. 'No, but Sandra only told Sam that it was Peter Ryan's baby, not his, just before it was born.'

Bradley looked puzzled. 'In that case, shouldn't Sandra's mother be responsible for bringing it up?'

Abbie sighed. 'Mo Lewis didn't think she could take on such a burden so in the end Peter Ryan persuaded his own mother to bring the baby up.'

She hesitated, wondering if she should tell Bradley that Peter had wanted her to either marry him or go and live with him, so that they could bring up the baby together, but she felt she had stretched his patience far enough.

'This situation becomes more complicated the more you try and explain it,' Bradley muttered. He placed a hand under her chin and raised her face so that he was looking directly into her eyes. 'I think it's a good job that you will soon be changing your name to Fisher, don't you?' he asked softly.

Abbie felt her heart thud. Her blue eyes widened in disbelief. She looked at him dubiously. 'I can't believe you still want to see me, or talk to me, even. I thought you would turn tail and walk away when you heard the whole story,' she said nervously.

'You've not got very much faith in the man who is planning to become your husband, have you!' he retorted.

She smiled, comforted by his words, but refusing to allow herself to believe that such a dream could ever happen. Life had dealt her so many unexpected blows lately that she had grown cynical and afraid to take anything for granted.

'Come on, finish your drink,' Bradley urged, 'and then I'm going to take you home.'

Abbie shivered. 'I suppose I ought to go and see if Maggie Ryan is back home and how she is. She'll know by now about Peter, poor woman. Peter and the baby. Two deaths in one night!'

'You're not visiting Maggie Ryan tonight, or anyone else in Bostock Street. When I said I was taking you home I meant you're coming home with me,' Bradley told her firmly.

'To Wallasey? To your house in Seabank Road?' Abbie looked stunned. 'I can't go there!'

He frowned. 'Why not? There's a spare bedroom. You'll be living there soon enough. In the near future it will be your permanent home.'

'You mean, if we get married we'll be living with your mother!'

'Yes, why not?'

Abbie shook her head. 'I don't think she would like that! When she knows the truth about my past she'll tell you to drop me and find a nice girl of your own sort,' Abbie told him flatly.

'Not a bit of it. I could see she liked you!'

'Tolerated me, perhaps, because she was being polite and gracious. But like me?' She shook her head, 'I don't think so!'

'Of course she did!'

'We're completely different types of people, Bradley,' Abbie persisted. 'In fact, I don't know how you can possibly like both of us; we are so very different.'

He laughed and squeezed her hand. 'No more arguing. I'm on early shift tomorrow so I have to be up at five a.m. Come on, back to Wallasey and leave all your problems until the morning. You'll find they'll be much easier to deal with once you've had a good night's sleep.'

'I can't come back to Wallasey! I have to go to work tomorrow as well, you know. I need my uniform.'

He frowned, remembering the expressions he had seen on some of the faces of the people who had crowded round the Ryans' front door. He was pretty certain there were going to be unpleasant repercussions in Bostock Street before the night was out and he didn't want Abbie to become embroiled in it.

'I don't think it is advisable for you to go to your own house tonight,' he said firmly. 'Come back to Wallasey with me and you can catch the same early ferry as me first thing tomorrow morning. That will give you plenty of time to sort out your clothes and be at Frisby Dyke's before nine o'clock.'

Abbie still felt undecided. 'What will your mother think, though, if I turn up with you at this time of night?'

'She'll understand. I'll explain that there has been a spot of trouble with your neighbours and that you are rather upset, and she won't ask any questions, I promise.'

*

Mrs Fisher appeared to accept Bradley's explanation with perfect equanimity. She lent Abbie a nightdress and provided her with toiletries.

'Now you run along and have a hot bath and then pop into bed,' she told her. 'I'll bring you up a hot drink to help you sleep.'

She was as good as her word. Abbie was revelling in the comfort of being in a feather bed when there was a tap on the door and Mrs Fisher appeared with a steaming cup of Ovaltine.

'Bradley is already sound asleep. He must have dropped off the moment his head touched the pillow, so I hope this will help to do the same for you,' she told Abbie. 'Perhaps you have too much on your mind, though, to sleep easily,' she added.

The words were said kindly, but Abbie sensed the undertone and resolved to put matters right. Bradley might be right in thinking his mother liked her, and she had certainly shown her great kindness, but she didn't want Mrs Fisher to be under any illusion about who she was.

As if reading her mind, Leonora Fisher commented, 'I recognised the name, Martin, the moment Bradley introduced you this afternoon. Is it your family whose name is always appearing in the *Liverpool Echo*?'

For a moment Abbie thought of denying it, saying her name wasn't really Martin, but one look at Leonora Fisher's sharp face and she knew she would be wasting her time.

'You'd really like to learn all there is to know about me so that you can judge whether I am a suitable girlfriend for your son, wouldn't you, Mrs Fisher?' she said stonily.

Leonora Fisher nodded. 'You are a strikingly pretty girl, Abbie, and I can see why Bradley has taken such a shine to you,' she admitted grudgingly. 'He is young and easily impressed by a pretty face.'

'And you think that is all there is to it, do you, Mrs Fisher?'

Leonora avoided Abbie's direct stare. 'I think it would be best if we laid our cards on the table,' she stated firmly. 'Bradley is my only child and very important to me. As a policeman he has a great future ahead of him and I don't want him held back in any way. He is already on the first rung of the ladder, he has been made a Sergeant even though he is only twenty-four.'

When Abbie said nothing, she went on, 'My husband was highly respected in the Wallasey police force. He was an Inspector, and I am confident that one day Bradley will be his equal.'

Abbie nodded as she drained the last of her Ovaltine and set the cup down on the bedside table.

'And you don't think I am the right sort of person to be the wife of an up-and-coming Inspector?' she said tightly.

Leonora's face froze. For Bradley to have Abbie as a friend was disturbing enough, but the thought of her ever becoming Bradley's wife horrified her.

'Not when you come from a family with a criminal record like the Martins have,' she said furiously.

'Criminals who keep your son in work,' Abbie said caustically.

'A mother who works in the cotton sheds and gets herself into fights on the dockside; a brother who is always drunk and is frequently arrested for brawling,' Leonora Fisher contended.

'What if I told you that my real name is not Martin, that Ellen Martin is not my mother and that Billy Martin is not my brother?'

Leonora looked taken aback. 'You *are* related to them?' she blustered.

'Yes, but not in quite the same way as you have been told.'

Abbie watched the changing expressions on Leonora Fisher's face, as once again that night she gave details of her true parentage and her complicated family relationships.

'Well, perhaps things are not quite as bad as I thought they were,' Leonora Fisher admitted reluctantly. 'Even so,' she added, with grim determination in her voice, 'they're very disturbing. I certainly don't think you are the sort of girl Bradley should be going out with, or thinking of marrying. Not the right sort at all.'

Chapter Thirty-Six

'What sort of time is this to come home! You been out all bloody night with that scuffer you're knocking around with, have you,' Billy Martin sneered.

Knowing it was not yet six o'clock in the morning, Abbie had let herself in as quietly as possible and tiptoed her way across the room, hoping not to waken Billy who was sleeping in the armchair.

'Put the bleedin' kettle on then, kiddo, I've got a mouth like the bottom of a birdcage,' Billy muttered as he sat up in the chair and rubbed a hand over the stubble on his grimy jaw.

Abbie shuddered as the rasping sound hit her ears. She was feeling pretty fragile herself, although not for the same reason as Billy.

He yawned and scratched. 'So where've you been, then?

'I spent the night at Mrs Fisher's house in Wallasey, not that it's any business of yours,' she told him quietly.

'Who the hell is Mrs Fisher. Is she that copper's mam?' he grinned.

'Yes, she's Bradley's mother.'

'Getting a bit above yourself for a feckless Judy from Scotty Road, aren't you,' he jeered. 'You should have come home, you missed all the bloody carry-on that was happening here. Flippin' 'eck it was better than a tanner's worth at the Trocadero!'

He gave a deep belly laugh, watching Abbie closely to see her reaction. 'We had the scuffers and the ambulance here twice! There's been a bloody murder and a suicide, and Farder Bunloaf was running round like a blue-arsed fly trying to stop any more silly buggers toppin' theirselves. Thought perhaps you'd heard all about it and you'd got yourself in a tizzy and slung yer 'ook.'

Abbie turned away, sickened by his sneering, taunting tone. She busied herself raking the fire back into life, putting the kettle over the red-hot coals, and washing up a couple of cups so that she could make some tea as soon as the kettle boiled.

Seeing how unresponsive she was, Billy changed his tactics.

'You know all about what happened here last night, don't you,' he accused. 'Right little bitch you are, an' all,' he scowled, 'clearing off and leaving Ma Ryan in the lurch. Reckon Farder Bunloaf was reading her the riot act and no maybe because Peter had topped himself. You were sweet on him once. Perhaps that's why he did it. Couldn't stand to see you bugger off with a scuffer!'

'Shut it, Billy!' Abbie kicked his feet out of her way as she leaned across him to lift the kettle off the fire. 'You've got a mouth on you like a barn gate and you haven't a clue what you're talking about.'

'So you do know!'

'Yes, I was here last night when Maggie found the baby. I don't know why it died. I saw her into the ambulance. Then I saw the police arrive to take Peter in for questioning. If you must know, I was the one who found him hanging there.' She glared at him, dry-eyed and stony-faced. 'Know all you want, now?'

'Whew!' He let out a long low whistle and then gave a snort of contempt. 'Hard-faced bitch, aren't you. Take it all in your stride. You must have a heart like a lump of bleedin' lead.'

'I learned early on that you needed one to survive in this house,' she told him in withering tones.

He pulled a face. 'Mam's not going to be too pleased when she hears you've spent the night shacked up with a scuffer,' he taunted.

'Trying to stir it again, are you? I wasn't shacked up with him, as you so crudely put it. I stayed at his house, but I slept in the spare bedroom, if you must know.'

He watched her through narrowed eyes as she poured the boiling water into the teapot. 'Me mam still won't like it. He arrested her once, it's not something she's likely to forget.'

'I know, and he's run you in a few times as well. So how do you think I feel about that? It doesn't do much for my reputation!'

'Your bloody reputation! Who the hell cares about that? You're a bloody bastard, don't forget! You bein' born killed my sister, and we've had

343

you, a poxy girl, lumbered on us ever since. How do you think me and Sam feel about that?'

'Sam and me were the best of friends,' she reminded him. 'Sam probably still thinks I'm his little sister.'

'Well, that's another bloody shock to add to the list for him when he comes home, isn't it!' He took the cup of tea Abbie had poured for him and spooned sugar into it and stirred it noisily. 'Bloody hell! Sam's going to find that his sister is his niece; and not only is Sandra dead but the little bastard she cuckolded him over is dead, too!' He guffawed loudly and took a loud slurp of tea. 'And that his wife's lover-boy has topped himself into the bargain!' He slapped his hand across his thigh. 'If our Sam's got any bloody sense he'll stay as far away from Scotty Road as he can!'

Abbie drained her cup. 'I'm going to see Maggie Ryan,' she told him as she picked up her coat from the back of the chair and pulled it round her shoulders.

'Sooner you than me!'

Maggie's face was so red-eyed from weeping, and drawn and haggard from lack of sleep when she opened the door, that Abbie's heart ached for her.

She reached out to put an arm round Maggie's shoulders, but Maggie shrugged her away.

'There's tea in the pot, pour it if you want a cup,' she muttered dully as she sat down again in the chair she'd drawn up to the fire.

'I've only just had one,' Abbie said quietly. 'I've not long been home. Bradley took me back to his mother's place last night,' she added by way of explanation.

'I heard you were the one who first found Peter,' Maggie said listlessly. 'Two of them gone in one night!'

Abbie kneeled by the side of Maggie's chair and once again tried to put her arm round the other woman's shoulders.

'I know how you must be feeling, Maggie. I only wish there was something I could do to help.'

Maggie's blue eyes were cloudy with sorrow as she looked at Abbie. 'Too late now, isn't it,' she said dully. 'If you'd looked after the baby for me yesterday evening like I asked you to do, then none of this would ever have happened.'

'If the baby was sick . . .'

'Sick? Who says the baby was sick? The baby died because it was left unattended. It rolled over on to its face and was smothered because there were too many covers on it. Peter must have put another shawl over it when I went out, thinking it wasn't warm enough. You would never have done something like that.'

'You don't know that was what Peter did.'

'He either did that or he smothered the baby on purpose.' Maggie shuddered. 'The police think he did it on purpose. Those smart-arsed scuffers that work with that chap you left my Peter for say he deliberately smothered it. If he hadn't hung himself then they'd have had him up on a murder charge. Do you know that?'

Abbie shook her head. 'I'm sure he wouldn't have harmed the baby. I realise we'll never know the truth, but there's no cause to think the worst of Peter, is there.'

'Why are you championing him all of a sudden?' Maggie asked bitterly. 'You refusing to help him out with the baby was the start of all our troubles.'

'Oh no it wasn't! Come on, let's set the record straight. It all goes back much further than that, doesn't it. If you and Ellen Martin hadn't lied to me and to everyone else about who I really was then Peter would never have thought about me in the way he did.'

Maggie stared at her without answering.

'It's true, Maggie. If Peter had known he was my uncle he would never have gone out with me in the first place, probably never even played with me when we were kids.

'What's more, if you'd all owned up to Michael being my father, and you had brought me up instead of letting Ellen Martin do it, my life would have been so much better, wouldn't it. Why didn't you?'

Maggie shook her head. 'You don't understand what you're talking about.'

'Then tell me! Put me right. What don't I understand?'

'Paddy wouldn't let me because he didn't want anyone to know that you were Michael's child. He battered me black and blue, and half killed our Michael, when he first heard about it.'

'So you let the Martins bring me up because they didn't worry about such things?'

'Jimmy Martin scarpered almost the moment he

heard his Audrey had given birth. Couldn't see him for dust!'

'And that's when Ellen took charge?'

'Audrey was her daughter. She hadn't counted on her dying like that. She was far too young to be preggers, of course, but she was fit enough. She should have sailed through it. When she died, Ellen hung on to you and didn't want anything to do with me or mine.'

'So you left it like that!'

Maggie sighed. 'Looking back, I suppose I should have acted differently and given it more thought. I never thought about how it would affect you in the future.'

'No, all you were concerned about was that the scandal was hushed up nicely and you could all get on with your lives.'

'I tried to keep an eye out for you, especially when Ellen Martin and that Billy were smashed out of their heads. I did what I could,' Maggie said defensively.

'You were my grandmother, yet you left me living in that hovel with those two drunken, abusive tyrants,' Abbie said bitterly. 'Have you any idea what I endured?'

'I tried my best to help you,' Maggie sniffed.

'And you were content to see me getting involved with your Peter, even though you knew how closely related we were and that someday he might want to marry me?'

Maggie shook her head. 'I prayed for guidance and I never stopped worrying about what I should do if you two ever did decide you wanted to marry. It never came to that, though, did it. When Peter came home from that reform school he'd changed; all he could think about was getting on in the world.'

Abbie shook her head sadly. 'I thought you were so kind, so caring, that I envied Peter. Yet all the time you were simply protecting yourself. You weren't even a good mother to Peter. You said you knew it was Billy who'd stolen the bike, yet you did nothing about it. You kept quiet and let Peter go to reform school rather than risk the truth coming out.'

Maggie sighed. 'None of us can turn the clock back.'

'I'm beginning to think that the only true friend I've ever had in the whole of my life was Sam Martin!' Abbie said dejectedly. 'I'm not sure how he'll react once he knows that I'm his niece, not his sister!'

As she opened the door to leave, Maggie called her back.

'Are you seriously thinking of marrying Bradley Fisher, Abbie?'

Abbie stiffened, her eyes glacial. 'I hardly think, after all that has happened, that it is any of your business,' she said acidly.

'Oh, but it is Abbie. Michael has said he doesn't want a scuffer brought into the family.'

'Michael! What business is it of his?'

'Michael is your father, Abbie! He can step in and stop you marrying him.'

Abbie smiled contemptuously. 'Let him try!

Rather too late in the day for him to say he's my dad now, isn't it?'

Chapter Thirty-Seven

Abbie found it was hard trying to keep her mind on her work next day. Twice she made mistakes that entailed sending the money and bill winging back in its little metal cage to make a correction.

She knew this would be noted down and she would be taken to task for it when they closed, but it made no difference. Try as she might, the happenings of the past couple of days went round and round in her mind, making her head spin.

No one at Frisby Dyke's had actually mentioned it, but she knew there had been a report in the morning paper, the *Liverpool Post*, and there would be a longer version in the *Liverpool Echo* about what had happened in Bostock Street the night before.

Since the first edition of the *Echo* came out just after midday she was pretty sure that some of the other staff, those who took a late lunch-break, had already seen it, and she hoped they wouldn't realise the part she'd played.

She had deliberately gone to lunch late so that she could buy a copy, and she had been horrified as she read all the grisly details that had been used to embellish the story.

The reporter's description of Bostock Street made it sound like the vilest slum in Liverpool.

Peter had been painted so black that she hardly recognised him. There was, fortunately, no mention by name of the Martins, or of her own part in the debacle.

She suspected, however, that Leonora Fisher would hazard a pretty shrewd guess as to her involvement, since she already knew the truth about her background.

Before she'd come to work that morning she'd packed the best of her clothes into a canvas bag and brought them with her, together with her savings which she'd kept hidden under her mattress.

Once the whole story was out, Billy would be so enraged and blame her and Bradley and refuse to let her back into the house. Now, after having time to think matters over for herself, she knew she didn't want to go back to Bostock Street ever again.

There was no longer anyone there that she cared about. The only person she would miss was Sam and she could only hope that when he did eventually come ashore he would get in touch with her. He knew where she worked so if he wanted to see her then he knew where to look for her.

She had no idea where she was going to find a place to spend the night, or where she would live from now on. All she knew was that she had to make the effort to break free of the past and from the influence of both the Martins and the Ryans.

As the hands of the clock came ever nearer to closing time she remained resolute in her decision not to go back to Bostock Street when she left Frisby Dyke's that night.

She was overcome with relief when she found Bradley waiting for her as she came out of the staff entrance. He was wearing grey slacks, a tweed jacket and a brown tweed cap, and she felt relieved that he hadn't come to meet her while still in uniform.

'I was hoping you'd see sense and bring your things with you,' he told her as he took the bulky canvas bag from her. 'I nearly came along to the store when I came off duty at three o'clock to suggest it, but then I thought it would be better if the decision was yours.'

'Where are we going?' she asked, as he took her arm and steered her towards a Green Goddess tram that had just pulled up.

'To the Pier Head to catch the next ferry to Wallasey and then a bus to Seabank Road, and you are staying at my place,' he smiled.

She pulled back. 'Do you think that's wise?' she asked hesitantly. 'I don't intend going back to Bostock Street,' she said quickly, 'but I thought I would try and find a room somewhere.'

'At my place?' He grinned broadly. 'Where else?'

'By now your mother will have seen the *Echo* and read the whole story of what went on last night.'

He shrugged. 'You're not mentioned by name.'

Abbie shook her head. 'That makes no difference. She came up to my room last night, after you went to bed, and I told her everything.'

He frowned, looking puzzled. 'Everything? What do you mean?'

'I told her I wasn't really Abbie Martin but Abbie Ryan, and everything else there was to tell her,' she said lamely.

'Crafty old witch! She never said a word to me about it.'

'No, she's too clever to tell you outright that she doesn't approve of me.'

'Rubbish! What gives you that idea, anyway.'

'She wants you to marry one of the nice young girls you've grown up with and known all your life. She has such high hopes of the kind of future you will have, and she certainly doesn't think that someone from the Scotty Road area will make you a suitable wife.'

He gave her arm a gentle squeeze and dropped a kiss on the top of her head. 'Then we will have to prove her wrong. You do want to, don't you?'

Abbie looked puzzled. 'Prove her wrong?'

'Yes, by marrying me,' Bradley grinned.

'I want to marry you more than anything else in the world, but I'm afraid it's going to upset too many people if I agree to do so.'

'You mean my mother?'

'Your mother, the Ryans and the Martins.'

'I can talk my mother round, don't worry about her,' he said confidently. 'Do any of the others matter?'

She shook her head. 'Not to me, not any longer. I wouldn't want to cause a rift between you and your mother, though.'

'You won't. She'll accept it.'

Abbie shook her head again. 'I don't think so.'

'She's only worried that I might leave, because then she'll be all on her own.'

'I can understand that. You are her life, Bradley.'

'There's a simple way round that,' he smiled, as they got off the tram and hurried to catch the next boat to Seacombe. 'She has talked incessantly about turning the house into two self-contained flats, so that we can have separate lives, but still go on living under the same roof. Up until now I've always scoffed at the idea, but if I go along with her plans she won't raise any further objections to us getting married, I'm quite sure of that.'

'Do you think it would work, living so close to each other?' Abbie asked as they found seats on the upper deck of the ferry.

'I don't see why not. We would have separate front doors!'

'She'd have to understand right from the start that we would live independently of each other,' Abbie said reflectively.

'Don't worry. She has quite a busy social life, you know. She belongs to all sorts of clubs and associations. She's out every day of the week. It's just the idea of being completely alone that bothers her. I think she'll be pleased to know that I've settled down at last,' he grinned.

Abbie stared out at the busy Mersey as she pondered on the idea of the house in Seabank Road being divided into two flats. It was certainly possible. There was plenty of space to do that, but would Mrs Fisher want to give up her lavish accommodation and exist in a flat that was only half the size?

'It wouldn't only mean she'd have to give up half of her home, but she would have to get rid of an awful lot of her beautiful furniture and she's so house-proud,' Abbie pointed out.

'She can always give it to us if she doesn't want to sell it. You leave it to me,' Bradley grinned as the ferryboat docked at Seacombe.

'There really won't be any problem at all,' he assured Abbie as they became part of the jostling crowd making their way up the floating roadway to the bus terminus.

Abbie still felt doubtful. As the double-decker bus took them along King Street, the nearer they got to Seabank Road the more insurmountable the problems seemed to become.

'Don't say anything to your mother about us getting married ... not yet,' she said anxiously as they reached the house and Bradley opened the wrought-iron gate.

'Why not?'

'We do come from very different backgrounds, you know. If she's read the paper then she's going to be horrified at the thought of meeting the Martins and Ryans at our wedding and having to introduce them to all her friends,' she grinned.

He frowned. 'Does she have to? Must they come?'

'No, of course not. I had no intention of inviting any of them,' Abbie said quickly. 'I never want to see any of them again. I was really thinking of the problem she would have introducing me to all those important friends of hers, all those nice girls that she had hoped you would marry one day.'

He stopped and looked at her in surprise. 'You do have a point there, Abbie. I'd not really thought about that.' He frowned. 'She certainly might find that a little tricky.'

Her face fell. Why couldn't she keep her big mouth shut, she thought miserably. Why, when everything was so wonderful and her wildest dreams were about to come true, did she have to go and ruin everything.

The fact that Bradley had seen the sense of her argument was not going to do her any favours at all. He'd listen to his mother's objections and realise that she was saying much the same thing so there must be more than a grain of truth in it. Then he was bound to come to the conclusion that he couldn't go against his mother's wishes.

She was so caught up in her own despair that at first she didn't comprehend what he was saying.

'What did you say?' she asked in bewilderment.

'I was telling you what the answer to that problem was,' he grinned.

She looked at him blankly.

'I said I agreed with you that we would say nothing to my mother about us getting married. Instead, we'll elope to Gretna Green and get married "over the anvil".'

Abbie stared at him incredulously. 'She'll disapprove even more if we do that!'

He shook his head. 'No she won't. Not when we remind her that it is fashionable in high society these days to elope. Do you remember the piece in the *Echo* a short time back about the heir to the Larrinaga Steamship Company eloping with eighteen-year-old Jessie Hands?'

'Jessie Hands?'

'Yes! All her friends called her "Midgy". She belonged to our tennis club and my mother talked about their daring exploit for months afterwards.'

Abbie looked puzzled.

'If we do the same, and if I tell her I was only copying what Midgy did, my mother will be impressed, and it will give her something to dine out on for years to come.'

Abbie looked at him in wide-eyed admiration. 'Do you think we dare do that?'

She'd never met anyone quite like Bradley before. He was forceful, confident, and so capable that he seemed to be able to achieve anything that he wanted to do.

'We're going to!' he assured her.

She frowned. 'Since I'm only seventeen I suppose I will have to get consent, but I'm sure one of my grandmothers, or perhaps even both, will sign the forms. Probably only too pleased to get me out of their lives forever.'

'Good! I'll arrange for some time off and you do the same. Keep what we intend doing a complete secret. I'll leave a note for my mother the day we leave.'

Abbie giggled. 'She probably won't let us back in the house when we come home again.'

'Oh yes she will!'

He put his arm around her shoulders, pulling her close as they stepped off the bus. 'When I tell her she either converts the place into two flats or we go and live in Liverpool or Birkenhead or somewhere like that, she'll fall in with our plans quick enough.'

'You're a devious blackmailer,' Abbie laughed, snuggling up to him. 'I can see I'm going to have my work cut out keeping up with you, or you'll be leading me a merry dance.'

Chapter Thirty-Eight

Curled up next to Bradley on the sofa in Mrs Fisher's lounge, Abbie felt wonderfully relaxed. She had never felt so happy, so safe, or so loved. She was almost unable to believe that before the year was out they would be married.

It still seemed incredible to her that someone so good-looking and so successful as Bradley could be in love with her as much as she was with him.

He was a tower of strength in so many ways. Tall and broad yet lean and imposing, whether in his policeman's uniform or out of it. Added to that he was strong-minded yet fair. She could never imagine him doing anything underhanded, or allowing any kind of injustice.

She looked down at the symbol of his love for her that glittered on the third finger of her left hand. The solitaire diamond was the most beautiful engagement ring she had ever seen.

They were not going to elope, romantic though that would have been. She had sensed that deep down he'd not really wanted to do that in case it upset his mother, so she had agreed when instead he had suggested that they had a very quiet wedding.

It would take place in Wallasey, and apart from his mother and the best man, who was one of his colleagues, there would only be one or two guests. To follow they were all having a celebratory meal at the Victoria Hotel in New Brighton. Afterwards, she and Bradley would leave for the Isle of Man on their honeymoon.

None of her relations would be there, neither the Martins nor the Ryans. She would have invited Sam, but he was on the high seas and she had no idea where he was, or even the name of the ship he was on.

Like her, Sam was trying to start a new life. They'd meet up again in time, she was sure of that. They'd been so close while they were growing up and she was sure that the bonds that they'd forged then were strong enough to survive the recent upheaval and tragedy.

She and Bradley would be married before Christmas and, for her, 1933 would not only be the start of a new year, but of a whole new way of life.

She wouldn't let herself think too much about the future or she became nervous and wondered if she was going to be able to live up to Bradley's expectations. His background was so different from her own. She had so much to learn.

When, tentatively, she had mentioned this to him, he had hugged her close and kissed her passionately.

'I love you exactly as you are,' he whispered, and kissed her again.

She knew he meant it, but she was also wise enough to know that at the moment he was blinded by love. She knew she had to make a lot of changes if she was to fit into her new role as Leonora Fisher's daughter-in-law.

She shuddered as she remembered the sort of area she had grown up in. There had been dirt, squalor, and the stench of poverty everywhere. Grubby, barefoot children, drunken, abusive men, women old beyond their years, their health ruined by lack of food and constant child-bearing.

The behaviour of the people she'd lived with and the way they spoke to each other would shock Mrs Fisher and her friends. She'd found it hard enough to adjust when she'd first gone to work at Frisby Dyke's.

'You managed OK when you started work there, so why not here?' Bradley had asked, lifting one of his eyebrows quizzically when she told him how worried she was.

'Yes, but that was different. I put on a posh accent in the same way as I put on my uniform. When I was wearing my black top and long black skirt then talking in a refined manner came naturally.'

Bradley thumped the heel of his hand against his forehead dramatically. 'Does that mean you are always going to have to dress in black after we're married?' he groaned.

She knew he was teasing her simply to show that it wasn't all that important to him, but it was important to her.

For the first time in her life she'd found someone who loved her and she didn't want that to change ... ever!

She never wanted the day to come when

Bradley wondered if he'd done the right thing in marrying her.

Abbie looked forward to 1933 not simply as being a whole new way of life for her, but one filled with happiness and contentment. She had always yearned for someone to love her and now that dream had come true at last.

As long as she lived she would never understand why, or even how, Ellen Martin and Maggie Ryan had kept the truth about her parentage from her for all those years.

They must have done it so that their own names and reputations wouldn't be sullied, she thought sadly. In the end, all they had done was cause her and so many other people a great deal of misery.

All she'd ever wanted was to be shown love and affection. She wouldn't have cared who her mother was, or about the scandal that had led to her birth. She was sorry about Audrey, of course, but she couldn't feel anything for her. She was just a name.

Learning about Michael Ryan being her father was different. A shudder went through her as she recalled his coldness towards her. Over and over again she asked herself how he could have been so abrupt, so disinterested in her, when he knew she was his daughter?

She'd always thought Maggie so kind, but looking back she wondered if perhaps Maggie hadn't been the most evil of them all. Ellen had made no secret of the fact that she didn't love her, didn't even like her and had no time for her. Maggie, though, had shown her affection, and turned a blind eye about her closeness to Peter even when she'd told her that she thought she was in love with him.

When she talked about this to Bradley, he hadn't seemed shocked or surprised. 'It was only natural that you were attracted to each other and that there was a closeness between you, since you were uncle and niece.'

'Yes, but I didn't know that. In my eagerness to get away from there I would have married him if he'd asked me!'

Bradley nodded understandingly. 'And what about Sam?'

'I thought the world of him, but I thought he was my brother. Even that was a lie.'

'That's all in the past and you should try and put it all behind you,' Bradley told her seriously.

'I know, but I shall never completely forget what a terrible tangle it all was.'

Abbie still felt it was incredible that, knowing so much about her, Bradley should still love her and want to marry her.

Living at his home she had never felt so safe and pampered. Now that Mrs Fisher knew that Bradley's mind was made up and that she was the girl he intended to marry, she couldn't do enough to help her.

There was still a dreamlike quality about all that had happened. She still couldn't credit that Mrs Fisher was willing to give up half of her beautiful home so that they could have a place of their own waiting for them when they came back from their honeymoon. She'd even offered them some of her furniture!

Her new home was going to be better than anything she'd ever known in her life. When she'd been growing up in Bostock Street she'd envied Sandra Lewis because her mother had been so house-proud. They'd never had wall-to-wall carpets on the floor, though, or a bathroom! She'd loved the cosiness of Maggie Ryan's place, but there hadn't been any of the comforts there that she would have from now on.

She wouldn't have to put up with any more cursing, shouting, drunken brawls or raging rows. There would be no more bullying from Billy or rejection from Ellen Martin. There would be no more lies or deception.

Never again would she have to comb nits out of her hair, or check her bed to see there were no cockroaches or fleas in it before she got into it at night. Nor would she ever again have to use the public baths.

She was looking forward so much to putting her own unhappy experiences behind her, and erasing the memories of all the tragedies that had taken place as well.

In the past year there had been so many of these, as well as devastating revelations about the past. Sandra dying, the baby being Peter's not Sam's, and then the baby's death followed by Peter committing suicide. All still haunted her.

On top of that, she had felt almost bereaved by the fact that Sam had been so brokenhearted that he had gone to sea.

When Abbie finally summoned up the courage to go back to Bostock Street to ask Michael Ryan, since he was her dad, to give his permission for her to get married, she found that the Ryans were no longer there.

'They've all gone back to Ireland, and bloody good riddance to the whole bunch of them,' Billy snarled.

'I'm surprised they went on living here as long as they did,' Abbie commented.

His shifty eyes narrowed. 'They couldn't leave, could they, their consciences wouldn't let them. Her bloody husband wouldn't let her bring you up, even though their Michael was your dad, but Paddy Ryan was determined she would see you every day of her life. It was his way of punishing her and Michael, making them watch you grow up in muck and misery,' he sneered.

'They could have afforded to leave here years ago but he was a sadistic bastard,' Ellen added. 'Bloody skinflints, the pair of them. She said he always kept her short so she could never afford to hand over a penny-piece to help with your keep.'

'She was kind to me,' Abbie argued.

'Only when it suited her. Half the time she only did it to rile me,' Ellen replied, scowling. 'Anyway, they've cleared off. He's given up the sea. The old bugger saved up enough to buy himself a farm in County Kerry and Michael's gone with them.'

'So who is going to sign this document so that I can get married?' Abbie asked worriedly.

'I'm not bloody signing no form that has

anything to do with scuffers. You must be out of your sodding mind to marry one of those buggers!' Billy told her.

'That's her affair! As long as she gets off our backs she can marry who the hell she likes, so you shut your great gob,' Ellen told him. 'Since there's no one outside of Bostock Street what knows any difference I'll sign the bloody paper.'

'You mean as my mother? Will it be legal when you're really my grandmother?' Abbie asked in alarm.

'Who the hell cares. No one's given a damn all these years, so who's going to worry about it now?'

Abbie handed her the form and watched with mixed feelings as Ellen laboriously scrawled her name.

As Ellen pushed it back across the table towards her, Abbie felt an overwhelming sense of relief. It was over. The past really was behind her.

As she stood up to leave she looked round the untidy room, at the table piled with dirty crockery, the grate with its ashes spilling out on to the hearth, and felt a surge of sheer happiness knowing that it would be the last time she would ever be there. Impulsively, she put her arm around Ellen's shoulders and kissed her on the cheek.

'Geroff, you smarmy little bitch!' Ellen slapped her hand and pushed her away. 'You've got what you came for, so bugger off.'

When Ellen had rebuffed her in the past, Abbie had been brokenhearted. Now she felt indifferent and found herself smiling complacently. She'd been afraid that Ellen might show a display of affection and want her to stay, or even expect to be invited to the wedding. As it was, she could now walk away from Bostock Street and all its memories without even a backward glance.